Praise for *Always Something There to Remind Me*

"Harbison serves up a deliciously light blend of 1980s nostalgia and women's fiction. She packs the teenage flashbacks with age-appropriate miscommunications and emotional indecision, and cleverly uses [a] present-day story line to bring Erin to a point of understanding. Harbison raises the emotional stakes and gives this story a little more bite without losing her fun, breezy style." —*Publishers Weekly*

"*Always Something There to Remind Me* is a riveting look at the tender agony of first love. Full of self-awareness and scathing wit, Beth Harbison deftly contrasts teenage romantic idealism with the reality of growing up. Touching, truthful, and profoundly satisfying, Harbison delivers her finest work yet." —Jen Lancaster, *New York Times* bestselling author of *If You Were Here*

Praise for Beth Harbison

"A fast and fun read . . . sure to appeal to anyone who came of age in the late 1980s." —*Library Journal* on *Thin, Rich, Pretty*

"Told with Beth Harbison's knack for thirty- and forty-something nostalgia, and heartwarming humor, *Thin Rich Pretty* will strike a chord with any woman who has ever looked in the mirror, or the bank account, and said, 'if only.'" —*The Province* (Vancouver) on *Thin, Rich, Pretty*

"Harbison continues to wow readers with particular chick-lit charm and genuine characters." —*Booklist* on *Hope in a Jar*

"Zingy and funny, and her light touch allows her to get away with the ridiculous situations in this nutty beach read." —*Publishers Weekly* on *Secrets of a Shoe Addict*

"Kick off your Keds (unless you're driving) and meet a motley group of D.C. women who bond over designer shoes. It's chick lit with heart *and* sole." —*People* magazine

"I would happily recommend *Shoe Addicts Anonymous* to anyone who loves shoes . . . or to smart, funny, realistic women." —Jennifer Weiner

Also by Beth Harbison

Shoe Addicts Anonymous

Secrets of a Shoe Addict

Hope in a Jar

Thin, Rich, Pretty

Beth Harbison

Always Something There to Remind Me

ST. MARTIN'S GRIFFIN
New York

ALWAYS SOMETHING THERE TO REMIND ME. Copyright © 2011 by Beth Harbison. All rights reserved. Printed in the United States of America. For information, address St. Martin's Press, 175 Fifth Avenue, New York, N.Y. 10010.

www.stmartins.com

Design by Kathryn Parise

THE LIBRARY OF CONGRESS HAS CATALOGED THE HARDCOVER EDITION AS FOLLOWS:

Harbison, Elizabeth M.
    Always something there to remind me / Beth Harbison. — 1st ed.
        p. cm.
    ISBN 978-0-312-59910-2 ([hardcover]) — ISBN 978-0-312-64183-2 ([pbk.])
    1. First loves—Fiction.   2. Loss (Psychology)—Fiction.   3. Psychological fiction.
I. Title.
    PS3558.A564A49 2011
    813'.54—dc22

                                                                2011006363

ISBN 978-0-312-59911-9 (trade paperback)

First St. Martin's Griffin Edition: May 2012

10   9   8   7   6   5   4   3   2   1

To him, of course

Prologue

I could tell you what he looked like—his height and physique and the way the contours of his body felt close to mine in the dark; the shape and exact color of his eyes and how they looked when he was happy, sad, pissed, or passionate; the lines of his forearms, biceps, shoulders, and elbows; the curve of his lips and the feel of his mouth against mine; and what his back, and hips, and legs felt like beneath my fingertips. I could tell you what he smelled like and what he tasted like. I could pick his voice out in the crowd at Times Square on New Year's Eve.

Even twenty-three years after the end, I could close my eyes and remember every detail of him, as clearly as if he were right in front of me.

But what would be the point in describing all that? All it would do—all it could possibly do—is diminish the whole into a rearrangement of features you would never see the way I saw them. He'd sound like your neighbor, or your brother, or that guy you work with, or some other person you couldn't possibly imagine inspiring an unending ache in someone's heart.

Everyone has a first love, one person they never completely got over, right?

Picture yours.

Because when you come down to it, it isn't really anything about the way they look that distinguishes them in your memory—hair color, physical shape, style—it can all change with time. It's the way you remember *feeling* when you looked at them.

When I looked at him, I felt real, unconditional love.

And I felt *completely* loved.

He was the only person I ever met whose soul I could clearly see in his eyes.

And I had more faith in him than I've ever had in another human being.

After I lost him, on the rare occasions when I saw him, I could feel the shape, the moving embodiment, of the hole in my heart.

Not that my life was about that. I moved on, of course. Dated, worked, ate, drank, laughed, cried. Had a child. Things happen, life goes on, and you have to keep moving and think about what's in front of you or you'll go insane.

So I pushed the part of me that belonged to him way beneath the surface.

Just like he did with me.

No one would ever have imagined this part of me existed at all, that a piece of my heart deep down was broken beyond repair, or that *that* guy—the guy who could have been *anyone* (or no one) to you or the rest of the world—was the cause of it all.

He was the only guy I was ever truly in love with. It took me years to move on.

Then he came back.

Chapter 1

March 1985

The music throbbed—John Cougar singing about Jack and Diane, drums pounding his point and rattling the windows—and Erin Edwards scanned the smoke-filled room, half hoping to see him, half terrified to see him.

Todd Griffith. The cutest guy in school. Classic in every way: dark hair, amber eyes that looked green in the right light, square jaw, great mouth, powerful body. He was beautiful to look at and also athletic, which was the only thing that kept him from being universally coveted at Benson Prep School, since there was a contingent of freaky pothead girls at school who weren't interested in anyone their parents would approve of.

But the guys were afraid of him, without exception. Which made him even more appealing.

No doubt about it. Todd Griffith was perfect.

But Todd wasn't who Erin was here to see. The guy Erin was really looking for . . . he'd be with Todd.

"Is he here?" her friend Jordan Tyler asked at her elbow. She was thinking Todd because that was who Erin had liked first.

"He's *got* to be."

Jordan squinted and scanned the room. "I don't see him. And I think that's good because, Erin, he's kind of a jerk. No offense."

Erin was only half paying attention to Jordan. "Who, Todd?"

"Yes, Todd. Who else are we talking about? You went out with him one time three months ago and all he did was try to get into your pants." Jordan raised an eyebrow. "Then he told everyone you gave him a blow job. I don't know how you can stand him after that."

Erin nodded. "But I'm not *sure* he said that. That's just what David Rutley said, and *he's* a jerk." There was no denying that David Rutley was a jerk, but she did half wonder why Todd hadn't set the record straight if he really hadn't said it. All the guys were cowed by him, it would have been nothing for him to just tell them to lay off. They would have fallen in line like baby ducks, just like they did anytime he said anything else.

"Okay. . . ." Jordan looked dubious. "Whatever. Oh!"

Erin turned, startled. "What?"

Jordan frowned. "Well." She pointed. "Todd's here."

Sure enough, he was. Along with a group of guys, including David Rutley and a couple of others Erin didn't recognize, as well as a sleazy-looking girl with dark hair, teased high and sprayed into a style that made her look like a Mafia girlfriend.

The girl wasn't even pretty. It was so obvious what he wanted from her. She was rounded, with huge boobs and a big butt, and a big round face that he probably put up with to get the rest. Without even talking to her, Erin knew her type, knew exactly what kind of girl she was.

But that's what Todd was all about. She'd known it ever since she'd heard the rumors of her blowing him.

She was over him.

Maybe he'd have better luck with this girl.

"Wow, who's the slut?" Jordan whispered.

"Just his type," Erin said.

"Aren't you glad you didn't do anything more than kiss him?"

"Yes." Erin wasn't interested in playing that game. She suspected—or hoped, anyway—the other guy wasn't like that.

Unfortunately, *he* didn't seem to be here.

"Are you going to say something to him?" Jordan asked, indicating Todd and his date.

Erin shook her head. "No point."

Jordan nodded like she understood. But she didn't. Not yet. "Good call. Do you want a beer?"

Normally she wouldn't. Erin hated beer. But she and Jordan had a ride home with Jordan's older sister, who was at the movies until after midnight, so it wasn't like Erin's mom was going to smell it on her breath before she got to brush her teeth. Plus she wouldn't mind having a little liquid courage in order to socialize with all these people.

"Yes," she said. It was going to be a dull party after all. "Thanks."

Jordan gave her a pat on the shoulder and headed for the keg, leaving a waft of Jōvan musk trailing behind her.

"Somebody's Baby" by Jackson Browne came over the speakers.

That's when Erin saw him.

Him.

The one she'd been hoping to see.

Todd's best friend.

She knew who he was because he'd come to baseball games now and then when Todd was playing and she'd asked someone about him. The story was that he was a fighter, mean as a snake and twice as aggressive as Todd, but he looked mild and sweet to Erin.

Which itself was intriguing.

They'd grown up together, they were practically brothers. They even kind of looked alike, only his build was slighter, his hair lighter, his overall look just a little less immediately striking. But he had amazing eyes. Large and kind. The sort of eyes that made people toss around terms like *old soul*.

She found him both compelling and disconcerting at the same time. From the first time she'd seen him, his image had been emblazoned on her mind, and when he stepped into view it was as if her mind closed over it like a trap. She didn't *want* to think about him, but she couldn't stop.

His eyes met hers and something clicked.

She backed away involuntarily, knocking into a warm body.

"Er*in*!" It was Jordan, holding two opaque plastic cups of beer. There was quite a bit of it on her sweater now too.

"I'm sorry!"

Jordan touched the large wet spot on her top. "Oh, my God, I'm going to reek now!"

"Go rinse really quick," Erin said. "It won't be any wetter than the beer, but then it won't stink. Come on, I'll wear your shirt and you can wear mine since it's dry."

"No, that's too much trouble."

"It's not that big a deal. Really." Erin imagined she could feel his eyes on her back and all of her systems were running on high. She had to run away or she was going to run right to him and everyone would think she was a psychopath. "Let's go." She led Jordan to the bathroom and closed the door behind them.

Jordan pulled off her sweater and started rinsing the spot in the sink. "What's going on? Who are you hiding from?"

"No one." Erin pulled her shirt off and waited for Jordan to hand over the wet sweater. "Todd's friend."

"Todd's *friend*?" She wrung out her sweater and handed it to Erin, taking the shirt. "Which one?"

"You don't know him."

"What are you talking about? *I* don't know him but you *do*?"

"No. But." But what? She felt like she did? That sounded stupid. Something about him made her want to run to him and away from him in equal measure. "He's Todd's best friend, so . . ."

Jordan nodded sagely as she strained to pull the buttons together across her chest. "So stay the fuck away."

"Yeah." Erin thought about his eyes and her breath quickened. "Far away." She dabbed at the sweater she was now wearing with a dry hand towel to blot the excess moisture.

They grabbed their beers and returned to the party, where Erin spent the next fifteen minutes straining to find him again in the crowded haze but didn't see him. She downed her beer and went to refill it.

When she turned around, he was right there.

"Oh!" She laid a hand to her chest.

The song changed abruptly to "Dreams" by Fleetwood Mac.

He looked at her directly. "Hi."

Good teeth, she noted. That was important. Straight. White. Masculine. Not like Paul Dyson in her math class, who looked like he still had his baby teeth.

"Hi." She gave a flustered smile. It was instantly obvious that she wasn't going to be able to play this cool. "I . . . I'm sorry, I don't know your name . . . ?" Did that sound even *remotely* true?

"Nate Lawson."

"I'm Erin." She drank some beer.

He smiled. "I know."

"How do you— Oh." He'd been there the night she was with Todd on that one date. She was reasonably sure she'd been a topic of some conversation after they'd dropped her off, though she was equally sure the accuracy of that conversation was low. "You're Todd's friend, right?" Arrgh! Stupid *again*. She sounded like she was trying to sound *so* casual that he'd have to be blind not to see right through it!

"Right."

Silence stretched between them.

"You don't go to Benson," she pointed out. Like there was any question as to whether or not she'd know him in a school of just over a hundred students.

He shook his head. "I go to Churchill."

"Hm." She nodded, as if that were something worth mulling over. "Are you here with someone?" she asked, suddenly self-conscious that she sounded both hyperactive and overinterested.

Her mouth was dry, so she drank more beer. It tasted terrible.

She didn't care, she drained it.

He looked at her curiously. "No. Well, with them." He indicated Todd and their friends.

She looked, as if she didn't know who he meant. She was getting a little light-headed. "Oh. Yeah."

What was it about this guy that made her *so* uncool?

"Have you known Todd long?"

"Since first grade. We went to school together, played on the same baseball team . . . you name it. We've known each other forever."

She nodded, unsure what to say to that.

He looked at her empty cup. "Do you want another beer?"

She looked at the cup too, like it was surprising to find it empty. "Sure. Thanks."

He reached for it, lightly brushing her fingers with his hand, and took it over to the keg. She waited, standing awkwardly in the one spot, her heart pounding stupidly. He returned shortly and handed her the full cup. She noticed he had gotten one for himself too. "So who are you here with?" he asked.

"My friend Jordan. She's—" She looked around to point her out. "Suddenly not here."

"I think I saw her with you when I came in."

"Probably." He'd noticed her when he came in? That was good. Wasn't it? It's not like she was being loud and sloppy and calling attention to herself.

Someone turned up the music. Billy Joel's "Only the Good Die Young." Erin hoped to God he didn't ask her to dance. Of the many things she was not good at, dancing was at the very top of the list.

So naturally the next thing she heard from him sounded like him asking her to dance.

"Oh, I'm sorry," she said, shaking her head, feeling the heat rise in her face. "I'm not really into that."

He looked at her quizzically.

She'd made a mistake. Clearly. "I'm sorry, I must have misunderstood. What did you say?"

This time it sounded like, *Are you almost done?*

Done?

Done with what? Was she supposed to be doing something?

"Done with what?" She leaned in closer and felt a buzz of energy sizzle between them. She could smell the leather of his coat, which he hadn't taken off.

"I asked if you were having fun." Wow, he had a nice voice, now that she could actually hear him. Really husky and low. Sexy.

"Oh." She relaxed fractionally. "Yes!" That sounded too eager. "I guess. Are you?"

"Now." He held her gaze for a minute, then his face colored a little and he looked away.

That's when she got it.

He was nervous talking to *her*!

Suddenly she felt a little braver. "Do you want to go outside and talk?" she asked, like she was the kind of girl who was comfortable suggesting that sort of thing. In truth, she was kind of desperate to get away from the noise and smoke and the embarrassment of repeatedly asking, *What*?

"Sure."

"Cool."

He signaled Todd, who looked from him to Erin and then back at Nate with a funny look she couldn't quite read.

"He's competitive," Nate said, in answer to her unasked question. "You're part of his domain."

"But I'm not!"

Nate laughed. "Don't worry about it. That's just Todd."

She could believe it. Todd was exactly the sort to only be interested in her if she was interested in his friend. God knows he hadn't demonstrated any interest in her after their one and only "date."

She led Nate to the front door, stopping to grab her pitifully thin jacket from the back of a chair on the way. It was going to be little protection against the elements, particularly since she was wearing a wet sweater. As soon as she stepped outside, she was cold. Really cold. Their breath came out in icy white clouds. It was frigid even for a February night.

"I'm going to die," she announced on a quivering white puff of breath. The wind lifted and blew her hair across her face in ghostly pale strands. She pushed it back and sniffed in the frigid air.

He laughed. "Do you want my coat?"

She looked at him and smiled, though her teeth chattered. "No, then *you'll* die. And I'm already wearing one. Sort of."

"It's fine." He took it off and draped it over her shoulders. It smelled good. And it felt good—still warm from his body heat.

But now he had to be freezing to death because all he had on was a T-shirt that said PUERTO RICO and pictured what looked like a cartoon frog. Her Spanish wasn't good enough to read the rest and get an idea of what the frog had to do with Puerto Rico, but she was pretty sure it didn't represent magical warming properties.

"Maybe we should go back in," she suggested.

"Or we could get in Todd's car," he suggested. It was parked right out front and he went and opened the back door of the blue Dodge.

She looked at him dubiously. Oh, God, Todd had probably told him his stupid blow job story and he'd believed it and thought she was an easy mark. "I'm not . . . you know . . ."

"It'll just be warmer in there," he said, like he understood. "That's all."

She believed him and climbed onto the icy leather seat, then turned to watch him get in and close the door to the tundra outside.

From there it got easy.

They sat in the car and talked until the windows were fogged and neither one of them was wearing the coat anymore. They talked about everything, from what they liked to do in their free time to what they thought about President Reagan (though Erin didn't really have a strong opinion about him) and everything in between. They agreed on just about everything. Sometimes when she was about to say something, he said the exact same thing, or vice versa.

It was just like the way people talked about soul mates, people who were so much like you it was like you'd never been strangers. Not that she was going to start planning a wedding or anything, but he was so comfortable to be around that she didn't want to stop even though it was getting later and later. She'd known him a couple of hours and already felt like she'd miss him when they went home for the night.

They'd started on opposite sides of the back bench seat, then gradually had moved closer together, but Nate hadn't tried a thing.

She was starting to get frustrated with that.

"So," she said, deciding it was time to figure out where he stood. "You . . . don't have a girlfriend?" Ugh. That was ballsy. What if he did? Then what would she do? Make up a boyfriend from another school? Go on and on about him like Jan Brady's "George Glass"?

"No." He looked away for a moment and even though it was dark in the car she could tell from the gesture that he was nervous. "You don't have a boyfriend?"

"No." Actually, she'd never had a boyfriend. He'd probably think she was a loser if she said that, though. Other kids had started "going out," whatever that meant, in sixth grade.

A tense moment passed between them.

Then he moved closer and reached his hand behind her back to draw her closer to him.

Finally.

She closed her eyes and when his lips touched hers she melted against him. It wasn't her first kiss now, they both knew that, but it was good. Really good. He moved his other hand firmly against her back, drawing her closer, making her feel warm and safe. And when his tongue touched hers, all of the muscles in her body tightened. Her pulse raced. Why hadn't they been doing this the whole time?

How long had they wasted the dwindling night, sitting here *talking*?

He smelled like winter air, leather, and soap. He tasted like . . . she didn't even know what he tasted like, he just tasted good. Almost familiar. Whatever it was, she wanted more. She drank him in, not thinking about what would happen next. It was like there wasn't even a question.

She was with him now.

Now he would always be part of her. She just didn't know it yet.

The next day, Erin slept in, partly because the beer had gone to her throbbing head and made walking around difficult, and partly because it was more fun to roll over in bed and remember kissing Nate over and over again than it was to get out of bed and actually start a day in which she didn't have any plans.

Eventually, though, she'd had to. And, true to form, the moment she got out of bed, her mother heard her footsteps and asked her to take the trash out to the garage. So Erin hopped gingerly out in bare feet, opened the garage door, tossed the bag into the can, and closed the door, turning around just in time to see a guy walking past on the street, looking at the house.

He had on a hat and winter coat, almost completely obscuring his face, but she'd know those eyes anywhere.

Nate Lawson.

Something inside of her thrummed to life and made the blood push through her veins like it was a race.

Nate was walking past her house, either to catch a glimpse of her or at least to see where she lived.

The uncertainty, the questions, the hope he would call, and the fear he wouldn't . . . all of that wasn't necessary this time.

He felt the same way she did.

She went back inside smiling.

Chapter 2

Present

I could not figure out how the bitch had made it to her sixteenth birthday without someone killing her.

Roxanne Tacelli. Brattiest fifteen-year-old I'd ever met, and I could completely remember being a rather difficult fifteen myself, so that really was saying something.

Yet here I was, events coordinator for the Farnsworth-Collingswood—one of the top luxury resorts in the world—planning the ultimate Sweet Sixteen party for her, under the doting eyes of her parents, the watchful eyes of my employer, and the electronic eyes of multiple VTV cameras, which were filming the entire event for a reality TV show that promised to suck the soul directly out of anyone who watched it.

The Farnsworth-Collingswood Hotel Group had two locations, one in Geneva, Switzerland, and one in Virginia, just outside Washington, D.C. Both were the same sleek, modern European style with quirks and bells and whistles galore—everything from indoor water parks to landing strips for small aircraft and the ability to acquire just about any amenity a guest could want (for a price) and so both were major party destinations. And we're talking *huge* parties.

My job as events coordinator was therefore, usually, a blast.

Usually.

"Okay, so, Erin, I want bowls and bowls of all green M&Ms," Roxanne, age fifteen, was saying. "I heard rock stars do that. With my face on them. They can do that, right?"

They could, but I didn't have time to answer.

"Or pink," she went on, nodding to herself, like I'd just pointed out how much prettier her already cosmetically altered face would be on pink. "What do pink M&Ms mean?"

At first I didn't answer, assuming she was just in the middle of her stream-of-consciousness list of *I wants*, but then I realized there was silence and all eyes were on me.

"Um. Erin?" Roxanne clicked her tongue against her teeth. "Hello?"

I looked up from where I'd just written *pink MMs, get high-res picture smaller probably better* and said, "I'm sorry?"

Roxanne sighed and rolled her eyes like little brown marbles circling my apparent ineptitude. Really, she was a cartoon. "What do pink M&Ms mean?"

They mean you're a spoiled-rotten little snot whose parents will piss away their money on just about anything, thereby proving everything every manifesto-writing wack job has ever said about the class system in America. I gave a wan smile and said, "They mean you're going to have the best birthday ever."

It was the same voice I would have used with my daughter when she turned six.

Despite the fact that Roxanne acted like a six-year-old, she was savvy enough to know when she was being talked to like one, and she didn't like it.

"Right." She snorted. "So green means you're horny and *pink* means *best birthday ever!*"

Her mocking of my own fake enthusiasm was incredibly insulting. Probably in part because of its accuracy.

But I could barely react to that before her mother's indulgent chuckle filled the air. "Roxanne, I don't know where you come up with this stuff or where you learned such words!" She touched a hand to her too-bright red hair (clearly an attempt to match Roxanne's copper color) and I noticed the lipstick she wore—almost the same shade as her hair—had smeared onto her whitened front tooth. Her face was smooth and lineless, forcibly so, but her hand, with its crepey texture and sun spots, showed her true age. Especially next to the artificial color of her hair.

I sighed inwardly. If *my* kid were saying that kind of thing to adult strangers, I'd take her by the ear, nun-style, to the nearest bathroom and wash her mouth out with soap. Or at least threaten to—I'd always found the threat of embarrassment was much more effective with Camilla than actually following through.

Of course, Camilla—who was also fifteen—was a thousand times more mature than Roxanne.

"All right, so pink M&Ms with your picture on them," I said, trying to rein this conversation back in. "Do you want them to say anything on the other side? *Roxanne Amber Tacelli 16*, or maybe something more personal to you?"

Roxanne wrinkled her fake nose. "Isn't that, like, *your* job?"

"Isn't what my job?"

"Thinking of that kind of thing. I don't know what they should say on them! You think of that!"

I smiled. "You might not like what I come up with." My phone rang and I looked at it.

There was a text from Camilla: *Can I go to a concert at Verizon Center with Lela tonight?*

"Excuse me a minute," I said to Roxanne, and texted back. *No way. Last time you went out with Lela I had to pick you guys up and she puked tequila all over the car. Not an ideal influence.* I returned my attention to Roxanne. "So what were you saying?"

"Just make a list of suggestions." She gave an airy wave toward my notepad.

I had a few already.

"What else do you want, honey?" her father asked, speaking for the first time in about forty-five minutes (the last time being when he asked how much to write the deposit check for, after which he had then, without flinching, written it).

"Horses."

"*Horses?*" I echoed.

She nodded. "I want pure white horses at the party. Just, you know, standing around. Decoratively."

"That's not possible—" I began.

"Wonderful idea, honey!" her mother exclaimed, like she'd just disproven one of Einstein's theories.

This was ridiculous. "But the party is in the water park." One of the big draws of the resort is that it has a large indoor water park, themed like a huge, sprawling shipwreck. It's Gilligan's Island on steroids. And the entire thing is constructed from painted cement, plastic trees, and corridors of chlorinated water, churning through the fake foliage and down elaborate, and sometimes hidden, slides.

I couldn't even imagine putting horses in that environment. It would be dangerous for absolutely *everyone* involved. Especially the horses. Why couldn't everyone here see that?

"Surely you could make it work," Roxanne's father blustered, and I could sense he was ready to pay to make it work, even though it was patently *impossible*.

"What about . . ." I thought quickly, trying to come up with something even more fun than horses. Something, perhaps, not actually *alive*. "Balloons?" If my daughter were just a little older I might have been better at coming up with age-appropriate suggestions, but nevertheless I was certain Roxanne, like every kid, could be distracted from anything as long as you presented another, shinier thing.

That wasn't going to do it, though.

Roxanne looked at me like . . . well, like I'd just suggested balloons. Let's face it, I wasn't exactly an ace at thinking quick.

"I want horses!" she cried, and turned her suddenly tearful eyes to her father.

I want an Oompa Loompa NOW, Daddy!

"Then you will have them," her father said, patting her arm awkwardly.

"And . . ." She bit her thumb, thinking—I was sure—of new ways to torture me. "I want to arrive in a helicopter."

I sighed. "Again, not compatible with the indoor pool idea."

"Take the roof off!" she cried.

"You know that's not possible, right?" I looked at her father. A man with that much money had to have at least a *little* sense about that kind of thing.

"What would it take to remove the enclosure and put it back after the party?" he asked, his hand jerking reflexively toward his checkbook.

I gaped at him in stunned silence for a fraction of a second before saying, "You saw the pool area, right? Enclosed or not enclosed, and it *is* enclosed, there's no way to land a helicopter in there."

I imagine they pictured it teetering atop the volcano slide or maybe hovering over the whole works while Roxanne slid, fireman-style, down a rope into the middle of her party.

"What if you have your guests leave the party area and congregate outside to see you arrive?" I saw her objection form first in her brows. "Or," I added quickly, "maybe not even come into the party area until you're there."

She clapped her hands together. "That's perfect! Then they can all follow me in! Like a bride or something."

God help her future wedding coordinator.

And divorce lawyer.

"Maybe we could just shut the pool area and turn the lights out until Roxy arrives," her mother suggested. "Then she could arrive in the helicopter and lead the way in. It will be like a surprise party, only the guests will be the ones surprised."

All right, that could work. I jotted *helicopter* and *unhappy guests* on my list. "No problem."

"On horseback!"

I was about to voice another strong objection to livestock when my boss, Jeremy Rambaur, walked up. Jeremy was in his mid-forties, and as tidy as you can imagine, from his perfectly slicked hair to his pencil-thin mustache. I think he imagined he looked like a modern-day Errol Flynn, but to me he looked a lot more like John Waters. He was so firmly in the closet that I'm not even sure he knew he was gay, though once, after a couple of peach daiquiris, he had confessed to me that he thought Paolo at the front desk was "pretty delish."

If we were in a seventies sitcom, he could have been played by Paul Lynde.

"How are we doing?" Jeremy asked, putting one hand on my

shoulder and one on Roxanne's. "How's our little star?" He was asking her, but I knew that Jeremy himself was totally ready for his close-up. He might even have been more invested in this VTV thing going well than the girl and her parents were.

Roxanne pressed her lips together and somehow managed to shrug with her eyebrows. "Well, *she* says I can't have horses at my party." She nodded in my direction.

"What?" He looked at me, puzzled.

"In the water park," I clarified, fully expecting an understanding to come into his eyes. "I said we can't have horses *in the water park.*"

"Oooh."

I nodded and waited for him to turn those lemons into lemonade for her.

"That"—Jeremy looked at her sympathetically—"*could* be a problem. Consider what would happen if, erm, nature called for one of them. You wouldn't want to be the girl remembered as having a sixteenth birthday that smelled of horse dung, now, would you?"

That was good. I had to hand it to him. He knew damn well how stupid it was to even suggest putting horses in that area, but the only way he could get through to this girl was to appeal to her vanity.

How had I missed such an obvious trick?

"Eeeew!" was Roxanne's predictable reaction. "No! Forget the horses." She looked at me, like it had been *my* unforgivably stupid idea in the first place.

"Okay." I pretended to scratch the item off my list.

When I'd turned sixteen, my best friends Theresa and Jordan had thrown me a surprise party in Theresa's living room. My boyfriend had lied badly about us needing to go by her house on the way out to dinner, so I knew something was up, but pretended to be surprised.

It was a small party, my two best friends, their boyfriends, and the two of us—and it was one of the best nights of my life.

Roxanne would never have understood that.

For her it had to be huge, glamorous, and completely about everyone watching and admiring her. You could just tell she was already thinking this party had to outdo any subsequent efforts by her friends to top it.

I made a mental note to suggest to my daughter that maybe her sixteenth birthday would be most gratifyingly spent if we did it while building houses in a disaster area or perhaps in an Appalachian outpost.

I didn't ever want Camilla to be as wretched and ungrateful as Roxanne was.

"Is everything else going well?" Jeremy asked, his voice overly solicitous. "Everybody happy?" He was desperate to keep this party—and the TV show—here. And already Roxanne had threatened to "just forget the whole thing" three times, a threat that apparently only I recognized as a total bluff. If she just forgot the whole thing now, even her parents and their bank account wouldn't be able to coordinate it all in another place half as nice with four weeks' notice. And there would be no guarantee it would be telecast.

"I guess." Roxanne pouted.

"The production company is going to start shooting tomorrow," Jeremy went on, a little lilt of glee in his voice. "It should be a *lot* of fun!" He didn't say it, but his voice held the words, *Oodles and oodles of fun!*

I saw my exit. "Well, with that in mind, I really better get back to my office—"

"What about those white birds?" Roxanne interrupted, leveling a challenging gaze on me.

I stopped. Oh, no. "I'm sorry?"

"You know, those white birds they let fly into the air on special occasions? What are they? Eagles or something."

"Doves?" I asked, picturing them lifting into the air in glorious celebration of Roxanne's birth, and then pelting, one by one, into the glass roof, only to fall down into the pool, broken necks contorting their bodies into little curved and feathered knots.

Where, if Roxanne had her way, they could then be trampled by drowning horses.

"Doves!" she said, looking into the distance and nodding. "I think so."

"Let's hold off on living creatures altogether for a moment," I said, then, feeling a warning look from Jeremy, added, "just long enough for me to get an idea of what kind of food you want."

That launched Roxanne into a long list of her favorite foods, everything ranging from Almas caviar (the mention of which made her father stand up a little straighter and clear his throat—a little telekinetic power, and his checkbook probably would have spontaneously combusted) to Cinnabon.

I jotted it all down, trying to figure out how a caterer was going to deal with this, but that wasn't my problem. I couldn't take it all on myself. It wasn't like I was going to be up in my kitchen for the next four weeks baking cinnamon buns for her.

When Roxanne finally stopped for a breath, I said, "You know, I want to get right on top of this so we can make sure we have the best caterer possible for your party." I gave her a quick smile. "You have my card, right? You let me know if you think of anything else you need or want." I turned to leave, but Roxanne caught me.

"I don't have your card."

I knew that, of course. As surely as I knew if she *did* have my card, I'd be hearing from her day and night. What could I do? It was my job. I stopped and was reaching into my pocket for one when Jeremy handed one over to Roxanne and each of her parents, shooting me a look in the meantime.

"I got these from your office just in case," he explained pointedly. "Something told me you might forget them."

I held up my hand with the card in it. "I didn't."

"I'll take that one too." Roxanne snatched it from me. "I'm always losing things and I want to make sure I can call you. Is your cell number on here?" She scanned it quickly. "Good."

"Good," I echoed. "So we'll talk."

"Fine."

This was going to be a long, long month.

⌣

Cam and I lived in a condo in McLean Gardens in Northwest D.C. Her father, Jake, had lived in Friendship Heights, about a mile away, which had made for easy handoffs between him and me when Cam was little, but Jake had been killed in a motorcycle accident when Cam was three.

She didn't even remember him now.

It broke my heart because he had loved her so much and would have gotten so much out of seeing her grow up, and she would have gotten so much from having a dad like him. He'd been handsome, quick-witted, fearless, and, unfortunately, reckless. The very thing that had attracted me to him in the first place—me, the typical goody-goody—had ended up killing him and depriving Cam of a father.

So it had just been the two of us for twelve years now. We'd done everything together. To tell the truth, I'd gotten quite used to having her as my constant companion and the adjustment when she'd gotten old enough to want her own social life had been embarrassingly difficult for me.

Of course, I did have a tendency toward the maudlin. On more than one occasion when she was in elementary school, I had found myself in her bedroom, holding her increasingly threadbare teddy bear and sobbing at the prospect of her getting older and going away to college and then on to her own life.

This, like many things, was a problem I had bought for myself unnecessarily. As it turned out, as Cam had grown up, so had I, albeit on a slightly slower curve. I'd learned to let go more and more with every passing year, to be flexible as her social life expanded into sleepovers at other houses, overnight camp, and so on.

Tonight Cam was staying at her grandmother's (Jake's mom's) and I had plans with Rick Samuels, a guy I'd been seeing for about a year now. Rick was a widower with a fifteen-year-old daughter named Amy, who went to Camilla's school. They were friends even before Rick and I met, but now they were as close as sisters. The whole situation was very comfortable.

I'd always worried that Camilla's untraditional upbringing had come at a cost to her. Yes, she knew she was loved—she would re-member and understand that her mother had worked very hard to raise her and be an active part of her life. My jobs in her youn-gest years had included working as a housecleaner—so Cam could come with me—and as a private cook, which took me away from her only two or three hours five nights a week since I did all the prep work at home. But those jobs didn't pay much and eventually I'd had to bite the bullet and put her into a day-care center near our house and go to work full-time. Still, I was glad to have at least spent so much of her first three years with her almost constantly, glad I was the one to nurse her through the madness of chicken pox and to sleep with her burning, fevered body during a particu-larly frightening bout with strep when she was only two and a half.

So I knew *I* had done the best I could, and I was fairly confident that Cam knew that too. But knowing your frenzied mother *tried* isn't the same as growing up in a security blanket composed of two stable parents and maybe even a sibling or two. An ideal that few people achieve? Maybe. But I'd had it and I wanted no less for my own child.

But we don't always get what we want.

As I got into the car after spending the afternoon dealing with Roxanne, I pushed her number on speed dial.

"Thank you," I said to her as soon as she answered.

"What for?" she asked.

"For being the perfect daughter." I didn't know how Roxanne's parents could stand dealing with her all the time. They must have wanted to tear their hair out.

Camilla didn't even ask for an explanation. "Sure! Now can I get an iPhone?"

"No."

"Mom—"

"*No.*"

"It was worth a shot," she said on a sigh.

I had to laugh. "Hey, I wouldn't respect you if you didn't at least try. Twenty times a day."

"You got my texts, then."

"Yup." I smiled thinking about them. It was always nice to check my phone and see the light blinking with a little message from her. Today she'd listed ten reasons she needed an iPhone. These included, *You will never need to feed it or clean up after it* and *I need to be able to access my Facebook and texts in case of an epidemic.*

"Seriously, Mom, it's like Edison's invented the lightbulb and we're insisting on using candles."

"Camilla, you are talking to me on a magic radio while I am in my car! It hardly needs four hundred thousand apps and a touch screen to make it a miracle."

"Yeah, but there's a *flashlight* app—can you imagine how handy that could be if there was a zombie invasion?"

"Are you kidding? Zombies go toward the light. Everyone knows that. There would be nothing more foolish in the event of a zombie invasion than for you to use your phone as a flashlight. Thank God you don't have one!"

She groaned.

"So are you set for the night?" I asked. "Have everything you need?"

"I've spent a lot of time with Nan, Mom. I think I can survive here."

"Well, if you can't, you can come home," I said, a little wistfully. "I can tell Rick we'll go out another time."

"Um, he's only been talking about this date of yours for *days* now," she said. It was sad when my fifteen-year-old was more mature than I was. "And Amy said he's totally exited about it. It would crush him if you canceled. Anyway, Nan and I are watching *I Am Legend.*"

"Ohh." I sucked the air in through my teeth. "So she doesn't know about the dog in that."

She laughed. "No way, she'd never watch it then. I've gotta run, Ma. I'm supposed to call Phillip before we put the movie on."

"*Who?*"

"I don't think I've told you about him yet. I'll tell you tomorrow!"

I didn't have time to say anything else before she clicked off.

Who the hell was Phillip?

So far she'd never been on a one-on-one date, but I knew it was coming and I was dreading it. As long as they stayed in groups—and, hell, even as long as they had to sneak to be alone, thereby preventing them from spending too much time doing so—she probably couldn't get too serious with a guy before she was ready.

I really didn't want her to make the same mistake I had.

It's hard to prevent a whole individual from making her own errors, of course, but it's not unheard-of for someone to heed good advice now and then.

I hoped Camilla would trust me on that one.

The idea of her grieving away what should be her happy, carefree teenage years—of her living a half-life of faked smiles, secret tears, and a distracted heart and mind—was untenable to me. I remembered beautiful blue-sky summer days when I felt like I was looking at the world from behind thick glass, unable to feel the easy optimism and simple pleasures that my friends did, going to the lake, the pool, the county fair, whatever.

After my breakup with Nate in high school, had my mother had *any* idea at all how I was crumbling on the inside? How, in that delicate brief place between childhood and adulthood, I had literally wanted to die rather than to surge forward into the rest of my life? Had anyone picked up on the depth of my anguish at all? Maybe not. Maybe not even Theresa and Jordan had realized how desperate the despair had been, how many times I'd stood at the precipice, looking over the edge and thinking how much better it might be to just . . . not exist anymore.

These were the memories that made me want to lock Camilla away in her room until she was old enough to really handle the fallout from a broken heart.

But when would that be?

We can understand the science of what makes a heart beat, but we can never stop it from breaking.

And some of us just never stop breaking.

Chapter 3

May 1985

It was the first outdoor party of the year, at Donny Frye's house on Mary Cassatt Drive. It had been hot for early May all week, and even the night was balmy and summerlike.

Erin, Jordan, and Theresa had walked there from Erin's house, and Nate was supposed to meet her there later, since he had something else to do first. She couldn't measure the time between her arrival and his in *time*, but it was about four beers from the keg and she was feeling tipsy and alive and happy. The music thrummed along and even the din of voices added to her good mood.

"When's Nate coming?" Theresa yelled over the music.

"Any minute."

"Lucky bitch," she joked, tossing her dark, glossy hair out of her face. As if she had anything to worry about, boy-wise. "You don't know what it's like for the rest of us, having to face these animals without the perfect boyfriend."

Erin flushed with pride. "You think Nate is the perfect boyfriend?"

"Duh." Theresa rolled her pale blue eyes.

"He's a great guy," Jordan agreed. She was always the more calm and reasonable one. If Jordan said something, you could believe it was true.

Theresa fixed her gaze on Dennis Maloney, who was on the soccer team and was one of the better-looking guys at school. "Though I could settle for *that* tonight."

This was why, in private, Nate referred to Theresa as a *penis flytrap*. She had dalliances with a lot of guys. A *lot*.

"Go for it," Jordan said. She'd long since declared to Erin that she wasn't going to keep worrying about Theresa's sexual habits, and instead was just going to watch them for the show that they were.

True to form, Theresa said, "I think I will," then flashed an uncertain look back. "Unless you guys want me to stick with you?"

"We'll be fine," Erin said with a laugh.

"Wish me luck!" Theresa sauntered off in Dennis's direction.

Jordan and Erin looked at each other and laughed.

"Want another beer?" Erin asked Jordan.

"Not right now. I'm going to run in and find the bathroom, actually. It's *that time*."

"Ugh."

Jordan nodded. "I'll catch up with you in a while."

"Okay." Erin went to the keg and tried to remember how to work it. Jordan was better at it than she was. That was why Jordan'd gotten the first four. After several embarrassing tries, she eked out half a cup of beer.

"She's Always a Woman" by Billy Joel started playing and couples on the terrace clasped themselves together to dance so slowly and so close that they might as well have gotten hotel rooms.

For some reason, that made Erin feel giggly.

"You look happy," Rick McClintock commented, coming up to her with a red plastic cup of mostly foam. He was in her history class, but he sat on the other side of the small room and somehow that meant they'd never really said much to each other before. "Drunk?"

"I haven't eaten anything," Erin said with a laugh. "Maybe that's the problem."

He laughed. "So . . . check out the real show." He gestured toward a small group of brave—or completely drunk—souls who were grooving on the patio.

She was about to produce one of the many excuses she had at the ready when it came to not dancing, when, despite the thick crowd, she became hyper-aware of one person out of about fifty in the darkness. "Excuse me. I'm meeting someone," she tossed distractedly to Rick, and took a couple of barefoot steps onto the slate patio.

She didn't even *see* him, there was no sight and recognition, it all moved too fast for that. She just *sensed* him, went straight to him, and threw herself into his arms, kissing him with a disproportionate hunger, before she was even a hundred percent sure it was him.

Except she was *sure* it was. She'd know the smell of him, the taste of him, the *feel* of him anywhere.

It was only later that the potential for humiliation occurred to her. Hurling yourself at a stranger and sticking your tongue down his throat is the kind of thing that can get you a challenging reputation in high school.

In this case, though, she was right and instead it served to deepen her certainty that what they had between them was a lot deeper than what most people had.

"Hey," he said with a smile when she drew back.

"What took you so long?" She kissed him again. She didn't know what it was. It was like the sight of him made her hungry for more.

She didn't bother to wait for an answer. After about five solid minutes of kissing, she wordlessly led him to a private spot on the grass at the far end of the yard, and they lay down and spent the next three hours or so making out under the stars.

"How much longer is this going to take?" Erin asked, watching Nate on a ladder, carefully painting around the door of her family's house.

"Hours," he said, giving her a quick glance.

"*Hours?*" She adjusted her sunglasses and leaned back in the lawn chair she'd dragged around to the front of the house so she could sit with him. "I'm just sitting here doing nothing."

"You could grab a brush and help."

She shook her head. "I'm not allowed. My mother says I'm too sloppy. Even when I try really hard to be neat."

He laughed. "I believe that."

She made an exasperated noise.

"You don't have to hang out here, you know. You *can* do something else."

"I know. I'm being supportive. Do you want a sandwich?" she asked, suddenly inspired to do *something* other than sit there like a lump.

"Yes," he said, focusing intently on the edging. He didn't get even a spot of paint on the brick. But what she really liked was the way his muscles flexed in his arm and back as he moved the paintbrush. "That would be great. Thanks."

"I'll get it." She got up and put her magazine down on the chair. "You want iced tea?"

"Sure."

"Okay." She went inside, and it took her eyes a moment to adjust to the light after coming in from the sun. The house was always dark and cool because tall shady trees blocked the side and back windows.

First she stopped in the bathroom and squirted some more Sun-In on her hair. It was already looking pretty pale, but she wanted to keep it that way, and using Sun-In with the sun instead of a blow dryer made her feel like it was happening more naturally.

Then she went into the kitchen and took out the bread, then went to the fridge and got mayonnaise and mustard, plus some turkey and ham deli meats. It was almost a club sandwich, but they didn't have any bacon.

However, there *were* Bac-Os in the cabinet. She'd often eat them right out of the canister.

So she toasted two pieces of bread, then spread the mayonnaise and mustard together on both slices, cracked some pepper over them, then sprinkled on a few Bac-Os. Then she layered the meats on and hesitated. There was no lettuce but there were tomatoes. She found a large red one that smelled of summer, and sliced it paper-thin, layering the slices on thick enough, she hoped, to make up for the lack of lettuce.

Then she mixed up some water and iced-tea powder, tossed in some ice cubes, and put the whole thing on a tray to take out to Nate.

Unfortunately, she wasn't paying attention when she opened the door and knocked it right into the ladder he was standing on, sending him and the paint flying into the bushes.

For a moment she stood there in shock, looking from the mess to the tray and back again, as if somehow she could reconcile the two.

Then her faculties returned to her. "Oh, my God!" She put the tray down and ran to Nate, who was recovering himself and the can of paint. "I'm so sorry! Oh, my God!"

"You *are* a mess around paint." He pulled a rag out of his belt loop and started cleaning up a couple of spots that had splashed onto the previously perfect brick. "Get the hose, would you?"

"Yes!" She ran to the side of the house and got the hose, dragging it across the newly cut grass. She handed it to him and ran back to turn it on. "Now?" she called.

He yelled back and she turned the faucet on full blast.

When she got back to the front of the house she was surprised to see his hair and shirt were wet, and the walkway was sprayed with water.

"What happened to you?"

"Someone turned the water on."

"I asked if you were ready!"

"Is that what you said?"

"Yes. And I thought you said yes!"

"I said *what*," he corrected. "Because I didn't know what you said."

"Ohhh." She couldn't help it, she had to laugh. "I'm so sorry. Really. I was just trying to help."

He laid the hose down by the bush to dilute the spilled paint, and went over to her. "Baby." He took her into his arms and held her.

"Ew," she said against his shoulder. "You're wet."

"You don't mind."

She didn't. "I guess I don't now." She ran her hands up his back and held on. He was solid against her.

"Okay, so what did you bring?" He drew back and went over to the tray she'd set on her lawn chair.

She followed. "My magazine is wet!"

He looked at her. "So's the sandwich."

"Oh, no!" She looked at it. Only a corner of the sandwich had really gotten it, but it looked like a soggy sponge. "Gross. I'll make you a new one!"

"Don't worry about it," he said. "It's fine."

"Are you sure?" she asked dubiously. She wouldn't have eaten it.

"It's great," he said appreciatively, his mouth full. "Seriously." Then he frowned. "Is there something chewy in here?"

"*Chewy?* You mean more than just the regular amount you'd expect from bread and lunch meat?"

He swallowed and opened the sandwich to reveal pink dots all over the meat.

For a moment she was horrified, but then she remembered. "Bac-Os!"

"What?"

"You know, bacon bits. Those things you put on salad. They're usually crunchy, but I guess either the hose or the mayo ruined them." She crinkled her nose. "That's really disgusting. Let me make you another one." She reached for it.

He held it back. "No, it tastes great. Really."

"Really?"

"Mm-hmm." He took another big bite and nodded.

"Okay. . . ."

He finished the whole thing quickly, then downed the iced tea. "Great. Thanks again." He kissed her cheek.

"No problem," she said, then looked over all the problems she'd caused. He was still soaked and water was still running off the garden, tinged pale gray with paint. "Now what?"

"We can turn off the hose now," he said, looking it over. "But I should give the wood a few minutes to dry before I paint it."

"No one's home," she said, raising an eyebrow.

He smiled. "What are you suggesting?"

"Nothing. But maybe you want to change out of those wet things." She frowned. "Well, the shirt anyway. Come on." She took his hand and led him into the house and up the stairs to her room. "Want to borrow one of mine?"

"No, thanks."

She turned on the radio. Air Supply was singing "Lost in Love." "You should take that off anyway."

He did, and she watched his muscles flex with the movement. He had a perfect body. Not that she was an expert on guys' bodies, but he was so much more muscular than the guys at school. They were all limp pansies who sat around smoking cigarettes and talking about getting high.

She took the shirt from him and draped it over the end of the bed, then she went to him and put her arms around his neck. "Are you sure you don't want me to help with the painting?"

He laughed in answer and kissed her. She pulled him over to the bed and they lay down, arms wrapped around each other.

After a while he moved his hand up her shirt, and she let him. He was still in bounds, as far as her celibacy rules went, and it felt good as he ran his fingertips across her skin until her breath quickened.

But when he went for the snap on her pants, she said, "No."

He groaned. "Come *on*."

She loved having that power. "Sorry."

He sighed heavily and kissed her harder, cupping his hand over the crotch of her jeans.

She arched against him, tempted to let him in.

But they hadn't known each other long enough for that.

That didn't stop her from reaching down to the outside of his pants, though, and tracing the contours of his desire.

"You're cruel," he said against her mouth.

"You want me to stop?"

"No."

They both smiled against each other's mouths.

Soon his hand trailed back up to the snap of her shorts. She let him linger there for a moment, playing with the sensation, wondering what it would be like to let him go all the way.

But when he started to slide his hand inside her waistband, she reached down and pulled it back out.

"Why not?" he asked, clearly gearing up for his Clarence Darrow argument on why he should be allowed to have his way with her.

"Because I don't want to get pregnant, for one thing."

"You won't get pregnant," he said. "I'd be careful."

"Hm."

"So—"

"No." She captured his mouth with hers, and wished she could go further. She was as tempted as he was, it was just . . . too much. She wasn't ready to do that.

He kissed her until she was dizzy and breathless. She could have stayed there forever, but eventually he drew back with obvious hesitation and said, "I have to go back and finish painting."

"Not yet. Just a little more." She kissed him again.

He kissed her back and somehow it felt more sweet than it ever had before.

It was like he'd lit a fuse in her. "I love you," she breathed, then realized what she'd said and panicked.

It was the first time she'd said it to him. Actually, it was the first time she'd said it to any guy.

During the nanoseconds of silence that followed, her humiliation level went from one to eleven. *Shit shit shit, shouldn't have said that, shit, how do I get out of—*

"I love you too," he said, in a way that was so heartfelt that she immediately started to cry. "Erin?"

"Good," she squeaked. The relief was profound, but even more so was the happiness she felt. He *loved* her. *Her!* The klutzy mouse who had never gotten anyone's attention until her boobs grew at fourteen, and that was attention for all the wrong reasons, was now actually *loved* by the nicest guy in the world. "Thanks for saying that."

He laughed.

Of course. Because everyone knew *thank you* was the worst possible response to *I love you*, though it was immeasurably better after *I love you too.*

And that was the point: he loved her too.

Chapter 4

Usually my intuition was pretty good. I don't know if it was my exhaustion that day or a general malaise over life, but for some reason I didn't see what was coming that night at all.

I was completely unprepared.

Normally the drive home at seven takes no more than thirty minutes, but today it took over two hours, thanks to some bonehead who thought he could switch lanes in an eighteen-wheeler without looking first. No one was killed, but the traffic was horrific. I was lucky my exit was miles before the scene. Some people had to sit on the road all night long.

As it was, I got home around nine fifteen and was in a foul, foul mood.

So, it turned out, was Rick.

I'd been dating Rick for a year—in fact, it was exactly a year that day—and we had plans for the evening that I was not up for. So he'd been waiting in my place for an hour and a half, growing more concerned by the minute that the big accident on 395 had somehow involved me.

"Why do you have a cell phone?" he asked. He was dressed up. He must have had a case in court today. His brown hair gleamed in the light, and there was just a hint of five o'clock shadow on his square jaw. He'd just spent a week in California and his skin was tawny from the sun—he was one of the fortunate ones who looked sun-kissed after five minutes outdoors—which made his eyes look even bluer.

In short, the guy was hot.

"So I can stay in touch!"

He laughed and kissed my cheek. The light, clean scent of his aftershave rested lightly in the air. "You never turn it on!"

"It's on. I was just talking to Cam." I dug it out of my purse. It was off. That was one of Camilla's complaints about our phones and I had to agree—they did tend to go off. I pushed the button and it sprang to life with a jaunty little electronic tune. "Better yet, I can turn it on if I need it. Saves the battery."

He gave a smile. Usually that would make my stomach flip, but tonight I was just too tired. "One of the other benefits of having a cell phone is that *other* people can call you if they need to," he said. "For instance, if they're going crazy thinking you caused a tractor-trailer to swerve into traffic on the highway."

I flopped down on the comfy chair that had once been my dad's. "Nope. Nothing to do with me."

"I'm glad. Now get changed, the latest I could move our dinner reservations to was nine forty-five."

Oh, yes, the dinner reservations. No getting out of that. Rick was all about this anniversary thing. I hadn't even realized it had been a year until he told me he'd scored reservations at the always-booked Naveen's. "Maybe we should go tomorrow," I suggested, wishing wishing wishing he'd agree. All I wanted tonight was to eat cold cereal over the sink and go to bed early with a good book. Then again, Cam would be here tomorrow, so that would make things difficult unless she had a friend come stay.

Rick's expression flickered with disappointment. "Probably not to Naveen's, but if you're really not up for it, we could go somewhere else." He took out his iPhone and started scanning, I knew from the Urbanspoon sound effects, for restaurants in the area. If I wasn't up for it, he wouldn't give me grief, but I could tell this was something he really wanted to do.

"No, no, that's okay." I hoisted myself up. This was the last thing in the world I wanted to do. "I've been dying to try Naveen's." Lie. Naveen's served things like rabbit and goat, and other foods that would have been tossed to the peasants in the old days, and called them "delicacies." But Rick was dying to try Naveen's and I knew that. "Just give me a sec."

I went to the bedroom, pulling my clothes off as I went and leaving them in a trail behind me. Naveen's was high-end. Top-of-the-high-end. As in Cinderella could have shown up in her ball gown and been underdressed. One look in the mirror told me I wasn't going to rate high enough for Naveen's tonight. My hair was in dire need of highlighting and looked, to me, like a dingy-dishwater dark blond. My eyes were the "red, white, and blue" we used to notice in the pothead students in high school, only I hadn't been smoking anything. It was sheer exhaustion creeping through every cell.

I took out a vintage Dior dress I kept for just such an occasion—it was so quirky and retro-modern that if it wasn't dressy enough no one would really be sure of it. Plus it was black. Black upped the glamour for everything. I hoped.

I was going to have to do some heavy lifting to make up for the tired and drawn mask of my face.

It took a few minutes to dig far enough into my closet to find my D&G heels, because they were perfect with the dress. I sat on the side of the bed to put them on, and languished, for just a moment, in the plush softness.

If only I could lie down for a few minutes . . .

"'Bout ready?" Rick asked, coming in, looking as sexy as a rock star with his casual stride.

"Almost."

"Wow! You pull together fast!"

"This is news to you?" I smiled and stepped into the bathroom. A little lipstick, a little dark eyeliner, and I was done. "You know I'm always running late. I had to learn to move fast when I could."

He laughed. "Sometimes fast . . . sometimes slow." He came up to me and put his hand on the small of my back. "You look absolutely beautiful." He leaned in and kissed my cheek.

I closed my eyes and inhaled his cologne. "Thanks. So do you."

"I appreciate that." He drew back and took my hand in his. "Happy anniversary."

"Happy anniversary." I felt sort of stupid saying it, considering the fact that I hadn't even realized it was our anniversary until he'd mentioned it yesterday.

His phone buzzed in his pocket. "Car's waiting."

"What?" I asked blankly. "What car?" Wasn't his car parked on the street, like usual?

"I hired a car," he explained, glancing at his phone. "So we could have some wine if we want to. Or . . . whatever."

This was exactly where I should have started to get suspicious. But no, I just figured he was being his usual fastidious self, thinking of everything, taking no chances. Rick was a corporate lawyer and details were everything to him.

So the car, the reservations, all of that just seemed like more examples of his careful planning than anything else.

Until I got outside, that is. Because the "car" was a stretch limo. "Rick!"

He gave a slightly embarrassed shrug. "I know. It's a little much."

"It's really . . . long." The sex scene from that Kevin Costner movie *No Way Out* came to mind and I felt a new wave of exhaustion.

He laughed. "Just what every guy wants to hear."

I had to laugh. "You are too much," I said, meaning every word, as well as the unsaid *for me* I didn't tag on the end out loud.

The driver got out and opened the door for me. I climbed in, feeling a bit Britney-esque and awkward as my dress lifted too much, and settled into the seat while Rick followed me a whole lot more smoothly.

There was a tinted window between us and the driver, so I barely saw his shadowy figure getting back in behind the wheel, and then the car glided forward.

"It's the closest I could get to a glass carriage in this town," Rick commented, reaching for a bottle of champagne on ice. Somehow I'd missed that when we first got in. He poured a glass and handed it, nearly bubbling over, to me.

I laughed. After the day I'd had, being washed in champagne was perfect. If he'd had a bathtub full of it, I would happily have jumped in with a straw.

Or taken it through an IV.

"Camilla and Amy would love this," I said, leaning back against the seat. "Well, not the champagne, obviously, but the car."

"I know. I thought about having the car come early and drive them home from school, but I couldn't get out of the office on time."

"You are so thoughtful," I said, and meant it sincerely.

"They'll have their chance." He poured himself a glass and held it up to mine. "Meanwhile, to the greatest woman I have ever known." Knowing I was apt to ask if he'd known Marie Curie, he added, "You," and tinked his glass against mine.

It would have been ungracious to suggest he was hard up for toasts, but, seriously, I was not the greatest woman he'd ever known. He was always saying that kind of thing to me, bless him, but I couldn't think of anything I'd done to really deserve his adoration.

"And to you," I interjected, not wanting the weight of responsibility entirely on my shoulders. Which was stupid, really, because how heavy is the responsibility of having a toast dedicated to you? "The nicest guy I know."

"Hmm." He frowned and looked thoughtful.

"Not sexy enough?"

He smiled. "You know what they say about nice guys."

"Then to you," I said, raising an eyebrow. "The meanest son of a bitch in town." I clicked his glass and took a sip. This was the real thing. Toasty, dry, with a crisp effervescence. A glance at the bottle confirmed my suspicions. That label started at a hundred and fifty a pop around here. "What's with this?" I asked. "Why the good stuff? What are you up to?"

"Nothing much," he said, raising his eyebrows in a never-you-mind-little-lady sort of way.

"Seriously, what are you up to?"

"Can't a guy just take his girl out for a nice night on the town without having some secret agenda?"

That settled it. "You *totally* have a secret agenda. Come on, what gives? Did you get a promotion? Or an inheritance?" My mind started to race with all the financially compelling reasons Rick might want to celebrate in style. "Oh! Did you find a house?" He'd been looking for the perfect one almost as long as I'd known him.

He took a long sip of his champagne, then let out a long breath and set the glass down. "I didn't plan to do this here, like this."

"Do what?" Okay, if I hadn't been so tired, I might have thought for a minute before asking that.

He dug his hand into his pocket.

Then—and only then—did I *finally* get an inkling where this was going.

And I panicked.

No, no, no, please not this, not now. Please please please don't go there. Things are so nice. Please don't do this! I don't want to think about this.

My thoughts roared in my head like an old engine turning over and choking out blue smoke. I had to stop him but I'd worked so damn hard to start him that it was clearly going to be impossible.

This was definitely the wrong timing for this. I had so many other things on my plate, the new job, a wedding over the weekend, the stupid sixteenth birthday party and TV show. This was a moment that should have been wonderful; I should be anticipating it, hoping for it, *praying* for it, glorying in all the ways it made perfect sense for us and for the girls, but instead it felt like my head was going to explode with the will to *stop him* at all costs.

But it was too late, he'd already gotten on his knee in front of me, jostling awkwardly as the limo bounced across K Street.

"Oh, Rick." My laugh sounded tinny and hollow, but everything in me wanted to stop this moment. "Come on, now, you don't have to tell me, let's just go have a nice dinner. I hear the desserts are pretty amazing too. Maybe not coffee, though, because it's a work night and if I have coffee, I will just never sleep. Did you know it takes coffee five hours to leave your system?"

I do this. I chatter when I'm nervous. I hear it and it annoys me as much as it annoys anyone else, maybe more, but I'm powerless to stop it.

"Frankly," I blathered on, "I think it takes longer than that. I'd probably be up until it was time to go to work . . ."

"Erin."

". . . and then I'd be dead tired. Which"—I yawned and gave an exaggerated stretch—"actually, I already am. Not that I'm not appreciating this elaborate evening, because I absolutely am, but it's just—"

"*Erin.*"

Damn it. It was going to happen. "Yes?"

"I'm on my knee in front of you."

"I see that." *Get up get up get up, don't do this.* "You're going to ruin your pants. Here, let me help you back to the seat." I reached for his arm and tried pulling. Actually, I sort of *tugged*, which sent him off balance and his hand shot sideways, knocking his champagne glass over.

"Oh! I'm so sorry." I grimaced and reached for some of the napkins next to the ice bucket. "Wow, I am so clumsy. Rick, please forgive me." I dabbed at the seat until he gently grasped my wrist and took the damp napkins out of my hand.

"It's okay." He put the napkins aside. "Are you really not seeing what I'm doing here?"

I hoped my look was blank. It should have been. That many emotions conflicting at once *had* to erase each other out. "Seeing what?" I asked in a small voice.

"Okay, here goes." He took a deep breath. "Erin, I love you—"

"I love you too," I said automatically. It was coming. I couldn't stop it. It was exactly like watching a fuzzy gray security-camera view of a car crash or Princess Diana heading for the Mercedes at the Paris Ritz.

"You have brought more light and fun into my life than I ever thought possible."

It was then that I realized he was holding a small black box in his hand. Not that it was a surprise at this point. I just hadn't noticed it up to then. Somehow I hadn't even wondered.

"I want to spend the rest of my life with you. And I would be honored"—he opened the box, revealing a perfect two-carat emerald-cut diamond, flanked by slender sapphire baguettes—"if you would become my wife."

And that's when I had the weirdest thought possible.

Nate.

Holy cow, where did *that* come from? I hadn't thought about him in *ages*.

I mean, he was there in my subconscious, obviously. Part of my experience in life. Periodically I had dreams about him—sometimes hot, sexual dreams and sometimes typical disjointed dreams where I'd pass him in the hall where he was watering the trash cans—and they'd always disconcert me a little but . . . that was normal, right? He'd been a big part of my life once, of course he'd be floating around in my subconscious.

That was different from really *thinking about him*.

This was terrible timing.

I was being proposed to by a great-looking, successful, young, vibrant, *available* (not a given anymore) man—he was telling me he wanted to commit his life to being with me and only me!

This was not the time to be thinking of a guy who'd left so long ago.

A new dialogue started in my head, one shooing Nate away in

order to give me the brainpower to think of an answer, or a way to stall, for Rick. Instead, it all came out as one big, jumbled mess. "I—I—I have to use the ladies' room. Oh, look, we're here." The car drew to a halt outside Naveen's, just in the nick of time. "Boy, that was a quick drive."

Rick was looking flummoxed. And who could blame him? "Erin, I just *proposed* to you."

I grimaced, probably only adding insult to injury. "I know."

The driver opened the door next to me.

"Not yet," Rick said sharply, and the driver, seeing what was going on—anyone seeing the scene could have known exactly what was going on—slammed the door shut.

I focused on Rick. "Look, I'm shocked. I mean, maybe I should have seen this coming, but I didn't, and it's not like in movies and books where you just have the perfect response at the ready, because I just *wasn't* ready. You had time to prepare." I gestured at the ring box. "You really prepared. It's beautiful. You must have known what you were going to say for days now."

"Weeks."

"*Weeks!* There you go." How had I missed it? I hadn't detected even a tiny sign of this. Was he that good at being covert or was I that blind to things that were going on right under my nose? "But I'm on the spot. Not in a bad way," I hastened to add. "Oh, Rick." I sighed. "I'm so sorry. I've made a mess of this."

He chuckled uneasily. "I understand. But my knee is starting to hurt sitting here like this, so do you *have* an answer?"

I swallowed hard. It would have been wise to say yes right away, to yank this fantastic man off the market before he realized what he was doing and rescinded the proposal. But I couldn't. I let out an unsteady breath. "No," I began.

He groaned irritably and snapped the box shut, moving over

onto the seat next to me. "I knew I should have talked to you about this first. It's too soon. Something in me told me that."

"Wait," I said quickly. "I didn't mean no I won't marry you, I meant no I don't have an answer yet."

He brightened fractionally. "So it's not a no?"

I shook my head and smiled. "No, it's not a no."

"Which means it could be a yes."

My stomach tightened. I swallowed again. "It could. I just . . . need to think. To process. There are so many considerations." I was in danger of expounding upon that ridiculously, so I pressed my lips together for a moment, then simply said, "I hope that's okay."

"Beats the hell out of a no."

I gave the brightest smile I could muster, as if I were a normal woman who was thrilled to receive a proposal from a wonderful man. Not a woman who had just received a proposal from a wonderful man and thought immediately of a guy who'd dumped her *twenty-three years earlier*.

"So what do you say we get fortified?" Rick asked. "I don't know about you, but I could use a drink. A few drinks."

The relief I felt at his practical tone was enormous. "Sounds like a great plan."

Rick opened the door, ignoring the driver, who was standing by outside waiting to do that for him. He got out of the car, then turned and took my hand, helping me out only a little more gracefully than I'd tumbled in.

Rick gave instructions to the driver about our return, and we went into Naveen's ornate interior.

It was the most expensive meal I've ever not tasted.

Chapter 5

July 1986

Another clear summer night.

Erin was newly sixteen and had all the freedom in the world, because her parents were gone for the weekend.

Of course, there was the problem of Aunt Cheryl, her father's sister, who was staying with her because they thought she was too young to stay alone. But Aunt Cheryl had actually turned out to be kind of cool. Where Erin had always thought Aunt Cheryl hadn't married because she'd missed her chance and life had passed her by, she was, in fact, a lot younger and more vibrant than Erin had realized. Although, to be fair, Erin hadn't really seen her since she was about seven, and at seven every adult seems ancient.

Turned out Aunt Cheryl was forty-five and had a boyfriend who, even to Erin's discriminating eye, was pretty hot. For a forty-five-year-old. He looked like Magnum P.I. but without the big mustache.

So the good thing about Aunt Cheryl was that she was so youthful. That turned out to be the bad thing too, since Erin wanted Nate to come over once Cheryl was asleep, and at 10:07 P.M.—and counting—that didn't seem to be anywhere close to happening.

"So you have a boyfriend?" Cheryl asked, coming into Erin's room. She was wearing a nightshirt and had her hair pulled back, so she was obviously close to either turning in for the night or mud wrestling.

Erin nodded, tucking her still-clothed body closer under the covers so, if all else failed, she could claim she was going to sleep, lock the door, and climb out through the balcony and trellis. "Nate."

"What's he like?"

Erin drew in a breath. She wanted Cheryl to sleep so she could see him, but, on the other hand, she loved to talk about Nate. "He's wonderful," she said, so ridiculously dreamy that she added, "really nice. Really."

"Really." Cheryl smiled. "Is he cute?"

"I think so. He's perfect." She thought of him, the mix of perfections and imperfections that he was, and how it made her feel when she looked at him. She gave an involuntary shudder. "He's perfect," she repeated wistfully, reflexively touching her chest where a locket with his picture in it hung beneath her shirt.

Cheryl chuckled. "Enjoy this while you can. You only have one first love."

"I didn't say I love him," Erin objected, but it was the diminishing term "first love" that bothered her. Because she *did* love Nate. But not in a "first love" sort of way—that implied puppy dogs and shared milkshakes and a small smile with the shake of a head later, musing over this tender, innocent time.

That wasn't how it was at all. She wanted to be with him forever. She wanted to see him get older, hear his opinion on changing world events forever; she wanted him to meet her at the altar, hold her hand through childbirth, and sit in a rocking chair next to her in old age. Somehow the assumption that that was where they were going had lodged in her mind, and Aunt Cheryl's implication that it might be a passing thing made her hackles rise.

"But I do," she heard herself say. "I do love him."

"Of course you do!"

Ugh. There it was again. That I-know-more-than-you, someday-you'll-understand smugness. Made worse by the fact that she obviously didn't mean it as smugness. She just thought she was stating a fact that they'd both agree on later.

Erin would never agree that this was just "first love."

Aunt Cheryl must have picked up on her discontent, because she lowered her brow and asked, "Is something wrong?"

"No, nothing." She didn't mean for it to sound like a pointed *nothingggg* but it did, even to her ear. She tried to soften it with, "I'm just tired."

That seemed to satisfy Cheryl. "Me too." She yawned, as if on cue. "Good night, sweetie." She came forward in a cloud of Shalimar perfume and bent down to kiss Erin's cheek. "Sleep tight."

"You too." Erin slunk deeper under the covers and tried to make her eyelids look heavy. "Could you hit the light on your way out?"

"Sure thing." Cheryl hit the switch and the room was cloaked in darkness. "See you in the morning."

Erin remained silent, hoping to perhaps give the impression that she'd already knocked off.

Then she waited in bed, fingering the locket on her necklace and listening to the cicadas outside her open window, until Cheryl had stopped moving around in her parents' room.

She reached for the phone and dialed his number, as she'd done a million times in the dark.

He answered after the slightest chirp of a ring. "Hey."

"Oh, my God, my aunt would not go to bed."

He laughed. "She's keeping an eye on you."

"Not a very good one, I hope. Come in half an hour?"

"I don't know." He gave an exaggerated yawn. "I'm getting kind of tired."

"Yeah? Maybe I should call someone else."

He never thought that joke was funny. "I'll be there."

"Okay, but wait in the car for a sec when you get here. If I don't come out it's because she's still up."

They hung up and Erin kept the light out, looking through the window at the nothing that was happening outside. Any car arriving at this hour was sure to call attention for anyone who happened to be up and looking. But when she opened her door and looked down the hall at her parents' door, she could see the light was out in there. She couldn't hear a sound from within.

Cheryl was asleep. Or almost. Why would she stay up? She'd mentioned at least five times tonight how she had to get up at six thirty A.M. and go to work and how she envied Erin the freedom of high school summers with no responsibility greater than reading good books and watching soap operas.

For all she knew, Erin was getting rest for another busy day of leisure.

After about twenty minutes, Erin snuck through her door, closing it behind her, and went downstairs. That was the worst of it. The house was entirely floored with hardwood and every board seemed to creak like a shrieking banshee when stepped upon, so she had to move as lightly and as stealthily as possible. Plus she had to do it fast, so if there was more than one creak, it would sound like one long one rather than footsteps. House settling, rather than escape.

When she got to the main floor, she froze, listening for any sounds from above. The hardwood floors worked to both their advantage: they could alert the chaperone to when a prisoner was trying to escape, but they also told the prisoner if the chaperone was rousing from bed and coming to investigate.

Fortunately, there was no sound at all.

She stepped onto the front porch and sat down, waiting for him. Soon she saw headlights swing onto her street and heard the familiar old Chevy engine make its way toward her house. A few yards away from her house, he turned off the headlights, then pulled up a bit short of his usual spot out front. If Aunt Cheryl looked out the window, she'd think his car was in front of the neighbors' house.

Erin's pulse quickened at the slamming driver's door and his footsteps coming up the street. She stood and ran across the sprinkler-dampened yard to him, throwing herself into his arms.

For a long moment, they kissed: mouths, chests, hips pressed together, arms locked around each other. She breathed in his familiar scent, part him, part Coast soap and Pert shampoo. Everything about him drew her in; it was the same every time.

"Where do you want to go?" he asked against her mouth.

"Inside," she said automatically.

"But she's in there."

"Downstairs."

He tightened his arms around her and kissed her more.

She didn't want it to end. Ever.

The cicadas buzzed hypnotically in her ears. In the distance, crickets joined the chorus. It was so loud she couldn't imagine Aunt Cheryl or anyone else could hear them over the sound, even if they yelled.

Finally, she pulled back.

She had A Plan.

"Come on." She ran her hand down his arm and twined her fingers in his, then pulled him toward the house. "Let's go."

He followed. He indulged her. Unless there was danger ahead, or another clear reason her idea was harebrained, he always indulged her. She recognized that, but figured it was usually worth it for him, one way or the other.

She amused him; they both knew it. In a way their roles just reflected a deal they'd made. She'd be flighty and needy and he'd be smarter and indulgent, and in exchange she'd be protected and he'd be adored.

It just worked.

Holding tight to his hand, she led him through the front door, closing it slowly and quietly behind them, then down the stairs to the basement. She always hated those steps because they were just thick wood slats with no back and ever since she was a child she had imagined a hand reaching through and grabbing her ankles as she ran up them after turning out the light.

Tonight she had no fear, though.

They reached the cold linoleum floor and worked past her mother's sewing table to an enclave that used to house a Ping-Pong table but which was now empty, except for some boxes of Christmas decorations and bolts of fabric her mother had laid out to measure and then left there.

That's where Erin stopped. Wordlessly, she drew herself in to him again and their mouths crashed together like he was a soldier going off to war. He cradled her face with his hands and moved his mouth against hers with a gentleness and control that far surpassed hers.

She wanted more. She was determined that this was the night, and her eagerness in kissing him was contagious. Soon his control was broken and he was sliding his hand up her shirt and unsnapping her bra, removing both with one fluid movement. All that remained was her locket.

She didn't even bother with his shirt, just went straight for his jeans, unbuttoning the hard snap and sliding everything off of him in one fell swoop. She was kneeling in front of him, and she took him into her mouth, clutching his hips.

She heard him pull off his shirt, then felt his hand on top of her head, absently tousling her hair while she brought him closer and closer to the end. But she couldn't do that tonight, as much as she loved the feeling of achievement she had when she brought him all the way.

She drew back, pausing for a moment before letting go of him and reaching up to guide him down to her.

Together they lay down, warm skin against the cold, hard floor. He unsnapped her pants and skidded them down across her hips and off. Erin reached for the fabric that was lying on the floor and pulled it underneath her before pulling him on top of her.

"I'm ready," she said breathlessly.

His breathing was strained in the dark. He was ready too. He was more than ready.

But he'd never let her do something she'd regret.

"Ready for what?" he asked cautiously.

She wrapped her legs around him. "Everything."

It was a long, tight moment before he said, "Are you sure?"

She thought about Cheryl's contention that this was young love, and about how she'd feel if they were ever to break up and she had to look back on this moment as an episode in a life that was full of people she didn't even know now.

The very thought made her want to cry.

She'd know him forever, wouldn't she? What would have to

happen to make this—what they felt right now—change at all? Unless it just got stronger. And surely that was what was going to happen, wasn't it? Wouldn't this just get stronger?

"I'm sure," she said. And as the words came out of her mouth, she knew she *was* sure.

She never knew how he'd gotten so artful with his mouth and hands, or if, perhaps, it was only her perception because she hadn't been with anyone else, but the moment she told him she was sure, he turned up the intensity, and within moments she was floating away, barely aware of anyone sleeping two floors up, or two doors down, or anyone anywhere else in the world.

His breathing was growing very strained from holding back.

"Now," she said, and swallowed her fear. "Do it now."

"You're really sure?"

But it was no longer a question. If it wasn't tonight, it would be tomorrow or next week or next month, but Erin could no longer see herself without him somewhere in her life, and there was no one she could even imagine being her first besides him.

She reached down and guided him toward her, then folded her arms around him and held on. She closed her eyes and he pressed against her.

"*Ouch!*" she cried involuntarily, then snapped her mouth shut and tried to breathe normally.

Now, *that* was some pain.

"I'm sorry," he said. "Is it bad?"

"Yes. *Ow.* Is it over?"

"Um. No."

She took his meaning. All that pain and he hadn't even broken through yet.

She took a deep breath. "Okay." She balled her hands into fists. "Try again."

He did. Several more times. And though the pain was intense, the result was always the same.

Nothing.

Finally, he rolled off her and said, "We're going to try this another way."

"What are you talking about?" she asked dubiously.

He laughed, then kissed her and gently trailed his hand down across her ribs, over her abdomen, and between her legs. He took his time, waiting for the throbbing to subside and her body to want more again.

Then he worked her with his hand, pushing the limits a little bit at a time with his fingers until finally she said, "I'm sure you can do it now."

He moved onto her again and started to press into her. She widened her legs and bit her lower lip, willing this to be over so she could find out about all the *good* stuff people talked about.

"*Ow ow ow*, wait a minute," she said, when she couldn't stand it anymore. "Just let me breathe for a sec."

"Are you okay?"

She nodded. "Yes. It's just . . . is it always this difficult?"

"I don't know. I've never . . . done this with a . . . you know . . ."

"What a *what*?"

"*Virgin.*"

"Who said I'm a virgin?" she asked, and they both laughed.

"Okay," she said, bracing herself like a boxer in the corner going in for another round. Hopefully the last round. "Let's go."

"I don't know, Erin, maybe we should wait."

"For what? For this to stop aching so we can start all over? No way. We're going to do this." Things had become decidedly unromantic. Now she was determined to lose her virginity.

So he tried again, distracting her moderately with his kisses, then, with a searing, earth-shattering pain that made her cry out, he was finally in.

They stayed still for a minute, half afraid to move and half afraid they'd hear Aunt Cheryl upstairs.

When a few minutes had passed with no sign of rousing, Erin whispered, "Now what?"

"We move," he explained. "You move your hips when I do."

He pulled out and she moved her hips up.

"You go the *opposite* way," he said, without a trace of the laughter she later learned would have been completely appropriate.

"Ooooh!" She wondered, privately, how that could work because wouldn't he just slip out if she moved down when he moved up? But she tried it anyway.

And it worked.

It didn't feel good that night. This was no romance novel where the heroine was taken by a handsome monster of a man and spent the evening moaning with pleasure at this newfound thrill.

But it did begin to hurt less. Or she got numb. Or something.

Before long, he pulled out and came onto her stomach.

It was one of the more triumphant feelings she'd ever experienced.

"Are you okay?" he whispered again in her ear after a moment.

"Yes. Just sore. And relieved." She touched his cheek. "I love you so much."

He kissed her, then said, "I love you," his lips next to hers. He kissed her again, longer, until they drifted off together.

They lay there for a long time, dozing in and out, but still locked together. Eventually, Erin noticed a faint light showing outside the high well window.

"It's morning!" She tapped Nate's shoulder.

"Hm?"

"It's morning. Aunt Cheryl will be down any second!"

He sat up and squinted at his watch. "It's five thirty."

"I have no idea when she gets up. She's been gone every day when I wake up." She giggled. One of the best things about summer was the complete freedom. Nate had a job, which was both good and bad, but Erin didn't have anything she had to do. "Of course, it's not like I'm waking up at six thirty or anything."

They collected their clothes and put them on in the semidarkness. Then Erin went and flipped the switch to turn on the light. The bolt of fabric they'd been lying on was marred with blood.

"Oh, my God," she breathed.

Even Nate's eyes widened when he looked at the amount.

She looked at him. "I told you it hurt!"

He nodded. "I'm sore too."

"You?"

"Yeah, I was bent, like, in half!"

She winced. "Sorry. Well, it's done now. You can't *un*do it."

He looked concerned. "Do you wish you could?"

"Nope." She went to the sewing table and found the only scissors she could, pinking shears. Then she cut the fabric off of the bolt. They'd ruined about two feet of it because of where they'd been.

"I kind of feel like I should save this as a souvenir," she said.

"Gruesome." He held out his hand. "Give it to me. I'll throw it out at my house."

She handed it over. "You just want to keep it as a trophy."

"Yup, you got me." He guided her to the stairs and they went up very quietly.

Erin heard a movement overhead and pointed.

He nodded and somehow managed to open the front door without a sound.

'Bye, she mouthed.

He kissed her silently, then laid his hand to her cheek for a moment before drawing back and closing the door as noiselessly as he'd opened it.

She stood there a moment, hand against the wooden door, heart still pounding with the memory of their time together.

Then she whispered, "I love you."

And she'd never meant what she said more than she did in that moment.

Chapter 6

Present

How long did he give you to think about it?" Jordan asked.

I continued my run down Wisconsin Avenue, answering her through my Bluetooth earpiece. I hated exercise, hated running, but it was better than sitting around on my sofa, spending the whole Saturday trapped in my condo *and* my head. Camilla was out with a bunch of friends at the zoo and the moment she'd left, I'd felt a strange, restless lack of purpose.

It was either stay in and let my brain melt or go out and run until my legs melted.

I opted for legs.

"It's not a contract negotiation. I can think about it until I have an answer."

"All right, so how long do *you* give you?"

"I don't know. Should I be timing it? I honestly thought the answer would come to me with some sort of magical certainty, but every time I try to meditate on it, I get distracted and start to think about other things." It was true, I had the attention span of a two-year-old child. If I was reading or working or trying to coordinate schedules on the phone, all I could think about was Rick's proposal. If I put the book down, hung up the phone, and decided to devote my attention entirely to the situation, my mind wandered. Too often it wandered to Nate, which freaked me out and made me search desperately for something else to concentrate on.

Suddenly I was the poster child for ADD.

"No, no, no," Jordan insisted. "You can't expect to have some psychic knowledge of what to do. This is a *practical* decision you have to make. Can you spend the rest of your life with this man? Do you want to have a family with him? Do you want to grow old with him?"

"Well, think about it, it makes so much sense! Cam would have a *family!* She loves Rick, she loves Amy, this completely makes sense!" I stopped at the light at Battery Lane and jogged in place, wishing with every step for clarity.

"You can't do this for Cam," Jordan warned.

But I disagreed. I completely disagreed. With her father dying when she was so young, she'd never had a chance. She'd been completely ripped off in the family department.

But Jordan wouldn't understand that because her whole life was about healing the individual, empowering the individual. Sacrifice, of any sort, didn't belong in there for Jordan.

"It's good for me too," I said. "*Rick* is good for me." If I were on *Survivor* and had to form an alliance with one person I knew and trusted the most, it would absolutely be Rick.

Most people probably didn't decide their futures by pretending they were on *Survivor*, I suspected.

"Okay, then pretend you have made the decision to marry him and really sit with it for a while, see how you feel."

The light turned and I continued forward, down the hill toward the Navy Medical Center and NIH. Every step was torture, but I had so much adrenaline coursing through my veins that stopping would have been even worse. "Perfect." I imagined I'd said yes.

I couldn't breathe.

"Tell me something," Jordan said suddenly. "What was your very first thought when he said it? Maybe your answer is that simple."

My breath caught as I remembered my first thought. Nate's image came to mind, a little faded like an old photograph. "I don't think so. It was . . . weird. My first thought was weird." I tried to shake it off mentally. "It's not relevant."

Jordan hesitated, then asked, "So are you going to tell me what it was or just be cryptic about it?"

So here's the thing. I would have told her the truth right up front if I hadn't found the thought so deeply resonant. Honestly, there were other guys I had dated—guys I'd dated longer than Nate—who could have come to mind and it would have made more sense and mattered less.

The fact that a guy who had dumped me heartlessly two and a half decades ago came to mind when a certifiably great man proposed embarrassed me to death.

"I don't mean to be cryptic," I said, hoping to sound airy. But I couldn't pull it off. "It's just . . . Nate. My first thought was of Nate."

This was not a proud moment for me. After the huge ass I'd made of myself mourning the end of that relationship, I wasn't eager to tell anyone who'd been there that the thought of him might be standing between me and my verdict on marriage to a great guy.

It was classic Stupid Girl Syndrome to prefer the asshole who wasn't interested. And while I wasn't *preferring* Nate, obviously, that I was even *thinking* of him was humiliating, even though it was Jordan I was talking to.

"*What?*" Jordan asked.

I stopped in the shade of a big oak and shook out my wobbly legs and finished, "The first word that came to mind was *Nate.*"

"Oh!"

"Yeah."

She let out a long breath. "Wow."

"I know."

There was a long pause while Jordan processed it. Finally, she said, "We never talk about him."

"Why would we?" I walked around in little circles on the sidewalk. My entire body felt agitated, from the inside out.

"Because he was a really important person in your development."

Let me pause here to say Jordan is a psychologist. Usually she didn't pull out the psycho-speak with me because she's been talking to me without filters since we were both idiot thirteen-year-olds and it's hard to take someone's professional opinion of your mental health seriously when you've personally witnessed her clinging to the back bumper of an ex-boyfriend's car while he drove away.

In this case, she was right, though. She was probably usually right, but the fact that Nate had been there for some major developmental stages was undeniable. Not all of them were pretty, but he should have expected that when he started dating a fifteen-year-old. I don't care how slowly boys mature, he was three years older than I was.

It didn't take a psychiatrist to figure out why that had been traumatic for me.

"Well," I said, impatient with the truth. "I'm pretty much developed now, so I don't see why he'd come to mind at all."

"You don't?" I could picture her leaning back on her office chair, thoughtfully removing her glasses. "Seriously?"

"Not really. I mean . . ." I tried to think what deep, dark thing she might be getting at. That was then, this was now, the 'tween didn't meet. "He was important to me once. Not anymore."

Her voice was measured. "Honey, you kind of had a nervous breakdown when you guys broke up."

I grimaced. "I wouldn't call running around the neighborhood in my underwear at midnight singing Bon Jovi songs exactly a nervous breakdown," I said.

I started running again.

There was an audible silence, before she asked, "You're kidding, right?"

I rolled my eyes to myself. "Yes, Jordan, I'm kidding." Like she wouldn't have known if I'd run around the neighborhood in my skivvies singing hard rock ballads. But the fact that she remembered me as so bad off that, even now as a professional, she found that conceivable was disturbing. "I got depressed. Had some panic attacks. It was a bad time, but not a serious psychological trauma."

"You dropped out of school."

"For *one* semester." Yeah, that was bad.

"Your parents took you to Chestnut Lodge!"

"They didn't *leave* me there!" It was an outpatient thing. A psychologist who was supposedly good at helping teenagers with anxiety problems. It wasn't like I'd really gone *crazy*.

"Mm-hm." Her chair squeaked and I knew now she was leaning over her desk, toward an imaginary me across from her. She was in full therapist mode. "It was bad. I don't think you ever got over that experience."

"Yes, I did!"

"You want my professional opinion?"

"That wasn't it?"

She laughed softly. "There's more. I think you need to find Nate and meet him face-to-face, to exorcise this demon once and for all. It will help you make your decision about Rick."

I laughed out loud. In fact, I had to stop running for a moment, the idea was so preposterous. "You're out of your mind."

"I'm serious," Jordan said.

"*That* is the worst idea you've ever had," I said shortly. "And you're the one who thought we could turn a Ping-Pong table into a raft and sunbathe on it in the middle of Conroy's Pond."

She clicked her tongue against her teeth. "First off, that wasn't *my* idea, that was *our* idea, and second, I didn't spend six years at Vanderbilt so some punk I've known since before we got our periods can tell me I don't know what I'm talking about. I *knew* you and Nate together. You were unusually close. You were way too young to be so close. My studied opinion is that it's still working on you on some really base level." She sighed, and I recognized it as a sound of sympathy. "I'm serious about this, Erin. It's not the first time I've thought this."

"What are you *talking* about? Nate has nothing to do with my daily life!"

"Really? It's not like you dated for just a few months, it was *years*. During crucial developmental years."

I didn't want to think about this.

"And you never really let another guy in," she went on. "Which, I think, is the root of your dilemma now."

"All right, so what if there is some kind of unresolved thing there? What good will it do to talk to a guy who might barely remember me? A guy who, in fact, might think I'm crazy to be holding on to any lingering thoughts. You know, if someone like Stuart

Heeley called me and said he had unresolved issues with me, I'd seriously think about calling the police and getting a restraining order just because it would be so wildly out of proportion to the way I remembered him." Which was barely at all—we dated long enough for me to remember his name, but not long enough for me to feel confident I'd recognize him in a lineup.

"This isn't the same," Jordan said, sounding a little impatient. "Don't play a playah, honey, you and I both know how he felt about you. Nate remembers you."

"I don't know," I said flatly. I didn't. I had no idea anymore. In fact, I had serious doubts that I'd ever really known him.

"Then that's another thing you need to find out," Jordan said, with the finality of a death sentence. "Find him and put this whole thing to rest."

I shook my head again even though she couldn't see me, and my audience in a Honda at an intersection had moved on when the light changed. "I can't do it." There had to be another solution. "Don't you have some sort of puppet I could talk to instead? Have a mock conversation to work this out?"

"I seriously doubt Mr. Snoodles would fool your subconscious."

"Look, I'd be willing to wrap Mr. Snoodles around a vibrator and pretend I love him if there was any chance."

"Find Nate. Talk to him."

My call waiting beeped. My first thought, as always, was Camilla. Child emergency. I was always braced for the worst. "Hold on a sec," I told Jordan, and switched over. "Erin Edwards."

"Erin, it's Jeremy." As if I'd mistake that voice for anyone else's. My relief that it *wasn't* a child emergency was short-lived as he continued, "Can you come to your office right away? We have a catastrophe on our hands."

A catastrophe. Good. That sounded like just what I needed to get my mind off of things. I switched back. "Jordan, I've got to run. But *thank you*, truly. I really appreciate your help."

"No problem. Think about what I said, okay?"

"I will." I wouldn't. No way. I'd tried hard to bury my feelings for Nate so deep, no one would see them again until my autopsy. I couldn't possibly open that wound again. "Call you later."

Forty minutes later I was on TV.

Had Jeremy mentioned the words "camera crew," I might have showered before hightailing it over to work. Possibly done something with my hair. Maybe put on some makeup so I didn't look like I was actually haunting the hotel instead of working in it.

As it was, I found him hiding in his office. "I can't be on camera!" he shrieked like a little girl. "I have a zit!"

Oh, for God's sake. I looked at his face and saw nothing. "Where?"

"Right *here*." He pointed at the nothing on his chin.

"I don't see anything, Jeremy." Why did he always have to get so hysterical over everything? And how was it he was still the boss, given that I had to take care of him all the time?

"You have to handle this."

Every muscle in my body seized. "Oh, no. No, no, no. The deal was that *I* have nothing to do with the on-camera stuff. You had me *cancel my vacation* to stick around and help with the specific codicil that I would not be on the show, even in a background shot. Remember?"

"They just need to do some establishing shots." As soon as he'd found out VTV was coming, he'd learned everything he could about television production and liked to toss the terms around like an expert. "And they also want to start getting some background information on the planning. They probably won't use it."

Right. Just like my mother wouldn't keep the unflattering blow-fish pictures she got of us every year extinguishing birthday candles. "Jeremy, I am telling you right now, there is *no way* I'm going on camera. You *agreed* to that, rather enthusiastically, when I told you that six months ago."

"Six months ago, I didn't have Mount Everest on my lip."

There was no point arguing. He wasn't going on, so I was stuck. Honestly, when Jeremy had called claiming there was a catastrophe and that I had to get over there right away, I'd pictured pipes spouting water. Maybe a sinkhole outside by the pool. Possibly even a guest with a broken limb in the water park.

Jeremy had counted on me thinking that way, of course. If he'd mentioned cameras and zits, he knew I wouldn't have come. Then he would have had to handle it himself. Now that I was here, though, I knew there was no way he'd leave his office. It was a game of chicken and he was a lot better at it than I was.

I made my way into the bar, where I saw three bored-looking guys with camera equipment and beers, sitting among a bunch of wires and power strips. There was a woman with them, with short red hair, dramatic makeup, and, I could tell thanks to the sleeveless shift she wore, seriously buff arms.

"Hello," I said, as professionally as I could, given my appearance. "I'm Erin Edwards, events coordinator here at the hotel. Mr. Rambaur told me you're here to do some establishing shots of the hotel?"

"We got those," the woman said, extending her hand. "Pippa Tanner," she said, shaking my hand with an iron grip. "I'm the producer in charge of this mess. What we need"—here she looked me up and down critically—"is to ask a few questions about the planning. Just a little bit of tape on that, because normally the party planner obviously isn't the money shot."

"Sure, what do you need to know?"

"Why don't you have a seat?" she suggested, gesturing at a seat being occupied by one of her crew.

The moment her hand swept in his direction, he sprang into action, picking up the camera while one of his coworkers picked up and turned on a rack of bright lights and the other started assembling what looked like a boom mic to hang over me.

"Oh." I felt Cindy Brady Syndrome coming on. If the camera started running, I was liable to freeze. I didn't sit. The camera hovered in my face and I said to the guy, "Can you turn that off for a minute?" To Pippa, I said, "I'm really not up for being filmed right now. I was out running and I got this call and I'm just a mess."

"How long would it take you to clean up?" She glanced at her watch, then back at me, the implication clear: *Time is money and you're wasting both of mine.*

This wasn't going well at all. Why hadn't they just looked at me, seen I'd make for awful TV, and let me off the hook? "Well, I'd have to go home and shower and it would really be more time than you'd want to spend—"

"You're not that big," Pippa interrupted. She was probably two sizes smaller than I was, but the way she said it you would have thought she was talking to Oprah in 1997. "I can loan you something from my room." That critical eye wandered over me again. "At least something you can put on as a suitable top and we can film from the shoulders up."

"I'm not borrowing your clothes." I didn't mean to sound snappish. "I mean, surely you can just wait until Jeremy . . . returns. I have a feeling it will be sooner than he expected," I added through gritted teeth.

"Fine. What did you think of Miss Tacelli when you first met her?" Pippa asked.

The lights guy swung around in front of me and I felt my pupils shrink. Anything I said now—even begging off and saying I didn't want to be interviewed—might be used to make me, and the hotel, look bad.

I had no choice but to answer.

I swallowed. "I thought she was delightful. A bright, vivacious young woman looking forward to a great future." Had they met Roxanne yet? Was there any way they would buy this?

Pippa gave me a smile that said she had and she wasn't. "Has she had any special requests for the party?"

I feigned ignorance. "What do you mean?"

"I don't know, balloons, limos, color-coded invitations"—she raised a knowing eyebrow—"horses?"

I looked her dead in the eye. "Nothing unusual or impossible." Game on. "We specialize in making dreams come true here."

My phone rang then, thank God. I didn't care who it was, I would be glad to talk to them for an hour or so. Salesman? Bill collector? Wrong number? Bring 'em on.

"Erin Edwards," I said, lifting my index finger to Pippa to indicate I had to take this Very Important Call.

"This is Roxanne," a weepy voice said.

My heart sank. "Yes, R—" No point in alerting them that their star was on the phone. "Yes?" I stepped away from the crew, lest their mics could pick up the sound. "What can I do for you?"

"Justin and I broke up."

"O . . . kay . . . ?" I'm not an idiot. I gathered, quickly, that Justin was her boyfriend and that he'd dumped her. What I didn't get, and what I was afraid to ask, was what it had to do with me. "Well. I'm . . . sorry to hear that. . . ."

She dissolved into sobs and I waited, trying to figure out the answer I'd give to various requests. Wants me to remove him from the guest list? No problem. Wants to cancel the party for time of mourning and/or finding new boyfriend? *Really* no problem. Wants me to have him killed? Against hotel policy.

"I need you to get him back for me."

Ah, she'd dialed the wrong number. That had to be it. She meant to call one of her friends, but she'd gotten me instead. "You must have hit the wrong number," I explained. "This is Erin Edwards, the event coordinator for your birthday party."

"I know!" she barked. "And you said"—she sniffed, sounding defiant—"that if there was anything I wanted for the party, you would handle it. I want Justin there."

I felt my brow knit involuntarily. I got stupid requests all the time, but this one took the cake. "But I don't know what I can possibly do about that. It sounds like you two need to have a talk or something, maybe straighten out a misunderstanding . . . ?"

"What I understand is that he's an asshole."

"Oh." Problem solved. "Then it's good he's not coming, right?"

"But I love him!" She took a wavering breath. "And he *has* to be at my party."

"Why would you want him there if he's an a—"

"I just do!"

Inspiration struck me. "You know who you should talk to about this? Jeremy Rambaur. Let me give you his number."

"*He* just gave me *yours*!"

I'd kill him.

This was becoming more of a pain by the second.

"Anyway, a man wouldn't understand," she went on, as if she and I had mind-melded. "You *get* it, don't you?"

"Well—"

"So let me give you Justin's number and you can just give him a call and get all the bullshit sorted out. He *has* to come to my party. He just *has* to. If he doesn't, the whole thing will be ruined!"

I looked longingly at the film crew. Five minutes ago, I had thought nothing could be worse than being interviewed on film. Now I'd revised my opinion. This was far, far worse. And it was about to reach new, lower levels of misery.

We specialize in making dreams come true. What a stupid thing for me to say when I knew full well I was dealing with crazy people. Well played, Universe. Well played.

"This isn't really a good time," I said to Roxanne. Then, hoping to appeal to her vanity by mentioning the TV stuff, I added, "I'm doing some preproduction stuff for your show."

Hope dissolved when she said, "Are you ready? It's two-four-oh—"

"Hang on," I said. "Let me find a pen."

I had experience calling estranged boyfriends, obviously, but it wasn't something I ever wanted to do again.

Particularly for someone like Roxanne.

This was ridiculous.

And yet, in some way, it felt like the universe was trying to tell me something. But whether it was saying I needed to contact Nate and resolve a few things, like Jordan had suggested, or that the whole idea of teenage romance and drama was ridiculous, I didn't know.

But maybe Jordan was right.

Maybe I needed to find out.

Or maybe—God, I hated thinking about this crap after so long—but maybe I needed to clear up the truth for him once and for all. To let him know, after all these years, that I truly hadn't done what he thought I'd done to him.

That I'd truly loved him.

Chapter 7

August 1986

They picked their way down the wooded path to the lake, Erin, Nate, Theresa, and Theresa's latest boy, JP, in the deep golden light of a late summer afternoon. They carried two six-packs of Champale, a drink pretending to be a cross between champagne and beer yet failing miserably on both counts, crossing creeks and stepping over branches to get to the lake in Potomac Falls.

Finally, the bramble cleared and the lake was there, stretching out for two or three acres in front of them, the sun dancing across the surface. There was a bigger stretch of woods across the way and to the right, and manicured lawns rolled out to the left.

"Let's sit," Erin suggested as Nate came to her side.

"Um, I think we're going to keep going a little farther," Theresa said with a giggle.

"Here." Erin handed her one of the sixes of Champale. She was glad they'd be alone. She'd been with Theresa and guys before and it always tended to be a make-out fest for them, and a conversation for her and Nate that made her feel like they were as old and prudish as her grandparents.

"Thanks!" Theresa and JP stumbled off down the path, on their way to who-knew-what secretive action.

Erin didn't care.

She and Nate sat down side by side on the dirt. She brushed some broken twigs aside and moved closer to him. The heat had been oppressive all day but as the sun went down and the wind picked up slightly, it was finally beginning to cool.

"We used to ride horses here when I was little," she said. "I loved to ride them into the lake and swim, but they were always losing their shoes in the mud right there"—she pointed to the bank—"and my mother got so mad because we had to keep having the blacksmith out to replace them."

"You swam on horses?"

"Well, we'd ride them into the lake, and they'd start to swim and we'd just sort of float along with them. It was great."

"I never thought about horses swimming," he said. "But I guess it makes sense. Like the ponies swimming from Assateague to Chincoteague."

"Exactly." She leaned against him. "Their bellies make them float like barrels." She yawned. "I want a horse again someday."

"Then you'll get one."

"That was easy." She tossed a rock in the lake while he pulled the tops off of two Champales.

"So is this like Michigan?" she asked, knowing that every summer he went to his widowed grandfather's house in Michigan and did a bunch of boating and fishing and nature stuff.

He laughed. "No."

"No?"

"This is a pond."

"This is a lake!"

"Around here, this is a lake," he said. "Anywhere else, this is a pond."

"Oh." She took the Champale he handed her. "Thanks. So what's it like at your granddad's?"

"Isolated." He took a sip from his bottle. "Quiet. The quiet is nice, though. You can go for a walk at night and if someone is having a party three miles down the shore, you can hear them. Water conducts sound really well."

"Three *miles*? There's that much water?" She looked at the small lake in front of them. No wonder he called it a pond. "That's almost like an ocean!"

A smile flickered across his face. "It looks like the ocean a little. But no waves. More like the bay."

"And are there loons?" They'd watched that movie *On Golden Pond* together, both of them in tears at the end, and decided they would be the old people in that someday. From a distance of fifty years, they could both see it.

"Yes." He slid his hand into hers. "There are loons."

"That would be good. I want to go there with you." She sipped from her bottle and looked contentedly at the muddy water, imagining a much bigger expanse and horizon. She could look into eternity in a place like that, all water and trees and silence. And Nate. Nate there by her side. That would be perfect. That would constitute her perfect day.

Someday they'd do that.

Meanwhile, they were here, and it was about as much peace and nature as they were apt to get in Potomac.

"Maybe this summer," he said. "In August we could drive up to my granddad's house."

His grandfather had a house locally as well, where they'd been many times, but it was all the same terrain to Erin. The idea of going someplace completely different was appealing.

Plus, she was good at fishing and crabbing, at least by Maryland standards, so maybe she could do it right up north as well. Or at least right enough.

"We should," she said, adjusting her grip on his hand and leaning against him. "We totally should." For a long moment she was silent, watching the water glimmer in the distance. "I love the light on the water. Remember that time we came here when it was a full moon?"

"Mmm." He nodded and drank from the bottle.

"That was the most beautiful thing I ever saw." It was like something out of a children's picture book, all perfect trees and perfect moon, and perfect reflection on both. "I wished on a star that night that I'd see a thousand more full moons like that one."

He frowned for a moment. "In a best-case scenario, that's eighty-three years' worth, without accounting for those times when it's overcast."

"That's what I was thinking!" she said, and laughed at their mutual practicality. "Some months you see nothing, so I thought I was covering my bases by asking for a thousand."

He smiled at her. "Smart baby."

"You'll be there for all of them, right?"

He looked down, but tightened his arm around her. "Of course."

"So that's a long time for us."

He nodded. "I'd be over a hundred."

"You *will* be over a hundred."

He shrugged. "Maybe so."

"It's not unrealistic." She raised her chin. She was certain that would be easily achieved by then. Especially by Nate, who was so healthy it was almost impossible to cut his fingernails because they were so strong. "I can see it."

"Me too." He nodded and looked at her in that way that gave her a thrill every time. "Me too."

She leaned against him and languished in the feeling of being completely safe and completely loved. There wasn't one thing in this world she wanted or needed right now, and she didn't care about anyone or anything other than this moment with him.

It was as relaxing as sleeping.

"Will you still love me when I'm a hundred?" she asked.

"I will *always* love you. No matter what."

For a long time they sat in silence, watching the setting sun glimmer on the small expanse of water, and listening to the distant sounds of what must have been Theresa and JP in the throes of passion.

"Ouch!" Erin was pretty sure she heard from Theresa at some point. "God, JP. Wrong hole!"

Erin and Nate exchanged glances and laughed.

"I'm so glad I'm not dating new people," she said to him. "Sounds painful."

A muscle tightened in his jaw. "You seem to want to date new people sometimes."

"What are you talking about?"

"I've heard you talking to your friends about guys you like at school or whatever."

"I don't." But she did, he was right. She just had no idea he had any awareness of it at all. She nestled closer to him. Someone approaching from the back wouldn't have been sure if it was one person sitting there or two. "Anyway, I'm going to marry you and spend my whole entire life with you. You're stuck." That was the point. He was forever.

"I hope so."

"Of course we are! But it doesn't mean we won't *notice* other people now and then."

"I don't look at other girls."

She wasn't buying that for a second. "Oh, bull!"

"I don't."

She drew back and looked at him. He looked like he meant it. And, actually, it wasn't the first time he'd said it. A pang of guilt stabbed at her. She noticed other guys all the time. Wasn't that normal? It would be weird to never even see that other people were attractive. She noticed pretty girls too. She was an equal-opportunity noticer. It didn't mean anything. "I don't believe you," she said.

"Why not?"

"Because it can't be true! People *notice* attractive people. It's just . . . the law of attraction."

"That's not what the law of attraction is."

"Whatever. It's still a fact. There's no way you can make me believe it's true that you never notice a pretty girl."

"It is true."

She looked at him in disbelief. "Okay. Right. You are never, in any way, *aware* of other girls. You never notice if someone's pretty or not. Not even in passing."

He thought about it for a moment. "I don't look."

"Okay, but do you *see*? Sometimes? I mean, look at Theresa. She's pretty. Don't you think?"

"Not my type."

Erin rolled her eyes. "Come off it, she's every guy's type."

"That's why she's not *my* type. Plus"—he kissed her—"she's not you."

"She's *kind of* like me. I mean, we do spend a lot of time together."

He looked at her and laughed. "Are you trying to talk me into Theresa?"

"No, *of course not*. That would be *totally* against every rule there is." She leaned against him again. "I'm just saying it's normal to *notice* when a girl's pretty. Pursuing it would be a whole different thing, but *noticing* other attractive people is normal. Girls notice attractive girls as well. If guys had any idea what made guys attractive, they'd probably notice them too."

He shook his head but he was still smiling.

A few minutes passed in easy silence.

The wind picked up and lifted the dank scent of water and earth over them. Erin inhaled it deeply. "I love that smell, don't you? It's like it could be another time, you know? In medieval forests it probably smelled just like this."

"Probably."

She leaned against him. "We should go fishing."

"When?"

She shrugged. "Sometime." She actually liked fishing and knew he did too. She could bait a hook, cast like a champ, once she'd caught a four-and-a-half-pound trout in New Hampshire. She'd do pretty much everything except clean the fish. How was it that they'd never done it together before? "Could we fish here, do you think?"

He shook his head. "I wouldn't want to eat anything I caught in here."

She wrinkled her nose. "I wouldn't want to eat anything I caught, period. I just like fishing."

"What?" He laughed. "But you don't keep the fish?"

"No way." The very idea grossed her out. "Taking that squirming, slimy thing and *eating* it? Yuck." Of course, she ate fish sticks or filets served in restaurants, but she preferred to think of her food as coming from big anonymous factories, rather than all googly-eyed and gasping for air as they're lifted from muddy, disgusting water.

"You are seriously nuts," he said, but he said it affectionately. "You know that?"

She wasn't buying that. "You like cleaning fish, seeing the eyes and the scales, and the flapping gills and anything else that's stuck to it, and then eating it?"

"Of course," he said easily. "You've just never had fresh fish before. I'll make you try it."

"Ew."

"You'll change your mind."

"I doubt that."

"We have trout for breakfast all the time in Michigan."

"Ugh!" Scales, fins, and eyes came to mind. "For *breakfast*?"

"Sure."

"I'm packing Pop-Tarts."

He sighed and shook his head, but his eyes were warm. He was used to all the things about her that drove him crazy. She knew it was amazing that he loved her so much, but at the same time she knew no one would ever love him more than she did and he was lucky to have her even if she didn't eat the same things he did. She was perfect for him. At least she thought she was.

They made their way through the Champales as the sun moved across the sky and finally dipped behind the trees.

"Should we go find Theresa?" Erin asked. Her mind flitted to all the horror movies she'd seen where camp counselors are impaled against trees in the woods in the middle of intimate acts. "Seems like it's been forever since we saw them."

"They're on their way," Nate said.

"How do you know?"

"I saw them across the lake about five minutes ago, walking to the path."

Erin was impressed. "You're a regular forest ranger, aren't you? Aware of everything within a ten-mile radius?"

"You've got to be alert so you don't get eaten by bears."

"There aren't bears around here!"

"Sure there are."

Fear crossed her chest. "In Potomac Falls?"

He nodded somberly. "There's a lot of wooded acreage back there." He gestured across the water. "Lots of wildlife."

She studied him for a moment, then noticed the tightening at one corner of his mouth. He was lying. She rolled her eyes and stood up. "You almost had me."

"Don't worry," he went on, dusting himself off. "I'll protect you."

"From guys in Izod shirts and penny loafers?"

"If that's what it takes."

She collected the empty bottles and dropped them into the bag they'd brought them in. "What would I do without you?"

The trees rustled several yards away, and Theresa and JP emerged, looking flushed and disheveled.

"Oh, my God," Theresa said. "Some old guy walking his dog just snuck up on us."

"Oh, no." Erin cringed, imagining the scene he might have walked up on. "What did he see?"

"Oh, yes." She nodded, confirming. "He got a good look at my ass."

"Probably made his day," Nate said, taking Erin's hand. He started walking up the path with her in tow.

She followed, tossing over her shoulder, "It wasn't someone you know, was it?"

"God, I hope not," Theresa said, raking her fingers through her tangled hair. "We didn't exactly chat."

"It was Mr. Beardsley," JP volunteered.

"*What?*" Theresa stopped and gaped at him. "You *know* him?"

"I know who he is, yeah." JP sounded unalarmed. "He brings his car to the service station all the time."

"Awesome," Theresa said dryly.

"He's blind as a bat, don't worry about it."

Theresa sighed and met Erin's eye. Erin shrugged and turned to follow Nate.

"I wouldn't do that in public," she said quietly to him.

"What about your beach fantasy?" he asked, suppressing a smile.

"Private beach," she said, imagining the horror of having someone walk up when she was in a compromising position like that. "Very private."

"I'll keep it in mind."

"Do that, because I think it would be amazing."

They picked their way through the dusky woods. Fireflies were beginning to bounce through the trees by the time they got to Nate's car on the road outside the path.

"My parents are away overnight," Theresa said, as they climbed into the car. "You guys want to come over?"

Erin looked at Nate. "Bedroom," she said with a smile. "With a lock. And a bed."

He smiled at her. "Whatever you want."

"Sold!" she said to Theresa in the backseat.

When they got to Theresa's they had a few beers and watched some TV, but around ten o'clock, Nate and Erin decided to go up to bed.

The guest room that had become "theirs" for these times when Theresa's parents were away had two twin beds and a private bathroom. They always wedged into one bed together, though. It never occurred to them to do anything else.

"'Aybe 'e should 'ove to 'ichigan," Erin said, brushing her teeth. She was wearing his Puerto Rico T-shirt to sleep in.

Nate came up behind her, still fully clothed. "What?"

She spit the toothpaste out and tried again. "Maybe we should move to Michigan. After you're done with school, I mean." She loved the idea of moving out with him after college. "What do you think?"

"I could do that."

"I think I could too." She pulled a length of floss off and started flossing. "You can buy real food there, right?"

"Nope, just fish."

"Damn."

He nudged her out of the way and reached for her toothbrush and put toothpaste on it. "You'll get used to it."

She dropped the floss into the trash can. "I'll starve, thanks."

"You'll still cook it, though, right? After my long, hard day of fishing?"

"Oh, sure." She opened the mouthwash and took a swig, swishing, then spitting, before handing him the bottle.

He did the same.

Across the hall, they could hear Theresa and JP at it again.

They exchanged a look.

"She's really loud," Erin commented, a little embarrassed.

He nodded, unflappable. "Some guys like that."

She was almost afraid to ask. "Do *you* like that?"

He took her in his arms. "I like *you*." He kissed her cheek, then her hair, and held her tight for a minute.

She relaxed in his embrace for a moment, then drew back and met his eyes. "So you don't want to date Theresa."

He laughed, and looked genuinely surprised that she would even ask. "No. I don't." He unzipped his pants and stepped out of them, tossing them aside.

"Good."

They went to one of the beds and climbed in together, nestling close. Nate reached up and turned out the light.

"It's freezing in here," Erin said. Theresa's family always had the air-conditioning turned way down low. "I'm opening the window. I bet it's ten degrees warmer out there than in here." She slid the window open and made sure the curtains didn't block it.

"You know the best way to warm up, right?" Nate asked as she came back to him.

"What?"

He reached a hand under her shirt. "Shared"—he pulled it off—"body"—he sat up and pulled off his own shirt—"heat." He lay on top of her and kissed her.

And he was right, she warmed up almost immediately.

"You'd never cheat on me, would you?" she asked.

He drew back. "Why would you even ask me that?"

She shrugged. "I don't know. Just making conversation."

"It's a stupid question." But he didn't ask her the same.

They slept, completely entwined, until the morning.

Chapter 8

Present

It had been one of those days filled with detail work—nothing very major, nothing very interesting, but all stuff that needed to be done in order for other things to get done, so by the time I was finished for the day my mind was positively numb.

Things for the Brettman wedding were falling into place, as well as an anniversary party that was coming in August and a private high school reunion that one of the class members was sponsoring, rather elaborately, for everyone else. A nerd-done-well, was my guess.

I had also effectively taken care of most of the current details for Roxanne's party, although any and all of her requests were apt to change at the drop of a hat, so virtually everything I did for that had an imaginary asterisk next to it.

But the good thing about a day filled with detail work is that when it's done, it's done, and I was able to leave work half an hour earlier than usual. The traffic wasn't quite as bad and the idea of quiet time at home beckoned like a siren's song. By the time I climbed the stairs to my condo, I wanted nothing more than to sit in front of the TV and watch *The Real Housewives of Absolutely Anywhere* and not use my brain at all.

So when I opened the door and saw Amy and Cam sitting on the sofa with their faces covered in dark green mud masks, I was taken aback at the unexpectedness of it. I had expected them to be at Rick's place, not mine, and even if I had expected to see them, it probably wouldn't have been like this.

I suppose that showed on my face because they both collapsed into fits of giggles.

"Ow! My face!" Amy shrieked, putting her hand to the cracked drying mud on her cheek.

"Mine too!" Cam said, but she couldn't stop laughing and cracking the mask.

"Wait till she sees!" Amy said.

"I know!"

"Wait till she sees what?" I asked, glancing nervously around, looking for some unholy mess that would turn the night into a living nightmare.

"Rick!" Cam said.

At the same time, Amy said, "Dad!"

"Where is he?" I asked.

He must have heard them shout his name, because before they could answer me, the bedroom door opened, and he said, "I'm coming, I'm coming. How long do I have to leave this on?"

I looked up just in time to see him see me, and both our eyes went wide.

For him it was more painful, though, given the fact that his face was also covered in a dry mud mask and contorting it into shock had to have hurt.

"Erin." He gave a stiff nod, though I could see the mud cracking at the corners of his mouth as it turned into a smile. "Good to see you."

"Well, well," I said. "Nice look. It works for you."

"Thanks. It's just a little something I'm experimenting with."

"Very hot."

"That's what I thought."

Cam and Amy shrieked with laughter, then both of them recoiled at the pull of the tight masks.

Rick glanced in their direction. "Is it time to rinse this mess off or is my humiliation still incomplete?"

"Oh, I can answer that one," I said, going to the foyer table to look for my camera. "Your humiliation is not complete until we have documented this digitally."

"No way," he said, and started back for the bedroom. "I don't care if I'm not beautiful yet, you are *not* putting this on Facebook."

"Wait! Wait! Dad, just a minute!" Amy scrambled off the sofa and ran over to block his way.

Cam was right behind her, grabbing his shirt and trying to stop him. "Rick, you *have* to let us take your picture! You look so funny! Please?"

"Yeah, Dad, come on. Please?"

He stopped and looked back at me for a minute before shifting his gaze to them and raising his arms in a broad shrug. "You have thirty seconds. After that, I'm rinsing, whether you've found the camera or not."

"In the drawer!" Cam shrieked, and she and Amy ran toward the table.

"It *will* be on Facebook, you know," I said to him.

"Oh, I have no doubt." He didn't sound very worried about that. I was glad. "Good thing I'm not on Facebook myself."

"Doesn't matter. They'll still tag you."

"I don't even know what that means."

I laughed. "It means they will make it so that if a cursor runs over the picture your name will pop up."

He shrugged. "I doubt we have the same friends."

"I dunno, hon." I shrugged. "I'm friends with both of them. So is Jordan. And probably a lot more people than you think."

He remained unconcerned, in the way that only a very confident person can be.

"There it is!" Cam cried, digging through the drawer. "Got it!"

"Stand still, Dad. No, wait, smile. That will look hilarious!"

"That's great, since *hilarious* is usually the look I'm going for."

"Not to worry," I said to him, knowing the girls were about to be very disappointed. "The camera battery is dead."

"*What?*" Cam looked as if I'd just slapped her. "What do you mean, the battery's dead?"

"Remember when you took the camera to Tristan's birthday party and then lost the charger in your room and swore up and down you would find it and recharge the battery?"

Understanding dawned on her face. "Oh, yeah."

"Yeah. And I asked you again and again to do that?"

Amy put her hands on her hips. "We're going to *miss* this picture because of that?"

Cam looked guilty.

Rick looked smug.

Amy looked like she was struck by a great idea. "Oh, no, we're not!" Faster than I would have thought possible, she whipped her phone out of her pocket and whirled around to take the picture of a surprised Rick.

"Whoa!" Cam said admiringly. "That was *smooth*."

Amy nodded and punched a couple of buttons. "And now it's

uploaded." She looked at her father. "So don't get any ideas about taking the phone away."

"Way to *go*!" Cam held up her hand and Amy high-fived her. "Now get me!"

Amy took several pictures of Cam hamming it up, then handed the phone over so Cam could get the same pictures of her.

I watched with pleasure as the two of them communicated with the same kind of shorthand Jordan, Theresa, and I used to have in high school. Understanding so deeply imbued with private jokes, late-night talks, favorite songs, and shared secrets that words were almost unnecessary.

They could have kicked serious ass on *Password*.

Rick, meanwhile, had disappeared into the bedroom and emerged several minutes later in basketball shorts, a tank top, wet hair, and—it was undeniable—a certain glow to his skin.

"You look radiant," I said to him.

"Very funny."

"Actually, I'm serious." I looked to the girls. "What kind of mask was that?"

"Dead Sea mud," Amy said.

"The stuff you got in New York last month," Cam added.

"Wow, that's right, I forgot all about that." How I'd forgotten a thirty-dollar mud-mask-treatment purchase, I don't know, but this experiment with Rick had reignited my feeling that it was worth it. "Go rinse off, let's see how pretty you look."

"How do you know when it's time to rinse it?" Cam asked.

"The guy at the store said you rinse when you can't smile any-more."

"So, like, when you're totally depressed?" My daughter had a gift for joking with a straight face, but the hard mud certainly helped.

"How about now?" I suggested.

She did smile then. "Fine fine fine!" She hooked her arm through Amy's and they ran off to the bathroom, where their laughter was amplified tenfold.

"Too bad they don't get along," Rick said, nodding in the direction of the laughs.

"I know." Truly, it made my heart soar to hear the girls having so much fun. "It's torture that we force them to be together like this."

He smiled and came to me, draping his arm across my shoulder and steering me toward the couch. "If only there was *some* way we could make sure they'd always have each other. Like sisters."

I bristled. And it was unfair because he was completely, totally, one hundred percent right.

And he was completely, totally, one hundred percent within his rights to try and get an answer to his proposal.

But I just couldn't give him one.

"They *are* like sisters," I deflected. "It's wonderful how close they are. They'll always have each other, just like Jordan and me. No matter what." God, it sounded so *pointed* when I put it that way, even though I hadn't intended for it to.

Of course, it *was* pointed, so it didn't matter whether I meant for it to *sound* that way or not.

And he knew it.

"Nice rebound," he said sagely.

"I'm not trying to—"

He put his finger to my lips. "I know what you're doing. You're mulling. It's what you do. Admittedly, it's hard to be patient while you mull in a situation like this, but I'm trying."

I looked into his eyes and felt better. "I appreciate it."

He smiled, and everything about him was warm. "Good. You pain in the ass."

We both laughed and sat down on the couch, where we passed

the rest of the evening companionably. No arguments, no problems, no passion, no steam . . . just . . . peace.

And I had to wonder if I was foolish in even wondering if that was enough.

———

When I was a kid, my friends and I used to hang out at Montgomery Mall and go to Woolworth's to buy Village Naturals beer shampoo, Maybelline Kissing Potion, Bonne Bell Lip Smackers (they were $2.50 then for the big size), and all the other products we saw advertised in *Tiger Beat*, *Teen*, and *Seventeen* that promised to make us more beautiful and irresistible to boys.

The mall has changed quite a bit in the past thirty years; Woolworth's is gone, as are Waxi Maxi's Record Shop, Peoples Drug Store, i Natural Cosmetics, the Magic Pan, and the Roy Rogers fast food restaurant. Now there's California Pizza Kitchen, Ann Taylor, Steve Madden, Coach, and Nordstrom. It's gone from a typical seventies suburban hangout to a pretty high-end shopping galleria.

And for her sixteenth birthday, Nordstrom Café was where Amy decided she wanted me to take her and Cam for lunch.

Nordstrom Café is awesome, I'm always surprised how much I like the food there, but Amy is not a fool—she knew if she got me into Nordstrom, she would leave with a nice bagful of things from the Brass Plum area. Cam did too. Look, I can't wear most of that stuff myself anymore, but it *is* fun to buy it.

So after a small shopping extravaganza, we made our way to the café with our bags and sat down in a big round booth that had enough room for us *and* our purchases.

"I'm totally wearing this blue shirt to school tomorrow," Cam said, stirring her tomato soup with a crust of bread.

"Wait, the blue shirt?" The blue shirt was kind of low in the front. It was for nighttime. Or maybe for someone older. Why had I allowed her to get that blue shirt? "That's not really appropriate for school."

"It is if you want Mason Bindeman to notice you," Amy said with a giggle.

"*Who?* Mason *who?*" It sounded like a soap opera name.

"Bindeman," Cam said, with a touch of exaggerated patience. "He's a senior. I have, like, two weeks to make an impression before he's gone forever."

"Oh. I see. And I just purchased an incredibly low-cut shirt to help you achieve that."

She smiled and reached over to pat my arm. "Thank you, Mommy."

"You were taking advantage of my momentary lapse in maturity."

Cam nodded. "I've learned to spot those and get while the getting's good."

"And *you* were complicit in this," I said to Amy, remembering how she'd pointed out the cute little pastel cardigans they had hanging on a rack near the dressing room.

Amy smiled. "Did I do something wrong?"

I sighed. This was an argument for another day. Tomorrow, to be specific. Not now. "So who is *Mason?* Wasn't it some guy named Phillip last week?"

"Ugh, he is *such* a jerk." Cam rolled her eyes. "We went out for, like, ten minutes and he expected me to totally give it up."

"He expected—"

"She *didn't,*" Amy said quickly, and suddenly I wished Rick were here to mediate this conversation.

"Well, *duh,* that's my point," Cam said. "If he can't understand why I might want to wait a *little* bit longer, then forget it."

"How much longer?" I found myself asking.

Cam leveled a gaze of pity on me. "Don't ask questions you don't want the answers to."

All right, if my mother had asked the same question of me at the same age, what would I have said? At sixteen Nate and I were seriously hot and heavy together wherever we could find a little privacy. It was a wonder I'd never had a pregnancy scare. No matter what happened during the day, or even during the night, I always knew that at the end of it, there would be no stresses, no Real Life issues, no big problems—at the end of every night the only thing that was looming was the fact that we were going to have steaming hot sex.

And it occurred to me, at this inopportune moment, that I really missed that.

Amy must have misinterpreted the look on my face, because she gave a shout of laughter and said, "Ohmigod, Erin, she's totally *kidding!*"

I looked at Cam and could tell, I knew right down in my heart, that that was the truth. She wasn't anywhere near the same place I'd been at her age. My daughter—and Amy, her best friend and potentially my future stepdaughter—was not emotionally and physically entangled with anyone, much less one guy who, two years into a seriously intense relationship, could dump her and leave her to twist herself into some damaged version of herself. A version that would take years to make right.

If, indeed, she could ever do it.

Fortunately, Cam and Amy were on such a shopping and eating high that they didn't pay much attention to my lagging reaction, so I was able to sit back and watch them, incredibly glad for the knowledge that they were going to be all right in a way I never would be.

To tell the truth, I envied them more than a little bit. They were so pure, it was obvious just looking into their eyes that they had never known even an inkling of the agony of that particular heartbreak.

Someday they would, of course. Everyone goes through it, at least to a certain extent, don't they? But watching these children talk a mile a minute and laugh so hard they couldn't breathe filled me with both happiness and melancholy.

How different would I be, if I'd never met Nate? Might I have had a normal dating life like Cam and Amy did, flitting from one guy to the next, never getting too serious or too invested in one while I was still so young? Who would I be if I hadn't endured the heartbreak of losing Nate and losing that part of myself that was built around him?

There are philosophical people out there—Jordan probably among them—who would argue that it was all important to making me the person I am today. And I guess that's true; what I went through definitely did contribute to who I am today.

But the thing no one understands when they say that is that I honestly think I might be a *better* person if I hadn't gone through that. Less neurotic, less afraid, more open to both people and experiences.

"*Mom!*"

I don't know how long she'd been trying to get my attention. That was probably just the second time she'd called me, but I'd been so lost in my melancholy that it really felt like I was being sucked back into my body from some weird astral travel. "Sorry, what?"

"Where *were* you?" Cam asked, and the look in her eye told me she'd picked up on the fact that it was more than just your usual run-of-the-mill distraction.

"Actually," I said, remembering something I'd heard a long time ago about telling as much truth as possible rather than telling a flat-out lie, "I was thinking about when I used to come to this mall as a kid. Just about your age, in fact." There was a rainy afternoon Nate and I had come—I can't remember why now—but later that night his friend had died in a car accident after they'd all gone to a party. I tried to push the thought out of my head. "It was pretty different here then," I concluded lamely.

"It's so weird that we're hanging out in the same mall you used to come to," Cam said, if not oblivious then at least losing interest in my nostalgia. Thank God.

"My grandmother is always talking about how different the town my dad grew up in is," Amy said, taking a crunch of her garlic bread. "All I know is that if that dinky Maine town was as boring today as it was when *he* grew up there, I'd go crazy every time I had to visit!"

"You know," I said, seizing the opportunity to keep us on a new subject, "you're probably right. Rick's told me about it. No malls, just a little drugstore and an outpost of Sears. You'd definitely hate that now."

"There wasn't even a traffic light," Amy said to Cam. "You know how the joke is that a town's so small there's just one light?" She shook her head. "There wasn't even that."

At the moment, that little lakeside town in Maine sounded idyllic to me, but there would be no point in saying that to the girls. Instead I just nodded and sipped my Pellegrino.

Soon they were off on another subject, and I tried to keep my attention on the conversation, even though part of me was lost in the past.

That's when I realized that part of me would probably always be lost in the past. That just seemed to be my personality: I was the one who couldn't stand change, who could miss something as innocuous as a bedspread if it was suddenly gone after a year of use.

No wonder I was thinking of Nate so much now—someone was offering to put a new bedspread on me and it was making me think of the ones that had been there before.

Particularly that first one. Maybe with a pale blue gingham pattern that was soft and neat and homey and orderly all at the same time.

So maybe it wasn't Nate I missed at all, so much as the firstness of him, and the sad fact that I'd never gotten a chance to say goodbye before he was hauled off to Goodwill.

I missed the idea of him more than he himself.

That was probably it.

Or at least I felt *fractionally* more comfortable when I told myself that.

Chapter 9

October 1986

"Pete Hagar has the hots for you," Theresa said to Erin at lunch. Erin looked up from her food. They called it "Benson Hash" and she wasn't exactly sure what it was. Some sort of chopped mystery meat. Possibly with onions involved. "Says who?"

"Says *him*," Theresa said triumphantly. "I asked him during history."

"Oh, my God, did you tell him I said he was cute?" Color flooded hotly into Erin's cheeks. Yeah, she thought Pete was cute. *Everyone* did. He was new and seemed normal and drove a cool car. All three of those things were rare at Benson Prep.

"Relax, no." She looked like she was lying. "I just asked him, hypothetically, if he'd like to go to the park with us on Sunday. And at first he said no, so then I said, 'Well, do you want to go to the park with us on Sunday if Erin is going?' and he was, like, 'Yes, I love the park' so . . ."

"*Really?*" Erin looked across the room to where Pete was eating. For a moment their eyes met, then she looked down. "Shit, he just caught me looking at him."

"Good."

"Good what?" Jordan asked, slipping up to the table behind them. She'd just had a conversation with the headmaster about why she didn't think she should be forced to say a prayer aloud before lunch, since every day one person was asked to lead grace and all the prayers were specific to God and Jesus, whom Jordan was just not that into. "What's going on?"

"Pete Hagar," Theresa said.

"Oh." Jordan nodded and sat down in front of her plate of meat. "This is gross."

"The mashed potatoes are okay," Erin volunteered, adding more butter. "And the rolls."

"I wish we could bring our own lunch," Jordan said.

"If you can't bring your own God, you can't bring your own lunch." Erin laughed. "But maybe you should have a talk with the headmaster about that anyway. Did you get anywhere?"

Jordan shook her head. "He just said it was only symbolic and that I shouldn't worry so much about it." She rolled her eyes. "Really helpful. But I don't have to recite it anymore."

"Well, that's pretty much what you wanted, right?" Theresa asked.

"It works."

"So he asked for your number," Theresa said to Erin.

"Who?"

"Pete," Jordan supplied. "Come on, you know how Theresa works. She doesn't do things halfway."

"He did?" Erin's stomach went on edge. "Seriously?"

"Yes!"

"But . . . Nate!" She just couldn't bear to think about Nate. Pete was cute, she was kind of interested, but she didn't want to hurt Nate or give him up. And, unfortunately, there was no way she could just put him on hold—freeze him like some scene from *Bewitched*—and come back if she wanted to.

This could be the end for them.

"Nate will get over it!" Theresa waved a forkful of mashed potatoes, then popped them in her mouth.

"I don't know. . . ." Jordan looked concerned. "Poor Nate."

"Ugh, don't *say* that!" Erin objected.

"You just did!"

Guilt tightened around her chest. She didn't want to make Nate feel bad. But, jeez, they never went anywhere anymore, never did anything in particular apart from hanging out at houses (hers, his, Theresa's, Jordan's). She was only going to be a teenager once, right? She wanted to know what it was like to be a normal teenage girl, with dates and everything, particularly since she was going to such a tiny, weird private school.

She had to grab normality wherever it presented itself.

And if Nate wasn't interested enough to try and keep her by treating her like he valued her, why should she just sit around and give up her youth on him?

"So did you give it to him?" she asked Theresa, determined to ignore Jordan's concerned looks. "My number, I mean."

"Of course!"

Erin met Pete's eyes again, and this time she smiled. He smiled back.

It was a very nice smile. Good, white teeth.

She was all about good teeth in guys. A great smile could make up for a lot of other flaws.

"Good," she said, raising her chin defiantly. She could do whatever she wanted. She didn't need to feel guilty! She was only sixteen, for God's sake!

Suddenly some small part of her felt an uncomfortable question wedge its way into her mind. Was she stupid to be spending so much time during these, her prime teen years, with just one guy? Yes, she loved Nate, but how could she know if it was *real* love, the kind that was supposed to last forever? She had nothing to compare it to. Things with Nate were so comfortable—wasn't "in love" supposed to be a constant thrill, pounding heart, quickening of the breath?

Maybe she wasn't "in love" so much as she "loved."

Because that was one thing she knew for sure: she loved Nate.

For just a moment she sank into that feeling. She loved him. He *did* make her heart pound a lot of the time. She *did* catch her breath still when she saw him. Sometimes. She didn't ever want things to be any different than they were now. But maybe that was just the problem—maybe she really needed to get out and see what else was out there so she didn't someday have regrets that would last forever.

Maybe the only way she could have *forever* with Nate was if she had *now* with a few other dates.

"Then I hope he calls." And she would ignore the nagging guilt and apprehension that already played at her psyche.

They dated for exactly a month.

She did have the decency to be honest with Nate about it in advance. She told him she wanted to date someone else, though the feeling she really had was that she wanted to be able to date someone else and see if it was good while still having the same thing going with Nate. There was no way to phrase it that way, of course, but they were so close that, in truth, she couldn't imagine *not* being close to him no matter what happened.

Nate was a constant in her life.

Surely he'd *always* be a constant in her life. Though it had been hard to ignore the deep pain in his eyes. He might have understood her need to try something else, but he didn't like it. It hurt him.

She didn't want to hurt him.

But she needed to get out there and date a little, didn't she? How could she say she wanted to *marry* Nate if she never even knew what it was like to be with someone else?

She couldn't!

And Pete was a perfectly nice guy. Yes, she had to pretend to like heavy metal at first and she couldn't really play her mix tapes in his car like she could in Nate's because his tastes ran more toward hard rock. But mostly she struggled with a matter of him never quite feeling familiar, the way Nate did.

She gave him a chance, she thought. A month was long enough to start to get used to someone. Or, alternatively, to see if you started to feel weirder with him.

In this case, she began to feel weirder with him.

Plus, she was in constant touch with Nate. It was like they were still together, really, but he was turning away and pretending not to notice when she went out with Pete.

As a result, she felt like Nate was still her boyfriend and Pete was, increasingly, a kind of boring friend with a cool car who paid for her dinner out and movies and stuff.

Finally one night after they went to see a movie, she faced the fact that what she was doing wasn't fair to him *or* Nate, and she wasn't really having any fun at it herself. So she had A Talk with Pete in the car when he brought her home.

"I don't think we should go out anymore," she said, when he pulled the car to a stop in front of her house.

He looked shocked. "*Why?*"

How could he be shocked? At first she'd let him kiss her, but she hadn't even done that for almost two weeks! "Well"—she couldn't tell him there was someone else, especially the Someone Else who had been there first, because that was just too insulting—"I just don't really want to go out with *anyone* right now." It was a limp lie, but not the first one she'd told and it wouldn't be the last. She could only hope he'd let her off the hook with it.

"Is there another guy?" he asked. Bingo! "Are you going to go out with Bennett?"

Bennett Laraby was the school Bad Boy and, yes, cute, but not someone Erin would *ever* go out with. "Absolutely not!" she said with complete conviction. "No *way*. It's really just me. Don't take it personally."

He gave a little scoff. "Kind of hard not to."

Of course. She'd feel the same way, in his shoes.

"It's that other guy, isn't it?" he said suddenly. "That guy you went out with before."

She swallowed and put her hand to her chest. "It's just *me*," she insisted.

Why had she gotten herself into this mess? It had never felt right, not once. The newness—the *foreign*ness—of him had been interesting at first, but only because Nate had never felt new or foreign to her.

He'd always felt like home.

She should have realized that was good, not bad.

But at her age, she wanted to shake it up. Or she thought she had. Now she thought she was a little old lady who didn't want shaking at all, but who wanted the easy, comfortable boy she could see herself in her nineties with someday.

"I'm sorry," was all she could say. At this point, she really wanted to get out of the car. She didn't want to have this conversation anymore. He was never going to understand. But she'd done what she'd needed to do, said what she'd dreaded saying, this should be over.

"Fuck it." He slammed his hands against the steering wheel.

Okay, so . . . did that mean she was dismissed? "I'll just go in now . . . ?" she said tentatively, one hand on the door handle so she could make a run for it if necessary.

"Fine." He kept his gaze fastened straight ahead.

She glanced at the clock. It was eleven thirty on a Friday night. She didn't have to be home yet. Good. "So . . . I'm sorry," she said again, opening the door. "Really."

He didn't answer, just gunned the motor when she closed the door, and she stood there a moment, watching him blaze down the street.

Then she glanced at her house—the lights were out, her parents were probably already asleep. Plus, she had till one A.M.

So she started to run.

She ran down the street, then stopped at the corner and took off the stupid leather shoes that had been killing her feet all night. She just left them on the neighbors' lawn, she didn't care if she ever saw them again. It was still warm enough, in early October, to go without them. So, bare feet pounding against the cold sidewalk, she ran almost a mile until she got to Nate's house.

His light was on, she saw as she stood in front of the house in the grass, trying to catch her breath. He was there.

She looked around for something to toss at the window to get his attention, and picked up a handful of landscaping gravel. But there was a screen on the outside of the window, so even if she was foolish enough to try and throw the gravel at glass, it would bounce off and probably hit her in the forehead noiselessly.

"Nate!" she called quietly, then waited.

Nothing.

Crap.

What was she going to do?

"Nate!" she tried again, a little louder.

Still nothing. Not a single movement in the room.

"Shit." She threw the gravel back into the garden.

"Erin?"

She whirled around, shocked to see Nate himself where she expected no one, and no one where she expected to see Nate.

Suddenly she was nervous. "Hey," she said, lifting her hand weakly. "How's it going?"

"What are you doing?"

There was no way to play this cool. "Yelling at your window."

"What did it do?"

"It ignored me." She smiled, but she was afraid he wasn't going to care. "What are you doing out here?"

"I was looking for something in my car. But I still don't get what *you're* doing here."

She sighed. "Well, I went out, and it ended early, and I was thinking about you, and"—tears started to burn her eyes—"miss you and stuff. And"—she swallowed—"I wanted to see you."

"Should I want to see you?" His voice was hard. Cold. "Don't you have a boyfriend?"

"No," she said quickly. She swallowed, downing her pride and everything else except the lump in her throat. "I mean, I *hope* so, but it's . . ." There was no clever way to say what she'd done. "You."

"You want me to be your boyfriend," he repeated flatly, without moving toward her. She was the one spotlighted by the streetlamp, but she could see his face well enough to tell his eyes were narrowed. His mouth was a tight line, his jaw clenched. "When you've just spent the last month with someone else."

"Yes," she said in a small voice, and a sob caught in her throat. He might say no. He'd be completely within his rights to say no.

He looked at her for a long, steely moment in silence.

Then he just shook his head and strode over to her, pulling her into his arms and kissing her hard.

She kissed him right back, instantly delirious in a feeling of relief and all being right with her world. It was amazing how quickly it took her over, this feeling of dizzying love and need that only he could—and would—fill. How had she ever done without it? Why had she ever thought she wanted something else?

They moved into the shadows, away from the watchful eye of the streetlamp, fumbling at each other in the darkness, urgency replacing ego and apologies and even forgiveness. Because every action he took showed her that he loved her even though she didn't know if he'd still talk to her tomorrow.

That wasn't what mattered right now.

What mattered now was that they were together, locked in the night, soul to soul in a moment that felt like it would never end.

A moment she hoped would never end.

He pushed her against the brick wall of the house, in the shadows of the side yard, and yanked up her shirt. She yielded to him eagerly, moving only enough to make it easier to free her of her clothing. The brick scraped her shoulder blades but she didn't care.

With his mouth still hard, but warm, against hers, he reached around and unhooked her bra, his fingertips cold against her skin, and shoved the heel of his palm against her breast. His fingers played roughly against her skin. Then his movement softened, like a mood shifting from anger to love, and he trailed his hand across her chest, her collarbone, and back down to her waist and hips, where he gripped her and pulled her against his hardness.

She gasped at the pressure and her desire skyrocketed. She reached her hand down to the snap of his jeans, flipping them open as she'd done hundreds of times before, and then used both hands to slide them, along with his underwear, down over his hips, where she knelt before him and took him into her mouth.

His breath caught and she smiled against him for a moment before doing all the things he'd taught her, long ago, about what he liked best. She closed her eyes, putting every ounce of herself into what she was doing. It seemed like only moments until she heard him hold his breath and felt his stomach muscles tighten in a way she knew well.

She slowed her movements, and, without looking, reached her hands up and entwined her fingers with his. He clenched his hands around hers, and exhaled, simultaneously releasing a month's worth of heartache and uncertainty into her.

She waited a moment, still and nurturing, not moving but not releasing him until she was sure he was through, that she'd taken in all of it for him.

She began to leverage herself up with her hold on his hands, but instead he knelt before her and cupped her face in his hands. "I love you," he said in a ragged voice.

Sorrow choked her. How had she risked this? How in the world had she risked this? "I love you too," she said, closing her eyes and burying her face in his shoulder. "So much. I'm so sorry."

"Don't," he said, again, as if there were just nothing else. "I love you."

"I hope so." Tears burned her eyes. She kissed his neck, his ear, his shoulder. "I love *you*," was all she could say. "I really really do. More than anything. I'm so stupid."

Then he kissed her, deeply, hot and wet, then lowered her to the cold grass beneath them. They hit the ground and lay clasped together, mouths locked, bodies entwined. They were still for a while. Wordless. But slowly touching each other, lacing and unlacing their fingers together, touching faces, hair, lips, cheeks.

"We should get married."

He laughed quietly and traced his fingertip across her palm. "Yeah? How do you figure that?"

"Because I know I don't want anyone else ever, ever again. Why wait?"

"Because you're sixteen." He smiled in the dark and put his finger to her lips. "Now, shhh."

"Okay." She relaxed against him.

They lay in silence for a few more minutes, but she started thinking about him, and about how stupid she'd been to leave him even for a minute, and she didn't want to say anything about that—just in case, by some off chance, he *wasn't* thinking about the same thing—so instead she just kissed him.

Things heated up quickly.

He worked at the button on her jeans and she raised her hips and helped him push them down.

If anyone came around with a flashlight now it would be pretty embarrassing.

But Erin didn't care. She kicked the jeans away and wrapped her legs around him, warming her cold bare feet on his heat as he moved on top of her and pushed into her. He was reclaiming what was his and she was allowing it with all of her body, heart, and soul.

She had no sense of time, no sense of the outside world at all, while he moved within her, and she clung to him, one single embodiment of love and fulfillment. There was nothing else then. No responsibility. No accountability. They were all emotion and hormones.

And they were good at this by now. She knew from the way he kissed her when he was about to come again, and she tightened her arms around him, instinctively wanting to make him feel protected, to fully feel every sensation he was going to feel.

His kiss deepened, in that way she recognized, and she let it, drinking him in, meeting his movements until he drew out and reached his climax.

He stilled against her.

"Nate," she said, reaching up and running her hands gently through his hair.

He drew back and looked at her for a moment, then just shushed her and lay his cheek against hers.

She didn't say anything else.

Some time later—she couldn't have said how much—they regained their composure (and their clothes) and Nate walked her home. Neither of them wanted to take the car. It would have been too fast, too soon to say good night.

So they walked the mile to her house, hand in hand, without speaking a word. The silence was warm between them and there was understanding in their touch. But nothing they could say to each other with words would mean more than what they'd just said to each other without words.

When they got to her front porch, she turned to him and finally asked the thing she'd been dreading. "Are we back together now?"

What if he said no? What if he said all of that had been a goodbye? Or even a fuck-you?

It would be a good one.

But Nate wasn't like that. He wasn't cruel. "You'll always be my little girl," he said, running his knuckle across her cheek.

"Does that mean okay, you'll take me back?" she asked, afraid to assume anything.

He smiled. Nodded. But his eyes were tired and sadder than anything she'd ever seen, including the weary-looking and creased ancient tribesmen in *National Geographic* magazine articles.

"I'm so sorry," she said, feeling it wasn't enough. But what else could she say? There was no way to fix whatever she'd broken during those weeks he'd waited for her. If she'd been in his position, what would she have done?

Probably not forgiven so easily, that was for sure.

He would never understand the deep feelings that had brought her here tonight. How could he, when she couldn't possibly come up with the words to express them?

So she shut up. Really, it was all she could do. She shut her mouth and leaned against him on her doorstep and hoped she could transfer all the feelings she had inside to him so, on some very subconscious level, he'd comprehend it.

Even then, she knew that probably wasn't enough.

But it was all she had.

Chapter 10

Present

It's weird how life sometimes decides to mirror and amplify your own issues when you have made the decision not to face them. Put off doing your taxes, and suddenly tax lawyer commercials are everywhere; decide to take a little time off between jobs, and suddenly unemployment is all over the news; put off your oil change, and cars are breaking down left and right.

The old saying is true: you just can't run away from your problems.

Which leads me to this question: You know what's harder than calling your own boyfriend after he's dumped you?

Calling someone else's boyfriend on her behalf, after he's dumped her. Especially when that girl is someone you don't really know. And don't particularly like.

Someone you couldn't recommend as a girlfriend to your worst enemy.

Like Roxanne.

Now, this seems like a good time to point out that I'm not particularly *wise*. I've learned a few things the hard way, but I don't actually feel very different than I did when I was fifteen, sixteen, seventeen. What I know about drugs, I learned from *Go Ask Alice* and *Sarah T.—Portrait of a Teenage Alcoholic*, and those were enough to keep me clean. What I know about romance, I learned from terrible seventies sitcoms and overwrought romance novels. What I know about parenting is a combination of real-life experience and *Brady Bunch* or, worse, *Leave It to Beaver* reruns.

In short, I've learned from popular culture and my own fuckups.

So Roxanne really could have picked a better advocate. Unfortunately for her, apparently she didn't have any choices in the matter.

I had to be the one to approach Justin.

Obviously I wasn't going to plead Roxanne's case for her; I didn't even know what her case *was*, though I was fairly sure it wasn't a really good one, based on what I knew of her.

I dialed the number she'd given me and heard, "Yo! You got me." I waited a minute, thinking it was a voice-mail message, but then he said, "Hello?"

"Hello, is this Justin?"

"Maybe." Sullen voice. Affecting some sort of rapperish I-don't-give-a-shit inflection. "Who wants to know?"

Okay, yeah, I knew who this guy was already. This was going to be a blast.

"My name is Erin Edwards, and I'm the event coordinator for Roxanne Tacelli's sixteenth birthday party and she asked me to call and"—it wasn't easy to make this sound like I meant it, but I gave it a shot—"make sure you had gotten the invitation and were saving the date."

"Hell, no! I'm not going to that!"

"I see." I did. Of course. This was no surprise. "So you do know about it."

"I've heard." He was trying to play it cool like only a dippy teenager can. I've known a few of them in my time—mercifully few, though. When I was in high school, my friends tended to be older than this.

And far cooler.

"Well, listen, just keep the date in mind, okay? It's going to be a great party. Really big." Maybe if he thought he could get lost in the crowd he'd reconsider. "Tons of people there that you know."

"Yeah, whatever."

What else could either of us say?

"So . . . okay, then. If you have any questions—"

He hung up.

"Thanks for your time, jackass!" I clicked off my phone and wondered how Roxanne could possibly be pining over such a dud.

Then again, she wasn't exactly the princess of charm herself. They were actually probably perfect for each other.

At least I'd tried. She couldn't ask for more than that. I mean, she probably would, but I couldn't reasonably be expected to do more than call. I couldn't have this punk kidnapped and brought to the party. I couldn't have thugs show up at his house and threaten to break his kneecaps if he didn't show up.

Unbelievably, I had to explain all of this to Jeremy in my office the next day. Not only had he handed off this impossible task to me, but he had very distinct ideas about how it should be executed and whether or not there was any wiggle room for failure.

"It's *very important* that she get *everything* she wants for this party," Jeremy told me. He was sitting on the edge of my desk, tapping his Montblanc pen on the surface for emphasis. "Our reputation *depends* on it."

It was so absurd, I had to laugh. "Jeremy, come off it, our reputation does *not* depend on this brat's equally bratty ex-boyfriend coming to the party!"

But he remained serious. "This is going to be *broadcast on TV . . .*"

"Where anyone watching will see how stupid the request was to begin with."

". . . and if this girl isn't completely happy with the party *we* throw for her, then our reputation as a special events venue will be adversely affected. Specifically"—he was being pointed now, lowering his chin and raising his eyes to mine with Heavy Significance—"our events coordination."

Whoa. "Are you saying my *job* depends on this?"

"No." He looked at me. "I'm afraid *mine* does."

He couldn't have played it better. If it was my own job I'd be less worried because I knew I could get a new one easily, but Jeremy? His . . . quirkiness . . . could be a problem for him in the job marketplace.

"What I'm saying is simply that you need to do everything you can to make Roxanne Tacelli happy," he went on. "Whether you think she's a brat or not."

It was ridiculous, of course. The entire thing was stupid. This idiotic TV show filming, the entire Tacelli family, Jeremy's personal investment in both of the above . . . all of it was comical, and yet it might be swinging over his job security like one of those blades in an Indiana Jones movie. The owner of the hotel was an aggressively masculine guy who wasn't crazy about Jeremy. If Roxanne were to go on national TV and tell the world, in a half hour's worth of tantrums and tears, that we'd fucked up the most important day of her life so far (because that was how I was sure she'd characterize it), the weight of that would fall on Jeremy's feeble shoulders.

So maybe thugs threatening Justin's kneecaps weren't such a bad idea after all.

Meanwhile, I'd try to talk reason into Roxanne. With great trepidation, I closed the door to my office and dialed.

"Hello?" Her voice was robust and cheerful. That was a good sign.

"Hi, Roxanne, it's Erin Edwards, from the Farnsworth-Collingswood. How are you doing today?"

I hoped, of course, that the answer would be something along the lines of, *Great! I have a new boyfriend, and he's sooooo cute, and I just love love love him!*

No such luck.

"Did you get Justin to say he'd come to the party?" she asked immediately.

"That's actually what I wanted to talk to you about."

"Is he coming?" She was like a child begging to go to the mall and see Santa Claus.

I leaned back in my chair and closed my eyes. "Well, I *did* call him, but he might have a scheduling conflict that day."

"Scheduling . . . ?"

"He might have something else to do."

"That is such a load of shit," she said, moving from cheerful to spiteful as if she'd flipped a switch. "He's a liar."

So I guess it was lucky that she was calling him the liar and not me. "If he's lying, then why do you want him at your party? Maybe he's not such a great guy after all."

"He's lying because he still loves me!"

Oh. Oh, no. There it was, the Great Lie that had been uttered from girlfriend to girlfriend throughout the ages, in every language from A to Z, including grunts and clicks: *He's not contacting you because he's afraid of how much he loves you.*

How many heartbroken women had comforted themselves with that perverse thought while they cried through the night over some guy who was probably not thinking about them at all?

I certainly had done my time with it. In fact, I'd spent *years* half believing that Nate only avoided me because of the depth of his feelings, because to talk to me would bring it all back to the surface for him and make him have to do something with it and he didn't want to face that. For my ego, it was a much more plausible explanation than *he's just not into you anymore*.

My brain, on the other hand . . . my brain called bullshit on the idea that anyone was so completely adept at compartmentalizing that they could completely ignore being that in love with someone.

My brain pointed out that, for a while, virtually every waking thought I had related to Nate, and if there had been any way in the world to get him back—stopping at nothing I could imagine—I would have dropped everything else in my life to do it because that love mattered more than anything else.

That kind of love, my irritatingly logical brain liked to argue, was the kind of thing no one could—or, more to the point, would—ignore.

Unfortunately, I think my brain was right.

And I always kind of suspected that, when my heart, and my friends, started nattering about how terrified Nate was to admit the depth of his love for me.

So here I was watching another dumb girl go through the same thing, wanting the same impossible outcome with a guy who just didn't care. But would I be doing Roxanne a favor by pointing that out right now? Would she even *hear* me?

I don't know if the Great Lie has ever been true, if a man has ever pushed those kinds of feelings away in order to protect himself, but even if it was, I was pretty damn sure that wasn't what Justin was doing right now.

Yeah, I was pretty sure Justin just wasn't interested in Roxanne, much less in love with her.

"I *know* he still loves me."

"What makes you say that, Roxanne?" I was trying to buy time, to come up with the appropriate response.

"Because we spent *weeks* together and now, suddenly, he doesn't answer my calls or texts."

Weeks. "How many times have you tried to contact him?"

"Dunno. Three or four . . ."

Wow. She had a lot more self-control than I would have expected.

". . . times a day," she finished.

Oh. Okay, she was *that* girl. I was that girl once too. We've all been that girl. "To start, I can tell you one thing I know is true," I said, preparing to give her the greatest advice she'd ever ignore. "As long as you're calling him, he's going to feel like he has the choice to take you or leave you, and as long as he feels like that's his choice, he's not going to feel compelled to do anything to get you back. Believe me."

There was a sniffle on the other end of the line and I felt sorry for her, despite what a pain in the ass she was, and would undoubtedly continue to be. "But I don't want him to forget me!"

Now, I can't say what it was about those simple words or their delivery from this girl I had so little regard for, but suddenly it was like a levee had broken deep inside of me, and emotion swelled into my chest.

I didn't want to be forgotten either.

I'd never forgotten Nate, despite spending half my life trying to forget him. I'd given him everything: my love, my body, my pride, and parts of my heart and mind that I could never get back.

And all at once, thanks to Roxanne whining about a guy she'd known for a few weeks, it hit me that deep down I'd wondered for years if Nate ever thought about me or if it had all blown away, forgotten, in the wake of whatever his real life had become.

If he had, what did that say about me?

"He hasn't forgotten you," I assured Roxanne, but my voice wavered a little over the sentiment and didn't have the confidence I was sure we both would have preferred. "I've got another call I have to take," I lied. "But I'll get back to you."

"But—"

I hung up. I had to.

If I didn't, I thought I might cry.

And I was never going to do *that* over Nate Lawson again.

———

"I thought I'd go to Maine for the holiday weekend, see my grandparents," Rick told me. His family lived near Portland. "There are some great deals on airfare if we leave on Saturday—do you and Cam want to come? The girls would have a blast up there at the lake together."

Did I want to go to Maine? When it was *finally* starting to get warmer here? "My mom's having that cookout on Saturday," I reminded him. "My aunt and uncle will be in town."

We were in the car, on the way home from one of the most boring movies I'd ever seen. It was a foreign drama, with lots of shadows and heavy dialogue. I'd fallen asleep more than once.

Rick said he'd slept the entire way through.

"We can still make it for some of the cookout," Rick said. "Maybe take the three o'clock flight out. I'd really like for you to meet them. I hate to say it, but they won't be around forever."

"That's a terrible thing to say!" The truth was, meeting the grandparents felt daunting to me. Like I would be making a commitment I wasn't yet sure I could fulfill.

"Well, it's true." He pulled into my parking lot. There was a space right up front. "They're dying to meet you." He thought for a second, then gave a quick, sly smile.

"Oh, my God, you're awful!" But I had to laugh.

"What time did your mother want us there?"

"Noon."

He nodded. "That works perfectly. I can go for an hour or so and then straight on to the airport from there. Can you get Amy from the Brodys' house around six and keep her while I'm gone?"

I nodded. Amy and Cam would love that. "Works for me. I'm easy."

"No, you're not." He pulled the keys out of the ignition. "If you were, we'd be setting a date for our wedding. And planning for you to meet the old folks."

As soon as he said it, I knew my stay of execution was almost over. He wanted an answer, and I was going to have to come up with one soon. Almost everything in me wanted to say yes.

So why was the small hesitant part of me holding everything up?

———

The Saturday before Memorial Day was a really weird day; sort of overcast and monochromatic, but balmy, with a breeze that was blowing straight from a different time.

The feeling I couldn't shake was that this was a leftover day from many years ago. The smell, the *feel*, the way the wind moved the reaching branches of the still-bare tall oaks in just such a way that you could almost hear them creak and scratch against the sky. There was a thickness to the air that made it seem old. It was a day between childhood and adulthood, lost in time, and carrying every question I'd ever asked, and every confidence I'd ever carried, and every tear I'd ever cried.

It made me restless.

Rick and Amy had stayed just long enough to make a great impression on the family and leave before eating the undercooked hot dogs from the grill.

Afterward, Cam went up to use my mom's computer and the rest of us sat around my mother's living room, talking to Aunt Sheila and Uncle Eb about their trip to Lourdes and the miracle fried egg Aunt Sheila had gotten at the hotel that looked exactly like baby Jesus in the womb. I wasn't sure what that would mean, but I was less interested in knowing than in sitting through a long explanation.

Apparently they'd tried to preserve it and bring it home, but what had seemed like a good idea—packing it carefully in Sheila's purse in order to preserve it—had turned bad when security at Charles de Gaulle Airport had searched her bag and pulled it out in slimy pieces.

Turns out it's bad form to laugh at stories of miracles that turned to mush.

I had to work not to giggle.

So I sat quietly and tuned them out, half in a dream world of remembered scenes from long ago: Nate and me making out on that couch where my aunt and uncle sat now, with *The Tonight Show* whispering from the old Zenith TV, soft enough so we'd hear if my parents came down the stairs; arguing in the front yard over something stupid and throwing his ID bracelet as hard as I could, only to spend the next two weeks searching through every blade of grass for it (and finding it right before the lawn mower reached it); a steamy scene in the powder room by the washing machine, interrupted by my parents coming home early. . . .

I could almost see our own ghosts, moving around this boring scene I now found myself in, confident and relaxed in a way I never would be again.

It was hard to believe I was thinking about Nate so much all of a sudden. For a long time, I'd wished I'd never met him, yet here he was in my head almost constantly since Rick had proposed.

For so long, I hadn't *allowed* myself to think about Nate. Now I was taking those feelings out of a box and they were as youthful and strong and unformed as they'd ever been. I felt like I was missing him; missing the way he made me feel. Like a wild girl being tamed, not like a goddess on Rick's pedestal. When I thought about Nate, in a way it made me feel *good*, and that was the compulsion right there. I *wanted* to feel the way memories of him made me feel.

I wanted *sex* to feel the way it had felt with him. Wild. Uninhibited. A perfect fit, perfect chemistry.

But it didn't with Rick.

"Rick seems like a very nice young man," Sheila commented, bringing my attention reluctantly back to the present.

I wasn't entirely sure if she was talking to me or to my mother, but when my mother looked at me, I said, "Yes, he is. Thanks."

"And his daughter and Cam get along," Uncle Eb said. "Any chance they'll be sisters someday?"

My nerves twinged. "It's possible."

It wasn't the big memories of the past that gripped me, it was the small ones. I was giving perfunctory answers about Rick, but in my head I was fifteen and having hot dogs and iced tea in the summer twilight right there on the screen porch with Nate.

"What's possible?" Cam asked, coming in with one of the Good Humor bars my mother *never* had on hand when I was growing up.

"How many of those have you had?" I asked, to divert her attention.

Cam bit some of the toasted almond crust off, exactly as I used to. "This is just the second one."

That meant it was at *least* her fourth. "Well, stop after that."

"What do *you* think of your mother's friend?" Uncle Eb asked her.

"Rick? He's great!"

Something pulled in my chest.

"Think he's good family material?" he pressed.

"Obviously! Then Amy and I would be sisters. Like, officially. We're already practically sisters."

"Of course, Rick and I don't need to be *married* in order to be together."

"Exactly the kind of nonsense Cheryl would spew," Aunt Sheila said to my mother and Uncle Eb.

Aunt Cheryl was my favorite aunt, though, so I felt I had to defend her. Or at least align with her. "And she'd be absolutely right; if people just want to date, they should date and not get married." I wasn't comfortable thinking about Rick right now. Every thought I had, however fond it might be, came with an accompanying stab of guilt because of the memories of Nate that would not leave me alone. I wanted desperately to get out of there. "Does anyone have the time?" They could have said fourteen o'clock and I would have told them I had an appointment now.

"Four thirty-three," Uncle Eb said.

I made a face. "I was supposed to give work a call at four thirty. We have . . . details to discuss. About . . . a party. . . ."

They nodded, as if understanding this stupid, generic lie I'd come up with.

"So I'm going to go out front," I said, grabbing my phone from the hall table as I passed. "I'll be a little while. Sorry to cut out."

"Do you want me to save any turkey tetrazzini for you?" Mom asked.

God, no. My mother was one for using every edible part of the bird. We're talking every *possible* edible part of the bird. Shipwreck cooking. I don't know how hungry I'd have to be for Bird Foot Bonanza, but I'm thinking I'd have to be in a plane crash in the Andes to even consider it. And even then it would have to be the *only* alternative to cannibalism. "I'll take some home, if you don't mind."

That worked for her. "I'll pack it up! I've got to run out to the grocery store to get some gravy anyway, I'll get some of those disposable boxes. You and Camilla can eat some tonight and freeze some."

Cam and I exchanged a look.

"Sounds great!" she said, with convincing enthusiasm.

"Thanks, Mom." Something pulsated inside of me. If I didn't get out of this room I was going to scream. Maybe it wasn't the day that was stuck in the past, maybe it was me. Put me in the old house, where the furniture and decorating had been the same for years, and suddenly I was a moody teenager, ready to cry over nothing at the drop of a hat, and so consumed by the gathering storm of angst in my stomach that I thought I might go mad if I had to be with people—anyone—for one more minute.

"Cam?" I caught her eye. "You okay for a bit if I go?"

She gave a reassuring smile. "Of course! I'll go with Nan to the store."

"Okay, I'll be back soon." I pushed the storm door open. The wind lifted as soon as I stepped out, as if it were sharing a secret with me.

I just wished I could understand what it was.

Chapter 11

January 1987

Y ou're being mean." Erin crossed her arms in front of her and tightened her jaw, looking out the windshield at Theresa's house, where they were supposed to be going for a party while her parents were out of town. It was cold and nasty out, she had PMS, and even while she *knew* she was acting on hormones and not on anything she'd done, she couldn't stop herself.

Too often lately her moods had been getting the better of her. She was restless and unhappy with everything. Unfortunately, Nate was the easiest target.

She saw it, she just couldn't stop it.

"What do you mean, I'm being mean?" Nate asked, exasperated. The conversation had been going on like this for about fifteen minutes now. "What did *I* do?"

She didn't really have a good answer for that. What *had* he done, besides not sensing her foul mood and coddling her? She'd started by saying she was depressed, and when he didn't pick up on that she immediately found herself going all-out with little jabs to prod him into a response.

She knew this was unfair, that she was being petulant and spoiled. It was absurd, even she could see that. She wanted so badly for him to take her in his arms and erase this dark mood, but all she could do was push him away. It made no sense. To either of them.

And these cramps weren't helping matters any either.

"You know what you did," she said, and tilted her chin up. "You're doing it right now."

He sighed heavily in the dark car. "This is ridiculous."

"So now I'm ridiculous?"

"I didn't say *you* were ridiculous," he began, then threw his hands up. "Fuck it. Do what you want." He got out of the car, slammed the door, and huffed into Theresa's house, where a bunch of people were already there and halfway drunk.

She watched him go and waited for the tears to come. She wanted to cry. She *needed* to cry. She needed this horrible mood to erupt somehow and dissipate before it took her over and strangled her.

Instead she just sat, upset, wrong, and so wound up she didn't know what to do. Her heart pounded. She wanted to go in, but it would be humiliating now to follow him there, tail between her legs.

It would be like admitting she was wrong.

Even though she was.

And for reasons she couldn't fully define for herself, she just couldn't bear to do that.

A knock at the window next to her startled her.

It was Todd.

She took a quick breath and tried to normalize herself, or at least her appearance, then opened the door.

"What are you doing in there?" he asked.

Pouting. "Nothing."

"Then come into the party."

"I will. In a minute."

"Now." He reached for her and grabbed her arm, pulling her out of the car. "Come *on*. You can't just sit there all night."

This was what she needed. Nate should have done this, just ignored her mood, ignored her whining, and just told her to get her ass into Theresa's party and socialize. It was probably the best way to get out of her own head.

And her own head was *not* a fun place to be right now.

She and Todd walked to the house in silence, but it wasn't tense silence like it had been with Nate. Apparently Todd didn't wonder what her problem was or he didn't care. He was black-and-white, and sitting in the car alone like a freak was black and going into the party was white.

He opened the door for her and she walked in. The smell of cigarettes and pot hung in the air already and her Tretorn sneakers stuck to the foyer floor in a way that suggested beer had already been spilled on the slate.

Theresa's mother would freak if they didn't get this cleaned up before she got back in town. But she and Theresa's stepfather were gone for another week, in Hawaii or Tahiti or somewhere, so there was time to put the house back in order.

They went to the stairs of the split-level and Erin assessed the crowd. She didn't know most of them, but Theresa had mentioned that a bunch of her brother's friends from the Walter Johnson football team would be there, so that was probably who they were. The only people Erin knew were Theresa, David, Todd, Nate, and Todd's friend Kenny.

Nate was at the top of the short flight of stairs, and she approached him with some shame at her behavior. She kind of wanted to run away, but, with Todd at her back, she had to keep going.

The crowd was thick at the top of the stairs and she stopped to wait for people to move. A guy she didn't know, with tawny skin, dark auburn hair, and mean little rodentlike eyes, stood leaning against the wall, blocking the way.

She made momentary eye contact with him and was shocked when he said, "Get the fuck out of the way."

Her jaw dropped. That was *all* she needed! After the night she'd had, the emotional roller coaster she'd been on, all she needed was a stranger to get in her face and cuss at her.

She met Nate's questioning eyes for one panicked moment, then felt a tap on her shoulder and Todd's breath at her ear.

"What did he say to you?" Todd asked, his voice low and tense.

"He told me to get the fuck out of his way," she told him, anger driving her to feed a fire she knew she shouldn't feed.

That was enough for him. Todd reached over her shoulder and grabbed the guy's neck. "You don't fucking talk to her that way—"

He didn't finish before someone else punched him in the side of the face.

That person had the misfortune to be standing in front of Nate at the time, and Nate's reaction was lightning-fast and brutal—he pounded him in the face and the guy went down.

Erin dodged out of the way as Todd, undaunted by the blow, surged forward for the guy who'd insulted her.

What followed was unlike anything she'd ever seen in her life. Even movies didn't get this dramatic when it came to fight scenes.

David disappeared like the mouse in *Goodnight Moon* and suddenly it was Todd, Kenny, and Nate against what looked like the entire Walter Johnson football team. There were at least twelve of them. Maybe fifteen. It was hard to say because everyone kept moving.

The noise was thunderous—the sounds of blows and impacts and grunts, and breaking knickknacks.

Erin watched in horror as everyone piled on and a group of them rolled down the stairs, Todd in the middle of the fray. There was a sickening thud, and she saw that one guy's head had hit the drywall and knocked a head-sized hole in it. Then Nate jumped over all of them and landed in the hall, pounding his fist against the guy who had started it all.

"Don't *ever* disrespect my girlfriend," she heard him say.

Something like pride nudged her heart, followed quickly by guilt for getting any satisfaction from this scene at all.

Todd plowed up the steps and halfway into the room, throwing punches at anyone who got in his way. Nate moved next to Todd, blocking the many people who seemed to be attacking now from all sides.

Soon it was just a tangle of bodies locked together, struggling against each other until they crashed into the lattice door to the kitchen and smashed it into pieces.

Erin stood, transfixed. Everything had happened so fast. One minute she was just going up the stairs, in her own little bad mood, and the next there was this huge brouhaha, ironically playing out her anger and frustration on life's real stage.

Theresa was screaming like a whistle, and crying. That got Erin's attention and she went to her and put her arm around her.

"It's okay," she said stupidly.

"No, it's not!" Theresa was wide-eyed. "Look what they're doing to the house!"

The destruction was amazing. And Erin had barely a moment to take it in before she heard Kenny shout, "I'm gonna *kill* you, motherfucker!" and saw him slam a guy twice his size down on the glass-top coffee table, smashing it in pieces.

"Ohh!" Theresa covered her face with her hands.

Erin scanned the room, looking for Nate.

She found him, back to back with Todd, taking on more people than it looked like they should be able to handle.

He caught her eye. "Call the police!"

She nodded quickly, and asked Theresa, "Where's the phone?"

"I—I—don't—"

Erin grabbed her shoulders. "*Theresa!* Where's the *phone?*"

"There." She pointed vaguely toward a bookshelf full of cookbooks.

Erin hurried to it, found a portable phone, and dialed 911.

"It will be okay," she said to Theresa while she waited for the operator to answer.

"No, it won't," Theresa said angrily. "This is all because of Nate and his stupid fucking friends!"

Erin's objection had to wait because the dispatcher came on and asked what the emergency was. She reported that a party had gotten out of hand and gave the address, then hung up and said to Theresa, "This is not Nate's fault."

"He and his friends are *animals*," Theresa said on a sob. "They didn't need to attack!"

"They *didn't* attack! Some guy said something to me, and Todd was telling him to shut up when one of those other guys punched him in the face!"

"And Nate just *pummeled* him! There was no need for that!"

Erin's heart filled with inexplicable pride. "I guess he didn't like seeing his friend attacked."

Theresa shook her head at Erin. Her eyes were smeared with mascara and shadow. "I can't believe you're defending this."

She couldn't either, actually. But she was. And more than that, she was really proud of Nate, Todd, and Kenny, because their opposition, she noticed, had dwindled to just a few, and her guys were still going strong.

Go team!

"It's your fault too," Theresa added sharply.

"*Mine?* How do you figure that?"

"Nate was pissed off when he came in here. Obviously you guys were arguing *again*. Now he's taking it out on my *house*! Why don't you two just break up and get it over with?" She dissolved into tears again and when Erin tried to put an arm around her shoulder, she shook it off. "Just leave me alone!"

Was it true? *Was* this Erin's fault? She heard a dull thud and saw someone fall to the floor. It wasn't Nate, but it could have been. Had she put him in danger by making him so frustrated that this was the only way he could take it out?

Finally there were sirens, which made a bunch of people panic and leave through the back door, taking with them their pot and whatever other substances they didn't want to be caught holding. The fighting stopped too, dwindling down to a last few weak punches.

The police came to the door and Erin, who fortunately hadn't had so much as one drink, stopped them there, assuring them that the party had broken up.

Clearly glad not to have to deal with too many details of a teenage party gone wrong, the police left, and Erin took a moment to assess the damage.

It was bad.

The house was a mess; there didn't appear to be one square inch that didn't need some sort of cleanup. Nate, Todd, and Kenny were the only ones who remained, a bit worse for wear too, except Nate, for some reason. She guessed it had probably been to his advantage that he was running on emotions ignited before the fight. He was red-faced from the adrenaline high but otherwise unscathed.

Todd, on the other hand, had a bloody lip and eyebrow from the sucker punch he'd taken right off the bat.

Erin laid her hand to Todd's cheek and said, "Thanks for defending me."

He gave a sly smile. "Anytime." And she knew he had accepted her as one of them now. She was Nate's, so she was all of theirs.

And, for the first time, she could see how that wasn't a really bad thing. As tired as she was of hanging out with all of Nate's friends, it meant a lot that they looked out for her.

At least most of them did.

"What happened?" David wandered into the room, looking a little too self-consciously dazed for belief.

"What do you mean, *what happened*?" Todd snapped. "Where the hell were you?"

"I've been upstairs. It looks like a bomb went off in here."

"It must have sounded like it too," Nate pointed out knowingly. "You didn't hear?"

"Fuckin' Hiroshima," Todd added, swiping blood off his lip with the back of his hand.

David's face colored and everyone knew he'd heard and known exactly what was happening.

Erin felt pity for him. He must have been terrified. It would suck to be expected to fight if you weren't any good at it.

"Let's get this place cleaned up," she said, going to Theresa, who was just shaking and mute, and hooking her arm through hers. "We've got a few days, right?"

Theresa nodded numbly.

"Nate—" Erin began.

"I can fix the drywall," he said, as if reading her mind.

"Just go now," Theresa said, then turned hard blue eyes on Erin. "Really."

Erin felt her face grow warm. "Okay. Well, how about if we come back tomorrow and start tackling all this?"

Theresa nodded. "Fine."

Erin was relieved to have at least some agreement from Theresa. "Your parents will never know anything happened. It will be just like in *Risky Business*."

Theresa rolled her eyes. "I seriously doubt that."

"You'll see."

"I'm really sorry about this, Theresa," Nate added.

She leveled a gaze on him. "You're an asshole."

Erin felt like she'd been slapped. "Theresa!"

"Forget it," Nate said, putting a hand to Erin's waist. "She's got every right to be pissed."

"It wasn't your fault," Erin said to Nate.

But he just shushed her, and led her out with a promise to Theresa that they'd be back in the morning to clean it up.

———

"I'm sorry," Erin whispered forty-five minutes later, as Nate pulled her jeans down off her hips. "I don't know what was wrong with me tonight."

They were on her bed, under the crocheted canopy, illuminated only by the old night-light she still had on the shelf by the door.

"Forget it," he said, trailing his mouth down her stomach.

Her breath caught in her throat. "But—"

"It's okay," he murmured, then fixed his hands on her thighs and lifted her to his mouth.

"It's just that," she breathed, "I was in this terrible . . . mood . . . and . . ." She stopped.

Nate's mouth worked her expertly. She clutched the pillow behind her head and bit down on her lower lip, arching against him.

"Seriously," she panted. "I'm . . . sorry. . . ."

He laughed gently against her. "Hush now."

"Okay, but—" She was able to get that out right before he plunged his fingers into her and doubled the sensation that was already sending her to the moon.

They were silent then, except for her rapid breathing and her fingernails trailing along the sheets.

Nate worked her just like always, easily taking her to the brink, keeping her there like a jumper on a ledge, then giving his all to the fall. And when she spilled over into wave after wave of pleasure, he moved up onto her and entered her, extending her ecstasy into something that felt way beyond the physical.

"I love you," she said, after he had released onto her stomach and lay, spent, on top of her. Despite the intimacy they had just shared, she felt like she was clinging to something that was slipping away.

"I love you too," he said, and kissed her cheek, touching her hair absently.

"Are we okay?" she asked in a small voice.

He hesitated. He would have denied it if she'd called him on it, but there was no doubt at all that he hesitated. "Of course."

"I'll always"—her voice broke—"love you."

He tightened his hold on her and pressed his face against her neck. "Me too, baby. Always."

It was two A.M. a week later. The sky was clear and brittle, the stars looked like something on a greeting card. Something about the

January sky always looked to Erin like an Ansel Adams photo. It was just more dramatic. Brighter. More starry. More everything.

Except warm.

It was definitely not warm.

Erin pulled her blue down coat closer around her.

Hopefully he'd show up. She'd asked him to. She'd begged him to. She was kind of banking on it now, standing out in the freezing-cold dark. But he was pissed. He might not show.

They'd had another fight. A little one. She'd told him she thought a guy he went to school with was hot and, if that wasn't bad enough, had proceeded to intimate that she'd think about going out with him . . . if it weren't for Nate, that is. . . .

Nate had told her she was being a bitch, but could he admit that he was jealous? No. What was his problem? Why was it so hard for him to ever step up and say he wanted her and he'd fight anyone to the death for her? Or maybe he wouldn't. Last week it had been Todd who'd fought for her honor—Nate had really just been protecting his friend.

Maybe it was an impasse. Or maybe—just maybe—she was being unreasonable in expecting big declarations and actions. After all, she did know he loved her. At least she felt like it *most* of the time.

Maybe it was their pattern; she'd be a brat, he'd get sick of it, they'd hang up or he'd leave, and then, after trying not to speak to each other, one of them would eventually say uncle and they'd get back together.

On some level, she knew that even that ridiculous cycle was them fighting to stay together. Every time they pushed and pulled, it was to make it work, and each time they succeeded in overcoming little obstacles. Could he see that?

She loved him.

The problem was that these things were happening more and more frequently. The relationship seemed more wobbly than ever, even though she loved him more than ever.

But she had moments when she realized it would be hard for him to believe that. She was always on the defensive, always ready to reject first. Inside, she was afraid that if she just told him she loved him all the time, and everything was peaceful, then maybe he'd get bored and disappear.

And she wouldn't even see it coming.

"Come on," she said, and her breath puffed out a cloud of white in the air in front of her. "Please show up."

Then a car turned onto the street, the headlights swooping across the houses and over her.

He pulled up in front of her and lowered the passenger window and simply said, "Hi."

She laughed in relief and got in. Tonight was not the night for standing there until he got out and opened it for her. There was chivalry and then there was idiocy. "Nate!" She slid across the seat to him and kissed his cheek, his jaw, his mouth. "I love you."

He expelled a long breath. "You're a pain."

"I know."

"Why are we doing this in the middle of the night?"

"Well, I thought it would be *romantic*." She didn't have any specific plans apart from that. "And it is! Don't you think?" She draped her arms around his neck and kissed his cheek again. Everything was okay now. "It's like eloping."

He shifted to put his arm around her and pulled her closer. "I should have brought a ladder."

"That's true, there's always a ladder involved in a good elopement." That didn't sound right. "Is that a word? Elopement?"

"Yes." He turned and kissed her properly.

It had been a year and a half and *this* never got old.

Sometimes other things did, like the fact that they spent so much of their time with his stupid friends and not going anywhere fun or doing anything interesting, which was what they'd argued about tonight, but the stuff that happened between them when they were alone was exciting every single time.

All thoughts of bad stuff disappeared quickly in the swell of physical need, as his hands moved inside her coat and under her shirt, sending a warm trail across her skin wherever he touched her.

"We're in front of my house." She smiled against his mouth. "What if they look outside?"

He didn't move his hands. "Where do you want to go?"

She drew back and looked out the windshield, considering.

Moonlight cast the street in gray light, and shone on the bare branches of the cherry trees that lined the front yards. It was a beautiful night. But it was hard to think of anyplace they could go in this suburb that wouldn't be just more suburbia. More houses that looked like hers, occupied by more people who knew her parents.

"Violet's Lock!" she said. It was a nice little cove along the C&O Canal, down River Road. On a nice day it got pretty crowded, but at night no one would be there. "Seriously, that would be so romantic tonight."

"Okay." He put the car in gear and accelerated. "But that's the kind of place all those stories take place with the bloody hook on the car door, you know."

She shuddered. "Do you think it's dangerous?"

He laughed. "I'm kidding! You're so easy."

She snuggled closer and put her head down on his shoulder again, sighing contentedly. Maybe she was nuts, but she always felt completely *whole* when she was with him. "Not easy for everyone."

His hands tightened almost imperceptibly on the wheel, but he didn't say anything.

Bad subject. It had only been a few months since Pete Hagar. The whole thing seemed stupid now, but at the time the idea of being picked up in that Porsche of his and going to restaurants or movies or other places without David, Todd, Robert, or any of Nate's other testosterone-heavy friends, was really appealing.

All the elements were there—Pete was a great guy, and he *did* take her on proper dates—but at the end of the night, it was always Nate she wanted to kiss good night. And he'd been ridiculously patient about it, waiting for her to get tired of the game and come back to him. He knew she would, apparently, and she did.

And here she was.

Pete, on the other hand, didn't appreciate being part of the game. When he realized she'd never given up ties with Nate while she was dating him, he came to her house to confront her. His timing couldn't have been worse. No sooner had he finished accusing her of "fucking me over by dating Nate at the same time" than Nate himself showed up and offered to kick his ass home for him if he wasn't out of there in three seconds.

Nate might have been gentle and easy with Erin, but guys found him intimidating.

Actually, that was just one—no, two—more things she loved about him.

She pushed one of the cassette tapes she'd made into the player and Bread's "Everything I Own" came on, the plaintive voice singing about love lost irreparably, grieving loss when it's too late. "This is a sad song," she said. The melody had haunted her since childhood.

The loss was like nothing she'd ever felt, yet when she heard the song, she *felt* it. "But pretty."

"This is how I'd feel if I lost you," Nate said, without any self-consciousness.

That struck her as exactly right. It was how she'd feel too. But she didn't want to acknowledge even such a possibility. "You're not going to lose me!"

She felt him shrug.

"You're *not*." She listened to the words with tears in her eyes. "But it's how I would feel too, if we weren't together." She could imagine it a little too well. The sadness, the longing . . . she would remember forever how warm and secure he made her feel. How could she ever live without that?

He turned right onto River Road and the lights of Potomac Village fell behind. They drove past fields and houses that got smaller on land that got bigger. The farther they got from new Potomac, the more rural old Potomac became.

"Theresa's parents are going away next weekend," Erin said after a couple of songs had played.

"Who's she going to have over? Sam or JP?" Nate paused, clearly amused. "Or Michael?"

"Ugh, I don't know." Theresa was kind of known for having a lot of boyfriends. All the guys liked her—she was petite and pretty and knew how to flirt like a champ—but she was just looking for one true love. Problem was, that one true love changed all the time. "I can't stand Michael. Or JP. I don't really know Sam—"

"You said he smelled bad."

"He did, but that might have just been the one time. Even if it wasn't, he's still better than the other two, so I hope that's who she picks."

"Are we going?"

"Of course."

"I'll try and get off work."

"Do that." She closed her eyes and listened to the words. It was nice that Nate said he'd feel that way about her if they broke up. She'd feel the same way about him. God forbid, if something happened and she lost him for good, she *would* give up anything to have him back. Anything and everything. "I love you," she said, and put her hand on his jeans-covered thigh. "I love you I love you I love you."

He laughed. "I love you too."

She smiled into the darkness.

After another ten minutes or so, Nate turned the car onto the dirt road that led down to the lock. "Your dad will kill me if he wakes up and realizes you're gone."

"We'll just tell him we ran off to Mexico together."

"And you think that would go over better than a drive in the country?"

"Maybe not. He's not a fan of hot weather."

Nate shook his head. "It's a good thing you're not eighteen yet."

"Why?"

"Because you probably would have talked me into doing something really stupid by now."

"Ah." She was sixteen. Nate was eighteen. They'd talked about getting married a million times. One night, on the way to the beach with Theresa and Michael, they'd even stopped at a house marked JUSTICE OF THE PEACE and pounded on the door, though Erin wasn't sure what she would have done if someone had answered. Luckily no one had. "Like getting married and running off to Mexico?"

"I'm not a fan of hot weather either."

She pouted. "Don't you want to marry me?"

"Of course I do. I just want to do it right."

Good. She was glad. "I don't want a big wedding, you know. Just a little courthouse thing will be fine." Actually, they'd already said they'd do it September 4 the year she turned eighteen, since September was her lucky month and 4 was her lucky number.

Who needed rented tuxedos and overpriced bridesmaid dresses? She wanted the guy, not the party.

He parked and looked at her. "You'll probably change your mind about that."

"No, I won't." She shrugged out of her coat. "Weddings are a big waste of money. I'd rather have the money. Maybe get a house."

"Aw, baby." He cupped his hand to her cheek. "You'll have it all." He kissed her, and again every other thought fell away.

The silence around them was thick and heavy. There was nothing but the sound of their breathing and her heart pounding. She loved him beyond expression. She loved this. It was intoxicating and she couldn't stop things now if her life depended on it.

She'd been waiting for this since he'd picked her up.

At this point, they had the choreography down pat: they could remove every stitch of clothing in the front seat of a car with their bodies and mouths locked together. Houdini could have learned a thing or two from them. Nate pulled her shirt off and snapped her bra off with one hand, she undid his pants and slid them down over his narrow hips . . . they'd done it all a thousand times before but it never lost its intensity.

Nate eased her back on the bench seat and her head hit the armrest. She laughed, the spell temporarily broken. "This is *exactly* the time the hook-handed guy is supposed to show up."

"I'll take care of you." Nate moved on top of her and glanced out the window above.

Her heart quickened. "You don't see anything, right?"

He shook his head and kissed her again, simultaneously entering her and making her feel safe from the world.

Time blurred. Erin couldn't have cared less when she got home or if she ever got home. All that mattered was this moment and that this moment continued.

He went slow, exploring her body with his hands, her mouth with his, until finally he reached his limit and quickened to his crescendo.

They lay together for a long time afterward, skin to skin.

Finally, Erin said, "It really is kind of spooky down here."

"Down here? You mean . . . ?"

She laughed. "The lock. The canal is beautiful, but there's something a little creepy about it, don't you think?"

He nodded. "But very private." He moved to sit up.

"I'm good with private," she agreed, and reached down to figure out which clothes were hers and which were his.

When they were dressed, they opened the windows to unfog them enough to drive.

Erin, exhausted from the hour and from everything she'd just spent in passion, wrapped her coat around her and lay down with her head in his lap while he drove. The road hummed underneath the tires and the radio sounded tinny and far away. This was just the way it felt when she'd fall asleep on long trips with her family in the back of the station wagon. Perfectly content. Not a care in the world.

She slept so deeply that when Nate tried to wake her, she was completely disoriented, even though it couldn't have been longer than fifteen minutes.

"You're home, baby," he said gently. "You better go in."

She sat up and blinked against the faint house lights. "I don't want to."

"Yes, you do. You were talking about your bed in your sleep."

Oh, no. "Are you serious?"

He nodded and smiled. "You were pissed that you couldn't get the covers up."

"It *is* still a little cold in here." God, how clearly did she speak in her sleep? Had she ever said anything else? Maybe something even more embarrassing?

"Come on." He started to get out of the car.

"That's okay, you don't need to freeze." She put her hand to his cheek. "I can make it to the door by myself." She kissed him.

For another five minutes or so, he kissed her back, then, before things started over again, he pulled back and said, "Go in to bed."

"One more," she said, and kissed him again. She didn't want it to end. Ever.

He moved his arms around her and drew her close. By the time they parted, the windows were fogged again and the sunrise was starting to light the edge of the horizon.

"Your mother is going to be up any minute," Nate said, nodding at the light.

"You're right." She forced herself away from him. "Want me to open the window?"

He looked dubiously outside. A cold wind was picking up. "I guess so."

She did, then turned to him. "Good night. I love you."

"I love you. Talk to you in a few hours."

She got out and pushed the car door closed slowly and quietly. He didn't move his car until she'd opened the front door and stepped inside. It was silent. No one had noticed she was gone.

She went up to her room and took off her clothes, slipped her Redskins shirt over her head, then got into bed and pulled the sheets up around her. She smelled like Nate now. Her mouth tasted like him too. She liked that.

Within minutes she was asleep, dreaming of her romantic tryst under the moonlight.

So maybe she and Nate didn't have the 1950s version of dating. They had each other.

And she couldn't imagine living without that.

Chapter 12

Present

I started to walk down the street I'd grown up on. The front yard of my mother's, and of the neighbors' house, smelled of the box-woods that had been growing, slowly, for thirty years. An earthy, solid scent that always helped me feel grounded.

I needed to think.

Rick was a great guy. I was one of the luckiest women on earth to be proposed to by someone (1) who was so hot, (2) who I was certain would be a fantastic husband, and (3) who would love me and take care of me and Cam for the rest of our lives.

God, I was being *such* a jerk, even just *thinking* about another man. Even if the Other Man was a specter who had been gone for ages.

I just needed an exorcism. But I didn't have a priest or even a smudge stick, so, I thought, maybe some perspective would do.

The sun was dipping in the sky, throwing a slant of amber light across the neat row of little brick Monopoly houses and cherry blossom trees. Everything was dramatic—the long, reaching shadows, the way the wind skittered fallen cherry blossoms across the street, and the faint smell of charcoal smoke hanging in the air, like something remembered.

I hated this mood I was in.

I knew there was another side to the mood—it wasn't normal for me to be dwelling on the past for so long. Granted, it hadn't been constant by any means—years had passed in which Nate was barely in my consciousness, perhaps just a passing thought now and then.

But now was somehow different. More intense.

I wondered if he remembered us as well as I did.

Then I chastised myself immediately for even wondering. I already knew I was nuts for still thinking about this. How could I even imagine that he was too?

I walked along Victory Lane and then turned right onto Parker Drive, where my old school sat nestled among green trees, grassy lawns, and stone walls.

I was still for a moment, looking at the school facade, thinking about how much history this building held for so many people. And everyone's story would be different. Every triumph would have a different prize, every heartache a different face.

I turned and headed back to the parking lot to leave. Passing the tall tree I'd passed every day on my way to and from Nate's car when he'd drop me off and pick me up. Somehow it was the tree that got to me. It made me tremendously sad, not just because of the time that had gone but because the time had somehow gone without me really noticing it.

For one crazy moment, I remembered what it felt like to walk this pavement without the weight of my world on my shoulders. To head toward the old blue car he drove and get in, tossing my books in the back and sliding against his familiar warmth.

Would Nate and I have the same memories of those times? Not all of them, of course, but if a police sketch artist were to somehow illustrate our time together based on what we said, would it look even remotely the same?

Or had I created a mind full of sunny days and starry nights because I knew I was adored? He'd had cause to doubt that, time and again—would his picture of the same time look bleak and sad, reflecting tension and anxiety instead of a powerful optimism that anything was possible?

It wasn't that I was a terrible girlfriend. I'd loved him more than I've ever loved anyone else—but I was so young and he was so sensitive. . . . I had a nagging fear that maybe the little jabs I'd tossed around to make him jealous or to bring a reaction out of him might have been more hurtful than I'd ever known or intended.

My adult perspective on the situation was much different than the selfish, childlike perspective I'd had at the time. I knew now that his home life had been turbulent, that his parents were on the verge of splitting up, and that he had probably spent a lot of time feeling out of place in an acrimonious atmosphere.

I just hadn't realized it at the time.

I left the parking lot and headed back out the way I'd come, pausing for a moment to see the echo of Nate's car, where he always parked, waiting for me after school.

Then I headed out, along the path I'd walked many times after that. But when I got to the corner of the road, I turned left toward his house instead of right toward mine.

I wasn't ready to go back to my mom's yet.

And, honestly, I wasn't quite ready to go back to the present yet. I'd delved this far into old memories, there didn't seem to be much reason to abort the mission now. Might as well go all the way.

So I walked down the hill, passing the little houses from the sixties that had looked outdated for as long as I could remember. I'd passed them all so many times in my life that under hypnosis I would probably be able to give an exact and detailed description of each. The only detectable difference between now and high school was the cars.

I remembered walking this way on many summer nights with my friends, and sitting outside of Nate's house, talking as dusk got heavier and heavier and eventually became night. In my mind's eye, all of those nights had been balmy enough to go swimming and get out of the pool without freezing. The sky in my memory was always filled with stars. And the neighborhoods were green and lush, and at night they smelled like earth and wet pennies from the sprinklers that hummed back and forth on the many manicured lawns.

It wasn't like that now.

The road at the bottom of the hill was under construction, with orange traffic cones rerouting cars that drove too fast on the residential street and clunked into and out of the potholes that the hard, salty winters had carved into the old pavement.

I longed for the heat of real summer.

I turned onto Nate's road, not stopping to think what I would say in the unlikely event that his mother happened to be outside and happened to recognize me (his parents had divorced around the time we'd split up—news he'd gotten the night before we'd broken up, as it turned out—and I had no idea if his father was even still in the area). A quick glance up the street told me there wasn't any obvious movement in front of the house, so I was probably safe.

I moved as if compelled by some force other than my own will. Next thing I knew, I was there, in front of the house. I remembered a cold night that felt like it had been a hundred years ago when I'd run here in bare feet to beg Nate to take me back after I'd broken up with Pete Hagar.

Odd, how time had shaken out those two relationships. I remembered Nate with crystal clarity, of course, but I had only a few memories of Pete and most of them were from school, not personal. Which was funny because Pete and I were Facebook friends now, so we shared brief exchanges now and then about meaningless things, yet when I looked at pictures of him now I could barely reconcile them with the heavily faded photograph of him in my mind.

Yet this—the house Nate had grown up in—was almost as familiar as my own. Obviously I used to pay a lot more attention to my surroundings than I do now, because the pattern of bricks on the walkway to the front door, the gold and black mailbox, even the small gap of cement where the garden was just a little bit lower than the front stoop, were all things I could draw with my eyes closed.

I stood out front. It was a stupid compulsion, I was completely aware of that. Under any circumstances, I'd feel like an idiot if anyone who knew me caught me down there because it wasn't exactly the normal route for a walk from my old house.

But I had to do it. I wasn't sure why. In a way, I think I kind of felt like if I saw the house, I could glue some pieces back together and not feel so fractured when I remembered those years.

Like I said, I know it was stupid, but I couldn't stop myself.

For years, every time I'd passed this street, I'd looked for his car in front of the house where I stood now. Obviously it hadn't been there; it had been an old model back then, so I'm sure it was long dead.

Still, it was weird standing where he used to park and having it not be there, since, like the rest of the landscape, not much had changed.

Suddenly there was the metallic clang of a trash-can lid from the garage.

I froze.

Oh, shit.

Shit shit shit.

Someone was there.

Someone who, if they saw me, would undoubtedly recognize me and mention to Nate that I'd been walking past, like a freaky stalker. I mean, really, how could this not seem weird?

I started to turn and walk back where I'd come from, but then I saw him.

And I couldn't move.

He was wearing ratty old clothes, splashed with paint. From this distance, he didn't really look very different, same presence, same posture. His jaw was shaded by a day's worth of growth, and added to the sense of him being older, yet his movements were as youthful and powerful as ever.

What the hell was he doing here? Hadn't he moved away ages ago? Last I'd heard he was in Arizona. How was it even *possible* that I was looking at him right here, right now? Had I somehow conjured him? Was this the first—or maybe last—step to going certifiably nuts?

Panic built in me, but I wanted to see him. Yes, I could have walked away undetected at just about any point up to then, but I had to see. It was like standing in front of an accident, terrified of seeing dismemberment but having to know.

He was putting bags into the trash can. Paint flecked his pants and forearms. As I carefully moved closer, I could see his triceps flexing as he moved them and was surprised to realize that the movement of his muscles was something I still recognized. The jut of his elbow. It wasn't like I hadn't seen a man's arms in years, but I still knew Nate's when I saw them.

Then he turned.

My first impulse was to hide. Turn around, dodge behind a car, dive into the sewer, maybe simply evaporate.

But there was no way to slip out of view. The stupid home-owners' association had insisted on planting Japanese maples all over these neighborhoods thirty-five years ago and they'd all gotten diseased and died and been replaced more recently by immature trees that afforded no hiding places.

So I stood there, feeling naked, in front of his house.

We made eye contact.

And there it was—recognition.

Now, I know the normal thing to do at this point would have been to perhaps wave, say hello, approach him with some sort of plausible reason I happened to be passing his house. Out for a run after a heavy meal of grilled burgers and wanted to stay off the main roads, maybe.

But I was mute. Really, I couldn't think of anything reasonable to say. Just about everything that crossed my mind would have been such an obvious ruse, including—and I'm embarrassed to admit I thought about this—pretending not to recognize him.

So I said nothing. I just watched the shock in his eyes as he took me in, and knew mine probably looked the same. Shocked, glad, scared . . . it was hard to read both what I saw and what I felt.

But I couldn't look away. And when I saw him try, I realized he couldn't either. He glanced down, a muscle in his jaw tensed, but then he looked back at me, still unspeaking.

And, following an impulse unlike anything I'd ever felt before, I walked toward him, holding his gaze the entire time.

As he held mine. Standing there. Silent. Watchful.

It's hard to describe what was happening because I don't entirely understand it myself. All I know is that one minute I was walking down the old streets, feeling melancholy and drenched in the past, and the next minute I was completely in the present, facing a Nate who looked the same only older and, to me, even more beautiful *because* of the years that were beginning to show in his hair and around his eyes.

Yet in some strange way I felt like I'd been looking at him the whole time, through all the years.

I stopped before him and, completely unable to come up with something clever or even coherent to say, I just followed a crazy, inappropriate impulse and reached out to touch his cheek. I laid my hand to the stubble, my thumb on that familiar cheekbone.

His hand shot up and grabbed my wrist.

There was a second of uncertain eye contact, then he pulled me hard against him. I softened against his chest, melting into him in a way I'd done a thousand times a thousand years ago, and the next thing I knew his mouth was on mine and I was drinking him in with the kind of hungry desperation usually reserved for shipwreck victims finding water and food for the first time in three days.

It was good.

Not just familiar, because that sounds too trite. In fact, anything I could say about it would sound trite. Too small for the emotion. It felt like it *fit*. A puzzle piece sliding into place and completing a picture that had been hidden for too long.

He held me so tightly I almost couldn't breathe, then moved his hands up and cupped my face, tangling his fingers in my hair.

Everything—the taste of him, the smell of him, the feel of his arms around me, the touch of his hand to my face, the expanse of his back and shoulders and everything else I touched—it just felt right.

I could have cried.

I don't know, maybe I did.

The moment was dark and dizzying, and I felt like I was spinning through time and space and never wanted to stop. If there is a way to recharge your soul, that was what was happening to mine at that moment.

I couldn't believe I was here, couldn't believe I was touching him. It was like touching a ghost. I'd wanted him so much twenty-three years ago but he'd kept me away. Now I'd just gone for a walk, it had felt like a hundred years later, and ended up living a moment I'd never dreamed I'd have again.

I trailed my fingertips down his back, slowly moving over the muscles I'd once known so well. How many times had I felt them flexing, moving under my palms as I clung to him while he slowly moved within me?

How many times had I thrown my arms around these shoulders and laughed or cried or just held on tight?

I moved my hands over his body, down his biceps, up his rib cage, across his lower back. It was tactile memory and I could feel it filling my heart and mind, like warm water spilling into a bath.

All the while he kept his mouth on mine, and his breath filled me and revived me. It was no longer a matter of me wanting this, I *needed* it.

I needed this and more.

We drew back and looked at each other and it was like all the weight of time arced between us. There was nothing to say. Nothing we *could* say that wouldn't be way smaller than the moment.

His eyes narrowed fractionally and his gaze traveled downward. Then he took my hand in his. It was warm, his grip strong, and he pulled me with him toward the front door and I went with him, followed without having any real idea where this would lead. But I knew we were alone.

There was a faint smell of fresh paint in the air, obviously the same paint that flecked his forearms and T-shirt right now.

We went up the stairs. The wallpaper was the same, if fading, and my knuckle grazed it where the handrail was still warped. The floors had gone from shag-carpeted to hardwood. In the upstairs hall, I looked into the warm brown eyes of the oil portrait of his great-grandmother that hung on the wall, as I'd done a million times before. He led me into his old room, which was almost exactly as I remembered it: a simple desk with books in the hutch, a double bed, a dresser, and two windows overlooking the side and back yards.

There was no time for melancholy, though. We tumbled onto the bed together, bodies locked as one, mouths hot, open, moving and communicating wordlessly. The span of time that separated this from the past dissolved like smoke.

It had been a long, long time since I'd felt this kind of thrill from a kiss, and we took it slowly, exploring for I don't know how long.

Then he pulled back slightly and we looked at each other. Really looked into each other's eyes, and I saw that same soul I'd always seen. I wanted to tell him I loved him, that I'd always loved him, and that life—and I—had never been the same without him there.

Instead, I just expelled a breath I think I'd been holding for years.

I wasn't even sure my voice would work if I tried to speak.

For a moment, I thought he was going to say something, but he just held up his hand in front of me. I looked at it, then pressed mine to it, and our fingers twined. His eyes were fixed on mine, but it was impossible for me to tell what he was thinking.

I couldn't even figure out what *I* was thinking.

He lowered our hands and shifted his weight, pressing the back of my hand against the mattress. Then, with more deliberation than I'd ever seen or felt, he laid his other hand to my cheek and drew me in for another kiss. It got deeper fast, more urgent. His beard stubble raked across my skin and I knew it would show on my face later, but I didn't care.

It was the first time I'd felt fully in a moment in as long as I could remember. I couldn't bear to think that this would ever end, that we'd have to speak, that we'd have to say good-bye, that I'd *ever* have to do anything but feel him feeling me. So I let go of all of that and drowned in him.

He ran his hands down my sides and pulled up my shirt. Seconds later, we were skin to skin, pressed together on top of the old brown quilt that had been there since he was a teenager.

He moved his mouth across my lips, my jaw, my neck, and skidded his hand down across my abdomen to my pelvis. I arched against it, moving his touch to below the zipper of my khaki capris.

There was no need to explain. He pressed his hand against me, only the fabric between him and me. The years blurred. I clutched the bed, but in my mind I felt the linoleum of my old basement floor, the rough bales of hay at the old barn where I worked in the summer. I was here, and now, but I was also swimming in the past, living these same motions we'd made so many times before.

I fingered the cold snap of his jeans, uncertainly for a moment, and his breath tightened. That small movement was enough to make up my mind, and I yanked the snap and pulled the zipper open.

As I slid the jeans down over his hips, I remembered things I hadn't let myself think about in ages: the muscular dent in his hips—unlike the soft curve of mine—the hard V of his abdomen, the perfect size of *him*.

There were times, when we were younger, when we might have taken our time, but our urgency was high now and he moved to whip my pants down so effortlessly it was like a magic trick.

Then he rolled on top of me and nudged my legs open with his knee.

Again, the calendar pages flew and I could close my eyes and see the canopy of my bed over me, I could feel the seat of his Chevy beneath me.

He put his hand between my legs and played me in a way that showed he'd never forgotten me.

I reached for him, our hands bumping, and nudged him toward me. This was a signal we'd worked out a long time ago. Slowly he removed his hand and moved it up to my shoulder, looking so deeply into my eyes that it felt like he could see right through me.

Then he bent down and put his mouth to mine, simultaneously pushing into me with such delicious force that it took my breath away.

It was like coming home.

I rocked my hips back and wrapped my legs around him, bringing him as deeply into me as I could.

For one endorphin-blurred moment I thought I could die right now and my life would have had perfect symmetry.

He cradled me in his arms and moved slowly, gradually building the urgency. I closed my eyes and tried to feel everything at once, his movement inside of me, the way the muscles of his back moved under my fingertips, the warmth and taste of his mouth, and the way his teeth would click against mine now and then when things got hungry.

He tightened his arms around me and we rolled over so I was on top of him. It had been a long time, but I remembered what he liked, and ground against him, watching him as he closed his eyes and his breathing grew strained. I stopped a moment, then moved again, and the muscle in his jaw tightened and ticked the way I'd seen it do before.

He was close, so I moved down and rolled us back over so he was on top. He didn't even open his eyes, his mouth just found mine, and he moved hard and fast, quickly taking me to the top.

I held my breath, living the physical sensation, the emotional fulfillment, the mental explosion. . . .

The release was tremendous.

And when he climaxed, he kissed me hard, hands gripping my shoulders, digging into my flesh. I remembered this too, the way he kissed me at that moment, the way he held me, the way he moved until he was spent.

Then he sank against me, his rough cheek against mine, his body heavy on me.

We breathed in sync, hearts pounding just millimeters apart.

I had forgotten sex could be like this. I'd forgotten it could feel like my soul was in it. Usually it was just my body—and, don't get me wrong, that wasn't bad—but this was so much better.

Afterward, we lay there for a while, still not speaking, but touching, hands, faces, hair . . . Finally, of course, I couldn't ignore the passing time. Cam would be waiting for me. Everyone would wonder where I was, though no one would ever guess.

"This would be a good time for me to say something really profound," I said, with half a laugh.

"I've been thinking you should," he returned with a smile. That voice. Something in me, some tiny part that had somehow made it through all of this intact, melted.

I ran my hand across his chest and sighed. "I've got nothing. I'm not even sure this is real."

"If it isn't, I'm the one who's dreaming it, not you."

"That's what you'd say in my dream."

"Mm." He nodded, as if understanding.

"What are you doing here?" I asked.

"I could ask you the same thing."

"I don't have an answer to that. I don't know what the hell I'm doing here. I was just out for a walk after my mother's cookout, and . . ." No point in finishing. He knew how that ended. "I thought you lived out West now."

"I moved back three months ago. I live down in Palisades now."

Palisades was an area of D.C. by the reservoir and Georgetown University. It was no more than five or six miles from where I lived, but in a city this populated and in neighborhoods as distinct and closed as the ones we lived in, it wasn't surprising at all that we never ran into each other. A lot of very recognizable people lived within a few miles of me—newscasters, musicians, politicians, and so on—but I never saw them.

"So you just happened to be here today. . . ."

"I'm doing some work for my mom. She's thinking about selling the house."

I felt a stab of sadness at the idea. "That would be a shame."

He shrugged. "It's a lot of house for one person. What about you? Where are you these days?"

"McLean Gardens."

He met my eyes and I knew he was going through the same thought process I'd just had: so near and yet so far.

For a moment, we looked at each other wordlessly. There was so much to say, yet it was all so big and so overwhelming that it was easier to say nothing.

Then he kissed me again, and it felt like we said more that way than words ever could.

A while later I tore myself away from him. I had to go home. Cam was waiting. Real life was waiting. And, in some weird way, I was eager to get away from this situation so I could think about it with some distance. So I went into the bathroom that used to smell of Pert shampoo and Coast soap to pull myself together as much as possible before facing everyone at my mother's house again.

I went to turn on the faucet.

And that's when I saw it.

A gleaming gold wedding band next to the hot water tap.

My heart dropped. I mean *dropped*. Moments before it had been soaring like an eagle and now it was like a Perdue roaster splatting on the kitchen floor.

I picked up the ring and looked at it, searching for some clue as to who it belonged to, even though I already knew.

It wasn't his mother's; his father didn't live here anymore.

He'd taken it off to paint. I would have done the same thing.

But the confirmation was engraved inside: *N & T Forever.*

I felt sick. All my internal systems went on full alert. I wanted to run, to scream, to smash something, to cry. But all I could do was stand there, frozen in shock.

Then I felt him move up behind me, his body heat pulsating toward me like an invitation.

But it was too late for that, and the air was thick with that fact. I can't say how, but I knew we both knew it.

I looked up. Our eyes locked in the mirror.

He glanced at the ring in my hand, then back at me.

Then he spoke, words that had been hanging in the air around us for almost two and a half decades, though I'd never wanted to acknowledge them before.

"I never wanted to see you again."

Chapter 13

February 1987

Winter stretched on and on.

By the end of February, Erin sincerely wondered if she was actually going crazy. Every day had been gray. The sky was gray. The street was gray. It was like looking at a faded black-and-white photo. It was hard to imagine there was anyplace in the world that was more depressing than Washington, D.C., in February.

She was restless. Depressed. Hopeless. Maybe it was the years of watching sunny romantic comedies like *The Love Boat* and *Fantasy Island*, maybe it was the books she read that were set in exotic, sunny locales like Crete and Majorca, but Erin felt like if she had to spend one more day trapped in this cold house in this depressing landscape going to that boring, bleak school she'd lose her mind.

The fact that the plan for the night was to go to one of those cheap-o dollar theaters to see some ancient Bruce Lee movie, *Enter the Dragon*, with Nate and his friends didn't help matters much.

But what was she going to do? Suggest a John Hughes flick? Not quite the same mood.

It was Todd's last week in Maryland before he moved to Seattle for some internship with a big computer company he was doing for school, and he was meeting them at the theater. Obviously they were going to want to do Guy Things, it was a wonder Nate had thought of bringing her along at all.

Nate and Todd had been doing Guy Things since they were in first grade and joined the local baseball team together. Thus began a love/hate, help-at-all-costs, win-at-all-costs rivalry that had characterized their friendship for more than a decade. If they were on the same team, they were as solid as a rock, fighting side by side to win together. Erin had witnessed that herself.

But when they were head to head, whether they were messing around fighting in the basement or playing one-on-one basketball, they could go at each other like enemies. Really, at times like that, from the outside a person wouldn't guess they were friends.

Erin figured that was normal best-friend stuff for guys, and a little voice inside told her that she shouldn't be going tonight, that this should be their thing and she didn't have a part of it.

But the plan was made. Everyone would probably think she was being petulant if she begged off. And anyway, she was bored, she didn't want to hang around this stupid house a minute longer than she had to.

She went downstairs and put on a down jacket to fight the cold, then opened the front door and waited for the swing of Nate's headlights at the end of the road. By now she knew the sound of his engine and was usually out the door before he had the chance to be gentlemanly and get out of the car to go to the door for her. Of course, it had been a while since he'd done that anyway.

Tonight was no exception. "'Bye!" she called to whatever parent might be listening, and closed the heavy door behind her. She ran through the cold, damp grass of the front yard to his car.

When she opened the passenger door, the dome lights came on and she saw David Rutley in the passenger seat.

Ugh. Not *again*. She frowned.

David understood. He knew he drove her crazy. "You can sit next to me." He gave the bench seat next to him an obnoxious tap. Did he seriously think she was just going to climb on in and sit on his hand while he slobbered filthy things in her ear with Nate sitting next to them?

Somehow, Nate never seemed to notice how David did this kind of weird stuff. Once he'd slapped her butt, another time he'd spent about half an hour saying how he'd like to trade places with Nate when she was leaning against him on a sofa at a party, but Nate didn't appear to take this as an affront at all. It was like he didn't even hear it, but he had to have. He just didn't care. Didn't take it seriously.

Well, she didn't like it. So, David sitting in her seat, telling her she could sit next to him and be groped all night?

No way.

"Get in the back," she said. Okay, technically it wasn't her car, but she had come to think of that as her seat.

"No."

She looked to Nate for help, but he just shook his head in a way she knew meant, *Deal with it yourself.*

"David, seriously," she insisted. "*Move.*"

"Forget it, Erin. I don't want to look like I'm being chauffeured—"

"David, get in back," Nate said quietly.

Then, as if touched with a cattle prod, David scrambled over the seat, muttering something like, "Fine. Whatever."

Erin got in the car and sat next to Nate. Something was wrong. She didn't understand why he let David spar with her.

"What's with you?" she asked.

"Nothing."

She sighed and looked out the window as they drove. He was like this lately—distant, preoccupied.

Maybe the weather was getting to him too.

By the time they got to the theater, the air was thick with a slow drizzle of cold rain. Todd was there with his brother and two other guys he went to school with.

Suddenly Erin felt ill at ease.

She was tired of guys, tired of always being the only girl in the group, tired of the whole damn group always being there. It seemed like she and Nate never went anywhere without David these days. That wasn't what dating at this age was supposed to be! She was too young just to be taken for granted this way.

What happened to the whole idea of the boy asking the girl out on a date, picking her up, maybe with flowers, and taking her to dinner and a movie *alone*? Okay, maybe the flowers would be a bit much, but she wouldn't mind the occasional romantic date.

They'd rarely had that. When they'd first started dating, he didn't have a car. By the time he'd gotten a car, they'd been dating long enough that he no longer had to impress her. And she loved him deeply, she really did—she was going to be with him for the rest of her life, she knew it—but she wanted to have memories of dating like a teenager, not hanging out with a bunch of guys while the rest of her friends had actual dates.

"Hey," Todd said, looking her up and down appreciatively when she approached. "Looking good, Erin." His breath smelled faintly of alcohol.

She flushed. She couldn't help it. It was flattering when a guy that good-looking complimented her. "Shut up."

"I'm serious." He looked at her with those amber eyes. His best feature. Along with that mouth. "If I had a girl like you here, I wouldn't be leaving."

She smiled. "That would be a pretty stupid reason to stay and not get a good job, don't you think?"

"I dunno. Could be worth it to stick around for a pretty face."

She hoped Nate was hearing this. It would be nice for him to get the idea that other guys might find her desirable, since he didn't seem to think about it anymore. "Well, you've got a pretty face, Todd," she said coyly. Of course, he knew that.

"Not as pretty as yours."

She gave a light laugh, again hoping it might raise at least a tiny bit of jealousy—or at least *notice*—in Nate. "You're ridiculous."

Maybe it did. Nate joined them and Todd knocked him in the arm. "Thanks for coming, man."

Nate's gaze shifted from Todd to Erin and back. "No problem. Won't be the same without you around here." The words were nice, but his voice was a monotone.

God, he couldn't even liven up for his friends! What was his deal? If she kissed Todd square on the lips, Nate would probably just yawn.

They bought their tickets and went in. Unsurprisingly, the theater was practically empty—there were not a lot of Bruce Lee fans in the area, and even fewer who were willing to brave the gross weather—so they didn't have any problem finding seats together.

Erin sat with Nate on one side and Todd on the other.

Throughout the movie, Todd made asides that only she could hear, and each time she laughed she glanced over at Nate's stony profile. He didn't even appear to notice. It was like he'd lost all interest in her; she might as well be a piece of old furniture.

It only served to accentuate how amusing and easygoing Todd was. Not that she wanted to trade Nate in; she couldn't see being without him. She just wanted him to be a little more fun, like he used to be. How could it be that his best friend in the world was so relaxed and easy and he was so stony and cold?

When the movie finally ended, and after they'd waited a few minutes to see if there was going to be a surprise double feature, they got up to leave. When Nate stepped away for a moment, Todd whispered to Erin, "What's your number?"

She was flattered. It had been a long time since she'd felt flattered by a guy. "Ask Nate," she said flippantly.

Todd groaned. "Give me a break. I just want to talk. Write your number down. It's harmless."

She looked him in the eye, then, with a small smile, reached into her purse and dug out a receipt from earlier. On the back of it, she wrote her number, adding *for emergency use only,* and handed it over to him.

He pocketed it subtly, not looking first.

"Let's go," Nate said, appearing out of nowhere.

"Where?" she asked. Now that she was out, she wanted to have fun. Pizza, maybe. Someplace with pool tables.

"Home."

"Are you serious?"

He shrugged and looked her in the eye. "Yeah."

"Let's go to Georgetown!" David suggested.

Still looking at Erin, Nate said, "I'm tired."

"Fine," she said crisply. She couldn't believe what a jerk he was being. How little fun he was these days. "Then drop me off first."

"David's is on the way."

"I don't care." This was becoming a standoff. "I want to go home." If she had to stay with this ice sculpture of Nate and that dimwit David one second longer than necessary, she'd scream.

"I'm going with Todd," David said, joining the others as they retreated. "Don't worry about me."

As frigid as it was outside, the atmosphere inside the car was even colder. Nate didn't say a word on the drive, and even though he was only a couple of feet away it felt like there was a huge chasm between them.

Erin pushed a tape into the tape deck and sang loudly along, not looking at Nate the entire time. It was hard to focus on the moving wet landscape outside for the entire twenty-minute drive, but she did it.

When he pulled up outside her house he turned off the tape.

Finally she looked at him. "*What* is going *on* with you?"

There was a long hesitation before he said, "I've just got some things on my mind."

"So you admit you're acting like an asshole?"

"I'm tired."

"Since when can you not talk to me? You know 'I'm tired' isn't the true answer."

"It's my answer."

She wanted to shake him. "Don't do this, Nate."

He looked straight ahead, didn't even glance at her. "I'm not doing anything."

"You're going to push me away until we can't get back," she threatened. Her heart was pounding. "Is that what you want? Do you want to break up?"

A muscle ticked in his jaw, but he didn't answer.

She waited for a moment, something plummeting in her chest with every moment that he didn't say anything. Was this really it? Was it really going to end this way?

Was he really going to *let* it?

It sure looked that way.

"*Fine!*" she yelled, suddenly irrationally angry. "Have it your way." She pushed the passenger door open, stepped into a freezing puddle, then slammed the door behind her. She huffed up to the house without even bothering to look back.

And he apparently didn't even bother to wait and make sure she got in all right, because she heard him peel out and drive away.

Two hours later, her phone rang. Her heart leapt, hoping it was Nate. Maybe he'd thought about how cold he'd been with her, maybe he was going to apologize, maybe he was going to come over in the middle of the night to reassure her that he loved her, the way she'd done for him that one time. Her anger had already melted, leaving a little pool of fear and heartache behind, but if this was him, and if they could just make it past this one hurdle, she was sure they would never fight again.

But it wasn't Nate.

It was Todd. He was drunk.

Erin's disappointment was enormous.

"Are you alone?" he asked.

He couldn't charm her now. "I told you not to call unless it was an emergency."

"'Sun emergency." His words were mushing together ever so slightly. "I might not get another chance."

She gave a dry laugh. "You don't have a chance now."

"Are you alone?" he asked again.

"Yes." She sighed. She was totally alone. Utterly, completely alone. "Why?"

"I'm coming over."

She looked at the clock. "It's after one in the morning!"

"So what? Are you going to deny a guy one little request before he goes off and leaves home?"

She laughed. "You're hardly going to a war zone."

"I'm on my way," he said.

"No," she protested feebly. "Don't come." But she was awake now, and angsty, and he had already hung up anyway.

There was nothing she could do to stop him now, so she got up and put on makeup again so she'd at least look good rejecting him. Twenty minutes later she was downstairs when there was a faint knock at the door. She hurried over and opened it as quietly as she could.

Todd was standing under the front porch light, smiling stupidly. No one else was around.

"Did you drive yourself here?" she asked incredulously.

He held up the keys. "Yup."

"Brilliant." She opened the door. "Come in. Want some coffee?" She didn't know how to make coffee, much less do it silently in the kitchen so it didn't wake up her parents, but she'd give it a try.

"No way, it might kill my buzz."

"That's the idea."

"I'm *kidding*." He leaned on her. "I'm not that buzzed. I was sober enough to call your number, wasn't I?"

"That's true." This didn't feel right. Without Nate here she felt a little bit out of her element.

But her element had grown pretty tiresome lately.

"Come up," she said, going to the stairs. "But be *quiet*." She led him to her room, flipped on the light, and sat down on the bed. "So what do you want?"

"What's going on with you and Nate?"

Did he know something she didn't? "Nothing. Why?"

He shrugged. "I don't know why he doesn't treat you better."

It was a classic woo-the-girl line, and they both knew it. She rolled her eyes. "You don't know how he treats me."

Todd sat down on the bed next to her and leaned his head against the wall. "I know he doesn't treat you like he wants to keep you."

She felt embarrassed. Was that everyone's perception? That she was some dumb girl in a relationship that was abusive on some level? "I don't want to talk about that," she said, hoping to sound breezy and unconcerned. But she doubted she was fooling him.

"He's kind of cold."

Exactly. *Exactly* her thoughts. But the bad thing was that he'd known Nate *way* longer than she had. In many ways, he knew him better. Maybe he knew, with certainty, things she could only fear.

"He's not, though," she said. *Not usually.*

He turned to her and touched her face. "You're really pretty, you know that?"

Heat rose in her cheeks. "Give me a break."

"I mean it." He touched her hair. "Really, really pretty."

She wished Nate could hear him. Maybe then he'd appreciate her a little more. Except that, of course, she *didn't* wish Nate could hear him since this looked bad, her sitting on her bed in her room with a friend of his at one thirty in the morning.

A friend who was suddenly kissing her.

Everything about it felt wrong. Foreign. He wasn't Nate. And she *liked* kissing Nate. This was just . . . weird.

She pushed him away. *"Don't."*

Her heart suddenly felt broken. She couldn't *un*do this. It had happened, even for a few confused seconds, and now she felt like she'd stepped off a cliff and was sinking through the air. She knew exactly how much it would hurt to hit bottom, but she couldn't stop it.

"Come on. No one will ever know." He leaned in to her again.

She pushed back again, harder. "There's nothing to know. There will *never* be *anything* to know. I don't want to do this."

"It's not like you're married or something."

"I don't *want* to be with you," she said, and she meant it completely. "So leave me alone."

This was insane! This was really stupid. But on the other hand, she couldn't put him in his car and have him drive away in this condition. Last year their friend Hank had been killed on his way home from having a few drinks when he hit a tree. There was no way Erin was taking a chance on being responsible for something like that. And there was no one she could call to pick him up.

So she was stuck with him, at least for a little while, until he sobered up some.

But now it felt tainted. It felt wrong. He was practically a stranger, the only thing that made him anything closer than that was the fact that he was Nate's friend, so he had no business being here with Nate's girlfriend.

And she had no business being here with Nate's friend, especially now that he was all over her.

It wasn't like Nate's friends hadn't been over before when he wasn't. It wasn't even like they hadn't sat on the bed with her and talked. It wasn't even as if they'd never made passes at her, but something about tonight felt like it had crossed a line.

She wanted him to leave, but she didn't want to be responsible for an accident, so she let him stay a while, just to talk. To sober up. Of course, Todd kept leaning toward her, heaving hot, alcohol-laden breath in her face and trying to kiss her again.

Repeatedly she pushed him away, but she couldn't bring herself to make him leave because he hadn't sobered up enough.

Finally, she picked up a baseball bat that she had leaning against the wall next to the bed—a silly precaution she'd taken when she got nervous in the house alone a few nights ago—and laid it between them as a boundary.

"Don't cross this," she said, completely straight-faced. "That's the rule."

He put his hands up in surrender. "Okay, I get it."

"I *mean* it."

"Yes, ma'am."

"I'm not afraid to hit you in the balls with it."

He must have seen then that she meant it. Once he stopped making passes, they actually had a pretty good talk. He confided that he was nervous about leaving everything he ever knew and acknowledged that Erin wasn't available but that he wanted a girlfriend to write to. Someone to make him feel like he had a purpose other than working. Then he said again, with sincerity, that he thought Nate was a fool for not treasuring her more.

But the thing was, even though Nate wasn't being what you'd call warm and fuzzy these days, she was really pretty sure he *did* treasure her. Maybe it wasn't fair to expect him to shoulder all the weight of romancing her at this point—maybe she just needed to accept that their relationship was already two years old and just wasn't going to have that new car smell anymore. But what did she really want? The excitement of a new relationship, or to be the lucky one who found her soul mate at fifteen and got to spend her whole, long life with him?

She wanted Nate.

This felt too strange.

Nate was quiet, dependable, the steady tortoise, while Todd was a good example of the flashy hare, and it was growing more painfully obvious by the second that *this* was getting old quickly. It was a lot more boring than what she was realizing was a pretty appealing predictability.

"You should go," she said, and as she said it she realized she really, really wanted him gone. Like, now. Like, an hour ago. In fact, she fervently wished he'd never come. It had been a long night.

It should have been Nate with her.

He looked at her, surprised, but didn't argue. "You're right."

"Are you okay to drive?"

He nodded. "Fine. It's been hours since I had anything."

"Okay." She stood up and he followed. Together they crept down the stairs, where she opened the front door with extreme care. She turned to him. "So . . .'bye. Good luck with the whole internship thing."

"Thanks." He leaned in to kiss her, and she turned her face so his lips brushed her cheek.

She met his eyes. "You're a jerk."

"I know. What can I say?" He smiled and stepped out the door. She watched him walk toward his car for a moment, then, satisfied that he was completely steady on his feet, closed the door.

———

The next morning she woke with a guilt hangover. She had been so *so* stupid to let Todd come over. Especially after she'd flirted with him all night when they were all out together. She'd led him on, probably; she'd certainly been disrespectful to Nate . . . the whole thing was a mess, one selfish mistake on top of another. It was all she could think about.

So when Theresa called and asked if she wanted to go to Rockville with her to run some errands, she was glad for the distraction.

Theresa picked her up and they sang along to her new Rick Springfield tape in the car. Erin wanted to tell her what had happened the night before, but her allowing Todd to come over had been so patently stupid that she just couldn't bear to admit it to another human being.

Better to just let time pass so that she and Todd would forget it ever happened and Todd would move on to some other way to try and one-up Nate, just like he always did. Last night she'd just been a pawn in that endless game of theirs and she'd be glad when he moved on to something else.

"Hello?" Theresa was saying.

"Sorry." Erin returned her attention to Theresa. "What did you say?"

"I said isn't that Todd?"

"What about Todd?" Erin asked sharply.

Theresa gave her a funny look and pulled the car over to the side of the road. "Isn't *that* Todd?" She pointed, then waved and put Erin's window down, letting a gust of freezing-cold air in.

Erin turned to see Todd Griffith walking over to them on the sidewalk. "Hey, ladies," he said with a devilish grin. The very one he'd probably hoped would have charmed her last night.

"Hey, Todd!" Theresa sounded delighted to see him, and all at once Erin realized Theresa was in flirting mode.

Erin's reflexive irritation with that turned quickly. This might be a good thing!

If she could hook Todd and Theresa up, maybe that would kind of *erase* what had happened last night!

"How are you, Erin?" he asked pointedly.

"Fine," she said, not quite meeting his eyes.

"What are you doing out here in the freezing cold?" Theresa asked.

"Walking home. Car died."

Theresa gave a snort. "Well, you're not walking home now, for God's sake. Get in!"

A tremor of apprehension ran through Erin, though she would have been hard-pressed to explain it.

"You sure?" Todd asked.

Theresa waved an airy hand. "Of course I'm sure. *Get in!*"

Aware that if she continued to be mute it would raise suspicions she didn't want to answer, Erin said, "Just get in, Todd, it's cold out there."

He shrugged and opened the door. Erin pushed her seat forward so he could get in the backseat behind her.

It was only a few minutes' drive to Todd's house, but Theresa managed to fill the time with plenty of innuendo. Erin had to give her a nod, she was masterful at luring guys in. Even Todd, who'd known her sort of tangentially for two years, seemed to be drawn into her charm.

"So you're leaving town soon, right?" Theresa asked him.

"Tomorrow."

"Oh." Her expression dropped.

Erin's too—that *did* put a crimp in the fixing-them-up plan. "But you'll be back in the summer, right?" she asked, turning to look at him.

He nodded. "Mid-June."

His eyes met hers and she felt a clamminess creep over her. She turned back around and looked out the windshield.

Theresa turned onto his street and said, "Which house is it? I think I've been there once, but I can't remember."

"Second on the left, here."

She turned into the driveway.

Erin opened the door and released the seat to let him out.

"Do you guys want to come in for a drink or something?" he asked.

"No, I've got to get back and—" Erin began.

But she was interrupted by Theresa's chipper, "Sure!" She flipped the ignition off and opened her door before Erin could object.

And, really, why *should* Erin object? Nothing had really happened last night, what she'd done wasn't that big a sin, and Todd was just being *Todd*. He was kind of a jerk and everyone knew it. If Theresa decided to take a chance on him, even knowing that, then fine. Erin's guilt was getting the better of her and she was making way too big a deal out of this.

She got out of the car and the three of them hurried to the front door. As soon as he opened it, a blast of warm air rushed out to usher them in.

"What do you want to drink?" Todd asked.

"We're not going to be that long," Erin began, but once again Theresa's hormones got the jump on her.

"Coke." Theresa smiled and gave a small shrug toward Erin.

The ideal situation would have been for Erin to clear out and come pick Theresa up later, but Erin didn't have her car. So she was stuck in the middle of this flirt fest and there was no telling how long it would last, given the fact that both Theresa and Todd seemed like they were in high gear.

"You sure you don't want anything?" Todd asked Erin.

"No, thanks." She knew she sounded cold, but apparently he didn't notice it.

He went to the kitchen and she hissed at Theresa, "I don't want to be here!"

"Why *not*? This is fun!"

"It's wrong without Nate here. It just feels . . . I don't know. I don't feel right."

She rolled her eyes. "You're crazy."

"Maybe so, but can you run me home and come back?"

Theresa pulled a face. "How would I manage that? I'd sound obsessive. *Erin wants to go, but can I come back please please please?*" She shook her head. "Please."

Erin shrugged, and Todd came back with a Coke for Theresa and led them down to his bedroom in the basement.

"Very Greg Brady," Theresa commented, looking around approvingly at the paneled wall and posters of Aerosmith and the Rolling Stones.

"He had the attic," Erin pointed out.

"What?"

"Greg Brady. He had the attic."

"Oh."

This was exactly the kind of thing Erin could talk on and on about, especially right now. "Remember? He had the beads and stuff and there was that one time they all pretended it was haunted. That was the creepiest— *What?*"

Theresa was looking behind her with an odd expression on her face.

Erin turned to see what she was looking at and it was clear immediately.

Nate was standing there, looking at her in a way she'd never seen before. His face was steely, his eyes looked black.

"Nate—" She moved toward him, but he shook his head.

"Fuck you!" It was like his soul had dropped out; his face was a mask of him, but his eyes had gone dark and dead. He wasn't in there. She knew what he thought he was seeing, even though there was no reason for him to think it, and she knew that this combined with last night made her less than innocent.

He was already up the stairs.

She followed him through the foyer and out the front door. "Nate, wait!" She caught up to him, grabbed his shirt, but he whirled around and knocked her hand away.

"Stay the *fuck* away from me! Last night, and now this . . ." He didn't finish. He didn't need to. He must have driven by last night and seen Todd's car out front.

It looked bad. It didn't even matter what had really happened, or not happened, he would never believe it. This was a betrayal to him. Just flirting with Todd had been a betrayal, but following it up by going to his house . . . that sealed it.

"*Please*, Nate." Her pleading rattled through her. She'd never felt anything so sincerely in her life. "Just listen to me a minute—"

The one word he said was both quiet and definitive and left no room for response. "*No.*"

She'd never seen him like this. Never.

"But this isn't what you think!" It wasn't! It wasn't! If he could get in her head, or in her heart, and see what she had really been thinking and feeling, he wouldn't be so mad!

Damn it, she was only there because Todd and *Theresa* were trying to hook up. Not *her*!

Nate didn't even look back at her. He got in his car and gunned it out of there so recklessly she completely expected to hear the impact with another car as soon as he was out of sight.

For a long time, Erin stood there, numb.

They'd fought before. Argued. Broken up and gotten back together. She'd never taken it seriously before, because she knew they were going to get married and whatever happened now was just them growing up.

But this? This was different.

The wind had shifted.

If only she and Theresa had taken a little longer at *any* of their stops today, they wouldn't have run into Todd at all and none of this would be happening.

If only she had ignored the phone when it rang last night.

A million things rushed through her mind, things that she should have done instead of what she did: *No, Todd, DO NOT COME OVER*, or maybe, *Todd, I love Nate and I'm not going to betray him.* Of course, no one really talked that way, the need for it was only apparent in hindsight.

What about just ignoring his flirtations at the movie entirely so he didn't even get so far as to ask for her number and have her— ugh—write it down there where anyone could have observed what was going on? Why didn't *that* possibility occur to her before it was too late?

She was a jerk, that's why. She'd traded a few minutes of flattery for Nate's heart. She'd flirted with his friend in front of everyone, tried to make him jealous so he'd pay more attention to her because . . . what? Why did she need *more* from him? He'd given her his heart. It was unbelievably selfish, she knew that already, but now it looked so much worse. She'd heaped on the disrespect over and over. On some level she must have known she was taking that chance, so on some level she must have decided that chance was worth it.

That was the thought that shamed her more than any other.

Why wouldn't he be pissed? She'd gambled his heart, his pride, everything, on a little ego from a pretty-eyed drunk.

She slowly turned back toward the house and saw Theresa and Todd had come out and were looking at her.

"Wow, I guess he's really upset about the divorce," Todd commented.

Erin looked at him like he was nuts. "*What?*"

"You know, his parents getting divorced. They told him yesterday."

He let out a breath and shook his head. "I didn't know he was so bummed."

Erin felt like she'd been punched in the stomach.

Nate's parents were getting *divorced*? On top of all of this, he'd just found out his parents were getting a divorce? No wonder he'd been so quiet last night! He'd just found out!

And instead of being there for him, Erin had, as usual, been there for herself, worried about him catering to her, trying to make him think he might lose her. . . . Her timing on that couldn't have been worse.

Now he thought . . . Oh, God.

She felt like she was going to throw up.

"He needs to know I didn't cheat on him," she said, half to herself. But he did need to know that nothing had really happened physically between her and Todd. He needed to know she hadn't slept with his best friend.

"Why would he think *that*?" Theresa asked, looking completely confused.

"Because . . . Todd . . ."

"But *I'm* here. Why would he think you're cheating on him with someone else here watching? That makes no sense!"

"It's not this, it was last night. I . . ." Erin sighed. She just couldn't explain right now. "Nothing happened."

"Do you want me to talk to him?" Todd asked her. He didn't look nearly concerned enough.

"Of course!" she snapped. "You need to tell him the truth."

"I will." He nodded and glanced down the street where Nate had driven and she wondered what he'd really say.

That couldn't be a conversation that would go comfortably.

"Take me home, Theresa," she said, suddenly nauseous. What

was she going to do? She had to call him. She had to get through to him. She could do that. He'd understand. "Please."

Theresa didn't argue. They got in the car and drove the longest ten-minute drive of Erin's life. She gave Theresa the overview, and Theresa almost had her convinced that Nate would see how small and silly this was by tonight and everything would be back to normal. Todd was drunk and stupid, he'd put Erin on the spot, she didn't want to send him out on the road drunk, she'd let him sober up and had kicked him right out of there. It wasn't a great situation, but it was no great sin either.

But something about that wasn't ringing true to Erin. When Theresa dropped her off at her house, it was beginning to snow, fat icy flakes slamming against the windshield and sliding down in wet rivulets. The cold outside now felt like it went straight to her bones, and she went inside to what she didn't fully realize at the time was a whole new life.

Chapter 14

Present

"You're m—?" I couldn't finish the word. I was still looking at his reflection in the mirror, my eyes fixed on the belt loops of the jeans he'd put back on. He looked ridiculously hot, but I couldn't turn and face him.

He kept his eyes on me. "Yes."

I guess I'd hoped there was some other explanation. When he confirmed there wasn't, the vulnerable heartache that had started in me froze into anger immediately. I slammed the ring down on the counter and turned to him, no longer conscious of my nakedness. "Fuck you," I said, well aware that I had done just that only fifteen minutes earlier. I shoulder-bumped him as I passed, glad for the dull pain in my body instead of just in my stomach.

The rest was a blur. I went to his room and shoved my clothes on.

He was *married*.

Nate was *married*.

He was someone's husband. Someone was his wife. They'd met, flirted, gotten to know each other, had first *I love you*'s, and had progressed through a relationship far enough to promise each other they'd be together forever.

So presumably he'd fallen in love with someone much, much more than he'd loved me.

It's not like the idea had never occurred to me, and I was certainly aware that he must have dated after we'd broken up—it had been a long time; it's just that I'd scarcely allowed myself to think about it. It had been bad enough to torture myself with thoughts of him making love to another girl back when I was still crying over him every night; and I'd imagined it all, his tongue in her mouth (or worse), his hands on her body, his thoughts on her instead of on me.

But he'd actually fallen in love with someone else and *married* her. Made vows. Wore her ring . . . at least sometimes.

Good God, did he have *kids* too?

"Erin—" he began.

I turned to him, ready to kill. "You have a *wife*."

And he had every right to have a wife. Despite whatever feelings of propriety I had about having been there first, despite all the childish feelings that he should always have wanted me first, no matter what time or distance separated us.

That part broke my heart.

But he should have told me he had a wife before he had sex with me.

That part made me angry.

He met my gaze. "Yes, but—"

"But what?" I challenged, perhaps hoping on some level that he'd . . . what? Tell me he was a widower? Divorced, even separated, but using the ring as a sink decoration? What could he possibly say that could make this better?

"It's complicated because—"

"Oh, *fuck* that," I snapped, well aware that I was careening toward shrill. "I realize this . . . what happened between us today . . . wasn't planned, but you *certainly* could have mentioned a *wife* before things went too far."

One side of his mouth cocked into an ironic smile. "If I had, you would have left."

Would I have? I'd like to think so, but I wasn't sure. But it didn't matter because he never even gave me a chance to make that choice. He'd lied by omission—to *me*, of all people!—and that hurt.

"I'm leaving now." I turned on my heel and hurried down the stairs. "Have a good life." This was humiliating. I was so stupid. Why did I just *assume* everything was just like we'd left it? There was no such thing as time travel, yet here I'd been, making out with my old boyfriend as if the passing years hadn't meant a thing.

Now, like a fool, I felt like I'd lost him *again*. How much could one person take?

I was a living, breathing cautionary tale.

He came down behind me, seeming to be right on my back even though he seemed to move with the ease of a lazy cat.

I threw the door open, my mind still racing with questions I'd never get the answers to now.

Or so I thought.

Because as soon as I stepped out into the twilight, a car pulled up. A neighbor? His mother?

But, no, it was worse. Far worse.

It was his wife.

The pieces came together for me with swift, horrible certainty as I realized who that was.

His wife.

Theresa.

———

When we were in high school, Theresa was always the one who was boy-crazy. She'd be with one guy one day, then another guy the next, and sometimes a third guy on the third day. Literally.

Not that she was a slut, really—she was always looking for love. The problem was, she was always thinking she'd found it, no matter how unlikely a package it was in or how obvious it was to the rest of us that she had picked another loser.

Nate used to be right on board with Jordan and me when it came to Theresa. He was kind to her, and about her, but he certainly never harbored any secret lust for her. I mean, he might have—one might even argue that he *must* have—but I hadn't seen it. And I was really sure I knew him inside out.

Evidently, something had changed.

But when I saw her out front of his parents' house, in that one brief moment between recognizing her and having to *say* something to her, time stood still and a million thoughts raced through my mind.

The ring. *N & T.*

They'd gotten married. They'd had rings engraved.

They must have fallen in love.

In love enough to get *married*. Grown-up love, not the youthful kind that ends in tears on the front stoop and calls that are never returned.

Had they always had a spark between them that somehow I'd just missed?

Two people I'd once imagined I'd know and love for the rest of my life had floated out of my awareness and into each other's. Was that not as shocking and devastating as it felt?

Maybe I had no right to be pissed or proprietary about that. But I was anyway.

How astonishing that on this day, which had started out weird and then had a delirious moment of completion, had now come to this.

"Oh, my God!" Theresa gasped. "*Erin?* Oh, my God, is that really *you?*"

"Yes," was all I could say. There were so many ways she might have meant it.

Of course, I had information she didn't.

She threw herself into my arms. She was skinnier than she'd been in high school. She felt bony against me. "I can't believe it! I just saw your mother at the grocery store and she said you were over at her place! I *actually thought* about going by!"

"Really."

"I swear it!" She beamed and looked at Nate. "Can you believe this?" She raked her hand through her short dark hair. It looked cute on her, I hated to admit. Sort of pixieish with her super-slim frame.

"No," he said evenly. His gaze was impassive, like he was looking at his neighbor or something instead of his wife. "What are you doing here?"

"Well, I had to take those old clothes over to the church for the women's shelter and I felt sorry for you, doing all this work on someone else's house, so I decided to stop at the Giant and get you some fried chicken. I hope you haven't been working on an empty stomach."

I felt like I could empty mine. "Theresa," I said, "it is so good to see you, but I just came out for a run and really should get back to pick up my daughter at my mom's house. She has a . . . thing tonight. A"—I thought quickly—"birthday party to go to."

"Oh." She looked disappointed. "Did you and Nate get to catch up, at least?"

I felt the blood race into my face and she *had* to have seen it. "A little bit. It was such a surprise to run into him, though, that we only had a minute. He was just telling me you two were blissfully married when you drove up."

She went over to him and slipped her hand around his waist.

It was a small gesture that would have gone unnoticed if her husband were anyone else, but we all knew she was doing it to mark her territory as surely as if she'd peed on him.

And there was a small part of me, there really was, that wanted to turn and run away from a scene that—as small as it was—felt like it might be more than I could bear. Because *that* gesture with *that* guy used to be *mine*. And she knew it, she'd known it then, she'd been around when it was NateandErin and none of us ever would have dreamed that someday *she* would be the one putting her arm around him and *I* would be the one who had no right to even think about it, much less feel jealous that she was doing it.

He was her *husband*.

Nate was Theresa's husband.

Theresa's.

It just didn't compute.

"This is so strange, isn't it?" she said to Nate. "We just saw Todd two weeks ago." She looked at me. "He lives in Sacramento now, has the *cutest* twin daughters, just two years old." She smiled, remembering, then added, "And here's *Erin*. It's like no time has passed at all!"

And there it was; the reason everything had gone so badly, the reason everything had blown up in my face, the reason Nate had not spoken to me for years, the reason my teenage years had ended up as shadowy memories of dark depression and anxiety, the reason—however indirectly it might be—that Nate was now married to Theresa and not me: Todd.

Todd, who'd gotten drunk, made a pass at me, been uneventfully rebuffed, but then had fucked up in getting the hell out of my space, and, in so doing, had *kind of* ruined my life.

Now Todd was happily oblivious to all of that, no doubt, living in Sacramento with his lovely twins and no doubt lovely wife, being visited by his pals, Theresa and Nate . . .

Todd hadn't paid one penny's debt for the mess he'd created, because Nate hadn't seen him as the bad guy. *I* was the only bad guy.

I owed the price. And I'd paid it. I'd paid it right into an emotional debt that had lasted for years.

"How *is* Todd?" I asked grimly.

"He's Todd," Nate said. "Same as ever."

I raised an eyebrow. "Do you see him often?"

"Last time was our wedding," Theresa said. She looked at Nate and tightened her arm around him. "So that was, what, a year and a half ago?"

"Huh." I wanted to go. I really wanted to get out of there. But I couldn't help but ask, "How long did you date?"

He shifted his weight and moved out of her grasp, his eyes fastened on me.

I moved my gaze from her to him and back again, waiting for her answer.

"Two years?" She wrinkled her nose and looked skyward. "I think it was like two years and two months. And maybe a week."

Oh, Jesus, leave it to Theresa to know the exact count. "That is really interesting. How did that . . ."—I looked to him again—"how did that come about?"

It was crazy the way this gave me the feeling I'd just missed as far as seeing him again. If it had only happened sooner, maybe he wouldn't be married to Theresa now. Maybe everything would be different.

He looked miserable. For the first time I noticed that his eyes, which had always been large and kind of sad-looking, were lined in a way that made it look like he'd had a lot of stress in his life. Of course, there were smile lines—he'd always been quick to laugh if something was funny—but the feeling I got from looking at him was that he wasn't happy.

And I wasn't happy about that, even while it was painful to imagine that he *was* happily married to my friend.

"We ran into each other at church," Theresa said.

Church.

I had to have misheard.

"You were in church?" I asked Theresa; then, to Nate, "*You* were in church?" I'd seen him in church exactly once, and it was for a friend's funeral. Apart from that, any talk of God or church had been pretty much limited to him teasing me for wearing a cross since I only did it because it was a cool-looking one, not because I was making a statement.

"My grandfather died," he said, going to examine the molding by the door. "The funeral was there. I was getting the flowers to take to my grandmother."

"Oh! Oh, wow, I'm sorry." I *was* sorry. But, of course, it had been many years and Nate's grandfather wasn't exactly young when I'd known him. He would have been well into his nineties now, which wasn't impossible, but still . . . I thought of the man as he'd been the last time I'd seen him, hearty and hale, at his farmhouse, telling ghost stories and cooking steaks on the grill over peach bark.

And I felt the loss.

"I was there helping with a charity thing they had going on," Theresa said, and smiled, glancing back at him, presumably to see if he was yet again within grabbing reach.

I couldn't just stand here and mourn the loss that was now years past for them. I focused my attention on Theresa as much as I could. "How nice of you!"

She shrugged. "I work for the National Coalition for Women's Rights, so we're involved in a lot of local charities."

Great. So she was adorable, and thin, and even nicer than ever, *and* she'd been there to help Nate through what I knew had been a tremendous loss for him.

"Good for you," I said, too heartily. "That's . . . wow, that's"—*maybe the only way possible to make me feel even worse about what just happened*—"just great." I had to get out of this twilight zone.

If I stuck around any longer, who knew what would come up next? Had she administered CPR to save his mother at some point? Cured some rare disease? Would two children toddle out and be introduced as their offspring, little Theresa and little Nate?

"I've really got to go," I said, my voice thick with emotion that I hoped they couldn't hear. "But I'm . . ."—I swallowed—"I'm really happy for you two." With any luck, I'd be able to act normal until I was out of their sight.

"Let me give you a ride," Theresa said, coming toward me jingling her keys. Suddenly she seemed like the least intuitive person I'd ever met. Or, wait, maybe the most. "I'd love to meet your daughter! Of course, I did meet her when she was born, but, my God, it's been how many years?"

"Probably fifteen since you saw her."

"Wow! Let me take you, then." She made a move.

"Oh! No. No, no." I shook my head. Kind of frantically. "No. Really. I need the exercise." I patted my stomach, which probably still had remnants of Nate's sweat on it. "I ate a ton earlier when we cooked out. Hamburgers. Hot dogs. You know my mom, always over . . . cooking." I was babbling.

Nate's eyes were on me.

Instinctively, out of a habit that should have been long dead, I turned to him for help.

He totally got it.

"I'll give her a ride," he said, neatly clipping the keys out of Theresa's hand as he walked past her. He took me by the elbow, his grip firmer than it looked from the outside. "I've got to go pick something up at Home Depot anyway."

"But—" Theresa sighed. "Wait! How about dinner next Sunday?"

We both turned back to her and asked, "What?" at the same time. And in the same disbelieving tone.

"All of us. Erin, your mom told me you're engaged."

I felt Nate turn and look at me.

"Bring him along and the four of us can have a nice dinner, maybe some wine, and get reacquainted. Or acquainted, in the case of . . . what's his name? Rick?"

Good God, she even knew his name? How long had my mother and Theresa talked?

Long enough to make this reunion as awkward as possible, apparently.

"Actually, I have an event on Sunday," I said.

At the same time, Nate said, "I'm already committed for Sunday."

"Where are you going Sunday?" she asked him, then said, "Never mind. Monday." Before I could come up with an excuse there, she said, "Or Saturday. Take your pick. We're free anytime." She narrowed her eyes at him, but it was more playful than anything else. They had private jokes. A private rapport. "Except Sunday, evidently."

"I'll let you know," I said vaguely. "Thanks!"

"Come on," he said under his breath, and bustled me to the car. Obviously I could have wrested my arm away and left, but that would raise questions neither of us wanted to answer.

So I was going to have to get in the car with him, drive down the street, and kill him when he stopped at the corner.

"I'll call you!" Theresa said. "Your mom gave me your number and e-mail address." She laughed and it made her look nineteen again. "I just can't get over what a coincidence this is!"

"Neither can I," I tossed over my shoulder, then looked at Nate and added, "Seriously."

God works in mysterious ways, all right.

I got in the midsized Honda sedan—probably registered in both their names—and looked straight ahead as Nate got in.

"It's better than her driving you," he said, clearly knowing I was pissed at being put in this position.

"Not really. At least I don't have *her* all over me. And in me." I couldn't help it. Tears started to fill my eyes. I swiped them away roughly. I couldn't even remember the last time I'd cried.

He was silent for a moment before speaking again.

"So you're engaged, huh? You didn't mention that."

I turned to him in disbelief. "One, I'm not, and two, you're fucking *married*. To *my* old friend! Which you failed to mention." I could have screamed. "That is *so* messed up."

"What is, that I'm married to her or that I didn't tell you?"

"Both!" I couldn't believe it. "Do you have kids?"

"No, of course not."

"There's no *of course* here anymore." It was everything I could do not to cry. "How could you have *married* her? You wouldn't even know her if it weren't for me!" The more I thought about it—and I was sure I was going to think about it plenty in the coming days—it *really* made me mad. "I mean, she was one of my *best friends*. She was there for me when I sobbed myself half to death every night after you blew Dodge with barely a word. What the hell is with you two hooking up? What's *wrong* with you?"

He shifted a glance in my direction. "I know, it sucks when you think someone who meant a lot to you hooks up with a friend."

"Oh. My. God." I could have strangled him. "How many times do I have to tell you *nothing happened*?"

"I know."

I wasn't expecting that. "You know? You know what?"

"I know nothing happened that night."

"Really." This was news to me. It took some of the wind out of my sails. "How long have you known that?"

He shrugged. "Todd told me the whole truth a couple of months after it happened."

Somehow that felt like a blow. As long as I'd felt Nate believed I'd truly wronged him, the wrongs he'd done me made some sense. I could justify the pain somewhat, understand his sudden and strong determination to stay away, because I knew he thought I'd really betrayed him. He thought I'd become someone unrecognizable and that made *him* someone unrecognizable.

But now to find out that he'd known—*known*—virtually the whole time that he'd hanged me for nothing . . . it was a shock.

"If you knew nothing happened," I said, the tension making my voice so tight I didn't even sound like myself to my own ears, "*why* did you let me suffer for it for so long?"

"Suffer for so long?" he repeated, as if the concept were foreign to him. "You moved on, dated other people. Maybe technically nothing happened with Todd, but the intention was there, you wanted something else, something other than me, and you got it."

This was so completely, insanely opposite of the truth that I didn't even know how to answer.

I just gaped at him.

"Look, you went out with other people several times while we were going out . . ."

"*Once.*"

". . . and I think it was pretty clear that you wanted to explore other options. You weren't totally innocent that night with Todd, you invited his attention."

It was true, I couldn't deny it. "I wanted *your* attention."

"Yeah, well, you got both. So even if you didn't really do anything physical, you told me a lot about where I stood in line."

"It had nothing to do with my regard for you, I was a stupid young girl, trying to make you jealous. I didn't *date* Todd. I didn't *fuck* him. I didn't *marry* him. You abandoned me and let me think, for *years* now, that it was because you believed I'd done something with your best friend. Then"—I gave a short laugh—"you ended up doing that very thing with Theresa!"

"It's not the same." He shifted his grip on the wheel.

Absurdly, the gesture made my heart ping. I remembered those hands so well. Long, dexterous fingers but bad knuckles from fighting when he was younger.

"It is *exactly* the same," I said, forcing myself to look away. "It's not different *at all*. Except that I was the wounded one, not you."

We were about halfway to my mother's house, directly in front of the high school. He jerked the car into the parking lot, stopped abruptly, and rammed it into park. "*You* were the wounded one?" he repeated, looking at me with dark eyes. "Only you?"

"Yes!"

"Bullshit." He said it like a slap.

The tears were rolling down my cheeks now. I didn't even care. "It is *not* bullshit. Nothing happened between Todd and me, and now I find out that *you knew it*. The way you did that, the way you left and wouldn't talk to me, nearly killed me. I swear to you that's not an exaggeration, it nearly *killed* me." And it *wasn't* an exaggeration, unfortunately. "And two months later, you were just fine and dandy with him again, but you never so much as talked to me again!"

"I couldn't."

"You *wouldn't.*"

He gave a small shrug. "Maybe it was a mistake."

A *mistake*. Such a tiny dismissal of such a colossal devastation. "You asshole." I sniffed.

A muscle twitched in his jaw and he looked away. "It was no harder for you than it was for me."

"Oh, clearly," I said, and my voice caught. "I mean, look at us. We're obviously on exactly the same wavelength here." I took a wavering breath. I had absolutely no control over my crying. None.

I *hate* that feeling.

He sighed, but still didn't look at me.

"It was pretty devastating to me too," he said quietly.

"Then why did you do it?" I implored. "You had all the choices. I had *none*. Okay, maybe you needed to 'punish' me for flirting or being manipulative, maybe you needed some time away from me, maybe we both needed to grow up a little on our own, but there were a million points over the years when you could have released that stranglehold you had on your anger a little bit so we could have at least talked. We might have worked things out."

"There were a lot of feelings, Erin. A lot of pain. At the time, I didn't think I'd ever get over it."

I took another ragged breath. "Tell me about it. It's a wonder you could even look at one of my friends afterwards without being reminded of me. It must have been torture."

"I couldn't," he said, ignoring my sarcasm. "I can't."

I looked at him sharply. "What?"

He shook his head. "Forget it. The point is, we were too young to have all those big feelings. It was bound to blow."

"I disagree. Completely."

"Think about it."

"*Think* about it? I've had plenty of time to think about it. Things didn't have to end the way they did. I'm not saying they didn't have to end, though I'm not sure they did, but it didn't have to go down the way it did. You were cruel. You have no idea how much damage you caused."

"You seem all right to me." He looked at me. "It wasn't that much longer that you were pregnant, had a baby, moved on. Now you're engaged. What's to complain about?"

"I'm not engaged," I said again. "And if I'd ever thought you might come back, I would have waited alone like a widow on a rooftop widow's walk for you, no matter how long it took." God, that was pathetic. What was even more pathetic was that it was true. If I'd known for a fact that he was coming back, even if it was twenty years in the future, I would have waited for him, chaste and cobwebbed.

"And if I'd had any idea you felt like that," he said slowly, "I would have gone to the ends of the earth to get you."

It took a second for that to register.

"But I *told* you!" I said, but . . . had I? At first, certainly, but things said in the heat of a breakup can't be taken to the bank.

He saw that cross my face. It was like he watched my entire thought process scroll across my forehead like the ticker outside *The Today Show* in Rockefeller Center. He studied me, then met my eye, and cocked his head, and I knew he knew exactly what I'd thought.

And he was right.

"I came back," he said, and I remembered it as if it were yesterday. My baby shower. Nate got back into town and called my mother's house looking for my number while I happened to be there. It was a casual conversation that had felt weighty at the time and had proven to set things in motion that I'd never anticipated. "Too late, but I came back. You were pregnant." He shook his head. "You got me again."

"It was . . ." It was wrong to say it was an accident. That reduced Camilla to a regret, and she wasn't. "Why *did* you call me that day?"

"When you told me you were pregnant?"

I nodded.

"Because I was finished with school, finished seeing the world, so to speak"—he hesitated—"and I guess you were just the one thing I couldn't forget. Especially once I came back into town. Everywhere I looked there was something that reminded me of you."

Another tiny crack in my heart. "Why didn't you tell me that at the time?"

"It was too late."

"I wasn't married."

He gave a short spike of a laugh. "You were clearly *involved*."

What could I say? Anything I said would be disrespectful to the child who had come out of that situation, no matter how unexpected and unfortunate the situation had seemed at the time.

"I didn't know how long this would matter," he added. "I believed what everyone said about young love, and how you get over it quickly because it's not the real thing. At the time *I didn't know* it would matter forever. I just . . ." He shook his head. "I didn't know."

"I need to go to my daughter," I said, looking out the windshield at the football field. There were some teenagers out there running the track. They'd probably heard everything we'd yelled at each other.

"I'm sorry," he said to me.

I'd had no idea how much I'd wanted to hear those words, or, rather, how much it would mean to me if he said them. The tears started anew, accompanied by hyperventilating sobs.

I felt his hand touch my cheek, and I let it stay.

It had been too long, and I was too tired from the years of keeping my feelings for him pushed down, to be self-conscious now. All the pain and angst bubbled to the surface and I had no chance of keeping them in any longer.

He could have opened the door and pushed me out of the car with his foot and I wouldn't have felt any more pain than I did right now.

But he didn't do that. He just held his hand against my cheek for another moment.

Then he let go and looked forward, his breath resigned. "About what just happened between us . . ."

"Don't." I held up a hand. "I realize we should probably talk about it, but I can't. I just—I have to calm down and go home."

And—I could feel it—he watched me with those big sad eyes until I'd collected myself enough to go home and be a grown-up for my daughter.

Chapter 15

May 1987

Erin couldn't sleep.

She'd had another dream about Nate and had woken up feeling like he was right there. As usual, it had taken a moment for her sleep-fogged brain to remember the facts, and for her heart to sink all over again.

He was gone. He never wanted to talk to her again. How could she have forgotten that, even for a split second?

Tears threatened—they were always quick to threaten these days—and she turned on the light and went to the bathroom to splash her face with icy water. She was sick of tears. Her eyes burned all the time now from crying so much.

It was raining outside. A car shushed through the wet street, leaving a hollow silence behind.

He'd come to his senses if she waited, she *knew* he would. She just had to be patient somehow. She wasn't all that good at it, but she had to try. Things would be okay, because she loved him and he loved her and people who loved each other that much *had* to be together.

Didn't they?

As soon as he stopped being so mad, he'd give her the chance to explain and he'd see it had all been a big misunderstanding. He'd probably feel awful for punishing her like this for something she hadn't done, but she'd forgive him because it *had* looked bad. And, of course, there had been a certain level of disloyalty on her part in opening the door—literally and figuratively—to that interpretation.

So she didn't blame him, really. But enough was enough. It had been months now and Nate wouldn't talk to her at all. It was the longest she'd gone without talking to him in two years and it felt really weird. Fifty times a day something little would happen and she'd want to tell him, but then she'd remember—again and again— that she couldn't. If she called, he'd hang up. If she went to his house, he wouldn't answer the door. If she went to his work, she'd embarrass the hell out of both of them.

She knew because she'd tried all of the above.

Repeatedly.

And, like gazillions of teenage girls before her throughout the ages, she'd written terrible poems, she'd plagiarized terrible poems, she'd made mix tapes, and she'd rewritten song lyrics that almost perfectly expressed how she felt. Worse, she'd offered up some of them to Nate as a means of expression for the things she couldn't say, or he wouldn't listen to.

She was pretty sure he threw them out.

The tears threatened again, but this time she couldn't stop them. She missed him so much she ached. Her arms ached, as if she'd been holding something heavy and dropped it.

Her heart ached.

The tears started anew.

There was a knock on her door and it opened a crack.

"Erin?" Her mother came into view, squinting into the light. "What's wrong?"

Erin turned her head and squeezed her eyes to make the tears stop. "Nothing, I'm fine," she said in a voice that indicated otherwise. How could she admit she was still such a mess? Maybe no one expected her to be completely *over* it now, but they probably thought it was weird that she was still crying over it almost all the time. She wished she could be angry instead. Part of her was.

But most of her felt guilty and was trying desperately to scramble back in time to undo the single stupidest thing she'd ever done in her life.

Time travel was out of the question, though.

Things were hopeless.

She felt the bed dip as her mother sat on the end. "No, you're not fine. Why are you so upset?"

"It's nothing. I was just . . . thinking . . . about something sad. . . ." She shrugged haplessly and sniffed.

A little flint of impatience came into her mother's eyes. "Did you talk to Nate?"

Erin shook her head. "He won't," she squeaked.

"I don't know why you won't just let go," her mother said. "You should have been over this already."

"I don't *want* to stop loving him." Something like panic rose in Erin. How could her own mother not understand even a *little* of what she was going through? "I just need to make him understand."

Her mother shook her head. "Forget about Nate. You need to get out, meet other boys. Date. The best way to get over someone is to go out with someone else."

That's what everyone kept saying. Erin wanted to ask her if

she'd just "go out with someone else" if her dad left, but decided against it, since it wasn't really comparable and it missed the point. "I don't want to," she said sullenly. Because *that* was the point.

She didn't want anyone but Nate. She never really had.

"Erin. You need to stop this." Her mother laid a cold hand on her shin. "In fact, your father and I have been wondering if maybe you should see someone. A professional."

So they thought she was crazy? Because she had a broken heart?

Erin had never felt so utterly alone in her life.

"There's a doctor at the Chestnut Lodge who specializes in teens—"

"The Chestnut Lodge!" Horror filled her. She couldn't believe what she was hearing. "You think I need to be *committed*?"

"Calm down. They have an outpatient program there too. You could just go for an hour a couple of times a week and break this cycle you're in."

It was clear that her mother would never understand.

So Erin decided her best course was to play along, to make her mother feel better in order to get her off Erin's back.

"I don't think that's necessary," she said, with a sniff and an attempt at a smile. It felt more like she was baring her teeth. "But you're probably right, I should just get out more, distract myself. Find some other guy." The words made her feel sick.

"That's right. Someday, when you're older, the right man will come along and you'll know it."

What if the right guy has already come along? she wondered silently. *What if fate screwed up and introduced us too young and I was stupid and he was stupid and now it's over and we'll never find that kind of love again?*

She tried to picture some anonymous man in her future, someone she would somehow adore and who would erase all memories of who came before him, but all she could come up with were suit-clad Ken doll look-alikes she could never, ever love as much as she loved Nate.

"And none of this will matter one whit then," her mother went on. "It already doesn't, you just don't know it."

Every word she said made Erin's pain worse.

She had to get out before Erin screamed.

"I'm sure you're right," Erin lied, snugging herself under the covers, implying that she was ready to go back to sleep.

Outside, the rain came down harder.

She wanted desperately to be alone. Her throat was tight and she could feel a sob working its way up her chest, like a knotted fist.

"Good. That's my girl." She patted with her cold hand. "Now get some sleep."

Erin gritted her teeth and squeezed her eyes tightly shut. "Thanks, Mom."

"No problem. Anytime you want to talk, I'm here." She turned out the light and made her way out of the room and down the hall, the floorboards creaking as she went.

There was no way in the world Erin was ever going to seek out her mother's advice again. She didn't understand at all.

No one did.

No one except maybe Nate.

He was the only one who could possibly know what she was going through. She was sure he did, somewhere deep down, he had to be feeling it too.

She had to get through to him. If he knew the truth—if he could just listen to her for ten minutes and actually *hear* what she had to say—he'd understand. Because he always understood. He was the one person in her life who had always understood her. He was the one person in her life who had always been there for her.

She could make him understand again.

Then everything would be all right.

Finally.

———

The phone rang three and a half times before he picked up.

"Don't hang up," Erin said quickly. "I just want to—"

He hung up.

Her stomach hurt.

She looked at the phone. The same yellow Princess phone she'd been whispering into while talking with him long into the night for two years now, scuffed from falling off the shelves a million times, splotched with specks of paint from when she changed her walls from white to pale rose. The plastic had held a million secrets, the wires transmitted a million laughs and tears.

Now it was just a cold, hard piece of equipment that had gone from representing something good to representing something bad.

She was sick of feeling this way.

She was sick of missing him. Sick of the wound that wouldn't seem to heal, no matter what she did.

She contemplated the phone. Calling back would be groveling. Humiliating. But she'd crossed the Groveling/Humiliating line a long, long time ago now. This was Desperation Territory, and Desperation Territory didn't ask for a passport proving intelligence, dignity, self-respect, or any other sort of personal virtue.

Desperation just needed intention.

And she intended to get through to him, even if it killed her.

At this point, it was really and truly feeling like it might.

She lifted the phone receiver, hesitated, punched in the digits again, then cringed to herself as the phone started to ring. He'd know it was her. Even if she hung up right now, he'd know it had been her and not, say, a wrong number or some absentminded friend of his mom's. She'd committed by dialing, now she had to see it through.

It was the rationalization she'd used almost every day since they'd split up.

Once upon a time, Nate had eagerly waited for her calls, answered on the half ring, called her himself, talked until they both fell asleep while the sun was coming up outside the window. Now it had come to this.

She was a fool. And absolutely everyone knew it.

She called again. It rang about thirty times. Finally he picked up. "What do you want?"

"You have to listen to me," she said, wishing she'd come up with the perfect thing to say in ten words or less. But that wasn't possible. There was no perfect thing to say, much less one that happened in ten words or less. She'd screwed up, but not to the degree he thought, and she had to make him believe her. "It wasn't what you thought."

"I don't care."

Yes, he did. That's what all of this was about! He hadn't just turned on her after two years because he *didn't care* anymore . . . had he? If he had, that wouldn't bring on this kind of hostility, would it?

Six weeks of this. She'd gone through six weeks of this already. Two months ago, this was a guy she was sure was going to love her forever. Two months ago, she'd been sure they were going to get married someday. Two months ago, they'd had a routine; she'd been flirty and charming and he'd been older and responsible and together they'd been in love, strong, solid. Everyone thought so.

How long was he going to punish her?

She'd learned her lesson. God *knows* she'd learned her lesson. She never should have taken him for granted.

Erin tightened her grip on the phone and swallowed back the impulse to puke. "Nate, I love you."

There was a hesitation. She knew he wanted to hang up, but, for that split second, he couldn't. He wanted to hear it. He *wanted* her to love him. He *wanted* everything to be all right. She knew it.

Then he said, "I don't care."

He might as well have shot her in the stomach. It would have hurt less than this.

She started to cry. She had no control over it. "Nothing happened," she said, but it came out weak. Like it didn't matter. Maybe it even sounded like it wasn't true. "It was just . . . stupid. But *nothing happened.* I'm *so sorry.*" If there was a word bigger than *sorry*, she wished she knew it. If there was an appropriate penance to pay, to prove her regret, her devotion, she would happily have performed it. Cut off a finger? She'd still have nine left. Shave her head? There were wigs. Stab herself in the heart? People had quintuple bypass surgery; the chances had to be at least fair that she'd survive. Maybe it would be touch and go for a while, but if anything, that might make him realize what he stood to lose, so maybe it would be worth it. . . .

"It. Doesn't. Matter." He was obviously speaking through gritted teeth. She had no reading, no sense, of what might be behind it, other than complete anger. But it seemed disproportionate.

She didn't understand.

"Why are you this mad?" she asked, pushing the words out hard with a voice that had no strength left. "Why won't you even *listen?* I don't get this at all. You've misunderstood *everything.* Don't you even *want* to feel better?"

Apparently not. "I told you," he said, his voice so hard it felt like blows. "We just weren't working. It's over."

Two months ago he'd cupped her face in his hand and pressed his body into hers and told her he'd always love her.

Just weren't working? It didn't make sense.

It wasn't true.

"I'm hanging up now," he said. "Don't call back."

"But—"

He was gone.

No point in calling back. It wasn't like if she did he'd finally say, *You know, it's good you called again, because I realize now that I've made a huge mistake. . . .*

She cried until she was empty, and fell asleep for the rest of the afternoon, curled up tight on the bed where he'd first told her he wanted to stay with her forever.

⌒

Though Erin had done her time as a drama queen, and Nate had certainly witnessed it time and again when they were together, she didn't like being depressed. Girlish tears over some semi-imagined slight were one thing, but the heavy dark cloak of relentless sadness she was beginning to carry everywhere was another.

It was starting to feel dangerous.

So when Theresa called that night, Erin forced herself to rise to the occasion.

"Ronnie has a friend," Theresa said, "who is apparently so gorgeous that some girl walked up to him in a bar the other day and handed him her phone number."

Erin doubted it. "Who does that?"

"I know. So the guy must be hot, right? Anyway, you're going out with him tonight."

Erin's first reaction was to say no. She didn't want to get dressed up. She was too tired to go anywhere. And she certainly wasn't interested in meeting any *new guy*, no matter how cute he was.

But this was getting ridiculous. She *had* to get out and shake off this depression. Maybe if the guy was really that great, she *would* start to forget Nate. It wasn't like Nate was being so gallant right now. He didn't really deserve all of the regard she was giving him.

Maybe he never had.

The idea took root uneasily in her mind. Could she have been wrong about him all this time? Had she invented him, in some way, to accommodate her ideas of what she wanted him to be?

Maybe he'd never really loved her.

In fact, maybe he'd just used her until something more interesting came along. Had he? She hadn't even thought about this before, but was it possible that he'd found someone else and that all of this supposed hurt-and-betrayal business was just a way to scrape her off so he could be with another girl instead?

Could she have been *that* wrong about him?

A couple of weeks before they broke up, he'd dropped her off at home and indicated he was going to his house, but he'd gone to his friend's sister's party instead. Erin had been kind of pissed, but she hadn't really made much of it. Maybe she should have. Except that she'd been really sure he'd just gone because his friends wanted to go. She'd trusted him enough to feel like there was nothing more to it.

Then there was the night David and Kenny had called her house, asking where Nate was, saying they needed a ride home from the gym, but then David's mother had picked up the phone and asked who was on the line. So they were obviously calling from his house, not the gym, but *why*? It was just . . . weird. But now she wondered if it meant something she should have read into, or if it was just Nate's stupid friends being their usual stupid selves.

She'd just chalked it up to everyone being a little immature and bored.

At this point she didn't know anything for sure anymore.

She returned her attention to the conversation with Theresa. Fuck Nate. She wasn't going to mourn him forever. She wasn't going to lose herself in this grief, no matter how awful he acted toward her. Enough was enough.

"What are we doing?" she asked.

"I don't know. Probably just go downtown or something. They're picking us up here at seven. Get over here and we'll get ready together. It'll be fun!"

Erin looked at the clock. It was five thirty now.

Something inside of her pushed her onward. It was well past time to move on. People broke up all the time. Maybe Nate had ended things badly, but that didn't need to be her burden forever. She wasn't willing to take that on. He was her first love. Big deal. Everyone had one, but most people didn't marry theirs. If she and Nate hadn't broken up now, and in this way, they would probably have done it at some other point in a different way. The end result was the same.

She needed to stop feeling like someone had died.

"That sounds great," she said, with forced enthusiasm. If she repeated it enough, she'd start to believe it. "I'll be right over."

She took her time driving through the winding Glen Road to Theresa's house, rolling down the windows and breathing in the first green scents of early spring. It was a beautiful evening. A tiny bit of optimism bloomed in the back of her mind. If she concentrated on one hour at a time, she could get through this, and this hour was fine.

It was only overwhelming if she thought about everything that had happened and imagined the rest of her life without Nate. But if she removed Nate from the whole equation and just thought about *now*, she'd be okay.

Hearts broke all the time. There were a million songs about it. And a million more about hearts being mended. She'd get through this. It was just going to take a little bit of time. And a super-hot guy wasn't going to hurt matters any.

In five years, she might not even remember Nate very well.

At this point, she hoped she wouldn't.

He *was* good-looking. His name was Brendan and, although she would never have done such a thing herself, Erin could see why someone had been moved to take a chance on giving him her phone number. Dark blond hair, light blue eyes, the kind of tawny skin that looked tan year-round. He could have been in a Coppertone ad or a beer commercial.

On top of that, he was charming—nice voice, intelligent, funny. He drove a Jeep, a nice manly vehicle. They parked in a parking lot off Wisconsin Avenue and as they walked over to Windsor McKay's, Erin couldn't help but notice that people were noticing him. He turned heads.

Better still, he seemed completely unaware of it.

It was a testament to how fucked up Erin really was that she wasn't into him. At all.

"What is *wrong* with you?" Theresa asked when they went into the bathroom together about an hour and two pitchers of beer into the date. "He's *gorgeous* and you act like you're sitting across from the Elephant Man."

Erin suspected her friends were tired of hearing about what was wrong with her, so she lied. "My head is killing me," she said, adding a wince that was slightly too small and slightly too late to be convincing. "It must be the beer." She'd had three of them so far and they'd done nothing to numb her angst.

"This is about Nate, isn't it?"

"No."

Theresa wasn't buying that. It would have been surprising if she had. "Yes, it is, you walk around looking like you're going to cry all the time. Snap out of it!"

"I *can't* just snap out of it! Don't you think I would if I could? Do you think I *want* to feel this way all the time? I hate it! I hate him! I hate me!" Tears burned, but she swiped impatiently at her eyes. She was *not* going to cry again. She was *not* going to drown in this. She couldn't let herself.

"Don't say that." Theresa pulled her into a hug, and Erin closed her eyes tightly against her friend's hair. It smelled like Flex shampoo and cigarette smoke from the bar. "Look." She pulled back. "You've got to understand that he has moved on. JP saw him and Todd out together the other night."

"He did?" It felt like a knife to her heart. Todd—the one who had committed the biggest betrayal—was right back in with Nate, yet Nate wouldn't even give her the time of day. It was devastating.

"Yes," Theresa went on. "Todd's back for the week. They acted like everything was normal, like nothing had ever happened between them, so he's obviously blaming you for everything, and *that's not fair.*"

"It's not!" Erin felt so sorry for herself in that moment. Pure, unadulterated self-pity. "I don't think I can survive this."

She cried.

Then Theresa cried.

Finally Theresa gave her a squeeze and said, "Maybe you just need more time. Just take it one tiny step at a time if that's all you can do."

"I need a lobotomy." It was one of many thoughts that had actually occurred to her as a viable solution to her problem. "I'm not giving him more time. Nate is an asshole. He knows what this is doing to me and he doesn't care. There's *no* excuse for that!"

"I agree. If he loved you, he wouldn't put you through this."

Wow, that hurt. The truth hurt. Especially coming from someone else. When Erin had had the same thought, she'd been able to dismiss it and replace it with a more comfortable thought, but when Theresa said it, there was no way to ignore it.

If he loved her, he wouldn't let her hurt this badly.

Because this was *bad*.

This was *way* beyond normal teenage blues.

Theresa put her hands on Erin's shoulders, looked into her eyes, and said, "Now you need to get out there and get into that guy, because he can't take his eyes off you."

"Who, *Brendan*?" She hadn't noticed that.

Theresa nodded and made a face that clearly indicated Erin was a blind idiot. "He's so into you. Don't ask me why." She laughed. "I guess he likes that distant, I'm-not-interested thing you've got going on. Whatever it is, you should take advantage of it. The best way to get over someone is to hook up with someone else."

It certainly seemed true for Theresa. She never seemed to spend too long mourning over a guy. And there was always—always—a new one waiting in the wings. Nate used to say Theresa was Teflon—she didn't let anyone stick around for long.

Erin wanted to be more like that.

She looked at herself in the mirror. She looked fine. None of the crap that was going on inside her head was visible on the outside. It was stupid to be moping around, weeping over a guy who obviously wasn't giving her a second thought.

"You're right," she said to Theresa, fresh resolution pushing her voice. She was going to go with this. She was going to go all the way with this. "I just need another beer."

"Sure it's not going to make that headache worse?" Theresa asked with a smirk.

Erin smirked right back. "It might just make the headache a lot better."

Four beers and two tequila shots later—bartenders in those days didn't card in D.C. unless you looked like a third-grader—Erin was in the seat next to Brendan, and he was telling her how beautiful she was.

She still wasn't into him.

But she pretended she was.

And when he came in for the kiss, she pretended she was into it. Fuck Nate.

In fact, what better way to screw Nate than to screw Brendan? And anyone else who appealed to her from now on, if she wanted to. Maybe she'd seek out Scott Koogan, whom Nate had once been jealous of, warning her that he was "bad news." She'd date everyone he'd been jealous of, why not? She'd already decided she would never fall in love again, so what did she need to hold out for?

A girl's first mattered. Losing her virginity was significant. But the second? The third? As long as she was careful not to get a disease or get pregnant, the rest didn't matter. They had no more significance than the second and third teams knocked out of the NFC East playoffs.

Her Super Bowl was already over.

She'd lost.

She leaned in to Brendan and put her mind elsewhere and pretended he was someone else, from the first kiss to his final release. She felt nothing but pretended to be as into it as he was.

It was a trick she would employ for a long time to come.

Chapter 16

Present

It's been my experience that the best cure for anguish or emotional duress is housework.

Go ahead and make June Cleaver jokes about me. I'll wait.

But that physical exertion, all of which makes a house a home, has always made me feel better about just about anything that was upsetting me.

Unless, of course, it made me confront memories that made me feel worse.

I spent the day after seeing Nate vigorously cleaning baseboards, organizing the pantry, digging stuff out of closets that had been there so long I didn't even recognize it all, and so on. Not one thing was interesting, but I listened to NPR while I worked and lost myself in the tasks at hand.

It was better than thinking about what had happened.

Until late afternoon, when I came across an old box of letters and pictures in my closet. They were from high school, and I saw the gingham ribbon that I recognized as flagging the pile of letters Nate had sent to me from his grandfather's summer place in Michigan.

Why is it that people always seem to find this stuff just when they're thinking about it or, more to the point, trying *not* to think about it? That's always the way it went in movies and books. It seemed like some big Foam Finger of Fate pointing something out, but I couldn't buy that.

Fate had already given me the finger.

"Okay, I get it," I said out loud. "He's an issue for me. Jordan was right. Got it."

"Are you on the phone?" Camilla asked behind me.

Startled, I dropped the box and turned. "Oh, my God, you scared me to death."

She laughed. "Um, not as scary as your mom going crazy and talking to herself."

"Believe me," I said, reaching to pick up the various papers and pictures that were now strewn on the floor, "some things are better said only to myself, not to you."

"What's that?" she asked, honing in on the pile of letters. How was it that kids always seemed to know and go for the things you don't want them to see?

I tried to shrug it off. "Just a bunch of old stuff." I dropped the letters into the box.

"Lemme see." She reached for a picture.

I moved it out of reach. "It's nothing interesting."

"You just pulled it away from me," she pointed out. "It *must* be interesting."

"No, seriously, Cam." I put the last of the pictures in the box and put the lid back on. "It's my high school stuff. *Really* dull."

That ignited a fire I wasn't expecting. "Oooh, I want to see it!" She grabbed the box.

At that point, I had two choices: I could either let her get bored with it by herself, or I could make it seem super interesting by taking it away from her. I'd been at this game long enough to know the better course of action.

"Suit yourself," I said, sitting down in the closet. "You'll be disappointed."

Her slender hands pulled an envelope out of the bunch and pulled one of his letters out.

"*Hi Baby,*" she read, then raised a questioning brow to me before continuing. "*Today we went to the mainland to check for mail and supplies but the boat broke down. I had to improvise a fix on a hose with Band-Aids from the first-aid kit until we got to land. I was glad there was a letter from you waiting for me!*" She looked at me.

"Date smart boys," I said, trying to sound light. "That's the lesson there."

She gave me a dubious look and continued reading. "*We're in tents tonight because we're starting fishing at three a.m. I know you will still be asleep but I'll be thinking of you and hoping I'm in your dreams.*" She set the paper down and asked me, "Um, was this guy, like, totally in love with you or what?"

I hesitated for a moment, feeling disconcerted. How could I explain Nate to Cam? He wasn't just another ex-boyfriend, yet how could I explain to her that he was anything but? I'd never had to before. I'd always skipped over Nate in the let's-talk-about-your-ex-boyfriends game.

I laughed, but it sounded hollow to my own ears. I just had to keep this light. "Yes. He was totally in love with me. Who could blame him?"

"No, seriously, Mom, what's the story about this guy?"

"He was my high school boyfriend," I said, making a face like, *Everyone's got one like this.* She would never know how much more Nate had meant and how completely blown apart that was now.

"Not everyone. Look at this stuff." She read from another letter she'd pulled out. "*It's three a.m. and I can't sleep. I want you. Now. I love you more than anything, my baby. Forever.*" She looked back at me. "I mean, that's not *Rick.*"

"No," I agreed, a dull ache in the pit of my stomach. "It's not Rick. It was just a little high school romance, that's all. Don't make this more than it was." It was already more than it should be.

"Are you kidding?" She slipped the letter back into its envelope and picked another one at random. "Who *was* this guy?"

I winced inwardly.

"*I want you, I need you, I miss you, where are you?*" she read, then looked to me for the explanation that was still not forthcoming. "This is intense."

I reached out and took the letter from her and put it back in the envelope. My hand shook slightly. I hoped she didn't notice. "No, it's not," I said, putting the envelope back into the box. "It's not that big a deal."

"What was his name?"

No point in lying. She'd never hear it again. That chapter was now officially over. "Nate."

"What did he look like?" she pushed. "Is there a picture in there? Is that a box full of him?"

Yes, it was. And over the past few years, I'd probably looked over the outside of the box a million times and just hadn't given it much thought. Why did I have to find it and drop it in front of its greatest audience ever?

"It's got a bunch of stuff in it," I told her, keeping a firm hold on it. She didn't need visual aids. "Mementos and letters and all the same kinds of things you save now, but no pictures. Nothing that interesting, truly. Do *you* have anything super significant in your closet?"

She raised her chin. "No, but only because I never had, like, a love of my life like that."

If she was lucky, she never would. "Who says this is the love of my life?"

"*He* does." She reached for the box and I held it out of reach. "He loved you, he wanted you, he needed you, he'd love you forever. Omigod, Mom, that's, like, huge."

"That's, like, youth," I corrected, standing up and putting the box back on the shelf. "And a few weeks spent apart. Find me a teenage guy who doesn't suddenly turn his ordinary girlfriend into the girl of his dreams when he can't see her for a few weeks and I'll show you a unicorn."

She looked disappointed. "But he sounded like he meant it!"

"That's what I thought too, honey." I felt sick. Somehow I'd gotten so tangled up in these memories that it hurt me too, to think he'd sounded like he meant it when he didn't.

I'd sincerely believed it was forever, and I'd believed, even more than that, that Nate would be there forever.

What a mess this had all become.

The past, the present, and all the stuff that lay in between. "At the time. But we were just kids." I looked at her with sincerity, since I believed what I was saying even though I thought Nate and I *had* shared something a lot more intense than the usual youthful relationship. "You don't meet the love of your life when you're a kid. You have to figure out a whole lot of things before you're ready to say what you want."

"So . . ." She looked at me tentatively. "Is Rick the love of your life, then?"

For the first time in years, I wished I could say yes to a question like that. I wished I felt like someone in the present, someone who was really *here* for me, was a great love of mine.

But I couldn't.

"Rick is *great*," I dodged. "Don't you think?"

"The greatest! Obviously!" She narrowed her eyes with a disconcerting amount of perception. "But . . . do *you* think so?"

"Of course!" I did! I really did! So why did I feel the need to point out his added value? "And it's a nice bonus that he has Amy, what with you two being so close."

"*Totally*." She looked at me intensely. "But I want to hear more about this Nate guy."

"There's really nothing else to say. It was a thousand years ago." And yesterday.

"Didn't your grandparents meet in elementary school?" Cam went on, raising an eyebrow.

It was true; we have a picture of my father's parents in their second-grade classroom together. "Yes, but that was a small town in the thirties. Things changed a lot over the next fifty or sixty years."

"But you never found anyone else."

"Um, besides Rick, you mean?"

She was young and romantic and obviously wanted this to be earth-shattering. "You've never been in love like *that*"—she gestured toward the letters—"again."

"Who says?" This was getting tricky. I was well aware that I was screwed up emotionally—I didn't want to encourage her to be the same. "I'm just not in love with *him* anymore."

She looked sad. "It's just so romantic. And so sad now."

"Yeah." I nodded and put my arm around her, closing my eyes against the emotion for a moment. "It is. It was. But it wasn't real." Funny how it made me sad to say that. Not sad that it wasn't real *now* but sad for the girl I'd been who was so completely sure she knew her heart and that Nate was the guy in it.

Boy had she been naïve.

"So if I fall in love with a guy, I can't believe it's real?" she asked, disappointed.

"If you wait and fall in love with a guy when you're emotionally ready, it will be amazing."

"Or it will be a complete failure and I'll be forty-five and single, like Lois DeMatto's mom, who shows up with a different ugly guy at every school event."

"That's not fair," I said. "For one thing, there aren't that many school events, and for another, you don't know what she sees in them. Not everything is about appearance, remember."

Cam gave a sarcastic shrug. "Maybe not, but isn't *some* of it about looks?"

"Some. For a very short time. And even then, everyone's different." I looked at her, and saw the baby she'd been not so long ago. I saw all of the people she'd been so far; the pudgy infant, the three-year-old who loved wearing one black patent-leather shoe and one white one, always with her rose-patterned dress; the six-year-old I'd made into a Twister game box for the first-grade play; the ten-year-old who cried to me that she was taller than everyone in her class and was embarrassed and awkward; and now this fifteen-year-old who was starting to bloom into the woman she'd become but who was still so much a child that it made me want to cry.

Suddenly I was a crier.

If I could go back in time and slow myself down from the insane drive to grow up at that age, I would. I'm not sure why my mother didn't. If I'd had a little more childhood, I believe I would have been a lot less wobbly in my adulthood. Particularly my young adulthood.

"I never want to be a desperate older woman, looking at creepy guys through new glasses and saying maybe they're not so bad after all," she said.

Wow. I didn't either.

"Well, how about you wait and see what happens?" I suggested. "I promise you, you're not going to lose anything by playing it cool with guys in high school." The chorus of "Sunrise, Sunset" swelled in the back of my mind. I ruffled her hair. "You are a *prize*. You need to be won, not hand yourself over. Never forget that!"

"Jeez, Mom, it's not like I'm going to *do it* with anyone right now!"

She might have been me, trying to sell my mother the same lie, even while I was Nate's personal amusement park at night after she went to sleep.

Not that Camilla didn't mean what she was saying now.

I would have said and meant the same thing at her age.

She just didn't know how quickly her hormones were going to change her mind. Especially after a few well-placed strokes from a boy she thought she loved.

I sighed. "Trust me, honey," I said, wishing she never had to learn anything the hard way. "If you want so much as a good kiss good night, he has to feel like he pursued you, not the other way around."

Cam shrugged. "Is that how it was with that guy and you?" she gestured toward the box of Nate's letters.

I nodded. The desperation to get away from this conversation was intense, but this was one of those defining moments in a mother-daughter relationship and I couldn't let the ball drop just because I'd been stupid enough to sleep with the guy again without knowing all the facts. "At first. He did all the traditional boy stuff he was supposed to. He called me, he asked me to do things with him and his friends, kissed me good night, the whole nine yards."

She narrowed her eyes. "Only at first?"

"Well, then we were going out, so we were equal. He didn't always have to court me. We talked all the time, all night long, we saw each other every day before and after school, but we never really had the thing where the boy calls and asks the girl on a date. It was all just . . ." I shrugged. "Hanging out."

"That seems okay to me," she said. "It would be weird if, after all that time, you had to wait for him to call you every time."

"True." And that wasn't the problem. The problem was that he'd never done anything that made me feel like he really wanted me. In some way, deep down, I had thought he had. I thought I'd *known* that was how he really felt about me, and the truth was he'd done a thousand little things to prove it—a thousand little things that would have been more than enough for the adult woman I'd become— but somehow they'd never added up, in my teenage mind, to mean the same as one single grand gesture.

"So why'd you break up?" Cam asked, leveling what may as well have been a loaded gun at me.

Ugh. I'd totally set myself up for this. I wasn't ready to tell her that particular story and she seriously didn't need a mental image of her mother sobbing on some guy's front step for days and weeks on end. So I employed the old rule about answering kids' questions exactly and not overexplaining. It had worked when she was six and asked where puppies came from ("The mama dog carries them inside of her until they're ready to come out and live in the world"), so I hoped it would work now.

"We grew apart," I hedged. "He finished high school and went off to college and I, of course, had to stay in school, so . . ." I gave an airy wave of the hand like, *It was just one of those things.*

And like, *I absolutely never called him, sobbing, forty-one times in one day.*

And I categorically deny having jumped into bed with him the other day without saying so much as hello first.

"Aw. So can I read the rest of the letters?" She reached toward the box.

A few things flashed into my mind. Intimate references she didn't need to see. "No," I said. "You'll get bored and leave them lying all over the place and I need to clean up."

"But—" she began, but then the Black Eyed Peas started wailing in the other room. Her phone ringer. Thank God. "Gotta go!" She didn't wait for an answer, just ran for it.

It's exactly what I would have done at the same age.

I started to put the box back on the shelf, but then thought better of it. She might get bored at some point and remember it was there. Instead, I put it in the one place I knew she'd never look—on the top shelf of the hall closet, behind the cleaning supplies.

Later, when I went to check my e-mail—again to keep my mind off of what had happened—I was shocked to see something there from Nate.

I know you don't believe it, he wrote simply, *but I never wanted to hurt you.*

I would have asked how he got my e-mail address, but Theresa had already said my mother had given it to her. I could imagine it tacked to some twee suburban bulletin board in their suburban country kitchen.

When? I typed back. *High school? College? Yesterday?*

The answer came later in the day. *Ever.*

I sighed. The I-never-meant-to-hurt-you cop-out has always been weak for me. *I never meant to hurt you* means *but that was a by-product of whatever I was actually doing and I was doing it because I wanted to.*

In other words, *Sorry if you got hurt, but I wasn't really even think-*

ing about you. I certainly wasn't thinking about you enough to try not *to hurt you.*

It would have been more gratifying, in some perverse way, if he actually *had* been trying to hurt me. That's what you do when you love someone so much and you're in a lot of pain—you try and strike back. Hurting someone inadvertently is like tripping over a cat you didn't see darting out from under the sofa.

But there was no way to say all of that. No reason to.

The problem was that now I didn't know how he'd ever felt about me. If he hadn't even loved me back then—if his characterization of it now would be it was "infatuation" or some similarly diminishing term—it would really hurt. Not because of what had happened the other day—maybe someday I could write that off as a midday one-night stand—but because he had meant so much to me that I'd carried some part of him around with me ever since.

And I'd given him some part of me I'd never get back.

Instead of writing all that, I simply wrote, *You should have told me before anything happened.*

His answer: *I couldn't think of anything but you.*

My heart pounded. I couldn't help it. I believed him, clichéd as the line might have sounded, because I had felt exactly the same way.

Why Theresa? I asked. There was no telling how long he'd be checking his e-mail, but I was eager for an answer, and checked back several times myself before he responded.

Because I could never have you, he said.

What???

She reminded me of you.

Wow. There it was. That was raw.

I swallowed a lump in my throat. I wanted to believe him so much, but dating her a few times because she reminded him of me would have been one thing; *marrying* her was another.

But you married her, I wrote. *You must have loved her. Were you always attracted to her, even when you were with me?*

No, of course not, was all he wrote, and I knew he was responding to the latter part of my question and not the part about loving her.

I wanted to ask him if he was happy, but part of me didn't want to know. I mean, I wanted him to be happy, of course. Because I really *did* love him and, although my own desires ran a really close second, the thing I wanted most was for him to be okay.

And for a long, long time after we broke up—even though the logical part of me knew that what I'd done hadn't been that big a deal and shouldn't have been *unforgivable* if he'd really loved me— I'd worried that I'd crushed something in him that would never come back. Optimism, trust, willingness to love . . . something. Maybe more than one thing.

But at the same time, if he was happy now, that would mean I really never had been meant for him. Yes, the adult part of me knew that it was silly to give solid credence to the romantic fantasies of teenage me . . . but teenage me was still in there and the idea that the relationship had ultimately meant so much less than I'd been sure it did kind of smarted.

So I left the question unasked, and unanswered.

With nothing clever to say back, I decided not to answer at all. Instead, I just shut my computer down and went in the bathroom to clean the shower.

Chapter 17

My dreams are almost never fully satisfying. Yes, I might dream I won the lottery and can go out and buy a new house and whatever else I can think of, but inevitably there is also a "grounded" element of the dream; for example, when the IRS comes calling.

I dreamed of Nate. At first it was promising. Romantic, intense. We were in the car, "Everything I Own" by Bread was playing, and we were making out, careening toward the hot sex that ended just about every date we had. His shirt was off, and I moved my hands across the broad expanse of his shoulders, remembering the light sprinkling of freckles on his skin, and that one on his ear that had been there forever.

Suddenly he grew cold. His body stiffened and he moved his arm away from me.

"Nate? What's wrong?" I drew back.

His eyes were fixed, like stone, on something in the distance. Or nothing in the distance.

Not on me.

I knew that look. It had been years and years, but I knew that look. He was shutting down, closing me out.

"Nate?" Panic grew in me. This couldn't happen again. He couldn't do this again. I couldn't stand it. "Nate!"

He wouldn't answer.

Something hit my leg, but when I looked down there was nothing there. A phone was ringing. Then everything around us faded and I slowly came to in my bed in McLean Gardens.

Rick was next to me, still sound asleep, despite his ringing phone. I tapped him, but he put the pillow over his head.

Made no difference to me whether he got the phone or not.

I rolled on my side and looked at his back, wondering when the last time was that I'd run my hands over it in ecstasy, feeling him inside of me.

I wish I'd told Nate how much he meant to me back when I'd had the chance. I wish I'd given more instead of just taking all the time.

I wish I hadn't done anything like trying to make him jealous.

There can't be anything worse for the ego than dating a teenage girl, you know? Honestly. No matter how she feels about you, you're still going to be dealing with someone who is insane with hormones and who has, almost inevitably, gotten her ideas about romance from TV, movies, and overwrought pop songs, sung by pretty-boy musicians who have mastered the art of manipulating tender hormonally driven feelings into dollars.

No matter what poor Nate had going on in his life—and now that I'm an adult I realize that there was plenty—I was always ready to squeeze a little more attention my way with a mention of, "I saw Derek today at the pool. He asked me out [casual laugh] [lingering ellipsis] . . ." or "Um . . . my other line is ringing, I'd better get that and talk to you later . . . ," whereupon I'd talk to Jordan into the night, keeping half an eye open for Nate to show up in my front yard with a boom box cued to "In Your Eyes" by Peter Gabriel like John Cusack in *Say Anything*.

It never happened.

Like I said, Nate wasn't one for grand gestures. But I still kept trying to pull one out of him. I guess it was a function of my age and immaturity, and maybe basic selfishness.

It had to be awful dating me.

Nevertheless, I loved Nate with all of my heart, I really did. I guess I just made it hard for him to see that. Or to believe it. In retrospect I guess I was just trying to believe he would love me as much as I loved him and the only way I'd ever seen that demonstrated, I thought—since my parents weren't newlyweds—was through the over-the-top antics of special guest stars on bad TV shows.

So I tried to work it out in my dreams, the way everyone does when they've stuffed things so deeply into their subconscious that they're in constant danger of imploding.

Fortunately, Theresa didn't show up in the dream.

She had nothing to do with this, really. At least she had nothing to do with the old issues I needed to work out.

Neither did Rick.

As if hearing my thoughts, Rick stirred next to me, resisting waking up for work. That was probably what had woken me in the first place. When Camilla was home, it was always her iPod screaming from the bathroom while she got ready for school that woke me.

But Camilla was at her grandmother's, and Amy was at a sleepover, so Rick had stayed over and it was his earlier-than-mine hours that got me up.

I turned away from him and closed my eyes, trying to bring the dream back to me, but it was too late. It was gone.

I turned onto my back and lay there, discontented.

"Good morning," Rick said, chipper. He was much more of a morning person than I am.

"Hey," I said on a slightly impatient sigh.

He laughed at me. "Don't poke the bear in the morning, huh?" He was quoting something I'd said once when he thought it was funny to goad me when I was too tired for good manners.

I looked at him through narrowed, puffy eyes. "It's never a good idea to poke the bear."

"But sometimes it's fun." He got up and stretched. I watched him. He really was a good-looking man. He had an amazing physique, and the kind of face that made fans of Disney high school movies swoon. Blue eyes, strong jaw, perfect straight nose, shaggy brown hair. He was Zac Efron with a few more years and an edge.

And he was mine.

Why wasn't I happier about that?

Because I was tired and work was a drag right now, that was all. It was nothing to do with Nate, I told myself. That incident needed to just be a blip on my radar. It was a one-night stand, although it was daytime, and Nate was just a stranger with a familiar face.

If anything, it made me more grateful for Rick. I mean, seriously, if you were going to compare the two, Rick was technically *far* better-looking. Any woman faced with both on a dating Web site would opt for Rick in a heartbeat.

Nate's charm was more subtle.

I hauled myself out of bed and gave Rick a peck on the cheek as I passed him on the way to the shower.

"Coffee?" he asked.

"Yes. Lots."

"You got it."

What was not to love about this guy?

Was I always going to be the idiot that pined for the one guy who would never really love me?

An hour later I arrived at work after twenty-five minutes of sitting still in bumper-to-bumper traffic. When I got there, Jeremy was off, but he'd sent me an e-mail regarding the Brettman wedding that was taking place now in two days—the bride wanted a champagne fountain, was it too late for that?

No, you can always get a champagne fountain. That's because champagne fountains suck. The wine loses its effervescence once it's spat out the tiny holes into waiting flutes, suits, and children's hair. Champagne fountains might as well be called Chardonnay fountains, but no one ever believes me when I try to warn them of that.

Still, I made a call to the future Mrs. Brettman, trying to make her see sense. She ignored my warnings and I went ahead and ordered the fountain, along with two cases of Prosecco, which she had agreed to because it would save her about seven hundred dollars over her initial choice.

By late afternoon, I'd finished everything that was on my day's to-do list and was sitting at my desk, bracing myself for the inevitable whiny call from Roxanne. She'd tried me three times already during the day and each time I told her to call me back later. The first time "later" had meant seven minutes to her, but then she had to go to the mall where the cell phone reception was bad, so it seemed I had a stay of execution until she was finished.

I checked my e-mail. Jordan wanted to know if I'd found Nate yet.

No, I wrote, a little stab of guilt at the lie. *I think I'm actually beyond that now.*

My phone rang not three minutes later.

"Okay, what's going on?" Jordan asked.

"I saw him," I said without preamble.

"*What?*"

"When I was at my mom's for the cookout the other day, I went for a walk and went by Nate's old house." I don't know why I couldn't bring myself to tell her what happened then. "He was there, painting it for his mom."

"*And?*"

I hesitated. "You won't believe it."

"*What?*"

There was a lot of stuff she probably wouldn't believe.

"He's married . . ."

Her sharp intake of breath told me she would be as blindsided as I was.

". . . to Theresa."

There was a long pause then. Finally, she asked, "Theresa who?"

She didn't know. Deep inside, I have to say, I was relieved. "*Theresa*," I said. Then added, though it was bitter in my mouth, "Theresa Lawson."

"You do *not* mean Theresa Carson."

God, just hearing her *name* made me feel nauseated. Made it that much more real. "Yes."

"No way," Jordan said. "You're full of shit and I'm not buying it. It's not April Fool's Day and you *know* I hate this kind of joke."

I closed my eyes tightly and said, "It's not a joke. Theresa is looking adorable, like a little modern Audrey Hepburn, working for charity, being basically the nicest person in the world and fucking my boyfriend. Only now he's her husband and I can't do any of those things. I never could have made him happy. I probably never did."

"There's no way he'd prefer her over you. Even *I* know Nate better than that."

"Neither of us knows Nate anymore," I said. And, seriously, I was sick of trying to figure him out. He seemed to be on my mind all the time lately. I was unraveling.

While I was giving instructions for the placement of the champagne fountain for the Brettman wedding, in my mind I was thinking about his tongue trailing down my abdomen.

Tallying my expense reports I could feel his breath on my neck, like he was right behind me.

And sitting here in my office talking to Jordan all I could really think about was his mouth, warm and open, on mine, his tongue touching mine. . . .

But that was never going to happen again.

Ever.

Trying to change the subject, I pushed her instead. "What's going on with you?"

"Nothing of any interest at all, but nice try. We were talking about *you*. Did anything else happen? Did you guys talk or just wave or what?"

We had hard-core sex on his old bed. "We just talked. It was awkward, especially once the Theresa thing came up."

"I bet. Oh, honey, I'm so sorry."

I sat down. "It's surprising how much it sucks. You know I've never been a jealous person in my life. Now, suddenly, a hundred times a day I have to push visions of them doing the deed out of my head. I mean, Nate and Theresa! It's just . . . I can't believe I'm able to be hurt by this so long after it ended, but it's killing me!"

"I understand that," she said. "But you need to have some perspective. It *did* end. A long time ago. Who they are today isn't who they were then; and even though I know this feels like a betrayal—and probably a huge one—it's *not*."

"I know. I guess."

"No, you know. It's been more than two *decades*. You've spent more time without him than you spent *alive* before you were with him! That's a *lot* of time."

Put that way, it made me feel like an even bigger loser than I'd already felt like. I was pining for a guy I'd known only two years. Granted, it was two formative years, two *intense* years, two unforgettable years, but it was two years out of almost forty now.

Being upset about this was crazy.

But knowing that wasn't going to make me stop feeling this way. It was only going to make me feel stupid *and* heartbroken. I had to get off the phone before Jordan pointed out any other big obvious problems with what I was feeling. "Listen, can we talk about this later? I've got to run now. I have a work thing."

"Sure! Anytime, honey. I'm here for you."

"I appreciate that." I hung up the phone, knowing she meant it. But I'd never felt so alone.

⌒

I suppose the timing was actually good, if I could say anything related to Roxanne's party was "good." It certainly kept me busy, and what kept me busy at work kept me from thinking about Nate so much. Not that the thoughts didn't creep in, because they did, but every time I had one it seemed like someone showed up with a crisis of some sort or other.

Roxanne, for her part, simply assumed no one around her had a private life. "Justin is telling people he's not coming," she complained to me one day when she was supposed to be picking from the samples the caterer had prepared.

"Maybe that's lucky for you," I suggested. Certainly if Justin wasn't there I was sure it would be better for *me*.

"How can you say that?" she wailed in a voice I had previously only heard her use on her mother.

"You're right," I said. "I shouldn't. But, Roxanne, I have been where you are, and I swear having some woman he doesn't even know call and hound him about coming to your party is *not* going to work." No point in sugarcoating things for her. "It's just going to make you look like a complete loser."

She gasped. "Did he *say* that?"

"No, but he might as well have." I sighed and gave her my most heartfelt advice. "The only thing that really interests certain types of guys—in fact, *most* guys—is if you're *not* interested. So if you could possibly resist calling him, texting him, and otherwise contacting him for a few days, you might find he has a turnaround."

"But . . . I *gave myself* to him! He owes me for that!"

"Wait." I didn't know how to process this. So much information. Too much. "You mean he was your first?" Not that he'd *owe* her anything for that.

Or would he?

"No," she said, like I was an idiot. "But, you know, we *did it*."

I sighed. But for a minute there I'd felt sorry for her and the reason struck me: if he'd been her first, *would* he have owed her something?

It wouldn't have been legally enforceable, in any way, of course. Even the moral police would have a hard time making a public case for it.

But something about giving your virginity to a guy makes you fragile where he's concerned, even if you're strong everywhere else. It's the most tender interaction a girl can have. And obviously virginity can never be retrieved, but it—and more specifically the loss of it—sure can work on you psychologically in a lot of ways for a long time.

Nate could never have understood that. He never could have understood all the things he broke, in my heart *and* mind, by leaving so coldly and not speaking to me again for so long.

But he should have known that, no matter what he thought I'd done, I'd given him the best of my love and that deserved more respect than that. It was hard to contemplate. I was mad and sad and a hundred years too old to be all of those things all at the same time.

Meanwhile, Roxanne was looking at me impatiently.

I handed her a chicken finger. "Try this. Parmesan chicken tender."

She took a bite, then nodded. "Is there ketchup to dip them in?"

"Well, there's a honey-lime aioli," I said, and then, upon seeing her blank stare, added, "And we can put ketchup out too."

"Sweet!" She took another chicken finger and scarfed it down as we moved through the appetizers and on to the mini-cheesecakes the chef proposed for dessert. "Do you really think if I ignore him, he'll come back?" she asked me after shoveling about twelve cheesecake bites in her mouth.

I chose my words carefully. "I think if he's going to come back at all, it will only be because he notices you're not hanging around."

"Do you promise?"

Why not? "Sure."

"But next weekend is Katie Anderson's pool party and I wanted him to go with me!"

I nodded. "That's the thing about breaking up. There's *always* something coming right up that makes it a particularly bad time to split up. The holidays, Thanksgiving, your birthday, Valentine's Day, a big party. There's always something." I just couldn't let go of the Virginity Debt idea. "It sucks."

She smiled then. "It does!"

For just a moment, we had a connection.

Then she said, in that determined-child voice, "But at least you promised he's coming to my party."

I blanched at that. "Whoa, whoa, whoa, I didn't promise he'd come to the party!" There was no way she was going to report to Jeremy that I'd made a promise that wasn't kept. "Only that your best bet for him reconsidering is if you leave him alone."

Her face crumpled. "It's hard!"

"Oh, boy, I know that." I shook my head in sympathy. My inclination was to put an arm around her, but I seriously thought she might rail at that. But I knew what *would* work. "It's the worst." I handed her another cheesecake bite.

She took it and popped it into her mouth.

Maybe I'd just follow her around her party with a tray of cheesecake—it seemed to keep her happy.

"So what happened with your boyfriend?" she asked me.

"I'm sorry?"

"You seem to know a lot about being dumped. What happened to you?"

Despite her sugared words, for some reason I didn't feel like confiding in her. "Oh. Well. He . . . went off to college. We lost touch."

Once again, it was like I felt his breath on my neck.

His mouth on mine.

His hands on me.

"Excuse me, ladies?"

Saved! I turned to see Bill Watts, the associate producer, standing there, a cameraman behind him.

"Yes?" I asked cautiously.

He gave a laugh. "Pippa was hoping for some footage of the tasting here."

I stepped back, too far for him to have both of us in the frame. "Get the food. And, of course, the birthday girl!"

He nudged me back into the frame. "And the party planner."

I looked at him pleadingly. "Is this really necessary?"

"It's Pippa's thing. Showing the help interacting with the privi-leged party girl." He shrugged an apology.

Of course, I knew he was just being honest. "What happened to Jeremy?" I asked, knowing that he would be more than willing to be *the help* in exchange for some air time. "I thought he was back in action."

"Here I am! Here I am!" Jeremy was speed-walking over, and even from a distance of twenty yards I could see that he was heav-ily made up.

"What's with the makeup?" Bill asked me under his breath. "Does he always do this?"

"Only for TV," I said, wincing as Jeremy came closer into view.

"Oooh." Bill chuckled, as did a few others around us.

"This gets me off the hook, right?" I asked.

"You bet. I'm sure Pippa will find it quirky and amusing." He met my eyes and smiled. "Personally, I'd rather look at you than Norma Desmond over there, but I know you don't want to do it."

"I really don't."

"Okay." He gestured to the cameraman to get some footage of Jeremy prancing over.

The minute he did, though, Jeremy assumed the blank look of someone who was pretending he didn't know the camera was on and he lifted his chin to reveal his left side—he'd told me earlier he'd decided that was his "good angle"—which meant he didn't see where he was going.

He tripped over the camera cord rather spectacularly, flying into the edge of the table. As a final insult, the leg broke and all of the food came tumbling down on top of him.

It was like watching a Jerry Lewis movie.

"Omigod, I didn't get to try all of that yet!" Roxanne shrieked, as if that were the point.

I hurried over to him. "Jeremy! Are you okay?"

He raised his head and I could practically see the stars circling around him like in a cartoon. "I think so."

Mascara or eyeliner—or more likely both—was smudged under his right eye, and the creamy cheesecake was smeared into his hair.

Already I could see his eye was beginning to swell.

"Looks like you're gonna have quite a shiner there, buddy," Bill said behind me, reaching a hand out to help Jeremy up.

"A black eye?" Jeremy raised his hand to his cheek and winced. "How much will it swell?"

"Less if you get ice on it right away," Bill said.

"I'll take you to get an ice pack," I volunteered.

"No, no, no, no, no," Jeremy said, waving me away. He was clearly coming to realize he would be less of a spectacle if he slunk off on his own to handle this.

Bill looked at me apologetically. "Looks like you're back on the hook."

I sighed heavily. "He's going to be out of commission for days, isn't he?" I remembered how embarrassed he'd been about his imaginary zit. A genuine black eye and swollen cheek were probably going to go over considerably worse.

"Any chance you'd let me go if I conked myself in the head?" I suggested.

Bill laughed and shook his head.

"Um, what are you going to do about the food?" Roxanne demanded.

The cameraman edged closer to her and asked, "Would it make you mad if they didn't have more for you to try?"

"But we—" I began.

Roxanne glared at the camera. "I will be *so mad* if they don't have food for me to sample! This is my *only* sixteenth birthday party and I want everything to go *just right*."

"She's a pro," Bill said quietly behind me. "She's obviously watched the show before."

I tried to keep a straight face as we watched the cameraman feed her questions that could later be edited out so that Roxanne seemed to be giving a standard reality-show "diary room" type interview.

She was amazing, I have to say. Ghastly. As snotty as you can imagine, but if she'd been improvising the role of one of Cinderella's evil stepsisters, she would have been heralded as a genius by critics.

"This might work," Bill said in a low voice. "She's got some good stuff going. Pippa will love it. You might just find yourself on the cutting room floor."

I nodded. A bitch fit like Roxanne was building up to would be too good for this terrible show to let go.

"And I wanted horses, right?" Roxanne was saying. "And they were all, *No, no, no we can't get horses.* Like *horses* are that hard to find!" She rolled her eyes. "And eagles! I mean, how many people have eagles fly away at their wedding? But noooo, we can't get eagles either."

Eagles. It was just preposterous.

But I kept mum and let her talk. And talk. And talk.

Finally she got around to Justin. I knew she would. "All I want," she lamented, "is for my boyfriend Justin to come back from . . . the war. On time for my party."

I shot a look at her.

"He's in Afghan," she finished, with a sad nod.

I closed my eyes. There was no way to save her from herself on this one.

"Afghan," the cameraman repeated. "That must be rough. For him *and* for you."

"Oh, it is. He calls, like, every day, of course . . ."

Of course.

". . . but he's got to stay in Afghan for another few weeks."

"How long has he been gone?" the guy asked, essentially handing her her own petard.

She hoisted. "They drove out there about three weeks ago. Maybe two. What? Why are you looking at me that way, Erin?"

I just couldn't stand to see her do this to herself. "You mean they drove to the airfield, right? Then *flew* to Afghanistan."

"Right. Yeah." She looked back at the camera. "They flew to Afghan. Istan," she added uncertainly, with a glance at me.

I nodded.

But, God, she did *not* deserve this pretend boyfriend.

Bill was smiling. "I understand," he said, before I said a word. "It was getting uncomfortable for me too."

"You're lousy at this job, aren't you?" I joked.

"Terrible."

"Can, um, can we get some food?" Roxanne asked, tapping my shoulder.

I turned to her. "Absolutely. Let's go pick out the rest of your menu in the kitchen, okay?" I looked at Bill. "Okay?"

He nodded. "I think we've got plenty to work with for now. Al, get the broken table. That will be a good fade-out."

I took Roxanne into the building. "I think you should drop the war thing," I said. "There are too many details they can call you on." *And Justin would sooner inhale carbon monoxide from his Porsche's tailpipe than join any military service and you know it.*

"But it makes a good story line for me," she objected. That's the way reality-show people talked now—about their "story lines." I'd seen the Real Housewives of various places say it more than once.

I opened the door and ushered her into the kitchen. "It's not really working," I said. "Trust me."

"You're asking me to trust you on a lot."

"I know," I said. "But I'm the best hope you've got."

After the filming debacle, I went back to my office.

The moment I sat down and had a moment of peace, Nate flew to mind as if I'd summoned him there with some Harry Potter-ish spell.

My intuition told me that somewhere along the line he'd lost his passion for life and was just going with the flow now. He had a wife he didn't seem to be in love with, he had a job during the week, he was helping his mother on the weekend . . . and so on. I didn't even know what his *so on* was, but I had a very strong feeling there was one, and that's what his life felt like to him.

One big line of duties. And *so on*. He had an amazing capacity, it seemed, for compartmentalizing. For putting things in whatever place he deemed proper for them and then only looking at what was in front of him.

Then again, maybe my intuition was completely off.

It wouldn't be the first time.

What I did know was that this ceaseless speculation on Nate's state of mind and state of being was making me crazy.

I had to get back to my *real* life. My work. My family.

The rest of my day was spent working on the last details for the Brettman wedding, which was due to take place in twenty-four hours, despite the bride's never-ending list of last-minute changes.

By the time the wedding party arrived in the afternoon, I had gotten so many calls and e-mails from the bride, Lisa, that I was ready to scream. Instead, I had to be cordial and welcoming. It was part of the job description, I'd been through it before and I'd go through it a million more times, but I have to confess it's not all that easy for me to pull off that kind of acting job.

It was a very busy afternoon of putting people into their rooms, receiving calls of complaint that the rooms weren't big enough or had the wrong view or some other problem, switching rooms, and going through the whole exercise all over again. Like I said, this kind of goes with the territory of planning big, once-in-a-lifetime (hopefully) events for people who have pinned all their hopes and dreams on the idea that it must go "perfectly."

By the time I got back to my office, it was almost eight P.M. and the minute I finished with the pressing matters of the day, my mind drifted back to Nate again.

This had to be what insanity felt like. Thinking the same thoughts over and over, expecting a different reality every time.

The reality was that Rick had proposed to me. He wanted to forge a life with me. I was *lucky*.

Really lucky.

So what was I waiting for? I just needed to get practical about it.

We both knew it was a good match, we were good together, and it was great for the girls. Amy's mom had died three years ago and Amy had really taken to me quickly when Rick and I got together. I *wanted* to be there for her. I wanted her to be there for Cam. I wanted the whole, perfect family unit that I'd failed to give Cam the first time I'd had the chance.

Was it selfish of me to be holding back?

Something about my relationship with Nate, or the end of it, had made me gun-shy about relationships. Maybe it wasn't even about Nate himself, just what that relationship and that time represented.

That was what Jordan thought, and I had to admit that it was plausible that maybe the excruciating pain of that breakup had gone some distance in making me want to avoid ever feeling that kind of love (and therefore that kind of loss) again.

This is how it is with psychological hiccups, right? A person can go fifty years avoiding, say, going outside on a rainy day and when they undergo hypnosis it turns out they slipped on a worm after a summer thunderstorm once and broke a finger.

Maybe Nate was just a broken finger.

Or a worm.

Or—whatever—the catalyst for a disproportionate fear of commitment in me that, *maybe*, was actually a fear of rejection. It certainly could be at work with me now, with Rick. Because Rick was a great guy—inarguably attractive and desirable. And together we had a nice, calm relationship. No drama.

A few days ago I'd had a taste of that old passion with Nate and all it had done was make me feel awful.

It wasn't worth it.

So Jordan had been right all along: I had something significant to work out with Nate before I moved forward. I had to work out that he was always going to break my heart as long as I was willing to let him in.

He wasn't coming anywhere near me or my heart again.

Chapter 18

I wasn't exactly in the mood for the Brettman wedding the next day.

But as it turned out, it was beautiful. I was busy running around, choreographing the caterers and waitstaff, but I did catch the bride's walk down the aisle and if I didn't know what a pain in the ass she was, I might have been moved to tears by the way her father was trying, clearly, to keep his emotions in check.

Afterward, when Mr. and Mrs. Adam Brettman were official, the reception was in full swing, and the new Lisa Brettman had complained that the champagne in the champagne fountain was flat—big surprise!—I found the grandmother of the bride sitting quietly by the butterfly garden in an isolated part of the garden.

"Hi, Mrs. Winger," I said, hoping she wasn't lost or disoriented. "Do you need any help with anything?"

She swiped at her eye and it was then that I realized she'd been crying. "No, dear, I'm fine."

I came closer and sat down on the cement bench next to her. "Are you okay?"

She gave a small smile and nodded. "Not to worry, I'm not a lost Alzheimer's patient."

It was exactly what I'd been worried about. "Of course not," I said, "but it looks like you're upset. Is there anything I can do?"

She sighed and looked at the fountain in front of her. "I was married to my Ronald for fifty-five years."

"Wow. That's a good long time."

She met my eye. "We met when I was sixteen and he died when I was seventy-one. That was eleven years ago now."

"Are you kidding?" I said, without thinking. "Of course you're not kidding, it's just . . . wow, what a long time." A *really* long time. It was a pretty astonishing thought. "You must miss him terribly."

She swallowed and raised a crepey hand to her eye for a moment, then fluttered it down in a way I took to mean, *Obviously I do.*

I wondered if she was clinically depressed. Eleven years was a hell of a long time to feel empty. Then again, fifty-five years was a hell of a long time to be married. How *would* you get over that?

If I wasn't fully over a teenage love that had lasted just two years, what would I be like after more than fifty? I shuddered to think.

There was nothing I could say that would matter. "I'm sorry."

Silence stretched between us.

"I wish I'd had sex with at least one other man," she said then.

I was so startled I thought I must have misheard her. "I'm sorry, you wish—"

"If I had it to do over, I'd be bonking men all over town instead of giving myself to that one son of a bitch for my whole life only to have him die and leave me on my own when I was too old to really sow my oats with handsome young men. Lots of them."

Okay, I was really out of my depth here. "It's . . . not too late . . . ?" It probably was, though. At least it was too late for her to go around doing the deed with a bunch of hot young guys.

The mental picture was not pretty.

"Today my granddaughter got married."

I was grateful for the change of subject, and hoped it meant the other topic had been an aberration. "Yes, she did." Jordan's words echoed in my mind. *Don't ever get married.* "And she looked beautiful."

The older woman scoffed and waved an airy hand. "I hope she bonked a few other young men before this."

Oooh, I was *sure* she had. But it seemed like it would be impolite for me to say so to her grandmother, no matter how much the older woman invited that response. "She seems . . . very happy with her choice," I said, hoping to sound diplomatic.

The older woman sighed. "I've never heard either one of them say they loved the other."

That seemed consistent with the Lisa Winger Brettman I had come to know over these past few months. "Well, if they both don't say it, then maybe they're perfect for each other. I mean, if they're both okay with that."

Mrs. Winger laughed then. "By golly, you may have a point."

"How many children did you and Mr. Winger have?" I asked.

"Just the one son." There was a pause. "We couldn't really even afford that, but we made it work."

I knew how that went. "That's wonderful. I bet you're glad you did."

"Oh, yes." She nodded to herself. "Oh, yes. There was that."

The birds sang around us and I felt, for a moment, like I was in a fractured fairy tale, talking to my fairy godmother in disguise.

"Are you married?" she asked me suddenly, eyeing my bare left hand.

I held it up. "Nope. Thinking about it, though."

"Oh?" She didn't ask, but I knew she was wondering how many guys I'd screwed prior to this.

"I sowed my oats first," I said with a smile, and thought of Nate again, gripping my shoulders and trusting me with the life he poured into me. I could have done without any other oat-sowing, actually, but to say so would have been too personal and also I suspected it might have disappointed poor old Mrs. Winger.

She tipped her head and regarded me. "That was very wise of you."

Yup, that's why I did it. Because I was *wise*.

"Are you in love?" she asked.

"I love him." I felt a little defensive. "I don't know about *in love*. That might be better for kids than for grown people trying to make a life together."

"Piffle."

It took me so off guard I laughed. "I beg your pardon?"

"You think being in love is just for kids? Why, I say that's just piffle. You look like a lady who would know better than that."

I nodded. "Maybe you're right," I said, trying to mollify her. "Maybe I should take that into consideration."

"You should." She stood, more briskly than I would have expected. "That's why you try a bunch of men. To find the one you can fall in love with and *stay* in love with." She sighed dramatically. "If that's possible."

If.

"How about I walk you back to the party?" I suggested. "Maybe you'd like a glass of champagne?"

"From the fountain?" she asked, cocking an eyebrow. "Fountains ruin champagne, you know."

I nodded. "They do. But I think we can find some at the bar," I said, wishing I could join her in a glass or two.

"What's your name, young lady?"

"Erin," I said. "Erin Edwards."

"Erin Edwards." She nodded, like she approved of the name. "I like you."

"Thanks, Mrs. Winger. I like you too."

We walked back to the bar together and made idle chitchat until she was finally swept away for pictures.

But before she went, she looked at me and said quietly, "Good luck to you."

———

Those words were still ringing in my ears when I got to my office and saw that Rick had called three times. I called him back, fearing an emergency, as usual.

It was bad news, all right. But not in the way I'd anticipated.

"We have a dinner party on Monday night," he said.

"Okay." Another of his work things, no doubt. Ugh. "Where?"

"It's a funny thing, you're gonna love this. One of your old friends from high school called right after you left."

Oh, no.

"Theresa," he went on. "Wait, I wrote it down. Theresa Lawson."

My throat squeezed shut. Of all the things I'd already thought about, all the ways I'd already, in this short period of time, tortured myself with thoughts of them together, somehow one of the most painful things was putting his name on hers.

I knew it was crazy, but the feeling of betrayal was overwhelming. I sat down. "Really."

"Yeah. She sounded really nice and we didn't have plans for Monday night."

"But Cam—" I began.

"Is fine with it." He was clearly pleased with himself for having handled all of this. "When I couldn't get ahold of you, I called to ask her if she had anything going on that we needed to know about before making plans. She said it's all clear."

I closed my eyes and pinched the bridge of my nose. Obviously I didn't want to do this. And I could get out of it, no matter how awkward it became to do so. If worse came to worst I could just say I was uncomfortable hanging out with my ex.

But part of me *wanted* to go. Some childish little bitch inside of me wanted to go with good-looking Rick and pretend I was happy and in love and that Nate didn't matter.

Pretend I hadn't just sobbed until I was dry and limp in his car.

"Amy's going to come hang out with Cam here, in fact," Rick went on.

All settled.

Great.

"Did you get directions?" I asked, wishing the not knowing where the house was would be enough to decline.

"Sure did!"

I felt ill. "Okay, then. Look, I've got to go wrap up all this stuff we're doing for the show on Saturday. I should be home at a decent hour, though."

We hung up and I sat back in my chair and closed my eyes.

Nate and I had had a relationship that was so sweet, so close. Yes, we fought sometimes—mostly that was me. And there had been some drama—again, mostly me. But when I looked back on it, what I remembered and felt was just intense love.

Truly, just adoration.

Somehow, there had been no self-consciousness, no posing, no trying to be cool. He'd sat with me for five hours by a drain in Theresa's basement while I threw up four thousand beers and my immortal soul. I'd sat by his bedside day after day reading him a suspense novel when he was recovering from an operation.

Yes, there had been sex, and a lot of it. And it was really good. But when I thought back on him, it wasn't my spine that tingled, it was my heart.

Would I go back in time if I could? No way. I wouldn't be a teenager again for anything in the world. The feeling that lingered for him in my heart wasn't a melancholy longing for a simpler time, it was a love that was independent of time and place.

Which could have been a really nice thing if it weren't for the fact that now it was muddied by time and place because he was with Theresa, and now I had to wonder if there had always been some spark of attraction between them that I had arrogantly missed because I was so comfortable—cocky?—that he loved *me*.

Had looks exchanged between them that I'd never seen?

Had touches lingered when I wasn't paying attention?

What had I missed when I'd introduced them for the first time? A buzz of attraction, quickly dampened by temporary loyalty to me?

What was the first conversation they'd had after they'd met at the church? *I always had a thing for you, but I was with Erin, so there was nothing I could do about it?*

When had they first kissed?

When had they first made love?

Had he kissed her the way he kissed me? Done the things with her that he'd done with me?

You know, I don't care if I was ancient history for both of them, the world was *full* of single people. Why in the world had they picked each other?

Especially him. He obviously wasn't in love with her or he never would have done what he did with me. He was living a life I know, from his reaction afterward, he'd never wished for himself. And he was doing it with my former friend.

It should have made me hate him.

I wished it did.

When I got home that night, Cam and Amy were lying on the floor watching *Gossip Girl* reruns and Rick was on the sofa reading a law journal.

"Hi, guys!"

Cam barely looked up. "Hey, Mom."

Amy waved without looking at me.

Rick put his journal down. "Hi, hon. How was work?"

"Ugh." I put my purse on the hall table. "I'll be really glad when this party is over."

"Can I come?" Cam asked. "It's going to be on VTV, right? Let me come!"

"No way. I don't want you tainted by that kid."

"What about me?" Amy asked with a smile. "I'm older than Cam. Can I go?"

I smirked at her. "Very funny."

"Told you," Cam said.

"Worth a try!" Amy laughed. "I hear *you're* going out Monday night," she said, looking at me with mild interest. "With some old friends. And Dad's going too."

Friends. Hm. "Yes."

Cam sat up and muted the TV. "Is that the Theresa you and Jordan talk about? From high school?"

"Yup."

"So who's she married to?" she went on. "Anyone you know?"

I leveled a gaze on her. How did kids have this ability to pounce on the one thing you don't want to talk about? *What's a vagina? Why are you kicking me under the table? What's that on Mrs. Holt's face?* "Yes. Someone we were both friends with."

"Cool!" Amy said, unaware.

"You know Theresa's husband too?" Rick asked me.

Did I know Theresa's husband? The question felt too sad to answer.

Suddenly it felt like an inquisition. I went into the kitchen and rummaged around until I found a box of Cap'n Crunch. "Yes." I dug my hand in and took a mouthful of Crunch Berries.

"That will be so neat to meet your old friends," he said, apparently unaware of the shift in my reaction.

It was uncharitable of me to find his use of the word *neat* unmanly, but I looked at him for a moment before I said, my mouth full, "Yeah. *Neat*."

"Were you all close at the same time?" he persisted.

A Crunch Berry lodged in my throat. I held my index finger up and went to the fridge to get some milk. I came away with a beer instead. Given the circumstances, it seemed like the better choice. "Theresa and I were friends from tenth grade to, I don't know, right around the time Cam was born."

"I broke up your friendship?" she asked, then nodded, as if she'd been known to do this.

"No, no, I was just busy. We lost touch." I took a sip of beer. It wasn't actually as bad as you'd think with the Cap'n Crunch.

"What about the husband?" Rick asked, and he was clearly just curious, there was nothing loaded about his question at all.

As far as he knew.

I set the beer down and the foam rose and bubbled out the top. I sighed and got a napkin to clean it up, saying, "What's *close* when you're that age?"

"What's his name?" Cam asked, narrowing her eyes at me.

I took a swig of the beer and looked at her evenly. "Nate."

She widened her eyes in recognition.

I nodded.

Amy continued to watch *Gossip Girl*.

Rick noticed nothing. "There was a guy in my dorm at USC named Nate. I wonder if it's the same one. What's his last name? Wouldn't that be funny?"

"It would be . . . hilarious." I gave a dry laugh. "But I doubt it's the same guy." Even God doesn't mess with people *that* much. Plus, Nate had lived in California briefly but it was after he was out of school. "So am I supposed to call her back?"

"You probably should, but I went ahead and got the directions and everything. They live down in Palisades."

I felt the blood drain from my face. "Great."

None of this was supposed to happen! It was all complete madness. What was I supposed to do now? Tell him I didn't want to go because Nate was my ex and, oh, by the way, I fucked his brains out the other day?

This was a mess.

Rick said, "It'll be fun. You never talk about your past. I'm looking forward to getting some insights."

There would be plenty of those for the taking.

"I'm not that interesting." I downed the rest of the beer.

"That's not true." Rick returned to his magazine. He'd noticed nothing about my reaction or my mood. Meanwhile, Cam was signaling frantically toward my bedroom because she wanted me to give her the whole scoop in private. Or whatever part of the scoop I could make appropriate for a fifteen-year-old.

"Um, Mom?"

"Hm?"

"Can you show me *that dress* you were telling me about?" She gestured toward the bedroom yet again.

"Sure." I picked up the box of cereal and looked at Rick. "Do you mind?"

"Not at all. I'll be in there in a few."

I nodded, hoping he'd give me more than a few minutes to collect myself after I answered whatever it was that Cam was so desperate to ask me.

"*Mommy!*" Her stage whisper was loud enough to be heard down the hall.

I closed the door. "What?"

"Nate? *The* Nate?"

"Yes. Same"—I plopped down on the bed and jammed my hand into the cereal box—"Nate." I put a handful of the sugary stuff into my mouth and remembered hearing it was more addictive than heroin.

I wished it could alter my mood like heroin.

"The one who was going to love you forever," she clarified, a heavy question in her voice.

"That's the guy."

"He married your *friend*?"

I felt ill. "Apparently so."

She was agape. "Why aren't you more upset about this?"

I have to say, I appreciated the fact that she was taken aback by it. "It was a long time ago. Everything's different now. I'm"—it was a small effort to choke the words out, but the sentiment was right— "happy for them."

"Well, *I'm* not," she said, indignation coloring her voice. "I think they're both jerks."

Amen to that. "Honey, you don't even know them."

"It goes against the most basic girlfriend rule and you know it." When did she get so smart? That was totally true. "You're not allowed to go out with your friends' boyfriends."

I nodded.

Apparently that nod didn't convince her. "So you see why this is messed up, right?"

I laughed. "I see why it looks that way, yes. But a lot of time has passed."

Cam snorted and rolled her eyes. "I don't care."

I had more cereal, shamefully gratified by her response and agreeing with it. "Okay, I admit it's a little uncomfortable for me," I said, mouth full, "but I'm not in high school anymore. He's not mine. He never really was."

"But he *was*!" She gestured helplessly toward the closet where the Box o' Nate had been.

"No, baby. You never own someone else. You can't dictate the rules they should live by. They're grown people and apparently they fell in love." I'd seen how Nate looked when Theresa had shown up. He wasn't in love with her. But maybe he had been once. They must have been. Once. "It's kind of cool, if you think about it. They met pretty young and are together still."

She considered that for a moment, then voiced what the inner child was screaming in me. "But they met because of *you*!"

"It's fine," I said, more to myself than to her. "That's just how it is sometimes."

"I think it stinks."

I nodded. Yup. It stank. "Sometimes that's how life is. It stinks."

There was a knock at the door and Rick came in. "Is this a private party?" It felt like an intrusion, but that wasn't fair.

I looked at Cam.

"It's fine," she said, though I could tell she felt it was an intrusion. "I have to call Sara anyway."

I'd never heard of Sara. She might have been made up.

"Good night, babydoll," I said to her, and she came over for a good-night kiss. I handed her the box of cereal. "Stick that in the kitchen, will you?"

"Are you sure you don't need it?" she asked, like she was offering me a glass of wine.

"No, thanks."

"Are you okay?" she asked me pointedly.

"Of course!" I glanced at Rick, who didn't appear to see anything amiss with her question. "Good night."

"Good night, Cam," Rick said. "Tell Amy I said it's time for bed, would you?"

"Sure. G'night." She left, looking a little deflated.

"Everything okay?" he asked me when she'd gone.

"Yes." I made a show of yawning and stretching. "It's just . . . boy trouble." True true true.

It was time to accept his proposal. I'd resolved to do it and he was waiting.

"Rick," I began.

"Mmm-hmm?"

"About that thing you asked me . . ." I took a breath.

"What was that?" He was focusing on his watch crystal, trying to clean it with the bottom of his shirt.

This was not the way to do this. Maybe it was even a sign. "Oh . . . nothing. We can talk tomorrow. I'm pretty exhausted."

He frowned at the watch, then shook his head and looked at me. "I'm sorry, what was that?"

"I was just saying I'm tired. So." There was nothing else to say. "Good night."

Chapter 19

So, yes, obviously I *could* have gotten out of dinner with Rick, Nate, and Theresa.

But not without questions I didn't want to answer, suspicions I didn't want to raise, and weirdness I didn't want to feel.

Part of me was curious about what their life was like. Well, *curious* sounds so light. I was dreading finding out the answer too. Maybe you could call it a morbid curiosity.

Yet I had to know.

Even still, my heart pounded out my dread every single minute of the drive. Every minute a new rush when I realized I was about to see Nate. That I was about to see Nate with *Theresa* . . . his *wife*. My old friend.

So even though it startled me at first, it was a relief when my phone rang and I saw it was Jordan. "What's going on?" I asked, glad for something else to think about for a moment.

"Are you alone?" she asked.

"Rick and I are on our way to have dinner at Theresa and Nate's house."

"What—wait, did you try to call earlier?"

"Um-hm. I left a message." I lowered my voice. "A rather plaintive one."

"My voice mails were all crackly this morning," she said. "I'm sorry. Wow. This sucks."

"I wish you could join us too."

"I bet you do. But this is going to give you some really important closure. Hopefully."

The GPS shouted, in a British accent, that we needed to turn left ahead.

"What?" Jordan asked.

"Nothing, it was the GPS," I said.

"Left where?" Rick asked, instantly impatient. "There are three lefts in a row."

"Keating Drive," I read off the LED.

"Cheating what?" Jordan asked, ultra aware of that concept lately. "Who's cheating?"

"No one. I said *Keating*. I was talking to Rick."

The GPS spoke again, demanding another left. Honestly, I don't understand why people need the sound on with those things, they have the little purple path showing exactly what road to take, in addition to showing the road names.

Rick always insisted that having the sound on was the safer option. Even though all it seemed to do was piss him off every time it said something, which struck me as the *less* safe option. "Now there isn't a damn left to turn onto, that's an alley."

"It's up there," I said, pointing to what was obviously a street in *front* of the houses that the alley ran behind. I returned to Jordan with a sigh. "This is going to be a weird night."

"Probably. But I want you to call me as soon as you get home tonight, no matter what time it is!"

"I will." Rick started arguing with the GPS again about whether or not we had, in fact, *reached our destination*, so I said to her, "I'd better run now, but we'll talk later."

"Good luck, sweetie!" she said.

"Thanks." It really made me feel so much better to hear her voice. "You too!" I hung up the phone and slipped it back into my purse. "What," I said to Rick, "is your problem?"

"That stupid thing is the problem." He gestured at the GPS, which was now showing a finish line, indicating we were at, or very near, the right address.

I looked at the directions, and at the GPS. "We're on the right street. There—forty-four-eleven, it's right there." I pointed at the house. It was a little Cape Cod that, in this neighborhood, probably ran close to a million bucks. My chest tightened at the place they called a home.

"Oh. *There*." He said it like he'd discovered it on his own, *despite* the opposition and interference of the electronic map.

We got out of the car and walked toward the front door, misgivings building in my chest with every single step. This was nothing short of masochism. Why was I doing it? I *should* have declined and let everyone think what they wanted, rather than putting myself through seeing the only guy I'd ever really loved, married and living with someone else. Never mind that the someone else used to be my friend.

"Nice house," Rick mused.

I made a noise of agreement.

Theresa threw open the door like she'd been looking forward to this moment all her life. "Hi!" She put her arms out and pulled me into a hug, then turned to Rick and said, "You must be Rick!" and hugged him.

Nate stood awkwardly behind her and stepped back to let us in.

He and Rick introduced themselves to each other and shook hands, then Nate turned to me and—because anything else would have been suspicious in and of itself—we hugged. Awkwardly.

The buzz of electricity when we touched was undeniable, and we drew back quickly. He looked away and I looked down at their impeccably clean floor. I swear I could feel heat pulsating from Nate to me.

We all ended up in the hall for a minute, where I noticed the house looked just like a Pottery Barn catalog, right down to the tasteful-but-generic paintings on the walls, accent pillows that were *just so*, and bold paint colors that made statements I couldn't quite read. But that was Theresa; impeccable, bold, and striking.

Yet there was something strangely impersonal about it all too. No family photos. Nothing to suggest it was a *home*. It might as well have been a builder's model.

"This is a beautiful house you have," Rick said, and I could tell he was admiring Theresa.

Who wouldn't?

My eyes flicked to Nate, but he looked at me and I looked away, feeling the heat in my face again.

This was going to be a long night.

We sat down in the perfectly appointed living room, where Theresa had set up a small bar that seemed to have the makings for just about any drink or bar snack you could think of. Seriously, if I'd asked for a sour apple brandy Alexander mojito with a Buttershots floater and a side of Kentucky beer cheese, she probably could have whipped them right up.

It was hard not to feel like I paled in comparison, honestly. I didn't have the home-decorating gene. If I didn't have girlfriends who did, my places would all look like college dorms, for the rest of my life. I also didn't have the entertaining gene. Organizing events by delegating responsibilities and tasks was one thing—doing the whole shebang myself in my home was quite another. Every time I entertained—and I mean *every* time—I ended up forgetting some critical part of the meal or appetizers: asparagus remained forgotten in the fridge, Pepperidge Farm crackers languished in back of the pantry while I frantically set out saltines and broken Ritz remains with Cracker Barrel cheese.

Normally none of this made me feel bad about myself—I have other assets that deflect these lacks—but sitting in this beautiful home, looking at this beautiful woman, who had married my most beautiful memory, I felt like a pair of ratty old sneakers at the foot of a D&G evening gown.

After a while, the conversation turned to a collection of Civil War artifacts Theresa had inherited when her father died ten years ago.

"For example," Theresa said. "There's an Emerson & Silver cavalry sword with a straight blade which is very rare and—"

Rick was beside himself. "I have *got* to see that!"

"It's right downstairs!" She glanced at Nate and me. "Would you mind excusing us for a moment . . . ?"

"Go right ahead!" I waved airily at her. "He loves this stuff!"

"It's this way," she said to Rick, and led him out of the living room. "My dad was a *huge* Civil War nut, he had ancestors on both sides of the war . . ."

I listened to her as she took him down the stairs to the basement. Rick would undoubtedly adore her by the end of the evening and I would feel even more frumpy by comparison.

What did Nate see when both of us were in the room together? I wondered.

"So," I said on a sigh.

"So." Nate leaned back in his chair and looked at me.

"This is . . . interesting."

He gave a laugh and nodded. "That's one word for it. But I'm not hating it. It's good to see you."

I felt a flush rise in my cheeks. "Yeah, well, it's good you're not seeing quite"—I lowered my voice to a whisper—"*as much of me* as you did last time."

He nodded. "You're probably right. That's probably best. Even if it doesn't feel like it."

"We shouldn't even talk about it again. It never happened."

"It happened."

"It shouldn't have."

"I don't regret it."

I didn't either. But I knew I *should*. "So how long have you lived here?"

"A few months. I think it was February when we moved in."

Only a few months and it looked like they'd been there forever! "It's really nice." Something deep inside of me started to waver. I wasn't sure I could do this. Maybe I should go find Theresa and Rick and just keep my eyes on Rick like a shipwreck survivor heading for the shore.

Because looking at Nate was too hard. That jaw, that chin, that mouth . . . how many times in my life—how many times in the past week—had I pictured kissing all of that and more?

I swallowed. "It really feels . . . homey." Funny, though, I wouldn't have thought of him as the type to go for the fussy furniture, the doilies placed *just so* under a vase, the abstract and clearly expensive artwork that evoked nothing but wonder.

In other words, it felt like her home, but it didn't feel like his. But what did I know?

He smiled, that wonderful crooked smile that made his dark eyes lighten to amber. "It feels like a grandparents' house, doesn't it?"

"Oh, my gosh, you're right—it feels like *your* grandparents' house!"

"You're sitting on their sofa."

"That's *right*! I thought this felt familiar!"

"A couple of pieces here are." He shrugged. "Most of them are Theresa's, though."

I nodded. A few moments passed in awkward silence. Finally, I said, "This is weird."

"I know."

"Do you remember that time I went out with Pete Hagar for a few weeks in high school?"

"Yes," he said immediately.

I met his eyes. "This is way worse."

He nodded and looked away. "I'm sure."

"I mean really," I went on, unable to keep from harping at least a little bit. "This was a shock in so many ways."

"I'm sorry. I handled it . . . badly. All of it. But not because I wanted to score something from you." He looked at me intently. "You know that, right?"

"I do." And I did. There were a lot of easy ways to hurl blame at him, but one thing I knew absolutely was that he hadn't had sex with me this time just to *get some*.

"If I could do things differently . . ." He didn't finish.

I didn't know what to say. This wasn't right. None of this was right. "Why are you doing this?" I asked.

He cocked his head. "Doing . . . ?"

"Why are you *married* to a gorgeous perfect woman and . . . doing what we did the other day?"

"I'm not in love," he said quietly. "With her. No matter how perfect she is."

"Then why did you marry her?"

He tightened his jaw. "Life throws curves."

"I'll say." I looked at him. God, he was cute. He still looked like My Nate. Those eyes, those teeth, those hands, that body . . . it was impossible to be so close to him and not want him. It felt *right*. Things trembled deep within me, and while I knew I should wish I wasn't there, what I really wished was that we were alone.

It was a good thing we weren't.

Instead I just sat there quietly, simultaneously wishing Rick and Theresa would hurry up *and* that they'd never come back, and feeling my heart break. If things had gone just a little differently— maybe even just that one night—Nate and I might have been in our house, not *their* house. It all felt alien, like something had gone terribly wrong and we'd screwed up our fate.

Then again, anyone who believes in fate has to be prepared to believe that whatever happens *is* fate, whether they like it or not.

"What about you?" he challenged. "Are you in love with Rick? Because I'm not seeing that."

"I'm not married to Rick."

"No, but you're thinking about it."

Before I could respond, Theresa and Rick came up the basement stairs, shrieking with laughter over some joke Theresa had told about the Gettysburg Address.

I'm not kidding.

"That's a good one," Rick said, apparently never having heard it before.

"Shall we move into the dining room?" Theresa suggested. "Dinner is ready whenever everyone else is."

Anything that took us one step closer to being finished and out of there worked for me. We moved into the dining room and sat at a perfectly set table with a centerpiece of fresh freesias.

And, really, it was a mistake. The whole thing, coming here, it was one big debacle and I should have known better than to try. In fact, I think I *did* know better, I just didn't know how to get out of it gracefully.

And there was some part of me that didn't want to lose contact with Nate, even if contact did come under these circumstances.

Theresa served a fantastic Chardonnay, which the guy at Pearson's Liquor Store had taken out of the back vault for her when she told him she was having her best friend from twenty years ago over for dinner.

"So, Nate," Rick said, leaning toward him. "I understand from your wife that you work as an aeronautical engineer at Quince."

It was the tone Nate's grandparents had used to ask me where I wanted to go to college.

I'm thinking about Southern Methodist University, I'd told them. Lucy Ewing had gone there on *Dallas*.

The grandparents had been thrilled. It was the family alma mater. From that moment on, they had just grown to love me more and more.

But now here I was, grown-up Erin, sitting at a dinner table with grown-up Nate, but with our significant others . . . not each other.

Which would have been fine; I'd interacted with adults many, many times in my adult life, of course. But never with Nate. This scene was just too uncomfortable.

Theresa said to me, "Isn't that funny, Erin?"

I dragged my attention back to the moment, blinking against the discrepancy of the *then* versus the *now*. "I'm sorry?"

"Didn't you always think Nate would be, like, an investment banker?" Theresa asked. "He's so good with numbers!"

She was his wife! How could she be so completely off base about him? "No. I thought"—I looked at him uncertainly and just went ahead and said it—"this is exactly what he wanted to do. Since he was really young." Suddenly I was uncertain. "At least I *thought* so. Right, Nate?"

For a moment, it felt just like it always had talking with him over dinner. But it wasn't. We both knew it wasn't.

He suppressed a smile but just met my eyes and gave a small nod. "It's a good fit for me."

A good fit.

My hands, holding knife and fork, started to tremble slightly. I tightened my grip on the utensils and tried to still the earthquake that was erupting inside of me.

Oblivious to my meltdown, Theresa said, "Of course, Nate could probably do just about anything he put his mind to. *You* know that almost as well as I do, don't you, Erin?"

Now, I know what she was trying to do. She was trying to validate my history with Nate in some way. To acknowledge it without handing it too much importance. And definitely without trumping *her* importance in the matter.

There was no way she realized what a terrible position she was placing me in by putting me on that spot, though. Now was *not* the time for me to reminisce aloud about the old days of Nate and me. In fact, probably *no* time would be the right time for that again.

"I'm sure," I said, not looking at him. "He can be very focused." God knows *that* was true. He'd set his mind on dumping me and keeping away and he'd succeeded.

I straightened in my chair, remembering. That was ancient history. It shouldn't be acting on me now. The problem was, *recent* history had made it difficult for me to see any of this clearly.

"That kind of focus is important," Nate pointed out. "It's an asset in my work."

"Sure, in *work*," I said, looking at him. "But maybe less so in personal relationships." I held his gaze for just a moment before realizing how inappropriate I was being. I cleared my throat. "For instance, in my work, I have to deal with difficult people all the time and, while I'd love to tune them out, what I actually have to do is tune *in* to them, determine the root of the problem, and solve it."

"Not all interpersonal problems can be solved, though, can they?" Nate said. "Sometimes, if you don't focus on the big picture instead of the details, you end up going under."

"That's for sure," I said, a little sharply. "If you don't have the cooperation of other people involved." This was really making me mad, but I tried to keep my cool. "Teamwork. That's key."

Nate shrugged. "That's the difference between you and me, I guess. Our work, I mean. I deal with facts, you deal with emotions."

"The problem with that is that everyone has emotions," I said. "Even if they don't want to acknowledge them."

"And there are always facts," he countered. "Even if people don't want to acknowledge *them*."

"I'm with Erin," Theresa said, and I couldn't tell if she'd picked up on what was going on or not. I mean, really, how could she not? But she didn't seem to think anything of it if she did. "I wrestle with emotions all the time, but I have to maintain my left-brain impartiality for work."

"Well, I'm not *wrestling* with emotions—"

"No, no, that's a *good* thing," Theresa said. But I didn't believe her.

And one quick look from those brilliant blue eyes told me, yup, she'd picked up on something. She knew Nate and I weren't talking about work.

Rick, on the other hand, didn't have a clue. "The world wouldn't run very smoothly without our left-brained engineers," he said, and gave a laugh. "We'd still be driving *around* the Chesapeake Bay to get to the beach."

Nate just ate, looking amused by the conversation. It might as well have been about someone else.

Rick asked Theresa a question about her work, and they got going in an animated conversation about a company they'd both done work with.

I turned to Nate and said privately, "Congratulations. I know you always wanted that. Quince, I mean."

"Thanks." He gave that smile that had always made me melt. "I know you're good at yours too. You were always good at making people feel . . . emotions."

I swallowed. "Not good enough," I said lightly.

"You'd be surprised."

My heart stopped. Meanwhile, Theresa chatted away with Rick, while so much heat buzzed between us that I was amazed neither of the other two looked over and asked what was going on.

"Nothing surprises me anymore," I said with a small smile. "How could it?"

"Life is full of surprises."

"These days, I prefer the predictable," I said. "Surprises aren't always pleasant, are they?"

He shifted in his seat, and the heat from his body whooshed closer to me for a moment. "No," he agreed. "They aren't."

"Erin!" It was Theresa again. This time there was a tiny impatient tinge to her voice.

"What?"

She raised an eyebrow. "You and my husband are so deep in conversation that you missed the big news."

My husband.

I guess I deserved that, but wow, it stung.

"What news is that?" I asked with dread. Had she had wine with dinner? Yes, she had. So it wasn't that she was pregnant. Thank God.

"Your *fiancé*"—did she draw the word out or was I imagining that?—"got a promotion today but hasn't had the chance to tell you!"

I looked at Rick, shocked that he would announce that to Theresa so she could make a production of it. "Is that right?"

"It's not that big a deal," he said, but he looked like the proverbial cat to my canary.

"If you call being made *partner* not a big deal," Theresa said, and waved a manicured hand. "We should get out some champagne!"

"Wow, Rick, that's really great," I said, unable to bring the enthusiasm the news needed, thanks to the awkward presentation.

"Yeah, congratulations, man," Nate agreed, and suddenly it felt like the two of us were the couple congratulating the two of them on their news.

I saw that register with Theresa, saw it flicker across her expression immediately before she stood up and said, "Does anyone want champagne?"

Everyone demurred.

Instead we moved back to the living room, which she had somehow reset for coffee between serving wine and dinner, and had, unsurprisingly, a delicious brew.

Finally, with cups drained perhaps a little hastily, I seized a moment of silence to suggest that Rick and I should be going since we had to work in the morning and he had still to tell me the details of his big promotion.

Theresa hooked her arm through Rick's and led the way to the door. Nate hung back with me.

"Sorry you had to do this," he said to me quietly.

"You too."

A moment passed, then he said, "I've thought about you a lot."

I wanted to know, but I didn't want to ask. "I don't know if that's a good thing or a bad thing."

"It's all . . ." He stopped and blew air into his cheeks before expelling a heavy breath. "It's a mess."

He just seemed so sad. I mean, I was too, but the ache of regrets I felt was nothing compared to the ache I felt when I looked at his drawn face. And yet, part of me wondered if he regretted what he'd done to us. He'd cut us off like it was nothing, like that kind of connection was expendable or easily replaced.

But now did he, who clearly still had feelings for me after all these years and who obviously knew I did too, ever regret detonating the single most loving and cohesive relationship either one of us would ever have?

"Well," I said stupidly, "we survived it anyway."

He flattened his mouth into a grim line.

"Good night!" Theresa flung herself toward me. "It's been so great to see you! We *have* to get together soon." She drew back and eyed me with surprising kindness, maybe even pity, saying deliberately, "Just us girls. There's a lot to catch up on."

More than she knew.

"We'll do it," I lied. "I'll call you."

"Thank you for inviting us," Rick said, shaking Nate's hand. He nodded toward Theresa. "You're a lucky man."

Nate's gaze moved to me. "You're not doing so badly yourself."

"I know it." Rick put his arm around me and it felt inappropriately intimate. But it wasn't, of course.

"Good to see you, Nate."

"You too, Erin."

The understanding between us was clear: there would never be understanding. The whole thing sucked.

And we both knew it.

Chapter 20

As soon as I got home, I called Jordan.

"How was it?" she asked immediately.

"It sucked. Of course. Theresa was completely enchanting; of course, Rick thought she was great. She *looked* great. Nate looked great too." Sudden, unexpected tears threatened. "It was pretty painful."

"God, I'm so sorry," Jordan said, her voice warm with compassion. "That must have been torture for you."

"You just have no idea. . . ." I recalled the feel of Nate's gaze on me, the way his heat found me when he got anywhere near me. "And, of course, Rick thought it was great."

"Sounds like a nightmare," she said. "I mean, literally, it sounds like a nightmare."

"Okay, so what does it mean, that Nate kept looking at me all night long?"

"It means you've been magically transported back to high school and you're asking your best friend to read a guy's mind for you."

"You're supposed to be an expert! Is this what your patients pay you two hundred and fifty bucks an hour for?"

"My patients pay me to be objective, which I cannot do with you. I didn't see how he was looking at you. But if he's the guy he used to be, or the guy I think he used to be, then whatever he's thinking is probably exactly what you think he's thinking, because you two were always sharing one mind."

Something in me deflated. That was true. But I would have preferred to discover, or finally feel, that ours had been the kind of teenage relationship that didn't have any real significance. Plenty of people could chuckle at themselves now and say that they hadn't known what love was back then and that they hadn't even known themselves, but, damn it, I knew exactly what love was—then and now—and I'd known myself as well then as I did now.

Maybe I was wrong about both, but if I was, at least I was as wrong as ever.

"Plus," Jordan went on, "he could always read you really well. If you were angsting tonight, he probably picked up on it and was concerned about you."

"It didn't take Carnac to figure *that* out."

"And maybe he picked up on the fact that you dream of having wild animal sex with him."

"*What?*"

"I'm *kidding.*" She laughed, but then I could imagine her arching her brow. "Aren't I?"

I closed my eyes and tried to blot out the torrid images that suddenly came to mind. They'd be back. They'd been dancing around there ever since we'd enacted them. "So, what, you're going to help me or just make fun of me and make me cry?"

That made her laugh even more, and I smiled at the sound. Maybe this, right here, was a good example of why you *shouldn't* marry your high school boyfriend or girlfriend—because you are never completely grown-up around someone you've known since you were thirteen.

"I'm sorry," she said, sobering slowly.

"Honestly, Jordan, do you think our relationship was unusual? Was it more than just the usual puppy love? Or am I making way too much of this?"

"No, no," she said. "It was unusual. For one thing, you were way too young to handle that kind of emotion, and for another, it went on way too long. How long were you guys together?"

"Two years." It *was* a long time. Eight long seasons. Two long D.C. winters, which in themselves seem to last years. Two Christmases. Four birthdays.

Two anniversaries.

"Then on and off and back and forth for another couple," I added.

She clicked her tongue against her teeth. "I wish your parents hadn't allowed you to do that."

"If they hadn't you wouldn't have had nearly so much fun," I said, though privately I'd had the thought myself that I wished my parents hadn't allowed me to spend *all* my time wrapped up in a relationship.

I would have hated them for it at the time, probably, but they would have been right.

"True," she agreed with a small laugh. "But I was probably a bad influence too."

"Probably." I loved her. I was incredibly lucky to have a friend like her.

"But that isn't the point now. It was what it was."

"Helpful."

"I wish I could help you."

I sighed. "I do too."

It wasn't that I wanted to steal him away or have him back for myself—it was impossible to even think about that—what I really needed was to sort out the past. I wanted to know what really happened and if he'd regretted it and how the years had shaken down his memories of me and feelings for me.

Were they gone?

Were they stuffed away like an old baby blanket in storage?

Had they, maybe, never really existed at all?

"You should talk to him about it," Jordan said.

"No," I said. "I can't. Not directly."

"Why not?"

"Because I'd sound like a psycho. He's *married*. I need to figure out a way to dance around the point until *he* lands on it."

Jordan groaned. "You *are* a psycho. And I have to hang up and go to sleep."

I glanced at the clock on my desk. It was almost eleven thirty. Sleep would probably be a mercy to me too. "Thank you," I said sincerely. "For everything."

"Please consider what I said. You really do have a little blip to resolve here and the best way to do that is just come at all this stuff head-on. It's not that big a deal, but if you keep sweating it and overthinking it, it's going to feel bigger and bigger until eventually you won't be able to keep your perspective when you think about it. That's how a little blip becomes a big problem."

I sighed. "You're a wise old woman, I'll give you that."

"I am, you're right. Now go to sleep yourself. You've had a rough night."

We hung up and I went to bed, but I don't think I slept at all.

All I could do was think about Nate. Weirdly, it wasn't all "Nate and Theresa," because the reality of the situation was beyond that. If they'd been clearly in love, then maybe I would have had some indulgently petty feelings about that, and I'm not sure where it would have gone from there.

But the fact that he looked so sad, so *haunted*, grabbed me by the heart and wouldn't let go.

And that was one of the reasons I knew I truly loved him.

Still.

———

Producer Pippa was dancing on my last nerve.

Roxanne's party wasn't the only thing we had going on. Granted, the fact that it was going to be on that stupid TV show made it a bigger deal and put our reputation on the line a bit more, but our reputation wasn't going to be too pretty if word got around that the place was crawling with TV cameras and wires, etc., and that the entire staff was so busy kowtowing to a bratty sixteen-year-old that they weren't paying attention to the other hotel guests.

But it seemed everyone except me was ready for their close-up.

Jeremy more than anyone.

"Where is Roxanne?" he asked me, kneading his hands in front of him. It had been days since he'd run into the table, and his eye was still caked in makeup, the swelling more obvious than he thought. Odd, considering how freaked he'd been about a blemish that *hadn't* been there, but I guess he had come too close to missing his opportunity to be on TV. Now he was willing to yield a little on his physical appearance.

"I don't think she's here," I said.

"She was supposed to be here half an hour ago. Pippa wants to show us discussing the options for her party."

"But we already discussed them." I looked at him more closely. "Is that *eyeliner* you're wearing over your black eye? So, like, you covered the black eye, then added black to it?"

He sighed. "I'm simply enhancing my eyes for the camera. So they look like eyes and not just"—he tossed his hands—"two shiny spots on my face."

I nodded. "Likewise the lipstick."

"I am *not* wearing *lipstick*."

"Jeremy."

"It's just a subtle little liner."

As subtle as Eddie Izzard. "Looks good, Jeremy, but they show this stuff in HD, you know. You better hope it doesn't look like makeup over a wound on camera. Unless, of course, that's the look you're going for."

He raised the back of his hand to his mouth. "Do you really think it's too much?"

"I think you should revisit it."

Pippa showed up then. Well, bustled up. She seemed to move in short, staccato, almost violent steps. "Erin, we need you to suggest these things to Roxanne." She handed me a sheet of paper.

I looked at it. *Fleet of Hummers to bring guests, forty-foot volcano, fortune cookie invitations and rejections* . . . This was ridiculous. "A volcano would go against the fire code, of course."

"Where there's a will, there's a way."

"But if this isn't *her* will, I don't see the point in borrowing trouble so she wants impossible things this way."

Pippa would hear none of it. "Nothing's impossible!"

"Yes, I think the volcano actually is." I looked at the list again. "And what are fortune cookie rejections?"

"Oh, they're excellent. She has a bunch of eager friends hanging around to see if they get invited and they find out by opening a fortune cookie!"

"So some will open a cookie and get a *no*?"

Pippa's eyes lit up. "Good, right? Tyra did something similar on *America's Next Top Model*."

"That's just mean."

"Good viewing, dear. Good viewing."

I went back to the list. "And there's just no way the health department *or* the ASPCA is going to let us have a hundred and one Dalmatian puppies milling around."

She sucked the air in through her teeth. "Yes, we did run into that problem once before. Best not to use the words *puppy* and *milling* in the same sentence, believe me."

Bill arrived then, thank God. "Pippa," he said, "the dog thing would be a mess, even if it were possible. Totally unpredictable."

Clearly she loved the idea of that being the big birthday catastrophe that put the drama in the episode.

Bill must have noticed that look come into her eye too, because then he added, "And you don't want the liability for personal injury or equipment."

That did it. The shrewd look came back into her eye and she gave a quick nod. "Well played, Watts. Now can you please talk to Erin here about her chat with Roxanne? We need something camera-worthy."

"Oh, I think now that Jeremy's back, he'll be doing anything you need done on camera," I said quickly.

"Jeremy?" Pippa looked blank.

"The guy with the makeup," Bill told her.

I cringed inwardly. Jeremy would be horrified. But, really, he shouldn't have put the makeup on if people noticing it was going to horrify him.

"Him! No, no, no, we're going to stick with you, honey, the camera likes you better. And he's clumsy, isn't he?"

"Thanks, but I'm really not interested."

"Nonsense, of course you are!" She was off without bothering to wait for an answer.

I looked imploringly at Bill. "I'm really not."

"The problem is you're the only one who's really telegenic. I don't think she's going to let up on this."

"But Jeremy went to take the makeup off," I said. "Or at last make it more subtle. He'll probably keep the cover over his bruises. Anyway, I'm sure he'll look a lot more telegenic now."

Bill laughed. "The makeup was just the icing. What Pippa's looking for is someone sympathetic for the audience to identify with when the snotty sixteen-year-old starts throwing a fit."

I had to laugh at his unexpected frankness. "A sacrificial lamb."

"Exactly."

"That sort of stinks."

He nodded. "Tell me about it. But, listen, let me tell you a little secret. If you refuse, Pippa's not going to give up the idea. She's just going to go ahead and use unflattering footage of you anyway. It'll still be better than she'll get from your friend. So if you want to have some control over this, you might consider just going with it."

Jeremy would be *so* disappointed. I could already picture his crestfallen lined and shaded eyes. "I just really, *really* don't want to do this," I said. "Really."

"Gotcha."

"But you're saying she'll find a way regardless."

"Yup."

I let out a long breath. "Can you help me sort of integrate Jeremy into the interviews? Maybe do both of us?"

He considered for a moment. "I can try. Yeah, I think I can do that."

"Okay. So what is it you need now?"

"Pippa gave you the list, I see." He nodded at the paper in my hand with a wry smile.

"I'm not saying this stuff."

"Of course not. What you'll suggest is all the things you've already suggested that she's already nixed."

"Oooh! Good thinking!"

He gave a nod. "Plus a few of the absurd requests that you're able to accommodate."

"There are a few of those."

"Believe me, there's always a train wreck of some sort at these things." He shrugged and ran a hand through his shaggy hair. "Pippa doesn't need to manufacture one. I just want you to be as prepared as you can be."

"Thanks." I gave a wave as he went back to production.

"Erin!"

I started, having rarely heard my name whined in quite such a screechy way.

It was, of course, Roxanne.

"There you are!" I said, falsely bright.

"Did you convince Justin to come yet?"

Jesus, she was like a tape machine playing the same thing over and over again. "Well, like I told you, I don't think he's going to do that unless he comes to the conclusion himself. But the guest list has tons of guys on it. Don't waste your time on one like that. He doesn't deserve you."

Her eyes filled with tears. I had the distinct impression she was able to do this on command and it had probably gotten her a lot of valuable goodies from Mommy and Daddy. "I'm *counting* on having a boyfriend there! Otherwise, I'll look like such a loser!"

I pinched the bridge of my nose, trying to stave off the migraine that was rapidly coming on. "Actually, Roxanne? I just can't control every—" I stopped. No, I couldn't control everything. But I might be able to control this, at least a little bit. "I've got a great idea."

Her eyes brightened. "What is it?"

"What if we picked out the absolute best, hottest guy and made him your boyfriend for the night?"

"But you said he wouldn't come."

Oh, please. Like the Justin I'd talked to was the best, hottest guy. There was no way. "No, I mean hire a model or actor." We'd done that on a number of occasions at the hotel, invited ringers to events to get out there and dance and be attractive and basically work the room to make it seem like the party was a success even if it was filled with dullards.

"You mean hire someone to fake it?"

I shrugged, afraid she was going to be offended. "Sure. That way you can make up whatever story you want about how you met, how close you are, whatever, and everyone will think you have this amazing boyfriend who goes to another school."

She scratched her head. "Hm."

I waited. It was the best offer she was going to get.

"Do you have pictures?" she asked.

"I can get them."

"Okay." She nodded. "Do it!"

Pippa ran over then, dragging a cameraman whose name, I'd learned, was Tiny (he was neither big nor small, so I have no idea why), behind her. "Get this!" she rasped to him in a stage whisper that I guess she thought Roxanne wouldn't be able to hear.

"Um." The camera was so close it almost knocked me in the cheek. I put up a hand to stave him off. "Roxanne." I saw her eyes drift over to the camera and then fill with tears again.

Uh-oh, she was eating this up.

"I . . . can't . . . live . . . without him! He *has* to come!" she wailed, obviously continuing an earlier scene in which she'd mourned the loss of Justin.

Shit. The camera swung over to me. "Roxanne." I licked my parched lips. "We *just* talked about this—" What was I doing? I should be saying *fuck fuck fuck* so it was unusable footage.

Too late. "Oh, *thank* you for helping!" She threw her arms around my neck and squeezed uncomfortably tight.

"Is this the guy in Afghan we're talking about?" Pippa asked with a smirk.

I looked at her. "He's back in the States now."

"Mmmn."

But it became clear that Roxanne was into the idea of a hired boyfriend. She was just creating a "boyfriend drama story line" . . . I'd come to understand something of the way she thought.

God help me.

———

"Mom, Jordan knew Nate, right?"

It was so strange to hear Nate's name coming out of Cam's mouth that I think I might have actually jumped a little. "Yes, she did."

"So did you talk to her after your dinner with him?"

Had Cam heard me talking to Jordan? I rewound what I could recall of the conversation, hoping I hadn't said anything incriminating. "Yes," I said evenly. "It was a little hard for me, so I talked to her about it afterwards."

Cam plunked down on the sofa next to me. "Why was it hard?"

What had I said? Was she quizzing me to see if I'd tell the truth when pressed? Did she already know too many elements of the truth for me to lie about it now?

"Because it's always emotional to see people you haven't seen in a long time," I said. "Especially if they're people you were really close to once."

"Like you and Nate."

"And Theresa."

"But . . ." She sighed. "Never mind."

She wanted to know more about Nate and me. I wasn't ready to tell her more, though. As a compromise, I told her, "Look, just because you get older doesn't mean you totally grow up. Part of me felt really weird seeing my old boyfriend and my old friend married to each other."

Cam eyes lit with interest. "Were there sparks between you and Nate? Did you feel the way you used to?"

I was very glad she covered her first question with the second. "No, I don't feel the way I used to. It's been a long time and we're not the same people we were."

"But were you jealous?" She screwed up her face. "Because I kind of am, and I don't even know them."

I frowned. "It was definitely disconcerting. And, honestly, if I'd known way back then that this would happen someday, it would have just killed me. I guess that's why we don't get to know our future until it comes to us in time, huh?"

"But maybe you could have stopped it!"

I'd done everything I could to get him back. There was no way I could have stopped this. "Things happen for a reason," I said, without really believing it. "We just don't always know what the reason is."

Now, normally I wouldn't be a fan of saying something to my daughter that I didn't really believe, but when I was her age there were a *lot* of days when having faith was the only thing that got me through.

I didn't need to inject her with cynicism about that.

"Did I ever tell you how I met Jordan?" I asked, trying to deflect the conversation off of Nate.

"How?"

"We were in the library and this obnoxious boy stole my purse and wouldn't give it back. He was just messing around, but he looked at her and asked her if he should give it back to me."

Cam laughed. "And of course she said yes!"

"Yup. A lesser girl would have taken the opportunity to flirt with him, but she made it completely clear she thought he was being a jerk."

"So he gave it back?"

"And left immediately, shamed." I smiled, remembering. Marvin Borniak. He had been *so* obnoxious, for the entire two years I'd gone to school with him. "Never knowing he'd planted the seed for such a long-lasting friendship."

"Wow."

"Right?"

She laughed. "You should find him on Facebook and tell him."

"I probably should." I reached out and ruffled her hair. "What do you think? Should we watch a movie tonight?"

"Actually, Amy and I were going to go do a *Glee* marathon at her house and eat tons of Ben & Jerry's. But I can stay here if you want."

"No, no, no, that's okay." I smiled. "A *Glee* and ice-cream marathon sounds like just what you two need."

She got up and took her dishes to the sink, started for her room, then stopped and turned back. "Mom?"

"Mmm?"

"I'm really glad *we* can talk."

My heart swelled and I went to her and pulled her into my arms. "Me too, baby. Me too."

Chapter 21

The universe sends signs, even when we're too stupid or bull-headed to see them.

When I went out to my car after work, I saw that the rear left tire was flat. Completely flat.

Now, here's a shameful admission—I never learned to change a tire. I absolutely *hate* the idea of having to count on a man for certain tasks, but, to me, car stuff and the removal of dead rodents would forever be the job of someone with a penis.

So I called Rick and asked him to come over and help.

While I waited for him to arrive, I sat on the hood of my car and looked at the stars and the moon. There was a night a million years ago that I could remember sitting by the lake in Potomac Falls with Nate, looking at the moonlight play on the water and the stars in the sky. It had been such a perfect children's storybook kind of evening that, ever since then, I'd come to associate it with happiness and love. All good things.

To this day, whenever there's a full moon I'm taken back to those carefree days and the feeling of looking at those stars, wishing on my whole, wide-open future.

It wasn't so wide open anymore, of course. Time had marched on and things had changed; being an adult wasn't nearly as exciting as being a kid looking forward to being an adult.

Once upon a time, Nate and I had been It. We'd talked all night on the phone, seen each other for hours every day, slept together, ate together, played together. Everyone thought of us as NateandErin. How had we gotten so far apart that it would be wrong for us to even talk to each other? If I were to call him and tell him I was thinking about him, it would be tantamount to adultery.

And we'd already done that.

I envied Roxanne and her stage in life. She had no idea how good she had it. She had no idea how many options were still open to her. Hell, if she played her cards right she could probably even still get that dimwit Justin back, though I didn't see her playing her cards right . . . or caring in a few months. They'd dated for all of a few weeks and, as far as I could tell, he had nothing to make him memorable apart from his complete asshole-ness. It was hard to imagine that even someone as shallow as Roxanne would miss that for very long.

God, I was such an old fogy. Sitting here thinking that youth was wasted on the young.

Rick drove up just when I was about to launch into a mental lecture about how far I had to walk to school as a child.

"I called Triple A," he said, getting out of the car and coming to me. He put his hands on my arms. "Are you okay?"

I frowned. "Well . . . yeah, it's just a flat tire. I didn't have an accident, you know."

"Well, it can be very dangerous to drive on a flat."

"I know. That's why I called you instead of driving on it." I considered for a minute. "Why did you call Triple A?"

"To change the tire."

"You can't change a tire?" This felt like something I should have already known.

He must have known his masculinity was slipping in my eyes because he said, "Can you?"

"Well, no, but I'm not a guy."

He was instantly defensive, of course. "Obviously I can change a tire, but I'm not exactly dressed for it. I came right from work."

He was right. He was in a two-thousand-dollar suit, it would have been insane for him to change the tire. But still . . . it seemed so *fussy* for a man to call Triple A for a tire change.

"They should be here in about an hour," Rick said.

"An *hour!*" I went to the trunk and opened it. "I'm going to try this myself."

He stood back, looking bemused. "You're going to try what?"

"Changing the tire." I flipped back the carpet and saw the spare tire pinned in by the jack. "I've seen it done before."

"Oh, for God's sake." He took off his jacket and loosened his tie.

I pulled the jack out and went to the tire to unscrew the bolts. "No, Rick, just go on. I've got this covered. I wouldn't want you to get your hands dirty." Okay, that was obnoxious. I really was kind of attacking his masculinity.

Fortunately, he had a pretty healthy ego and an even healthier sense of humor. "Okay. Let's see how you do, then," he said with a laugh, and he leaned on his BMW to watch me.

You know what's not self-explanatory? Assembling a jack. I was trying to get the pump thingy into the notch.

"Need help?" Rick asked.

"No!"

"That's the wrong end you're trying to fit in there."

"But the other end won't fit in this tiny hole!"

He came to me and turned the jack around. "No, but it will fit there." He indicated a bigger hole that suddenly seemed like the obvious place for the pump. "Here, let me do this."

It was immediately obvious that I wasn't able to do this myself and that I had made a big stupid ass of myself by suggesting I could. "I don't want you to get all messy."

He rolled up his sleeve. "It's fine. Call Triple A on my phone and cancel."

"Okay." I stepped back. No need for me to stand on pride. Within five minutes, he had the tire changed and the old one put back in the trunk.

And there was just enough grease on his two-hundred-dollar shirt that I knew it would never be the same.

I felt like such an asshole.

"You're lucky this is a full-sized spare," Rick said. "But we should still replace it."

I nodded. "Right. So, it's safe now? I can drive on it?"

He turned the corners of his mouth down, looked the car over, and nodded. "Yes."

"Wow. Thanks. I really appreciate it. Sorry I . . ." What? *Goaded you?* "I should have just waited for Triple A."

"Forget it," he said, in a way that made it obvious to me and anyone listening that I totally should have waited. "Look, it's been a long day, so I'm going to go on home. The girls could probably use some supervision anyway."

I nodded. "Talk to you tomorrow?"

"Sure." He got in his car and drove off.

And for the first time I really realized that I didn't have forever to make a decision about him and that, if I didn't straighten up, I might not be the one to make the decision at all.

Chapter 22

⁓

"Okay, Roxanne. Pick your fake boyfriend." I laid three eight-by-ten glossy head shots on the desk in front of her, each guy more gorgeous than the last, in that teen-movie sort of way.

She looked at them wide-eyed, then up at me. "Can I keep one?"

"Picture? Yes. Guy? No. You don't have that kind of budget."

"You've got good taste," she said, her eyes scanning the pictures. "I'm surprised."

I sighed. "Well, yes, I can vaguely remember what hot was way back when I was your age."

She nodded. She didn't get it at all. "I think this one." She pointed to Troy, who, I thought, was the least attractive of them all, thanks to his girlishly long eyelashes and full lips, but I knew that was in right now so I'd added him to the choices.

"You got it." I picked up the phone to call the modeling agency.

"But wait!"

I hung up.

"No, go ahead. That one."

"Are you sure?" I asked, my hand on the receiver.

"Yes." She said it impatiently, like I was the one holding things up. "God!" She pronounced it *goiy-d*. I was so sick of hearing it come out of her mouth over the past few weeks I could scream.

But the party was in three days now, and then it would be over.

"All right, stand by." I picked up the phone again and made the call, securing Troy for the party and arranging for him to arrive early so he could make his grand entrance with Roxanne. "It's done," I said when I hung up.

"Thanks." She did look delighted. "So I can keep the picture?"

"Of course." I was glad this had worked out, I have to say. There were times when I would have given *anything* to have a person like me there to create every illusion I wanted to present to the world. "Here's the story. You guys met at a baseball game a couple of weeks ago. You went with a friend, maybe from another school. Troy was playing, you caught the foul ball, and the rest . . . is history."

Her jaw dropped. "Did you come up with that?"

I nodded. "Not bad, huh?"

"It's perfect! My friend Denise in Delaware invited me to a minor league game just last week!"

"Well." I picked up the pictures of the other two boys. "Good that you went, then."

"Does *he* know the story?"

"He will. Troy hopes to be an actor someday"—like every pretty boy who looks like him and does musical theater—"so he's looking forward to the chance to use his acting chops."

"Oh, my *God*!" she squealed, and jumped up to shuffle around the desk in her stilettos and give me a hug. "You're so good at this! I'm so sorry I told everyone you suck."

"You told everyone I suck?"

She didn't even look embarrassed. "Well, when you couldn't get Justin to come . . ."

"Hm. That's the other thing. Justin *is* coming."

"*What?*" She started jumping up and down. Visions of broken ankles danced in my head. "Are you being completely serious with me right now?"

"Yes, but here's the thing, Roxanne. Don't throw yourself at him. You *have* to trust me on this. He'll be jealous when he sees you with Troy." *Because he's a total douche canoe who only wants what he can't have.* "You'll have your chance then to get him back, I think. Though I don't recommend it."

"Ooohh!" She squeezed me around the neck again. "This is *so* awesome! This is like the *best party ever!*"

"Good!"

"Where's the camera crew?" she wanted to know. "I have to go tell them you kick ass after all."

"They're out back getting more establishing shots and talking to Jeremy. And actually . . ." I took a breath and said what I had to. "Jeremy had a lot to do with this. He's the one you need to thank, not me." I am no saint. I really hated giving credit for what I'd done to someone else, but if I let her go out there and credit me, they were going to want to interview *me* for the camera, and that was the last thing I wanted. Better to let Jeremy take the credit.

He was the one who needed to know I'd done a good job. He'd get it once Roxanne started talking.

"Okay!" She shuffled out of my office and I got up and closed the door behind her.

I couldn't wait until this damn party was over.

———

Instead of going home that evening, I found myself turning toward Palisades. Toward Nate's house.

Okay, Nate and Theresa's house.

Why was it that I had such a continuously hard time factoring her into the equation? The fact of her should have been so troubling that she was never far from my mind, but somehow that was so big, or so bad, or so *crazy* that I just couldn't add it to the equation.

And that was where my wrong thinking began.

Because what equation was this? The equation to getting back with Nate? For one thing, he hadn't offered, and for another, we hadn't known each other in a long, long time.

But, you know, there had been an ease to being around him that I found surprising. I hadn't even realized I'd missed that in other relationships until I was with Nate. And I don't just mean when I was naked—though that was certainly a good example—it was also when we were at his house and he just *got* it.

I've found it's hard to find people who *get it*. I could put a Journey song on and he'd know the words; I could make a *Good Times* reference and he'd know the mom's name was Florida; I could say *On Golden Pond* and he'd remember the same scene I was thinking of; and I could recall the time Jordan was catsitting and we all took over the apartment and the cat fell off the balcony and he'd remember the name of the maintenance man who broke the news.

He'd been there for so much of the stuff that formed me.

And that compelled me on as I steered onto MacArthur Boulevard, and then onto Keating, and—it's awful to admit this—past his house. Seriously, it was like being sixteen again. Driving past my ex-boyfriend's house. Maybe hoping to spot him in the window.

Unless spotting him meant spotting him and Theresa. Together in some way.

The lights were out, thank goodness. Nothing to see there. No reason to stop or even slow down.

No way to get myself into trouble.

Shamed, I accelerated out of his neighborhood and got back onto the anonymous safety of MacArthur. My heart was pounding, my hands were shaking, my mouth was dry.

This was too much emotion for something so long dead.

Something so clearly hopeless.

I saw a CVS ahead on the left and pulled into the parking lot. For a moment I sat in the car and flogged myself mentally for the stalker I'd become. This was crazy. I hated it.

I wasn't the kind of woman who sat up drinking wine and reading old love letters from a high school boyfriend. I wasn't the kind of woman who then obsessed over that old boyfriend to the point of driving miles out of the way to pass his house.

What was *happening* to me?

How had I unraveled so quickly, so *completely*?

I got out of the car and strode purposefully into CVS, determined to shake this budding obsession. I found a Vitaminwater in the refrigerator section, paid for it, then paused outside the door to take the lid off and throw the protective plastic away.

When I looked up I saw him.

Seriously. There he was. Right in front of me.

His face reflected the same surprise I felt.

"Nate."

He shook his head and looked down for a minute before meeting my eye. "A little far from your neighborhood, aren't you?"

"Yes." I nodded, holding his gaze. "I was stalking you by driving past your house."

"Yeah?"

I nodded again. "I'm about one tequila shot away from making you a mix tape."

He laughed. "And what would be on it?"

I swallowed, then remembered my water and took a sip before saying, "A whole bunch of songs that say what I can't."

His gaze traveled from my eyes to my mouth and back again. "Like what?"

"Like nothing that would be appropriate for me to say now."

Our eyes locked for what felt like a long time.

"Come here." He came to me, took me by the arm, and led me to his car. "Get in."

I did. Why? I don't know. I should have argued, stood my ground, refused to be manhandled, pointed out that we had other people and other obligations; in short, I should have been some sort of grown-up, I don't know.

But instead I willingly—eagerly—got in and sat in the passenger seat next to him.

Okay, actually I do know why. I wanted to know what he had to say. Standing my ground on some stupid principle would have deprived me of the one thing I wanted.

I wanted him to say something that would make me feel better.

He got in, closed the door, and turned to me. "I had *no idea* this would ever matter again."

"You had no idea what would matter?"

He shrugged. "*Anything* I did. As far as you're concerned, I mean. You were gone and I was the one who'd sent you away and by the time I got back it was too late. After that, I never even imagined our paths would cross again."

"We live within twenty-five miles of each other *and* of where we grew up!"

"In the capital of the free world! A metro area in excess of six million people! Look how long we've gone without running into each other at all!"

I nodded slowly. And if I hadn't actually walked past his mother's house on a holiday weekend, we might not have seen each other at all, possibly even for the rest of our lives.

Yet here we were.

"It's a big place," I agreed. "And it's been a long time."

"And for things to go . . . the way they did when you came by the house . . ." He shook his head. "I don't regret it." He met my eyes defiantly. "I'd do it again. But I wouldn't have anticipated it."

"Me neither." It was all I could say. Once upon a time I'd dreamed about it. A lot. Of course, Theresa knew that. Jordan knew that. Hell, even Nate probably knew that.

But I had long ago given up hope of ever having that particular brand of satisfaction.

"Erin." His hand moved toward me, but he didn't touch me. Still, the heat came at me as surely as if he had. "I made a huge mistake."

"Me too."

"Not as big as mine." He closed his eyes for a second, then looked at me. "When we broke up it hurt. A lot. But I had no idea how minor the stuff with Todd was compared to what happens in the real world. At the time it felt like everything. Only later I realized it was nothing. And then"—he shrugged—"it was too late."

"Why?" I had to ask. "Why was it too late?"

"Because you'd moved on."

"There was a lot of time between us breaking up and me getting pregnant," I pointed out. But how stupid, really. Quibbling about the years between major events, and who should have done what when.

This was an argument better suited to sixteen-year-olds than adults.

And that was exactly what I felt like: a sixteen-year-old, facing the boy who broke her heart and wanting to know *why*.

"I didn't want *feelings* to get in the way of what we needed to do with our lives."

"What the hell does *that* mean? What matters more than feelings?"

"That's exactly what I didn't want to think."

"What, the truth? We *loved* each other. How lucky were we for that? How stupid to let that go!"

"It didn't make sense to hold on to it just for its own sake," he said. "There were so many other things to do before either of us could settle down."

"Couldn't *logistics* have been figured out later?"

He met my gaze. "I couldn't go halfway with you."

Maybe I couldn't have either. Unless it was the only alternative to nothing. "It was better to be without me?"

He tightened his jaw. "I kept thinking it wouldn't matter soon. I just kept thinking that."

"How long did that take?"

A long tense moment passed between us.

"I'm still waiting."

My heart throbbed. Might as well go all the way with this. "Tell me about Theresa." I swallowed hard. "Tell me about you and Theresa."

"What do you want to know?"

"You know what I want to know." *Everything*.

He braced his hands against the steering wheel. "It wasn't . . ." He paused and tried again. "We were both living in Phoenix—"

"You *were*? *Both* of you? By coincidence?" Or was it fate?

He nodded. "Well, she was in Phoenix, and I was just outside, but we ended up having mutual friends and running into each other at a party. It was a lonely time in my life. I was working all the time, didn't know anyone outside of work, felt like a stranger in a strange land. . . ." He shrugged. "When I saw her, there was something so . . . familiar about it that I couldn't resist. We started seeing each other and even though it never reached that point of really being *in love* I just never got around to ending things."

"Never *got around* to it?" It was unfair to be so angry now, to be mad at fate or whatever had brought them together in addition to holding it against him, but I couldn't help it. "Wow, you wasted *no* time with me."

He winced. "It's not the same. This didn't matter as much. In the same way. And pushing her away would have felt a little like pushing you away too. Again."

"I don't see how. She's not me."

"No. She's not. I guess that was the problem."

"Surely you realized that before you married her." Despite myself, I was sad at the idea of him having what had to be a pretty difficult home life.

"Yes," he said. And it was clear there was no questioning it now. It had been a mistake and it no longer mattered why he'd made it or what he'd been thinking when he did.

"Nate, why are you staying in a marriage you don't want?"

"I thought it was because I'd made a promise I had to keep," he said, then looked at me again. "Now I don't know."

I did. Because sometimes in life you do something that seems right even if it doesn't *feel* right.

I cringed, picturing him planning it out, getting on one knee to propose, when, practically reading my mind, he said, "When Theresa suggested we get married, it seemed . . . reasonable."

When Theresa suggested . . . It didn't erase the facts, but it certainly added to them. "Why?"

"Because there was nothing else." He met my eyes. "There wasn't going to be anything else. There was no chance, I knew there was no chance, of really falling in love again."

Oh, God. I knew that feeling.

And sometimes grown people, who have actually *learned* something from their mistakes instead of just being doomed to repeat them until they die alone, needed to do the *right* thing, even if it wasn't the most gratifying thing.

"What a mess," I said to him. I wanted to reach for his hand, I wanted to touch him so badly, but it wasn't my place anymore.

"Big mess," he agreed.

He had no idea how big a mess this had become.

It had been almost two decades, yet part of me yearned for days that seemed like only moments ago, when Nate and I were free to do what we wanted, when we wanted, with each other, and no one would ever think twice about it.

Those days were long gone, tangled by the threads of more lives than I could even count at this point.

After a moment, I said, "I'd better go. I should have been home an hour ago."

"Is Rick waiting for you?"

"No." I swallowed. My lips ached to kiss him. My hands tingled, wanting to touch him. "I just shouldn't be here."

He nodded.

I got out of the car and went to mine, a few spaces over. He watched me go, I could feel it.

And it took all my willpower to keep moving and not turn back and run to him.

Chapter 23

Yes, I was nervous about Roxanne's party the next day, but that wasn't the reason I did what I did.

Well, *nervous* . . . I'm not sure that's the right word. I wasn't afraid of things going wrong, I was just wondering how many things *would* go wrong and how many Blame Balls would be lobbed at me for them.

Pippa had ordered what felt like hours of taped interviews and establishing shots. She'd talked to me, Jeremy, the chef, the parents, the most attractive *and* the most unstable friends, and absolutely anyone else who might have slipped up and said something unflattering about Roxanne.

Helicopters were out at the last minute—it didn't make for the most desirable sound—and somehow Pippa had talked Roxanne into a whole mermaid theme, which would begin with her being driven up in a giant fish tank. It looked something like a parade float, or something out of a Busby Berkeley film for synchronized swimmers.

It promised to be very embarrassing for anyone with the sense to feel humility.

So far that was only me. And that made me tense.

So when I got home that night and found Cam in my walk-in closet, surrounded by vestiges of Nate and me—in the form of letters, a prom garter, dead corsages, etc.—I nearly flipped out.

As in Nancy Grace could have talked about me for a week.

"What the hell are you *doing?*" I demanded, as soon as I saw her. Yes, she was my daughter, my flesh and blood, but this felt like a *huge* violation of my privacy.

"I'm doing what you *should* be doing, Mom," she patronized, better than a fifteen-year-old should have been able to. "I'm trying to figure out where things went wrong and how to fix them."

"Where *what* things went wrong?" I went over and started snatching things from the floor and putting them back into the box.

"Your relationship." She began picking up letters and holding on to them. "You are in love with this guy."

"*Was.*" I went to her, now competing to grab the letters off the floor around her ungracefully. "I *was* in love with him. I don't even know him anymore!" That was the truth.

And that was the hell of it all.

"You had dinner with him the other night!"

"Yes." I continued to pick up the envelopes, ticket stubs, and other memorabilia she'd strewn around. "And that was the first time I'd seen him in . . ." *Years* would have been perfect, but untrue. "*Ages.*"

"So all this"—she gestured now at my hands, because that's where most of the letters were—"is all meaningless? All those feelings you had, all those feelings *he* had and said to you in such *huge* ways, were all just fake?" Her voice was sharp with emotion. She didn't want it to be untrue.

"Give me the letters." I held out my hand.

"But—"

"*Now.*"

She handed them over and I shoved them into the box. My emotion took over. I had no control. My eyes burned like I'd gotten acid in them, and I turned away from Cam and sat on the end of my bed, still holding the box like a six-year-old getting ready to bury a beloved hamster. "Just go to your room. We'll talk about this later," I said, hoping to sound normal. Angry. Maternal. But normal.

Not like a fifteen-year-old basket case.

Unfortunately, basket case won out.

And Cam wasn't fooled. "Mom!" She rushed to me, kneeling before me with her hands in my lap. "Are you okay?"

Was I okay? How could I answer the one fate I couldn't live without—my daughter—that I *wasn't* okay because of the other fate I could never forget?

It wasn't even just Nate. It was the whole life we'd laid out, as two individuals together; a life that had been totally in line with who we essentially were because we'd planned it when we were too young to have piled on the baggage of realistic expectation.

Yet now, with the wisdom of more than twenty years past, I saw that the intentions of my younger self were more true to what I needed than anything I'd built on the details of my subsequent life. My ideals had disappeared somewhere along the way and I didn't even know where or what they were anymore.

I just knew they once felt like "me" and now very little did.

And I had to wonder if that was what was the most painful part of this episode—though, if it was, I don't know why Nate's face always had to be painted across the emotions.

"I'm okay," I said to Cam, in a fairly even voice considering, though we both knew it was untrue.

"Wasn't it real?" she asked after a moment, with something that looked like desperation in her face. "Didn't you *really* love each other?"

And that's when I lost it.

It's one thing to try and be a grown-up and hide your childish emotions to protect your child, but it's quite another to be pushed to the limit where you can't hold your emotions and, moreover, you can't even be sure that keeping them secret is the best thing for that child.

In short, in that moment, I had to make a decision whether to perpetrate the endless lie of *You'll meet The One when you're older* and *You'll know him when you see him*, or to just admit that, yes, sometimes maybe you meet someone perfect for you when you are a kid and you should try to scramble over all the childish impulses that come naturally to you in order to keep him.

Because I was honestly sure that—Cam aside—I would have been far happier all these years with Nate than without him.

And that was taking into consideration all the great things that had happened to me in my real adult life.

It still would have been better with him.

Now, how could I hide that, as it came to me right when Cam started questioning me?

Maybe someone stronger could have, but I couldn't.

Still, I tried to be the adult. As much as I could, that is, when I was obviously in tears. "Look, Cam," I said, opening up all the doors to honesty that I'd tried to keep shut. "Yes, I really, really loved him. And I think he loved me too. The same way. But I'm really torn about telling you the truth here, because I just don't *know* what would have happened." I shrugged. "And I really don't want to give you the impression that you're supposed to find the love of your life as a teenager, because most people don't."

"I know *that*," she said. "Obviously."

I was surprised. "You *do*?"

She looked at me like I was a pitiable moron. Which, maybe, I was. "Obviously. None of the coolest couples meet in *high school*." She rolled her eyes. "No offense. But it's not like I'm going to be trying to imitate that."

I had to smile. "Good."

She was on a roll. "I mean, can you imagine Brad and Angelina meeting in high school? I mean, I know they're kaput now, or so everyone's saying, but either way most normal hot relationships don't start in civics class. Jeez."

She was *so* right. Not only about Brad and Angelina—who were said to be totally kaput—but about the unliklihood of teenage romance ever meaning anything. I didn't know anyone who thought anything more than *I wonder how X is doing now* about their high school sweetheart.

I mean it, I really, literally didn't.

Why was I the lone exception that looked back, wishing, still, to be understood or forgiven or—maybe this was the big point—fought for?

Yet even that didn't feel right. What I longed for was just the everyday life I always thought I'd have with him: the intellectual equality, the same sense of humor, the same values . . . and I knew that Nate would feel like home to me no matter where we ended up living.

Nate was home, and I hadn't felt at home in years.

And I could go the rest of my life like this, don't get me wrong. This was reality and I'd certainly learned to adapt to that reality. I didn't love it, I'd never *loved* it, but I lived with it pretty well.

But it was a life spent denying something that had once felt important to me. Something that had once felt as obvious to me as breathing. And I don't just mean Nate; I mean the way it felt to love him and be loved by him. I had taken for granted that *that* was what love felt like, and that *that* feeling would always be part of my life.

That's the assumption, right? When you're young, you wonder who you'll marry when you grow up. Because, at least in my circle, marriage and family were always obviously going to happen.

Even into my twenties, as a single mother, I'd kept a tenuous hold on that assumption. *He*—whoever he was—was out there.

So it was kind of jarring to realize maybe that wasn't going to happen. Then it was depressing.

Then it was just how it was. I was resigned to the fact that passionate love wasn't going to be part of my adult life the way I'd assumed it would be when I was a kid.

Actually, I'd assumed that was how it was for everyone. Then I started noticing that people around me, people my age who had been married for years, still seemed to be in love. Jordan and her husband Curtis were a good example.

I didn't know where all this left me. All I knew for sure was that my life wasn't fulfilling in all the ways it could be and now my daughter was learning all the wrong things from me about relationships.

"Do you miss him?" Cam asked, interrupting the swell of thoughts and guilt that were taking over my mind.

"Nate?"

She nodded.

I hesitated. There had to be a way to say this properly. To phrase it like an Oprah interview somehow. I ran my hands through my hair and took a breath that felt like it came from underwater.

"Until recently, I hardly ever thought of him," I said. True. Yet the reason was that it was too painful to think of him. There was no resolution, just an open-ended question. Who needs that?

Cam furrowed her brow. "That's just really sad."

"Sad? Why? Isn't it better if you move on and don't hold on to that kind of thing?"

She shrugged. "You wrote all this stuff in your diary about how much you loved him and what it was going to be like when you were old together. Like that movie you both saw—"

"Whoa! You *read my diary* too?"

"Well, it's *ancient*! Do you really care if I read something you wrote when you were fifteen?"

Um, *yes*. There were enough details in there to lose me credibility in just about every arena with her: sex, alcohol, sneaking out. . . . Of course I didn't want her reading it! "Cam, that's private stuff no matter how old it is. How much did you read?"

I saw her trying to guess how much she could play this to her advantage and realized, right away, that she hadn't gotten any real dirt. "Just a little," she admitted. "There was stuff, like, about him going to the barn with you and you wishing on a star that you'd marry him. That's what's so sad. You loved each other *soo* much. You wanted to *marry* him! And now you're just all, *Yeah, I saw him, it was nice, la-di-da. . . .*"

I sighed. "Okay, well, it wasn't nice, and it definitely wasn't *la-di-da*. But once you're grown, you can't really sit around your room sobbing to old records about the one person you'll never forget. You have to move on and live your life. Sometimes that means not allowing yourself to indulge in those melancholy thoughts."

She really did look sad. This had affected her, whether it should or not, in some sort of real way. "Then how do you ever trust anything you feel? Are all my feelings wrong right now? Will they be in two years?" A challenge rose in her voice. "When do you reach the point where you can *believe* what you feel? Eighteen? Twenty-one? Do you even believe anything you feel now? I don't see how you could."

Some small, teenagery part of me resented her assault on me like this, but now wasn't the time for me to be adolescent.

"Cam," I said, quietly but firmly, "you know in your heart what's real and what isn't. The mistake we tend to make as teenagers is that we believe it all without really thinking about it. That's why you make deals with God to please please please let you marry some punk you've got a crush on and a month later the sight of him makes you sick."

She laughed reluctantly. "But that's not how it was for you."

I hesitated. "No. It wasn't. If I had it to do over again, I'd treat the whole thing with a lot more respect. I would have honored my feelings more and understood that, even though I was young, they were real and rare. And I would have honored his feelings a lot more too. I would have treated him with a lot more respect. That's the lesson to take out of this—don't treat someone in a way that you wouldn't want to be treated. You can quote me on that."

She persisted, ignoring my levity. "What *happened*? Why did you break up?"

I considered her for a moment. "Because I flirted with one of his friends."

She waited for a moment, then her jaw dropped. "That's *it*? That's *all*?"

"Well . . . I think I kissed him for a few seconds. I can't honestly remember for sure now. But he came to my house in the middle of the night, and . . . it looked bad." I thought back on it. "It looked really bad."

"But that was *all* you did?"

I nodded. "It was enough."

She lowered her brow. "That's just weird. If he loved you so much, why would he let you go because of something so small?"

Exactly! That had been *exactly* my question at the time. Now I understood a little more, though. A little, I thought. "He took it as a measure of respect, or, more specifically, *lack* of respect. It didn't ultimately matter what I did or didn't do; as he saw it, the intention to flirt with someone else was there and it didn't matter to me that it was his friend or that his other friends would see it. That was bigger to him than one mistake."

"What a douche!"

"Cam!" I cautioned her. I hated hearing that kind of thing come out of her mouth even though I said worse all the time. "This is what I'm saying: you have to see someone else's point of view. I didn't treat him with enough respect and finally that broke us."

"Sounds like a big ego problem to me."

I sighed. "The night it happened, his parents had announced they were getting a divorce. I found that out later. I guess he wasn't feeling all that up on relationships in general." It was a big deal. I knew later it had been a *very* big deal to him. Of course.

But honestly, at the time I'd been such a selfish adolescent that even if he'd told me, I probably still would have argued that he wasn't being nice enough to *me*.

Cam rolled her eyes. "So much for love."

I shook my head. "Listen, Cam, seriously. You need to hear me telling you this, because it's one of the most important lessons you can learn. If you love someone, you should make sure they know it every day and make even more sure you never hurt them in the name of gratifying your own ego, which was what I did."

"You mean because it flattered you that this other guy was interested."

"Yup." At that age, still so close to a particularly awkward and gawky adolescence, I had been very vulnerable to ego gratification. I looked down. "I knew Nate was off that night, acting weird, but I didn't even ask him what was going on." My hands felt shaky, thinking about it. I laced my fingers tight. "That was pretty crappy of me."

And it had never *once* occurred to me to consider how that might have made anyone else feel. At least not until Nate dumped me.

"I don't know." She looked skeptical. "I still can't see how he let that end everything when he loved you so much."

"Maybe he didn't." I shrugged. "Or maybe he did and he regretted it later." I remembered his words from just the other day.

I had no idea this would ever matter again.

"We both should have listened to our hearts more," I added. "We just didn't know it at the time. Neither of us knew it."

"I think it sucks," Cam concluded.

"It did." I went and gave her a hug. Suddenly this conversation was too heavy for me to carry. "Now you know everything you need to know about my deep, dark past. So go clean up your room and stay out of my private stuff from now on, would you?"

"I'm sorry. I really thought it wouldn't matter because it was so old."

"Hey. Calling me old isn't going to help!"

She laughed, then sobered and said, "So tell me one more thing. When did everything change?"

"What do you mean?"

"When did you decide not to listen to your heart anymore?"

"Who said I'm not?"

"Are you in love with Rick? I mean, I think you're talking about marrying him, but I don't see you acting like he's the big love of your life or anything. You haven't doodled *Mr. and Mrs. Rick Samuels* or *Erin Samuels* on *anything*."

Another diary reference. I could tell these were going to get old fast. "Yeah, well, I also haven't doodled *Erin Lawson* anywhere in a while either, so your example proves nothing." Except it did. I hadn't even toyed with our names together, Rick's and mine, in my head. Rings, names, retirement plans . . . none of the stuff that usually came with marriage had entered my mind at all. "So, Cam, I have a question and I want you to answer it honestly. Please."

"Okay . . . ?"

"If things didn't work out with Rick and me, would that be a problem for your friendship with Amy?"

I thought she'd think about it for a moment, maybe wince or pale or have some other telltale sign of concern, but instead she looked at me like I was nuts. "No!"

"No?"

"Um, *no*."

"Okay, elaborate. I need more than *no*. How could that just be okay for you two?"

"Because we're not friends because of *you two*. Jeez, Mom, I'm not a baby. You don't make or break my friendships." She looked at me and her tone softened. "I mean, I *appreciate* that you care, I really do, but Amy and I were friends before you and Rick got together and, in some ways, we'd probably be better friends if you *weren't* together."

"Really?"

She shrugged. "Well, I don't know, obviously it's cool if we become, like, sisters. But there's a little bit of my-real-dad-versus-your-dad, and my-real-mom-versus-your-mom between us, and it would be kind of cool to *not* have that." She paused for just a second before adding, "Not that it's a problem. I mean, don't break up with him because of that. But, Mom, seriously. If you never got over someone else—not that I'm saying you never got over someone else"—she looked at me pointedly—"but if you didn't, you would be stupid to marry Rick."

Stupid.

The mouths of babes.

"I'll take that into consideration," I said, already considering Nate for the forty millionth time that day. His lips, his tongue, his hands, his . . . everything. His everything. "Now go," I said, because I wasn't really holding it together all that well. I wanted to be alone. "You've got things to do that *don't* involve violating my privacy."

"Fine, fine, fine. But promise me you heard what I said."

"Oh, I heard you. Loud and clear."

"Good. And good night." She went.

And as I put the letters back in the box, touching them slowly and with great sadness, I wondered when, exactly, I'd gotten to be such a basket case.

And how, in the process of me trying to explain to her that she needed to keep her life fun and light for as long as possible, I had instead ended up explaining how very dark mine had gotten because I lost a boy at a young age.

Instead of encouraging her to believe the very thing I wished I'd believed and followed with my whole heart—when you're grown up and truly ready for it love will find you—I'd ended up telling her I'd lost the love of my life as a teenager and I never found another one.

As things go, this was not my greatest parenting moment.

But it *was* a decent human being moment and my talk with Cam had served to remind me how important it was for me to treat Rick with the respect he was due, instead of just thinking about how all of this affected me.

It was time I learned from my own mistakes.

And then, just like that, I broke down. Sitting there, a grown woman, surrounded by the relics of a life that didn't even feel like mine anymore, I cried like I hadn't cried in twenty-three years. It was the kind of sobbing that just propelled itself: I couldn't breathe, couldn't see, couldn't do anything except cry out this deep, primal grief.

When it finally subsided, I was spent. I lay down on the floor where I was and just closed my eyes until the past receded and I fell asleep.

So when I asked Rick to come over and talk the next night, and sent Cam to her grandmother's place instead of off with Amy, it wasn't because my nerves were raw and I was at the end of my rope. That wasn't the right place to make this decision from.

I made the decision because I'd realized that Rick deserved to spend his life with someone who loved him so much that, if they were separated, she'd spend two decades pining for him.

Clearly that wasn't me.

The ugly truth was that I had considered accepting his proposal even after I'd realized I would never love him enough. It would have been easy. Good on paper. He had a good job, good benefits, if we decided to have more children and I wanted to stay home with them I could. He was good-looking, smart, and just about everything a woman could want in a man.

Believe me, I was not proud of the fact that I had to be the exception who wanted something else. It wasn't because I took him for granted or didn't see his assets for what they were.

Rick was in his mid-thirties. He had a long life ahead of him and he deserved passion and romance and blind, loving devotion.

I couldn't give that to him.

That didn't make it an easy conversation.

"Have you come up with an answer?" he asked eagerly after I ushered him over to the sofa.

Oh, no. He thought this was going in a different direction. "That's what I wanted to talk to you about."

Somehow he missed the clear signal in my tone. "Okay." He looked at me expectantly. "What'll it be? Yes or yes?"

"Oh, Rick . . ." I touched his hand.

"Erin." He really wasn't getting it. Every syllable he uttered was confident.

I guess we really believe *no news is good news* on a very deep level.

So I had to just get it out quickly. "You don't want me to marry you," I said. That was awkward. Backward.

He frowned. "Yes, I do. That's why I asked." He reached for my hands, as if to reassure me, then stopped. "Wait a minute, is this a blow-off?"

"No, I'm not blowing you off," I argued, adding quickly, "I'm trying to be fair to you." Even as I said the words, I could hear what a hollow consolation they were, however sincerely I meant them. "You need more than I can give you."

His expression hardened. "So it's no, then."

"It's no, but it's because I really care about you and want you to have everything in life that you deserve."

He paused, then sighed heavily. "May I ask if there's someone else in the way?"

Someone else *in the way.*

That sounded so easy to push aside.

"No," I said. Because, really, I was the only one "in the way" of this. "Of course there isn't."

He looked dubious. "Are you sure?"

"This isn't about someone else. It's about you and me. It's about me not loving you the way you should be loved if you're going to commit your life to someone. You deserve someone who will love you with all her heart and soul forever, not someone who will take your life, and your love, and 'make do.'"

Okay, the minute I said it, I knew it had come out way worse than I'd intended. I mean, it was true, and I did mean what I said, I just didn't mean to imply that I had been "making do" with him in the time we'd been together, or that I would have had any right to continue to do that into an indefinite future.

"All right." He stood up. His face was grim.

"Rick, please don't—"

He held up a hand and I stopped.

Instead I nodded. "I'll be at work all day tomorrow. That VTV thing."

"Great." His voice was flat. "I'll leave the key on the counter when I go."

I felt immeasurably sad and stood up to walk him to the door, but again he stopped me.

"I'm so sorry," I said idiotically, standing in the middle of my living room. "I know it sounds like a cliché, but I'd really like for us to be friends. Maybe not right away, I know that might be hard, but someday. . . ." That was a shitty thing to say at a time like this. Even though I meant it sincerely, that kind of thing could only sound like the offer of a lame consolation prize.

A white "participation" ribbon instead of the blue.

"I'll pass," he said briskly.

I sighed and watched him go. There was nothing else I could say. Anything nice I tried to eke out would only sound condescending. I just had to let him go.

And actually I knew from experience that anger was preferable to tears. Lucky Rick—he could huff out and tie one on, grousing about how awful I was, until finally some pretty young thing distracted him.

Honestly, that was my biggest hope. It would be a huge relief for me to know he'd moved on with someone better for him.

In the meantime, here I was, alone in the wreckage of another failed relationship. I didn't want to be a bitter old curmudgeon at my age, but I really had to wonder if this was worth it. I'd been breaking up with guys for twenty-three years now.

It was getting old.

I went into the kitchen and heated up water for tea. While I stood there, bare feet on the cold linoleum, I remembered Pete Hagar suddenly. That had been, what, eleventh grade? I'd gone out with him for a month and then broke up with him in his car at the end of a date.

Then I'd run to Nate's house and begged him to take me back.

I'd wanted to break up with Pete for at least a week before doing it in that case, but had put it off, dreading the fallout. We went to school together and it was bound to be awkward afterward.

And it was.

But the only regret I had was that I'd ever gone out with him in the first place. I'd come so close to losing Nate that even after he'd taken me back that night and told me he loved me, I went home and cried like I'd watched *Brian's Song* three times in a row.

I wished I could run to Nate now.

I wished I could run anywhere that would make me feel safe and sane and less alone.

Instead I just went to bed.

———

I had warned everyone it might rain. Obviously, it might rain. The forecast said there was a fifty percent chance.

They should have had a contingency plan.

But no one would listen to me when I suggested that, so when

Roxanne was carted in as a "mermaid," in her giant fish tank pulled by the cab of an eighteen-wheeler, I was hoping against hope that there wouldn't be any thunder and lightning.

Her guests waited, shivering and cold, in the downpour and watched Roxanne do a little swim show that had the overall impression of being a stripper show. Then she climbed the ladder and was assisted out of the tank by two gorgeous gay actors I'd hired for that purpose.

Unfortunately, the rain made the edge of the tank even more slippery and she stumbled, falling back into the water with an unceremonious crash.

To her credit, though, she did a little flip like the whole thing had happened on purpose and climbed out again. I was probably the only one who noticed how white her knuckles were as she held on to her escorts.

They helped her off the float and led her to her date for the evening, Troy, who hooked his arm through hers and led her like a queen into the indoor water-park area.

Everyone else followed gratefully.

As she passed me she muttered, "*That* was not cool. You should have made sure it wasn't slippery."

I simply smiled and held my hands out. Surrender.

"Turn up the heat in the pool area," Jeremy said into his walkie-talkie as he came over to me. "The guests are freezing to death." He put it away and gave me a look. "That? Was a disaster."

I shrugged. "Could have been worse." Thunder rumbled in the distance as if on cue. "See?"

"Let's get inside before we're killed," he said, taking me by the arm.

We went into the pool house and there was faint music playing in the corner. Kind of like a cheap tinny music box. "Is that the band?" I asked, cocking my head and listening.

"Yes." Jeremy rolled his black-lined eyes. "One of their speakers blew, so that's as loud as they can play."

"What a weird problem," I said. I'd never run into this before. Having a band playing quietly was more annoying than having them play too loud. It created the impression of ignoring someone, which was a subtle distinction—but important—from talking over them. "We have to have someone bring the sound system from inside and set it up out here."

"Obviously, I have already gotten the men working on that," Jeremy said. "In the meantime maybe we should sing along, loudly."

I laughed. "Yeah, because *that's* what we want to see on TV. You and me caterwauling like drunk karaoke barflies."

He appeared to consider that for a moment before agreeing. "That wouldn't be very hot."

I looked at him. "No. Not hot. Not cool. Now, you check on the activity, since that's where the cameras are most likely to be, and I'll check on the food."

He gave me the thumbs-up and went off in search of his close-up.

The next thing I knew, Pippa had sidled up next to me. "I really thought there was going to be lightning when she was getting out of the tank," she commented.

"Oh, I know, can you *imagine*?" I looked at her and saw that, yes, she *had* imagined.

And she was apparently disappointed that it hadn't come to fruition.

"Wow," I said despite myself, and shook my head. "This is an ugly business."

She glanced at me sideways. "Someone's got to do it."

Yes, and unfortunately there was always someone willing to have it done *to* them. Front, back, and sideways.

The thing that sucked here was that it was the *parents* who had to consent and the kids who might regret it all later.

"I'm going to check on the food," I said, and didn't wait for an answer before leaving. If I'd let fly with what was really on my mind, she would have magically summoned a cameraman and I would probably become the next YouTube idiot making the rounds for a few days.

The food was beautiful, I'm glad to say, even the small seashell-shaped peanut butter and jelly sandwiches Roxanne had requested. But I noticed as I looked it all over and talked with the caterers that it was getting oppressively hot in there.

I summoned one of the waitstaff and asked him to go tell the engineer to turn the heat down. Five minutes later, he returned with a message that the heat was malfunctioning and engineering was working on the problem.

What better time for them to wheel in the ice sculpture of Roxanne as the little mermaid?

Everyone cooed and clapped and Roxanne stepped up to the sculpture to admire its "likeness" . . . except it really looked more like Daryl Hannah, which was probably who they had an old mermaid mold of.

It didn't take long before someone said, "Look! The ice mermaid is crying!"

Dread clutched my chest.

Roxanne's glance shot to the ice sculpture, which was, indeed, beginning to melt. From the top down.

At the moment, it looked a little like a Miracle from Lourdes. My aunt and uncle would have been thrilled.

I grabbed a waitress. "Get a fan. Quick!"

She looked at me uncertainly.

"*Ask* someone, if you can't find one," I said, then practically shoved her away. "It's warm in here," I told Roxanne. "But they're going to take care of this. Meanwhile, how about . . ." I racked my brain, trying to think of some reasonable diversion, but none came to mind.

Which didn't matter, since I was interrupted by Roxanne, wailing like a siren. "You've made my mermaid cry!"

Now, what do you say to that?

The cameras, of course, swooped over like vultures over road-kill.

A waiter was running toward us with a fan, but it was too late to save anyone's dignity. The high points of the sculpture were melting first, which meant it also looked like Roxanne's mermaid was lactating.

Or, as she put it, "What's with the boobs?"

The fan proved to be little help. The pitiful small breeze only nudged the melting water into strange rivulets down the mermaid's body; it didn't do much to stop the melting.

At this point, even the ink images of Roxanne on the M&Ms were starting to melt and look more like the Jesus image people claimed to see in pancake burns, grilled cheese sandwiches, and misshapen potatoes.

"Open the doors," I told the servers, then got on the phone and called the engineers myself to find out what the progress was on fixing the air-conditioning.

"Not there yet," said Carlos, who had worked there longer than I had. "The system hasn't been used since March and we really should have cleaned it up and serviced it before turning it on."

"Can you send in some more fans?" I asked, watching the ice melt like the wicked witch in *The Wizard of Oz.* "As many as you can find?"

"Sure thing."

The combination of the fans and open doors alleviated the problem somewhat, but not enough to make it what you'd call comfortable.

Jeremy got the band back in business, though, and once they started blasting Lady Gaga the party loosened back up some. Roxanne stopped crying over the sculpture and led a group of her friends like the Pied Piper back to the other end of the room, away from the smell of rapidly ripening food.

It felt like I just had a moment to lean against a fake palm tree and breathe when Roxanne approached from behind, crying, "Erin!"

I turned, finding it hard to muster the energy to deal with yet another tantrum. "Roxanne."

"You know the date you set me up with for the evening?"

I looked at her uncertainly. I thought she was going to pass him off as a guy who was legitimately interested in her. "Your date . . . Troy?"

"Yes, *Troy*." She didn't seem to care that people were around who could hear her. That was a bad sign. "Do you know where I just found him?"

"N-nooo . . . ? Where?" Please, God, not floating facedown in the mermaid tank outside.

"Making out with a *server* behind the Coke machine! A *male* server."

Now I understood. She could either blame me or look like she was so unattractive she drove her boyfriend to other boys. "There must be some mistake," I said.

Bill, behind the cameraman, shook his head. No mistake.

And they'd captured it on film.

"I am so sorry, Roxanne. I had no idea he was . . ." Gay? Of course I had. Unreliable? He was an actor. ". . . Behind the Coke machine with anyone."

She turned on the waterworks then. "This is the worst Sweet Sixteen party *ever*." But then her eyes alighted on someone coming in from the locker room area.

I turned to see who it was, expecting Brad Pitt or someone equally worthy of shutting her up, but there was just a skinny kid in a tracksuit, schlumping in and trying to look cool.

I realized who he was just as she said his name: "Justin!"

She ran over to him and tackled him, kissing him in a way I was pretty sure would be edited later for decency.

"Hold on, hold on," Justin said, making some sort of splayed-finger rapper gesture with his hand. "I wanna say something." He strutted over to the band and, right in the middle of a song, stepped between the lead singer and his microphone.

The band petered out the song and looked to Jeremy for an explanation, but he had no answer beyond a pale-faced, wide-eyed panic.

"Yo! Can everyone hear me?" Justin said over the mic. It buzzed and zinged with feedback. "I just wanna say, I'm here for Roxanne on her birthday. We've had some rough times, but I'm here for my girl." He paused and there was a small smattering of applause.

"Happy birthday, babe!" he said, and there were more cheers.

She blushed and gave a little wave.

Her parents beamed.

"So now I'd just like to do something I haven't done for a couple of weeks and I've missed it," Justin went on. "Come here, Roxy." He reached out a hand and drew her up to him, where they kissed sloppily and with loud, horrendous noises that bounced around the room courtesy of the speakers Jeremy had managed to score.

They left the stage, hands up like triumphant wrestlers, and Roxanne looked thrilled. "I can't believe you did it!" she whispered to me as they stopped near me. "What a great surprise! You were so right about staying away so he'd miss me!"

I may have been right about that, but I realized now I'd been really wrong about something else.

For all the times I'd complained that Nate hadn't made any grand gestures when we were Roxanne's age, it had never occurred to me what the grand gesture truly was at that time.

Justin had made an ass of himself, as far as I was concerned, but what he'd done had completely made Roxanne's day. No, probably her month. Maybe even her year. To her, this was *the* romantic gesture.

But I saw it for what it really was: a public masturbation of Justin's own ego. He hadn't done that for Roxanne. He hadn't sacrificed anything to step up to that microphone; he knew before he walked into the place that she was desperate for him to be there.

He hadn't laid his heart on the line in any way.

He'd just flexed what muscle he could, for a captive audience.

I couldn't believe that after all this time it had taken that punk to show me that real love was quiet and steady, not showy and loud and self-congratulatory.

Though make no mistake, that showy, loud, self-congratulatory performance had done some heavy lifting as far as salvaging the night. Everything that went wrong, and there was a lot, was a source of giggles for Roxanne once Justin arrived. Ultimately, her review of us for the VTV cameras had been glowing, intoxicated by her infatuation.

Worked for me.

And, for now at least, it clearly worked for her.

Chapter 24

June 1993

Apart from the fact that it was *hers*, Erin Edwards had found the baby shower to be really fun.

She saw friends she hadn't seen in ages, laughed at the old stories of their decadent pasts together as well as the foibles of being grown-ups now when no one really felt like one, and got presents. That was always fun, even though they weren't for her, really, and most of the tiny shirts and outfits served more to make her feel like a big fat whale—at seven months pregnant—than a joyful Madonna figure.

But that was probably normal, right? Get pregnant accidentally at twenty-two and you're not necessarily going to be feeling all that naturally maternal and benevolent.

There she was: twenty-three, a year out of college, still unsure of what she wanted to do with her life, faced with an uncertain future involving a small dependent being she'd never met and had no real sense of as a person. A small being that, up to and including now, felt more like a medical condition than someone she was going to bond with and love and know for the rest of her life.

Also, she was unmarried. A fact her mother was not thrilled about. Erin had been raised better than this—it was unbecoming for someone like her to get knocked up. And stupid—she and Jake had split up already. She'd stopped taking the pill because it made her feel like crap and there was no point in continuing it. Once they'd split up, that didn't seem to matter.

Until that night, one bored night, when she had a lot of mescal and a little mistake with Jake, and the next thing she knew . . . six positive pregnancy sticks lined up along the sink.

It was the easiest test she'd ever passed.

There followed several months of vomiting, losing weight then gaining it, and telling a seemingly relieved Jake that she didn't see the point in making one mistake into two by getting married.

That was followed by more vomiting and two hospitalizations for dehydration *from* the vomiting.

It was not the best time in Erin's life.

So when her friends Theresa and Jordan suggested a baby shower once she felt better, it really didn't feel like much of a reason for a party. Also, it didn't happen until she was seven months along and had gone from feeling half dead and constantly sick to feeling sick only some of the time and huge and awkward all of the time.

But she was also broke, so the baby shower was genuinely helpful and she appreciated her friends coming together for her that way.

"So you guys aren't getting married?" her cousin Susannah asked after Erin opened a gift from her, a box of onesies for the baby and a filmy negligee for Erin, who couldn't imagine ever fitting into it. Or wanting to.

"No," Erin said quickly. She'd been waiting for this question, and the judgmental raise of the eyebrow that accompanied it. "We're just . . . going to coparent. It will be fine. Good. It will be good." Their attraction had been short-lived, and had burned itself out fairly quickly. However, the basis of the attraction—their friendship— was solid. Had been, ever since Erin had met him when they were on a white-water rafting trip near Harpers Ferry. The good news was that, even if it weren't for the baby, she and Jake would proba- bly still be friends.

Maybe not super-close friends, but at least stay-in-touch friends.

"But aren't you in love with him?" Susannah pressed, crinkling her nose and appearing to *try* and understand the hedonistic creature she was apparently related to. "You must have been at one point!"

Susannah was from the more religious side of the family. It was bad enough that Erin had had sex before marriage, but they would never understand how she could have done it without being in love.

It was just easier to say, "Yes, of course."

But for her part, Erin didn't believe in being *in love* anymore. She'd given Jordan a long diatribe about that very thing, upon being questioned, but the upshot was that *in love* was—in Erin's theory—a form of infatuation that was as highly unpredictable and flammable as stibine gas.

Lives couldn't be built on chemistry, they had to be built on logic: compatibility and similar goals.

She and Jake had neither of those. And frankly they didn't have even a little bit of the chemistry anymore either.

"Whoa, let me help you carry those," Jordan said, seeing Erin piling the shower gifts on top of each other in order to make fewer trips to the car at the end of the party.

"Thanks." Erin handed over a pack of diapers and Jordan took the pile of clothes Erin was wrestling with as well.

They walked out side by side to Erin's Camry and Jordan opened the back door of the car for her to put the gifts in.

"So I'm leaving for school again tomorrow," Jordan said, leaning against the passenger door of Erin's car. The late afternoon light slanted down and cast them both in amber, but the mid-June breeze was unusually cold. "I won't be back until it's time for the baby to come."

The baby's due date was two months away. Now it was Jordan's school break. Their old friend Theresa had planned the shower now on purpose because she knew it would be important to Erin to have Jordan there. Theresa had never been as close to Erin and Jordan as they were to each other, but she'd been there through a lot nevertheless and she knew how important it was that Jordan be part of this.

"I wish you didn't have to go." Erin sighed, then smiled, hoping to disguise just how badly she wished Jordan weren't leaving. "Why couldn't you just stop at a BA like everyone else?"

"Just contrary, I guess." Jordan laughed. She was going for her Ph.D. so she could be a counselor, so this school thing was going to go on for quite a while.

Erin knew it was selfish and unrealistic to wish things could be more like they were in high school, when the two of them could gab all night on the phone, see each other all day in school, and then hang out afterward, but it didn't stop her from missing those days sometimes. Things were so much easier then.

But she knew things would never be like they used to be.

Erin went to her and hugged her, holding on tight for a long time despite the belly bulge that kept them at a slight distance. "I'll miss you so much!"

"I'll miss you too!"

Erin let go reluctantly. "Call. Often."

"I will," Jordan reassured. "But remember, you can call me any-time. Absolutely anytime. I can be here in a flash."

"Thanks." Erin smiled, but she was suddenly overcome by emo-tion. She was tired, and lost, and didn't want to be playing this role she'd found herself in. It felt like she was on the slow part of a roller coaster, climbing the tracks, and it was about to get fast and crazy and completely out of control.

There was no stopping it.

"Erin," Jordan began, then bit her lower lip.

"What?"

There was a long moment before Jordan let out a pent-up breath and said, "I don't want you to get mad at me for asking this, but it's my job as your best friend to ask if you're sure you don't want to look into adoption before you commit completely to the idea of single motherhood."

Erin closed her eyes for a moment, wishing it could be so simple. "I did. I can't do it. I would always wonder, every single time I saw a child about the same age. . . ." A lump formed in her throat.

"But are you *ready* to change your life like this?"

Erin didn't necessarily want to give the *true* answer to that, be-cause she hadn't allowed herself to dive too deeply into it, but she did have the *correct* answer at the ready. "Yes, Jordan." Her voice sounded confident, even to her own ears. "I'm ready. I'm sure."

Jordan smiled, and it almost completely disguised the doubt in her eyes. "Good." She started to go, then turned back. "I'll help however I can. You know that."

Erin raised an eyebrow. "Cool. So you're moving in? Which diaper shift do you want?"

"You think you're joking."

"I *am* joking."

Jordan looked at her for a long moment. "Call me if you need me. I don't care what time it is."

"I always need you, you know that. But thanks."

They said good-bye and Erin went back into her mother's house, where the shower had taken place, to get the last of her things and help with any residual cleanup.

"You just got a call," her mother said from the kitchen after the storm door slammed shut.

"Yeah?" Erin asked absently. God, she had to pee *again*. She never thought a catheter would seem like a luxury. "Who?"

Her mother kept putting utensils in the dishwasher, the clanking sound so loud it almost obscured the answer. "Nate."

Erin froze.

"I thought you'd left," her mother went on, as if she were just relating the news that a telemarketer had called about her *People* magazine subscription. "So I told him I'd let you know he called."

Nate.

Nate.

Erin's first thought was that something had to be terribly wrong for him to call her, but her second thought was that she couldn't imagine what could possibly go so wrong that she was the only one who could help him with it.

She took small tentative steps toward the kitchen. She *had* to have misheard. Misunderstood. Maybe she was dreaming it. Maybe she was dead.

Did pregnancy cause hallucinations? Was it a sign of premature labor?

Now was no time to think about the past. Especially *that* past. She wasn't up to that.

"Did he say what he wanted?"

Her mother shook her head and met her eyes, her own betraying nothing. "I didn't ask him that. Just told him I'd tell you he'd called." She returned to the dishes. "We should have used paper plates."

Erin swallowed and ignored the paper plate complaint. "Did he leave his number?"

"He's at his parents' house."

The number flashed in her mind like she was Rain Man or something. She was twenty-three now, not seventeen, and sometimes she forgot her extension number at work, but Nate's number was safely tucked away in her brain with her Social Security number, bank account number, and GFEDCBA piano scales.

This was it. He was back home. She knew it. After all those years away, and all but out of her head, he was back and he'd called her. He'd finally realized what they had and he'd come around to it now, of all times, when it was without question too late.

She tried to find her voice. "I'm going to . . ." She cleared her throat. Her hands were shaking like she'd had too much caffeine, though, of course, she hadn't had a coffee or Diet Coke in months. "I'm just going to run upstairs and . . . you know . . . call back and see what he wants."

Her mother nodded and returned to the dishes in the kitchen sink. She must have realized that Erin was freaking out; in fact, in all likelihood Erin didn't seem nearly as composed on the outside as she thought she did, but her mother let it go without comment.

Erin hurried up the stairs to her old room, hoping the burst of exertion would get rid of some of this nervous energy, and closed the door behind her. The latch of the lock gave a familiar click, and the bed squeaked as she sat down on the edge.

She was sixteen again.

And yet she was so, *so* far from being sixteen again. From being carefree, and flopping onto the bed to call Nate. Then it would have been *What are we doing tonight?* Or *Are you on your way over? Hurry up!* Or *Meet me on the corner at midnight.*

There would be none of that today.

After a moment, she picked up the phone and dialed.

He answered the same way he always had.

Something deep inside of her moved in its sleep.

"Nate," she breathed. Her heart was pounding. This was just sad. "It's Erin."

"Hey."

That voice! That *voice*! One word, and it was like fourteen thousand memories sprang to life.

"Hey." Her stomach was in her throat. Of course, it almost was. Literally.

But she didn't want to feel this.

Not now, and not ever again.

There was one small part of her that was still subject to this kind of broken heart, a part of her that was so distant it might have been close to subconscious, and she'd just tapped right into it.

"So," she said, the word too small, the feelings too big. "My mother said you called. What's up? Are you back?"

He'd been away at school for years. He'd gotten a bachelor's and then a master's. She knew that much from talking to his mother every now and then, but they had eventually lost touch too. She had no contact with Nate. She'd never told him she wanted him back. It was pride, maybe. Or the feeling that he should have known. The wish that *he'd* come after *her.*

But he never did.

It had been six years or so since she'd talked to him or seen him now. She'd grown up a mile from him, but before they'd met, and certainly since the last time he'd left, they might as well have lived on different planets, for all that their lives intersected.

"Yes, I'm starting a new job in D.C.," he said. He sounded a little nervous. Like he wasn't sure how to act either. "Now I'm just looking for a place to live."

She'd thought about this day a lot once. "Well. Welcome home." She twined the phone wire around her fingers and looked out the window. The leaves were rustling on the cherry tree outside one window and the magnolia scraped the other window when the wind shifted.

She knew this wasn't his usual call. Something in him had finally yielded, she could feel it.

She'd give anything for a different reality right now.

"Was it good?"

He laughed. "There was good and bad."

"I bet."

"What about you? What have you been up to?"

Her first impulse was to lie. Or, rather, to omit. To not mention the pregnancy, the shower she'd just had, the baby in eight weeks, but there was no way to get away with that. Even now it felt weird to tell him anything about her life that was so solidly Not To Do With Him, which was stupid since he was the one who'd made the choice that they should go their separate ways and it had been a long time since he'd done that.

She should have told him about the baby joyfully—she should have been so excited about this new chapter in her life that nothing else mattered—but something told her this call was pivotal.

If her life had gone a different way, if she hadn't met Jake—or even if she hadn't had that one last night with him—this was the call that might have given her and Nate the chance to see if they still had anything together. That was a question she'd had for a long, long time.

Or at least the chance to put a bandage on the open wound that their split had become.

But they were never going to get that chance now. "Actually, I'm pregnant," she said through a tight throat. There. It was done. Out. She'd said it. "The baby's due in two months," she added, in case there was any question left.

There was a pause.

"Oh. Wow, that's great!" He sounded chipper. Too chipper. "Congratulations, Erin, really. Are you— Who's the—" Another pause. It was a hard question to ask regardless of who you were asking.

"The father is a guy I went out with for a while," she answered. "Jake. We're not married. We're just . . . going to see what happens." She couldn't shut up. It was like she was in a confessional or something. What was she hoping? That he'd say he didn't care if she was pregnant, he wanted to see her anyway?

What guy would say that?

"Wow, you always liked kids," he said, in a tone that was utterly unreadable apart from the fact that it seemed disproportionately cheerful. "That should be good for you."

"Yeah." Wow, she really wished she believed that. She really wished she had the enthusiasm and excitement he seemed to be assigning her.

"A baby," he said, and she could imagine him shaking his head. "Wow. Big news."

It was stupid for her to be disappointed that he didn't sound more upset at her news. Why would he? This wasn't a significant call, it was just a guy calling an old friend because he'd just gotten back into town and was probably feeling kind of melancholy.

Now they'd chat for a few minutes about nothing, and hang up, and she'd never hear from him again. He'd be gone.

Again.

She didn't want that to happen.

But what choice did she have? She had a time bomb ticking away in her womb. There was no putting this off, no playing both sides, nothing.

Now it was even more awkward. They talked for ten more minutes, making idle conversation, both knowing there were other things to talk about that now had no place in this conversation. She watched the tree branches sway outside the window and wished things were different.

Finally they brought it to a close, Erin saying, "So . . . it was good to catch up with you . . . ," and Nate agreeing and probably neither of them meaning it.

Then it was over. The call was over. The contact was over. Everything was over.

Again.

How many good-byes was she going to have to suffer through with this guy? And why did it always hurt as much as the first time?

This one, though . . . this one was hers. She might as well have been telling him she was dying, for all the finality that her pregnancy held.

She had no idea what he was thinking, of course, but she was seriously disconcerted. In a way it wasn't surprising that he'd show up unexpectedly—after all, he'd *not* shown up when she *had* expected, and hoped, and prayed, for several years. Eventually she'd reached a kind of acceptance of that, if not a peace with it, so there was no way for him to appear again without surprising her.

But on the day of her baby shower?

If Nate had *ever* given *any* indication *at all* that he was thinking of her, that he was coming back, that he wanted to talk to her, *anything*, then she might have made that her priority.

Then again, maybe she wouldn't have. She might have met Jake, been taken by all the things that were so sexy about him, and followed the same course anyway, thinking of Nate with fondness instead of angst and this terrible lack of resolution that had hung from her like a loose thread for all these years.

She'd never really know now.

Two months later, she had the baby on schedule—Jake and her mother were there—and loved the little girl as soon as she laid eyes on her. She named her Camilla because she was reading a book about a heroine named Camilla when she went into labor. She and Jake tried to make a go of it, but it was over before it began and they settled into a friendship that made for a surprisingly easy co-parenting experience.

For the first year, her life was so consumed by parenting that she didn't have the time or inclination to think about romantic regrets.

As Camilla got older, and Erin began to date again, now and then she had the stray thought about how things could have been different. But she didn't regret how things had gone. She didn't regret having Camilla.

The only thing she wasn't completely glad of was the fact that she'd let that opportunity with Nate go. Not the opportunity to get back with him, but it had been a chance to finally *talk* to him. To feel some semblance of resolution to an issue that had plagued her for years.

She'd wanted that so desperately for so long—why had she blown it when she finally had the chance?

Nate had called and she'd essentially sent him on his way without taking so much as ten minutes to talk honestly before dropping her bomb on him. Instead she'd given him what clearly seemed now like the ultimate dismissal. She'd told him she was pregnant and left no room for discussion, even if he was inclined to discuss.

What she'd really wanted, though she only started to realize it a lot later, was for him to make some grand gesture. But what was he going to do? Swoop into the delivery room, like Dustin Hoffman at the end of *The Graduate,* to proclaim some undying love for her?

Even if that was what she wanted—or maybe something a little less grand—he wouldn't do it. Man, if there was one thing she knew about Nate by now, it was that he was never going to be the guy who makes the big gesture. It wasn't a fault of his or anything, just a fact. He'd no more step in and claim her as his girl than strip naked and dance in a fountain.

She was always the one more likely to strip and dance in a fountain.

The problem was that she'd always hope, despite knowing it wasn't in his nature, that—just once—he would fight even half as hard as she had to get back together.

If he had, she would have given him everything—her heart, soul, her life if that's what it took.

Then again, she'd already done that.

And he hadn't wanted it.

Chapter 25

Present

There are a lot of ways I might have expected this to end. It would have to be a huge grand gesture, right? Because that's what he never did before? Maybe some sort of skywriting overhead when I was leaving for work, apologizing for his lack of vision, vowing his eternal love and devotion. Or perhaps even a simple mix tape, like the one I'd been assembling in my head for months now, saying every flowery romantic sentiment he had but couldn't put to words.

Well, none of that happened.

What actually happened was that six months passed with no contact from Nate at all. It was six months during which I had to work to get over him—to get him out of my mind—all over again. Age had brought me some wisdom in this way, but the heart never learns to stop loving very quickly or easily.

So it was hard.

Then, one frigid December night, the doorbell rang while I was doing the dishes and I heard Cam talking to someone who had a vaguely familiar tone to his voice.

Obviously the sound of Cam talking to any man at the front door would draw my attention, so I dried my hands on the dishrag and went—garbed in Mickey Mouse sweatpants and a V-neck T-shirt that was a little bit tight in the bust but good enough for around the house—to see who it was.

And even though on some level I'd known the voice the moment I'd heard the timbre of it, it was still a shock to see him standing there: high cheekbones, chiseled jaw, cleft chin, soulful eyes, and that particular stance of his that always seemed like he was equally ready to relax or fight.

Odder still, there he was standing next to Cam. Two people I never thought I'd see together.

"Nate," I said stupidly, taking a step toward him, my unglamorous sweats crying *Oh, boy!* in Mickey's voice with every step.

He met my eyes. Same penetrating gaze that had met mine a million times before, same fringe of lashes that stopped short of being girlie and always made my heart trip, and the same curve of the lips I had long ago memorized and fallen in love with. I knew what it felt like to my fingertips and to my tongue.

"Erin."

I glanced at Cam, who suddenly seemed like a strange being placed out of time, then back at him. I didn't know what to do, what to say, who to say it to. "What are you doing here?" I heard myself ask him. "Is Theresa okay?"

Like if Theresa wasn't okay for some reason, he'd come running to tell me. *Quick! Only Erin can help!* It was a stupid question, but I wasn't capable of conjuring a good one now.

"I'm sure she is," he said, holding my gaze and speaking quietly. Gravely. "But I haven't seen her in five months."

Something in my chest lurched. It was immediately dampened by caution. After everything I'd been through with this man, and all the time in my life I'd spent getting over him, there was no wisdom in jumping to conclusions. "You haven't?"

Five months?

"No."

More information, please. I tried to still my pounding heart and had the passing thought that if this visit didn't mean what I was sure, deep down, it did, then I might never get over it this time. "Why is that?"

He looked at Cam. "Would you mind," he asked, "if I took your mother out in order to talk? I think we have a lot to catch up on."

"Absolutely!" she said with a smile.

"Wait, don't I have a say in this?" I asked.

"Not really," Cam said.

He smiled at her, then turned his gaze to me. "You heard your daughter. Maybe we should talk about this, just the two of us."

"I . . . don't know." I didn't know anything.

"Erin. Please."

I swallowed hard. There was a lump in my throat that I was pretty sure would never go away. "Maybe it's too late." I straightened my back, as if that would lend credibility to the idea of my lack of interest.

He sighed and leaned against the doorframe, a half smile playing at his mouth the way it always did when he knew I didn't mean what I was saying.

And he was totally right, of course. There was plenty to say.

Which made tears spring to my eyes. "I can't do this," I said to him. Then I looked at Cam and said, clearly about five minutes later than I should have, "Go to your room."

She looked like she'd just been caught watching something

wildly inappropriate on her computer. "Oh! Sorry. Okay." She scurried off.

I watched her disappear down the hall and around the corner into her room. Then I returned my attention to him. "This is crazy."

"It has been for a long time."

"I don't know what you want, but I'm not sure I can go through this."

He took a step toward me. "You know what I want."

I shook my head. "I don't know anything."

"What do *you* want?" he asked. "That's the question."

It took a little while for me to find my voice. Because I knew what I wanted. Of course I knew. On some level, I'd always wanted it. But did that make it *right*? "It's been a long time since that was your question," I said to him. "I'm scared to answer it."

"What are you scared of?"

I sighed and shrugged, holding back tears with everything I had. "Everything."

"Mom?" Cam called from around the corner. "Can you come here just for a minute?"

I held Nate's gaze. "Not right now!"

"*Please?*"

I broke eye contact. "Fine!" This was ridiculous. "Wait here," I said to him. "I'll be right back."

He nodded his assent. Like he was ready to stand there in my foyer all night if that's what it took.

I started to walk away, then turned back to him. "You'll really be here when I get back?"

He gave a laugh. "I promise. I will wait forever."

A sigh caught in my chest.

I went to Cam's room and the short walk felt like it took forever, each step taking me treacherously away from what might well turn out to be another one of those realistic dreams I had about him.

I wanted to stay with him, to keep him there, to keep him *real*.

"What are you *doing?*" she demanded as soon as I got to her door.

I was taken aback. Her words were like cold water on me, bringing me right back to the present. "What are you talking about? I'm trying to handle a *very* difficult situation. What do you think *you're* doing?"

"I don't know, maybe trying to stop you from making the same stupid mistake you've made over and over?"

"The same stupid mistake *I've* made?"

She nodded impatiently. "You've made, he's made, everyone's made. *God.*" For a second there, she sounded just like Roxanne. "What*ever.* It's late on a freezing winter night and he just showed up here saying he hasn't seen his wife, or maybe his *ex-wife*, in months. Even *I* know what that means! Now is your chance."

I shook my head and found myself pacing back and forth in front of her. "No, now is *your* chance. At least it *was*. But my stupid romantic choices have cost you over and over again. You had a chance to have a normal family, a *sister*, a father figure who lived in the house with us and was there full-time, and I blew that. I blew it for you. Because of silly, childish notions about romance and love and ideals that couldn't possibly have withstood the test of time." Tears burned in my eyes and spilled over uncontrolled. "I'm sorry."

"Mom—"

I held up a hand. "If I go out there and chase a teenage dream off into some John Hughes movie sunset, I will be the worst mother who ever lived!"

"*Why?*"

"Because . . ." Well, why? Because I didn't marry a man I wasn't in love with? Because I'd held out and now the man I *had* been in love with for twenty-three years had shown up at my door with what seemed to be his heart on his sleeve? Because if I went with him, I showed my daughter that there is power in true love, and faith, even if you have to wait for a long time to get to it?

I was going to him. It had been over for so long, but now I knew—I *knew*—this was it.

"See?" she said smugly, and for a moment there she was much older than her years.

And I was much younger.

I looked at her, and could see—just barely—the child she had been, there in the face of the woman she was becoming. I had no regrets. If I had done all the things I'd just spent so much time wishing I'd done differently, then I wouldn't have had her, and that thought was simply untenable.

My life *had* gone right; it had gone exactly as it needed to in order to bring me here.

"Mom," Cam said firmly, clearly sensing my wobbly uncertainty. "*Please* do this. You *need* this." She put her hands on my shoulders and looked into my eyes. "You've spent my whole life sacrificing yourself for me. *Please* do this one thing for yourself."

She was right.

"You stay here," I cautioned her, following a sudden urgency to move the earth, if necessary, to do this thing. "I'm going out for just a little while. I'll have my cell phone if you need me."

She beamed and clapped her hands together quietly. "Yay!"

"We're just going to talk."

"I know!"

Were we?

Would it stop there?

"Keep the door locked," I said unnecessarily. I'd stayed home alone all the time when I was fifteen, almost sixteen, I don't know why I worried so much about her, but I knew tonight was one night I really needed *not* to worry.

"I *will*." She giggled. "And Mom . . ."

I stopped. "Yeah?"

"He's really cute."

My heart thrummed. "Yeah."

She paused and frowned. "Shorter than I expected, though."

I laughed. "But good-looking."

She nodded. "Totes. Have fun!"

I went back to the foyer. Nate was fiddling with the knick-knacks on my foyer table.

It was nice to see him like that, looking strangely at home in my place, with my stuff.

I caught myself. It was stupid to start thinking that way. Yes, my instincts told me where this was going. He'd intimated as much too. But neither of us knew where it would end tonight.

Or maybe both of us did.

This was no time to start counting on my assumptions. I might as well just beg him to kick me in the heart and get it over with.

"Sorry," he said when he saw me. He set down a picture of me holding Cam as a baby. He came toward me and put his hands on my shoulders. "I didn't mean to ambush you like this. I'm not all that great at this kind of thing. The . . . romantic move."

The warmth of his touch was comforting. "It's okay." It had been too long for me to play coy. It *was* okay. It was more than okay.

In fact, I'd never been so glad to see anyone in my life.

"Oh, Nate . . ."

He looked toward the bedroom where Cam was singing loudly with a Weezer song and then said, "So . . . you want to go outside and talk?"

"Sure. Yes." What I wanted was to take him into my bedroom for a solid week. "Good idea." Given what had already transpired between us, this conversation had to be between us alone. We needed to *feel* alone.

I grabbed a sweater from the hook by the door and followed him out, shrugging into it.

Nevertheless, I was immediately cold in the brisk air.

Without asking questions, he took off his coat and put it over my shoulders, just like he'd done the first time we'd met. It was warm and smelled like him. I pulled it closer around me.

"So what happened with you and Theresa?" I asked. "Did she leave you for greener pastures?"

He laughed quietly and shook his head. "Not exactly. That would have made things easier."

I stopped. "You left her?"

"I had to." He turned to me and put his hands on my shoulders and looked into my eyes.

"Why?" I breathed.

There was so much weight on his answer. So much. This was the moment that could change not only our futures, but also our past.

But Nate didn't seem to feel any weight pressing on it at all. "I'd rather love you and be alone than love you and be with her," he said simply. "Or anyone."

And there it was.

Finally.

The moment I had waited for, for so long.

"You love me?" I tried to swallow, but my throat was tight.

He kept his gaze fastened unwaveringly on mine and gave the smallest nod. "I love you. I have *always* loved you. And it's pretty clear to me now that I always will."

"And even if I say no to you right now, even if I tell you it's too damn late and you blew it a long time ago, you'd rather be alone than go back to the beautiful and perfect Theresa?"

"Baby, I'd rather be in a monastery than live my life trying to convince myself that one more woman could hold a candle to you."

His use of *baby* made me come unglued.

He moved in and put his arms around me, holding tight, stilling my shaking emotions with his deep calm.

He drew back and looked into my eyes. "I love you," he said, with more sincerity than I'd ever heard from a man.

"But—"

He kissed me. And whatever I was going to say or ask disappeared with our breath, rising into the cold air.

Because whatever had gone wrong—with him, with me, with us—I knew what was right.

And I was never going to let that go again.

We stood there, clutched together, for a long time, breathing each other's breath, drinking each other in. Then it hit me—the only possible next move.

"You want to go for a ride?" I asked, excitement building deep within me.

"A *ride*?"

I nodded. "You know. In the car?"

"Sure." He looked a little confused. "Where do you want to go?"

I tipped my chin up and looked at him, smiling and crying at the same time. "Now, where do you think I want to go?"

Understanding dawned in his eyes. He smiled, that charming thief smile of his. "Down River Road? Violet's Lock?"

He remembered.

And heaven knows I remembered.

The weight of heartbreak fell off my shoulders like a bad costume. There was a lightness in my heart that I almost didn't recognize.

Almost.

But I *did* recognize it. It was myself. It was deeply, elementally me. And I loved this man.

"Perfect!" I said, but my voice was tight with emotion.

He smiled and reached for my hand and we started to walk.

We crossed the parking lot, hand in familiar hand, got into his car, and drove, away from the present, away from the past, and straight into our future.

Acknowledgments

Thanks to the people who kept me sane in various ways while I wrote this unusually difficult book: Patrice Luneski, Paige Harbison, Jamie Taylor, Steve Troha, Annelise Robey, Meg Ruley, Mike McCormack, Dana Carmel, Kim Amori, Nicki Singer, Mimi Elias, Anita Arnold, Connie Atkins, Devynn Grubby, Jami Nasi, Mike Beall, Carolyn Clemens, Martina Chaconas, Russell Nuce, Mark Bozek, Cinda O'Brien, Sue Conversano, Susi Keffer, Tatjana Kruse, Zarathustra, Melodious, Rose and Lily, and THM.

Thanks also to Sean Osborn and Dan Luneski for hitting the road in emergencies. And sometimes doing the clean-up afterwards.

As always, thanks to Jen Enderlin for her brilliance in every way, and for seeing things I can't.

And finally, thanks to those guys who were there, then, and raised me to be the monster I became, much to the dismay of later boyfriends: Gregg, Doug, Jamie, Brian, Roger, and Eric. I appreciate the fact that you taught me to throw a punch, and that you threw them on my behalf now and then, but sometimes I wish you'd taught me to block better.

Here is a sneak peek at
Beth Harbison's new novel

When in Doubt Add Butter

Available July 2012

Chapter 1

When I was twelve, a fortune-teller at the Herbert Hoover Junior High School carnival said to me: "Gemma Craig, you listen to me. Do *not* get married. Ever. If you do, you'll end up cooking for a man who'd rather eat at McDonald's; doing laundry for a man who sweats like a rabid pig, then criticizes you for not turning his T-shirts right side out; and cleaning the bathroom floor after a man whose aim is so bad, he can't hit a hole the size of a watermelon—"

This man sounded disgusting.

"—make your own money and be independent. Having kids is fine, but get married and you will be miserable for the rest of your life. I promise you, *the rest of your life.*"

This chilling prediction stayed with me long after I realized that the fortune-teller was, in fact, Mrs. Rooks, the

PTA president and neighbor who always gave out full-sized 3 Musketeers bars on Halloween, and that her husband had left her that very morning for a cliché: a young, vapid, blond bombshell. Mrs. Rooks had four kids, and at the time, I thought of her as really old and I didn't quite get why she cared so much if she was married anymore or not.

She was thirty-seven.

I was thirty-seven last year.

But for the most part, I have followed that sage wisdom she imparted, whether it came from a place of deep inspiration or, maybe, from a place of bitter day drunkenness. It had an impact on me either way.

Dating was fine. I love men. I love sex. I love having someone to banter with, flirt with, play romantic tag with, and finally yield to. Many, many times I have thought, in the beginning of a relationship, that *maybe* this guy could be different and the relationship might last against the odds my young brain had laid out.

But inevitably things soured for me, usually in the form of boredom, and *always* within two months. Seriously. This was consistent enough for my friends to refer to it as *two months too long.*

The good thing about a breakup at two months is that there usually isn't a lot of acrimony or anguish involved. The bad thing is that it gets tiresome after a while. Honestly, I'm a normal woman, I'd *love* to be in love. I'd love to have a family to take care of and to surround me as I navigate the years.

But once I hit thirty-seven, I had to wonder if that was really in the cards for me.

And if that was the case, I was okay with that because I had a career I loved that allowed me some of the better parts of June Cleaver–dom, along with the ability to hang up the apron at the end of the day and be my own, single self.

I am a private chef.

Being hired to cook for people is really different from standing around a kitchen with friends, drinking wine and making snacks. It's different from making a whole Thanksgiving dinner for family. It's vastly different, even, from cooking for strangers at the soup kitchen, where the pride of creating something delicious is just as compelling but somehow . . . easier. Less judgmental.

Cooking for people in their homes *can* be like cooking for friends, but more often than that, it's like cooking for the meanest teacher in elementary school: someone you want to shrink away from, hide from. Someone you hope to god won't call on you or make you speak in front of everyone else. Someone you're pretty sure will yell and scream at you if you do one little thing wrong.

The many scenarios include—but are not limited to—taking the fall for a failed party ("the food wasn't good enough"), taking the blame for a neglected hostess ("you shouldn't speak with the guests even if they talk to you first"), shouldering the blame for the burden of unused ingredients ("I have to do something with the rest of these onions now, thanks a lot"), and other failures of life in general ("my husband doesn't want to come home on time for dinner, but if you made something he couldn't resist, then he would!").

Fortunately, most of the time I'm treated as if I'm invisible. Which is okay with me, except the dodging out of the way of people and not making eye contact can sometimes be challenging.

Still, I prefer that to being faced with accusations.

At first, I didn't see this coming. I always loved to cook, and got pretty good at it early on—though a few major mishaps come to mind (root beer extract in cupcakes was . . . a mistake)—but it never occurred to me that I could make a living this way. I guess that seemed too domestic for me at the time.

When I was working in Manhattan right after college, my mother tried to convince me, time and again, to meet a nice man and settle down. She wanted me to open a retirement account, and my legs, and start a future and family.

Not me. After what I'd been through, I think I was seeking some form of anonymity. What I would have said at the time was that I simply wanted to be free to go wherever the wind blew me. Like I was just a whimsical spirit, blowing through life and open to everything.

The problem was, the wind wasn't a reliable headhunter, so I moved from one go-nowhere job to another, proving my mother's fears more correct every day. Every time I found a job I liked, something happened to ruin it: like when I temped in the props department for a local morning

show in the city, and I mistakenly got a Cat in the Hat costume out for a celebrity guest who was supposed to be
Uncle Sam for a special Fourth of July segment, but in my
defense, the electricity was out and it was very hard to see
in the storeroom. (And who would have thought they'd
have a Cat in the Hat costume at all? Seriously, how often
could that have come in handy?)

When I hit twenty-six, I started to question if I was being irresponsible and immature by continuing my "free-
spirited" ways. To my mother's delight, I settled into some
good corporate jobs with excellent benefits. Three years in
the research department at the local CBS affiliate led to
two years at the Discovery Channel—and a routine rut that
would have bored even the most patient yogi in Tibet.

But as I settled into a routine life and watched the years
fly by like the calendar pages in a movie, I started to feel
old. That was all. Not pious, correct, responsible, or anything else, just *old*. Suddenly I realized that actors and ac-
tresses and singers and even pro football players were *younger*
than me.

Ten years ago, my life was *I have plenty of time to figure
out what I want to do.*

Five years ago, I reached *Hmmmmm.*

Two years ago, I found myself teetering on the edge of
Oh-oh, and looking straight down the barrel of *Oh, shit.*

I quit my tedious job, got myself a place that was tiny
and modest but it was *my own*, and I followed my passion
into a cooking career. I loved it. I *love* it. I'm my own boss,
I meet interesting people all the time, I'm never bored, and

whatever small part of me has a maternal instinct to take care of people is satisfied by nourishing them.

Then leaving.

Monday nights, I cook for the Van Houghtens. The pluses included: the location (Chevy Chase), beautiful kitchen (the marble counters, stainless steel *everything,* and one of those fridges that blend into the cabinetry), and the stability of the job. I'd been doing it for a year now. Minuses included Angela's attitude, and the fact that they had the ugliest pantry you've ever seen in your life.

Not cosmetically, it was the stuff inside it. Angela had very specific and spare tastes. Think of the fussiest eater you've ever known, and Angela makes them look like a glutton. Honestly. There is so much she *can't*—or, more appropriately, *won't*—eat that it is astonishing that the woman even has functional bones, much less any flesh on them. And really, there is very little of that.

No dairy. In fact, no "moo food" of any sort: no steaks, milk, sour cream, cheese, and check every package of bread for signs of whey, casein, and so forth.

No onions. Not dried, not powdered, not within three feet of anything she eats because "the essence will permeate it" and it will have to be thrown away.

No soy. Including soy lecithin, mono-diglyceride, guar gum, even citric acid.

No nuts. No nut derivatives. Nothing that was processed in a plant anywhere near nuts, even if the plant was in Georgia and Jimmy Carter lived five hundred miles away.

No honey. Nothing even vaguely connected with bees,

including certain plants. So, yes, it was easy to avoid honey, less so to avoid anything Angela considered "honey related," but I did it.

No cinnamon or "warm" spice.

No garlic.

No fun.

Every time I looked at Peter and Stephen, her unfortunate and emaciated husband and son, I just felt an overwhelming urge to make them a pot roast with caramelized onions and a big ol' coconut cream pie.

"Peter," Angela would coo, narrowing her eyes and scrunching up her nose at him as he reached for another meager portion of romaine lettuce (beets were too sugary, radishes too "hot on the stomach," whatever that meant, and onions already established to be out of the question), "do you *really* think you need more?"

It was as if she were talking to her son and not her husband. Yet it didn't hold any maternal kindness. Just bossiness.

Once in a while he'd say yes, and eat it anyway, but for the most part, he'd set the bowl down with a dull thud and level a burning look at her once she looked back down at the bowl she was slowly working her way through. I like to think that was only when he had a witness—me—and that normally he'd tell her exactly where to stuff it. It's hard to understand why a smart, hot, successful man would spend his life being whipped by a switch like her.

Perhaps it was because of Stephen. How he had gestated in Angela's slight body, I cannot imagine. Maybe that was before she adopted her radical diet. But at six years old now, he'd never known any other diet, I'm pretty sure.

In fact, maybe the post-pregnancy weight was the *reason* she adopted her radical diet. I don't know. All I know is that in their pantry, where any normal American kid might find Oreos (or Newman-O's, I can be flexible about hydrogenated oils and organic ingredients), there was some kind of faux melba toast, made from spelt, and unseasoned almond butter. That was his after-school snack.

You just know if that kid ever went to a birthday party and got a bite of the manna that is sheet cake from Costco, he'd never want to come home. I can picture him there, in a wild-eyed eating frenzy, face smeared in icing, wondering why on earth his parents never told him of this bliss before.

It's like those people who grow up without TV. Move them into the real world and plop them in front of *Wheel of Fortune,* and they're not getting up until the national anthem is playing. If it's on cable, the only hope of having them move is if nature calls.

Believe me, I had a roommate like that once. I don't know how he managed to avoid TV into his thirties, but when I was watching *The O.C.,* I'd feel him creeping up behind me, and he'd just stand there, eyes glued to the set, like he was a caveman wondering at the magic box with the tiny people in it.

"Want to sit down, Darryl?" I'd ask, because there's nothing creepier than someone standing behind you, rasping their breath through their perennially stuffy nose. Especially if you're eating a bowl of popcorn, as I usually was.

"No, no," he's say vaguely, eyes dilating like something out of a 1950s alien movie.

And there he'd stay.

"Seriously, Darryl. Since you're gonna watch, anyway, why don't you just sit?" Elsewhere. Anywhere. Not there.

"I'm on my way to the kitchen."

And forty-five minutes later, he'd finally make it the other three yards to the kitchen, where he would prepare some vile midnight snack along the lines of a bologna and onion sandwich. I'd like to think his distraction by the show was what caused this revolting food choice, but alas, it was just one more slightly off thing about him.

Anyway, Mondays at the Van Houghtons were challenging. To say the least.

But Angela Van Houghton was also the events coordinator for the country club where my most profitable work was—usually one banquet every other week, though sometimes it was more—and that made the pressure of working for Angela that much greater. I needed to keep her happy so she'd keep recommending me to people who were having parties.

Tuesday is a lot more pleasant.

Tuesday was Paul McMann, a lawyer I never, ever even caught a glimpse of, but for a long time I imagined him to look a lot like Fred Flintstone, based on his culinary tastes.

Paul—or Mr. Tuesday, as I like to think of him—is a big

fan of June Cleaver–style comfort food. Pure back-of-the-box stuff: noodleburger casserole, onion soup mix meat loaf, beef pot pie, chicken 'n' biscuits, Philadelphia cheesecake, and so on. He probably would have been perfectly happy if I made him Hamburger Helper every week.

Butter, sour cream, white flour, cheddar cheese, canned Campbell's tomato soup, macaroni noodles . . . all that stuff that was missing on Mondays, I got to make up for with Mr. Tuesday. Even iceberg lettuce, which is nutritionally dull, but culinarily fun to slice and embellish, was A-OK with him.

I *loved* cooking for Mr. Tuesday.

He worked late *all the time,* it seemed. I never saw him, though I did arrive between five and six, and I suppose it was possible his workday started at noon. Nevertheless, he was a mystery to me.

For example, he was clearly a man's man: no frills, no fuss. It showed in his food tastes, his books, and especially in his choice of very spare décor. It works for me. I really kind of enjoy the clean wood and leather feel of his apartment. Decidedly masculine, but for some reason I find it reassuring. It's like sitting in an executive office, waiting for a big inheritance check from an elderly and unknown relative to be cut and cashed.

So, whereas I usually do most of the prep work for my people at home and take the food to their places to heat and serve it (no, this isn't strictly legal, since I don't have a commercially licensed kitchen, but no one really cares), I usually take all the raw ingredients to Mr. Tuesday's place in Friendship Heights and spend hours relishing in the glorious peace of it. Sometimes I'd take the remote from its usual spot and blast some Wham! through his mounted Bose speakers, and sometimes I'd just crack open a window and listen to the nothing outside.

Always—*always*—I would look forward to the notes he'd leave for me.

After I'd noted my disdain for peas, which I regard as fake vegetables since they are green but almost as starchy and sugary as Skittles, he wrote:

All I'm saying is give peas a chance.

His response to the appetizers I'd left for a party he was having for his office staff:

Everything was great, but I especially loved the things that I know weren't Snausages but looked just like them. Is it unreasonable to ask for them with dinner sometime?

They were chicken and sage sausagettes that I got from a local butcher and wrapped in homemade pretzel dough, minus the salt but painted with butter. They are incredible, so I gave him points for good taste *and* I gave him Chickens in Throws, as he later jokingly referred to them, in a freezer bag the next week so he could have them whenever he wanted them.

And on one memorable occasion, he taped a hundred-dollar bill to a broken Corningware casserole dish I'd left with him and wrote on a Post-it:

I hope this wasn't your grandmother's or some other senti-mental antique. I also hope you're wearing shoes because the vacuum cleaner hasn't worked the same since I acci-dentally sucked up a toupee. Not mine. I'll explain over a beer if we ever meet.

My guess was that he probably had a lot of stories I'd enjoy over a beer if we ever met.

Other than that, though, the guy was a mystery. I had a pretty good handle on most of the people I worked for—if nothing else, you can tell a lot about people by the things they surround themselves with in their homes—but Mr. Tuesday had very few clues to his personality in the main part of his apartment, and I'd never been into his bedroom or anything. Essentially, it was like trying to figure out something about the last person in your hotel room.

Wednesday was a different story. Wednesday was Lex Prather, who was usually there for at least part of the time I was. Personality-wise, he seemed to be the exact opposite of Mr. Tuesday, flamboyant where Tuesday was under-stated. Social, where Tuesday seemed to just be working all the time. But Lex was almost as much fun to cook for, though his tastes were far more highfalutin.

Until a year and a half ago, he lived with his mother in this two-bedroom flat in the old Westchester, off Mass

Avenue. She was like Perle Mesta, and he was Felix Unger—they must have been quite a pair. Anyway, when she passed away, he hired me to cook all his old favorites, which consisted of the kind of fussy white tablecloth dishes one might have found on the menu of the *Titanic*. Shrimp Louis, oysters Rockefeller, Waldorf salad, even the occasional molded Jell-O dish incongruously made it onto the menu. He apparently had no problem drawing the line at mint jelly, however.

Lex is tall and thin, and always impeccably dressed, which is appropriate, since he owns the venerable old Simon's Department Store downtown. It outlived both Woodward & Lothrop and Garfinckel's department stores, though I believe its reputation might be wobbling a bit now in the shadow of Nordstrom and everything you can find in Tysons Corner and the Galleria.

Anyway, the movie version of Lex could be perfectly played by Tony Randall. He is of completely indeterminate sexual orientation—though by "indeterminate" I mean that I don't know if he's gay or completely asexual; straight does not appear to be an option, although it's *possible* I'm wrong about that, I suppose.

A social butterfly, Lex often had me cooking for his mystery book group or his annual Christmas, New Year's, May Day, Fourth of July, Labor Day, and Halloween parties.

The upshot is that Lex had champagne tastes and a champagne budget. This made him pretty fun to cook for in and of itself, but he was also just a really great guy and I enjoyed seeing him every time. That's a luxury I don't always have with my clients, and it's particularly nice since work is basically the only social contact I have at all.

Which takes us to Thursday.

Thursday nights were with the Oleksei family, which was sheer chaos. Not really *bad* chaos, necessarily, just *crazy* chaos. The Oleksei family consisted of a grandfather, Vlad, who was clearly the patriarch of the family, often holding court in a mysterious back room I never saw but from which people would come and go at all hours, often leaving looking fearful or even in tears.

I half suspected that they were part of the Russian Mafia.

Seriously.

They made me a little nervous sometimes.

Vlad Oleksei's wife had died years earlier, leaving him with three strapping sons—now in their thirties and forties—and a handwritten recipe book I could not read, because it was in Russian. Fortunately, my sister's boyfriend worked in the Russian department at American University and was translating the recipes as best he could for me, though the metric translation was still a bit of a challenge for me.

The Oleksei sons—Borya, Serge, and Viktor—were all nice enough to me, and always politely appreciative of the food I prepared, but there was something . . . *off* about them, too. They owned a dry cleaning and tailoring store, which I knew from *The Jeffersons* could be profitable, but it was just hard to picture the three of them going into one little dry cleaner every day and whistling as they busily worked out a stain in the collar of a shirt.

Nevertheless, assuming that wasn't a cover for their actual work with the Russian mob, that was what they did.

Viktor was the only one who was married. His wife was American and stood out in that family like a sore thumb—blond, big-lipped, brash, and boisterous. It was hard to imagine how she lived in such a traditional old-world atmosphere. I could picture her much more easily in a football jersey, tailgating with a bunch of burly blond lumberjack types than this dark, moody family.

Fridays I had the Lemurras in Georgetown.

What can I say about Marie Lemurra?

For one thing, she was a social climber to the nth degree. In the short three months I'd worked for her, I'd watched her try to get in with politicians, a few former B-list movie stars who now lived in or outside D.C., and most recently, local famewhores on the D.C. *True Wife Stories* reality show.

For another thing, she seemed to hate me, though that *had* to be impossible, given that she knew me *only* in a professional context and even that involved me doing her bidding and not arguing. Nevertheless, she was a woman who didn't seem satisfied with acquiescence of any sort; she wanted it to include at least a small measure of pain. I think Marie Lemurra needed other people to be wrong so that she, herself, could feel right.

It wasn't an ideal work situation, believe me, but I don't think very many people among us would say their work is always 100 percent awesome.

Marie Lemurra, and those like her, was the price I had to pay for having a job I otherwise loved.

So that was my week right now: the Van Houghtens, Mr. Tuesday, Lex, the Olekseis, and the Lemurras. They ran the gamut, in every way.

With the banquet work added on the weekends, my life felt full and secure.

Famous last words, huh?